PENGUIN BOOKS

Adrian Mole: The Wilderness Years

Sue Townsend, with *The Secret Diary of Adrian Mole Aged 13¾* (1982) and *The Growing Pains of Adrian Mole* (1984), was Britain's bestselling author of the 1980s. Her hugely successful novels are *Rebuilding Coventry* (1988), *True Confessions of Adrian Albert Mole, Margaret Hilda Roberts and Susan Lilian Townsend* (1989), *Adrian Mole: From Minor to Major* (1991), *The Queen and I* (1992), *Adrian Mole: The Wilderness Years* (1993), *Ghost Children* (1997), *Adrian Mole: The Cappuccino Years* (1999), *The Public Confessions of a Middle-aged Woman (Aged 55¾)* (2001) and *Number Ten* (2002). Most of her books are published by Penguin. She is also well known as a playwright. She lives in Leicester.

D0956255

Adrian Mole

The Wilderness Years

Sue Townsend

PENGUIN BOOKS

PENGUIN BOOKS

Published by the Penguin Group
Penguin Books Ltd, 80 Strand, London WC2R 0RL, England
Penguin Putnam Inc., 375 Hudson Street, New York, New York 10014, USA
Penguin Books Australia Ltd, 250 Camberwell Road,
Camberwell, Victoria 3124, Australia
Penguin Books Canada Ltd, 10 Alcorn Avenue, Toronto, Ontario, Canada M4V 3B2
Penguin Books India (P) Ltd, 11 Community Centre,
Panchsheel Park, New Delhi – 110 017, India
Penguin Books (NZ) Ltd, Cnr Rosedale and Airborne Roads,
Albany, Auckland, New Zealand
Penguin Books (South Africa) (Pty) Ltd, 24 Sturdee Avenue,
Rosebank 2196, South Africa

Penguin Books Ltd, Registered Offices: 80 Strand, London WC2R 0RL, England

www.penguin.com

First published in Great Britain by Methuen 1993
Published in Mandarin Paperbacks 1994
Reprinted in Arrow Books 1998
Published in Penguin Books 2003
1

Set in 11.25/13.75pt Monotype Minion
Printed in England by Clays Ltd, St Ives plc

To my sisters, Barbara and Kate

'What's gone and what's past help
Should be past grief.'

William Shakespeare
The Winter's Tale

Winter

Tuesday January 1st 1991

I start the year with a throbbing head and shaking limbs, owing to the excessive amounts of alcohol I was forced to drink at my mother's party last night.

I was quite happy sitting on a dining chair, watching the dancing and sipping on a low-calorie soft drink, but my mother kept shouting at me: 'Join in, fishface,' and wouldn't rest until I'd consumed a glass and a half of Lambrusco.

As she slopped the wine into a plastic glass for me, I had a close look at her. Her lips were surrounded by short lines, like numerous river beds running into a scarlet lake; her hair was red and glossy almost until it reached her scalp and then a grey layer revealed the truth: her neck was saggy, her cleavage wrinkled and her belly protruded from the little black dress (*very* little) she wore. The poor woman is forty-seven, twenty-three years older than her second husband. I know for a fact that he, Martin Muffet, has *never* seen her without make-up. Her pillow slips are a disgrace; they are covered in pan-stick and mascara.

It wasn't long before I found myself on the improvised dance floor in my mother's lounge, dancing to

'The Birdie Song', in a line with Pandora, the love of my life; Pandora's new lover, Professor Jack Cavendish; Martin Muffet, my boyish stepfather; Ivan and Tania, Pandora's bohemian parents; and other inebriated friends and relations of my mother's. As the song reared to its climax, I caught sight of myself in the mirror above the fireplace. I was flapping my arms and grinning like a lunatic. I stopped immediately and went back to the dining chair. Bert Baxter, who was a hundred last year, was doing some clumsy wheelchair dancing, which caused a few casualties; my left ankle is still bruised and swollen, thanks to his carelessness. Also I have a large beetroot stain on the front of my new white shirt, caused by him flinging one of his beetroot sandwiches across the room under the misapprehension that it was a party popper. But the poor old git is almost certain to die this year – he's had his telegram from the Queen – so I won't charge him for the specialist dry cleaning that my shirt is almost certain to require.

I have been looking after Bert Baxter for over ten years now, going back from Oxford to visit him, buying his vile cigarettes, cutting his horrible toenails, etc. When will it end?

My father gate-crashed the party at 11.30. His excuse was that he wanted to speak urgently to my grandma. She is very deaf now, so he was forced to shout above the music. 'Mum, I can't find the spirit level.'

What a pathetic excuse! Who would be using a spirit level on New Year's Eve, apart from an emergency plumber? It was a pitiful request from a lonely, forty-nine-year-old divorcee, whose navy blue mid-eighties suit needed cleaning and whose brown moccasins needed throwing away. He'd done the best he could with his remaining hair, but it wasn't enough.

'Any idea where the spirit level is?' insisted my father, looking towards the drinks table. Then he added, 'I'm laying some paving slabs.'

I laughed out loud at this obvious lie.

My grandma looked bewildered and went back into the kitchen to microwave the sausage rolls and my mother graciously invited her ex-husband to join the party. In no time at all, he had whipped his jacket off and was frugging on the dance floor with my eight-year-old sister Rosie. I found my father's style of dancing acutely embarrassing to watch (his role model is still Mick Jagger); so I went upstairs to change my shirt. On the way, I passed Pandora and Bluebeard Cavendish in a passionate embrace half inside the airing cupboard. He's old enough to be her father.

Pandora has been mine since I was thirteen years old and I fell in love with her treacle-coloured hair. She is simply playing hard to get. She only married Julian Twyselton-Fife to make me jealous. There can be no other possible reason. Julian is a bisexual semi-aristocrat who occasionally wears a monocle. He strains after eccentricity but it continues to elude him. He is a deeply ordinary man with an upper-class accent. He's not even good-looking. He looks like a horse on two legs. And as for her affair with Cavendish, a man who dresses like a tramp, the mind boggles.

Pandora was looking particularly beautiful in a red off-the-shoulder dress, from which her breasts kept threatening to escape. Nobody would have guessed from looking at her that she was now Dr Pandora Braithwaite, fluent in Russian, Serbo-Croat and various other little-used languages. She looked more like one of those supermodels that prowl the catwalks than a Doctor of Philosophy. She certainly added glamour to the party: unlike her parents, who were dressed as usual in their fifties beatnik style – polo necks and corduroy. No wonder they were both sweating heavily as they danced to Chuck Berry.

Pandora smiled at me as she tucked her left breast back inside her dress, and I was pierced to the heart. I truly love her. I am prepared to wait until she comes to her senses and realizes that there is only one man in the world for her, and that is *me*. That is the reason I followed her to Oxford and took up temporary residence in her box room. I have now been there for a year and a half. The more she is exposed to my presence, the sooner she will appreciate my qualities. I have suffered daily humiliations, watching her with her husband and her lovers, but I will reap the benefits later when she is the proud mother of our six children and I am a famous author.

As the clock struck twelve, everyone joined hands and sang 'Auld Lang Syne'. I looked around, at Pandora; at Cavendish; at my mother; at my father; at my stepfather; at my grandma; at Pandora's parents,

Ivan and Tania Braithwaite; and at the dog. Tears filled my eyes. I am nearly twenty-four years of age, I thought, and what have I done with my life? And, as the singing died away, I answered myself – nothing, Mole, nothing.

Pandora wanted to spend the first night of the New Year in Leicester at her parents' house with Cavendish, but at 12.30 a.m. I reminded her that she and her aged lover had promised to give me a lift back to Oxford. I said, 'I am on duty in eight hours' time at the Department of the Environment. At 8.30 sharp.'

She said, 'For Christ's sake, can't you have one poxy day off without permission? Do you have to kow-tow to that little commissar Brown?'

I replied, with dignity, I hope, 'Pandora, some of us keep our word, unlike you, who on Thursday the second of June 1983 promised that you would marry me as soon as you had finished your "A" levels.'

Pandora laughed, spilling the neat whisky in her glass. 'I was sixteen years old,' she said. 'You're living in a bloody time warp.'

I ignored the insult. 'Will you drive me to Oxford as you promised?' I snapped, dabbing at the whisky droplets on her dress with a paper serviette covered in reindeer.

Pandora shouted across the room to Cavendish, who was engaged in conversation with Grandma about the dog's lack of appetite: 'Jack! Adrian's insisting on that lift back to Oxford!'

Bluebeard rolled his eyes and looked at his watch.

'Have I got time for one more drink, Adrian?' he asked.

'Yes, but only mineral water. You're driving, aren't you?' I said.

He rolled his eyes again and picked up a bottle of Perrier. My father came across and he and Cavendish reminisced about the Good Old Days, when they could drink ten pints in the pub and get in the car and drive off 'without having the law on your back'.

It was 2 a.m. when we finally left my mother's house. Then we had to call at the Braithwaites' house to collect Pandora's overnight bag. I sat in the back of Cavendish's Volvo and listened to their banal conversation. Pandora calls him 'Hunky' and Cavendish calls her 'Monkey'.

I woke up on the outskirts of Oxford to hear her whisper: 'So, what did you think of the festivities at Maison Mole, Hunky?'

And to hear him reply: 'As you promised, Monkey, delightfully vulgar. I enjoyed myself enormously.' They both turned to look at me, so I feigned sleep.

I began to think about my sister Rosie, who is, in my view, totally spoilt. The *Girls' World* model hairdressing head she had demanded for Christmas had stood neglected on the lounge window sill since Boxing Day, looking out onto the equally neglected garden. Its retractable blonde hair was hopelessly tangled and its face was smeared with garish cosmetics. Rosie was dancing earlier with Ivan Braithwaite in a manner totally unsuited to an eight-year-old. They looked like Lolita and Humbert Humbert.

Nabokov, fellow author, you should have been alive on that day. It would have shocked even you to see Rosie Mole pouting in her black miniskirt, pink tights and purple cropped top!

I have decided to keep a full journal, in the hope that my life will perhaps seem more interesting when it is written down. It is certainly not interesting to actually live my life. It is tedious beyond belief.

Wednesday January 2nd

I was ten minutes late for work this morning. The exhaust pipe fell off the bus. Mr Brown was entirely unsympathetic. He said, 'You should get yourself a bicycle, Mole.' I pointed out that I have had three bicycles stolen in eighteen months. I can no longer afford to supply the criminals of Oxford with ecologically sound transport.

Brown snapped, 'Then *walk*, Mole. Get up earlier and *walk*.'

I went into my cubicle and shut the door. There was a message on my desk informing me that a colony of newts had been discovered in Newport Pagnell. Their habitat is in the middle of the projected new ring road. I rang the Environmental Office at the Department of Transport and warned a certain Peter Peterson that work on the ring road could be subject to delay.

'But that's bloody ludicrous,' said Peterson. 'It would cost us hundreds of thousands of pounds to re-route that road, and all to save a few slimy reptiles.'

That is also my own private point of view of newts. I'm sick of them. But I am paid to champion their right to survive (in public at least), so I gave Peterson my standard newt conservation lecture (and pointed out that newts are amphibians, not reptiles). I spent the rest of the morning writing up the Newport Pagnell case.

At lunchtime I left the Department of the Environment and went to collect my blazer from the dry cleaner's. I had forgotten to take my ticket. (It was at home, being used as a bookmark inside Colin Wilson's *The Outsider*. Mr Wilson is Leicester-born, like me.)

The woman at the cleaner's refused to hand over my blazer, even though I pointed to it hanging on the rack! She said, 'That blazer has got a British Legion badge on it. You're too young to be in the British Legion.'

An undergraduate behind me sniggered.

Enraged, I said to the woman, 'You are obviously proud of your powers of detection. Perhaps you should write an *Inspector Morse* episode for the television.' But my wit was lost on the pedant.

The undergraduate pushed forward and handed her a stinking duvet, requesting the four-hour service.

I had no choice but to go home and collect the ticket, go back to the cleaner's, and then run with the blazer, encased in plastic, slung over my shoulder, all the way back to the office. I have got a blind date tonight and the blazer is all I've got to wear.

My last blind date ended prematurely when Ms Sandra Snape (non-smoking, twenty-five-year-old, vegetarian: dark hair, brown eyes, five foot six, not unattractive) left Burger King in a hurry, claiming she'd left the kettle on the stove. I am now convinced, however, that the kettle was an excuse. When I returned home that night, I discovered that the hem was down at the back on my army greatcoat. Women don't like a scruff.

I was twenty-five minutes late getting back to work. Brown was waiting for me in my cubicle. He was brandishing my Newport Pagnell newt figures. Apparently I had made a mistake in my projection of live newt births for 1992. Instead of 1,200, I had put down 120,000. An easy mistake to make.

'A hundred and twenty thousand newts in 1992, eh, Mole?' sneered Brown. 'The good citizens of Newport Pagnell will be positively inundated with amphibia.'

He gave me an official warning about my time-keeping and ordered me to water my cactus. He then went to his own office, taking my paperwork with him. If I lose my job, I am done for.

11.30 p.m. My blind date did not turn up. I waited two hours, ten minutes in the Burger King in the town centre. Thank you, Ms Tracy Winkler (quiet blonde, twenty-seven, non-smoker, cats and country walks)!

That is the last time I write to a box number in the *Oxford Mail*. From now on, I will only use the personal column of the *London Review of Books*.

Thursday January 3rd

I have the most terrible problems with my sex life. It all boils down to the fact that I *have* no sex life. At least not with another person.

I lay awake last night, asking myself why? Why? Why? Am I grotesque, dirty, repellent? No, I am none of these things. Am I normal-looking, clean, pleasant? Yes, I am all of these things. So what am I doing wrong? Why can't I get an average-looking young woman into my bed?

Do I exude an obnoxious odour smelled by everyone else but me? If so, I hope to God somebody will tell me and I can seek medical help from a gland specialist.

At 3 a.m. this morning my sleep was disturbed by the sound of a violent altercation. This in itself is not unusual, because this house provides a home for many people, most of them noisy, drunken undergraduates, who sit up all night debating the qualities of various brands of beer. I went downstairs in my pyjamas and was just in time to see Tariq, the Iraqi student who lives in the basement, being led away by a gang of criminal-looking men.

Tariq shouted, 'Adrian, save me!' I said to one of the men, 'Let him go or I will call the police.'

A man with a broken nose said, 'We *are* the police, sir. Your friend is being expelled from the country, orders of the Home Office.'

Pandora came to the top of the basement stairs. She was wearing very little, having just left her bed. She said in her most imperious manner: 'Why is Mr Aziz being expelled?'

'Because,' said the thuggish one, 'Mr Aziz's presence is not conducive to the public good, for reasons of national security. Ain't you 'eard there's a war on?' he added, ogling Pandora's satin nightshirt, through which the outline of her nipples was clearly visible.

Tariq shouted, 'I am a student at Brasenose College and a member of the Young Conservatives: I am not interested in politics!'

There was nothing we could do to help him, so Pandora and I went back to bed. Not the same bed though, worse luck.

At nine o'clock the next morning, I rang the landlord, Eric Hardwell, on his car phone and asked if I could move into the now vacant basement flat. I am sick of living in Pandora's box room. Hardwell was in a bad mood because he was stuck in traffic, but he agreed, providing I can give him a £1,000 deposit, three months' rent in advance (£1,200), a banker's reference and a solicitor's letter stating that I will not burn candles, use a chip pan, or breed bull terrier dogs in the basement.

I shall have to stay here in the box room. I need to use my chip pan on a daily basis.

Lenin was right: all landlords *are* bastards.

Somebody who looked like Tariq was on *Newts At Ten*; he was waving from the steps of an aeroplane which was bound for the Gulf. I waved back in case it was him.

Correction: I meant, of course, to write *News At Ten*.

Friday January 4th

Woke up at 5 a.m. and was unable to get back to sleep. My brain insisted on recalling all my past humiliations. One by one they passed in front of me: the bullying I endured from Barry Kent until my grandma put a stop to it; the day at Skegness when my father broke the news to me and my mother that his illegitimate son, Brett, had been born to his lover, Stick Insect; the black day when my mother ran away to Sheffield for a short-lived affair with Mr Lucas, our smarmy neighbour; the day I learned that I had failed 'A' level Biology for the third time; the day Pandora married a bisexual man.

Then, after the humiliations came the *faux pas*, a relentless march: the time I sniffed glue and got a model aeroplane stuck to my nose; the day my sister, Rosie, was born and I couldn't remove my hand from the spaghetti jar where the five pound note for the taxi fare to the maternity hospital was kept; the time I wrote to Mr John Tydeman at the BBC and addressed him as 'Johnny'.

The procession of *faux pas* was followed by a parade of bouts of moral cowardice: the time I crossed the road to avoid my father because he was wearing a red pom-pom hat; my craven behaviour when my mother was stricken with a menopausal temper tantrum in the Leicester market place – I should not have walked away and hidden behind that flower stall; the day I had a jealous fit, destroyed the complimentary tickets for Barry Kent's first professional gig on the poetry circuit and blamed the dog; my desertion of Sharon Bott when she announced she was pregnant.

I despise myself. I deserve my unhappiness. I am truly a loathsome person.

I was relieved when my travelling alarm clock roused me from my gloomy reverie and told me that it was 6.30 a.m. and time to get up.

> *Nipples by A. Mole*
> Like raspberries
> taken from the freezer
> Inviting tongue and lips
> but warning not to bite
> Not yet
> soon
> But not yet

I am on flexitime and had agreed to start work at 7.30 a.m., but somehow, although I left my box room at 7 a.m., I didn't arrive at work until 8 a.m. A journey of half a mile took me an hour. Where did I go? What did I do? Did I have a blackout on the way? Was I mugged and left unconscious? Am I, even as I write, suffering from memory loss?

Pandora is constantly telling me that I am in urgent need of psychiatric help. Perhaps she is right. I feel as though I am going mad; that my life is a film and that I am a mere spectator.

Saturday January 5th

Julian, Pandora's upper-crust husband, has returned from his Christmas sojourn in the country with his parents. He shuddered when he walked through the front door of the flat.

'God!' he said. 'The pantry of Twyselton Manor is bigger than this bloody hole.'

'Then why come back, sweetie?' said Pandora, his so-called wife.

'Because, *ma femme*, my parents, poor, deluded creatures, are paying mucho spondulicks to keep me here at Oxford, studying Chinese.' He laughed his neighing horse's laugh. (And he's certainly got the teeth for it.)

'But you haven't been to a lecture for over a year,'

said Dr Braithwaite (12 'O's, 5 'A's, BA Hons. and D. Phil.).

'But my lecturers are all such boring little men.'

'It's such a waste, husband,' said Pandora. 'You're the cleverest man in Oxford *and* the laziest. If you're not careful, you'll end up in Parliament.'

After Julian had thrown his battered pigskin luggage into his room, he returned to the kitchen, where Pandora was chopping leeks and I was exercising my new sink plunger. 'So, darlings, what's new?' he said, lighting one of his vile Russian cigarettes.

Pandora said, 'I'm in love with Jack Cavendish, and he's in love with me. Isn't it absolutely marvellous?' She grinned ecstatically and chopped at the leeks with renewed fervour.

'Cavendish?' puzzled Julian. 'Isn't he that grey-haired old linguistics fart who can't keep his plonker in his pants?'

Pandora's eyes flashed dangerously. 'He's sworn to me that from now on his lifestyle will be strictly non-polygynous,' she said.

She stretched up to replace the knife on its magnetic rack and her cropped T-shirt rode up, revealing her delicate midriff. I thrust the plunger viciously into the greasy contents of the sink, imagining that Cavendish's head was on the end of the wooden stick, instead of the black rubber suction pad.

Julian neighed knowingly. 'Cavendish doesn't know

the meaning of the word "non-polygynous". He's a notorious womanizer.'

'*Was*,' insisted Pandora, adding, 'and *of course* he knows the meaning of the word "non-polygynous": he is a professor of Linguistics.'

I left the plunger floating in the sink and went to my box room, took my *Condensed Oxford Dictionary* from its shelf and, with the aid of the magnifying glass, looked up the word 'non-polygynous'. I then uttered a loud, cynical laugh. Loud enough, I hoped, to be heard in the kitchen.

Sunday January 6th

Woke at 3 a.m. and lay awake remembering the time when Pandora and I nearly went All the Way. I love her still. I intend to be her second husband. And what's more, she will take my name. She will be known as 'Mrs Adrian Albert Mole' in private.

> *On Seeing Pandora's Midriff*
> The glorious shoreline from ribcage
> To pelvis
> Like an inlet
> A bay
> A safe haven
> I want to navigate
> To explore
> To take readings from the stars

To carefully trace my fingers
Along the shoreline
And eventually to guide my ship, my destroyer,
    my pleasure craft
Into and beyond your harbour

6.00 p.m. Sink still blocked. Worked for three hours in the kitchen, adding vowels to the first half of my experimental novel *Lo! The Flat Hills of My Homeland*, which was originally written with consonants only. It is eighteen months since I sent it to Sir Gordon Giles, Prince Charles's agent, and he sent it back, suggesting I put in the vowels.

Lo! The Flat Hills of My Homeland explores late twentieth-century man and his dilemma, focusing on a 'New Man' living in a provincial city in England.

The treatment is broadly Lawrentian, with a touch of Dostoevskian darkness and a tinge of Hardyesque lyricism.

I predict that one day it will be a GCSE set book.

I was driven out of the kitchen by the arrival of that wrinkled-up ashtray on legs, Cavendish, who had been invited to Sunday lunch. He hadn't been in the flat two minutes before he was pulling a cork out of a bottle and helping himself to glasses out of the cupboard. He then sat on *my* recently vacated chair at the kitchen table and began to talk absolute gibberish about the Gulf War, predicting that it would be over within months. I predict that it will be America's second Vietnam.

Julian came into the kitchen, wearing his silk pyjamas and carrying a copy of *Hello!*

'Julian,' said Pandora, 'meet my lover, Jack Cavendish.' She turned to Cavendish and said, 'Jack, this is Julian Twyselton-Fife, my husband.' Pandora's husband and Pandora's lover shook hands.

I turned away in disgust. I'm as liberal and civilized as the next person. In fact, in some circles I'm regarded as quite an advanced thinker, but even I shuddered at the utter depravity that this introduction signified.

I left the flat to get some air. When I returned from my walk around the Outer Ring Road two hours later, Cavendish was still there, telling tedious anecdotes about his numerous children and his three ex-wives. I microwaved my Sunday lunch and took it into my box room. I spent the rest of the evening listening to laughter in the next room. Woke at 2 a.m. and was unable to get back to sleep. Filled two pages of A4 devising tortures for Cavendish. Not the actions of a rational man.

Tortures for Cavendish
1) Chain him to the wall with a glass of water *just* beyond his grasp.
2) Chain him naked to a wall while a bevy of beautiful girls walk by, cruelly mocking his flaccid *and* aroused penis.
3) Force him to sit in a room with Ivan Braithwaite, while Ivan talks about the finer details of the Labour Party's

Constitution, with particular reference to Clause Four. (This is true torture, as I can bear witness.)

4) Show him a video of Pandora getting married to me. She radiant in white, me in top hat and tails, putting two gloved fingers up at Cavendish.

Let the punishment fit the crime.

Monday January 7th

Started my beard today.

Some of the Newport Pagnell newts have crossed the road. I telephoned Peterson at the Department of Transport, to inform him. There has obviously been a split in the community. I expect a female newt is at the bottom of it: *cherchez la femme*.

Wednesday January 9th

For the first time in my entire life I haven't got a single spot, pustule or pimple. I pointed out to Pandora over breakfast that my complexion was flawless, but she paused in applying her mascara, looked at me coldly, and said, 'You need a shave.'

Spent ten minutes at the sink with the plunger before going to work, but to no avail. Pandora said, 'We'll have to get a proper man in.'

Does Pandora realize the impact the above words,

so apparently casually uttered, have had on me? She has disenfranchised me from my gender! She has cut my poor, useless balls off!

Thursday January 10th

Brown has advised me to shave. I refused. I may have to seek the advice of the Civil and Public Service Union.

Friday January 11th

Applied to join the CPSU.

Pandora found Cavendish's A4 torture list. She has made an appointment for me to see her friend Leonora De Witt, who is a psychotherapist. I agreed reluctantly. On the one hand, I am terrified of my unconscious and what it will reveal about me. On the other, I am looking forward to talking about myself non-stop for an hour without interruption, hesitation or repetition.

Saturday January 12th

Pandora's most recent ex-lover, Rocky (Big Boy) Livingstone, came round to the flat today, asking for the return of his mini sound-system. At six foot three and fifteen stone of finely honed muscle, Rocky is a 'proper' man, if ever I saw one. Pandora was out, meeting some of Cavendish's children at the Randolph Hotel. So, in her absence, I gave the sound-system to him. Since he and Pandora split up, Rocky has opened new gyms in Kettering, Newmarket and Ashby de la Zouch. He and his new girlfriend, Carly Pick, are still happy.

Rocky said, 'Carly's a real star, Aidy. I respect the lady, y'know.' I told Rocky about Professor Cavendish. He was disgusted.

He said, 'That Pandora is a *user*. Just 'cos she's clever, she finks she's . . .' He flailed about for the right word and finished, 'clever'.

Before he went he unblocked the sink. I was very grateful. I was getting sick of washing the pots in the bathroom hand basin. None of the saucepans would fit under the taps.

I went to the window and watched him drive away. Carly Pick had both her arms around his neck.

Sunday January 13th

The Gulf War deadline expires on the 15th, at midnight. What will I do if I am called up to fight for my country? Will I cover myself with honour, or will I wet myself with fear on hearing the sound of enemy gunfire?

Monday January 14th

Went to Sainsbury's and stocked up with tins of beans, candles, Jaffa cakes, household matches, torch batteries, paracetamol, multivitamins, Ry-King and tins of corned beef and put them in the cupboard in my box room. Should the war spread over here, I will be well prepared. The others in the flat will just have to take their chance. I predict panic buying on a scale never seen before in this country. There will be fighting in the aisles of the supermarkets.

Appointment with Leonora De Witt on Friday 25th of this month at 6 p.m.

Tuesday January 15th

Midnight. We are at war with Iraq. I phoned my mother in Leicester and told her to keep the dog in. It is twelve years old and reacts badly to unexpected noises. She laughed and said, 'Are you going mad?' I said, 'Probably,' and put the phone down.

Wednesday January 16th

Bought sixteen bottles of Highland Spring water, in case water supply is cut off owing to bombardment by Iraqi airforce. It took me four trips from the Spar shop on the corner to the flat, but I feel more secure knowing I will not go thirsty during the coming *Blitzkrieg*.

Brown has not mentioned my beard for some days now. He is preoccupied with the effect that 'Operation Desert Storm' will have on the desert wildlife. I said, 'I'm afraid I regard Iraqi wildlife as being on the side of the enemy. I'm more worried about my dog, at home in Leicester.'

'Ever the parochial, Mole,' said Brown, in a lip-curling manner. I was quite insulted. Brown reads nothing, apart from journals on wildlife, whereas I have read most of the Russian Greats and am about to embark on *War and Peace*. Hardly parochial, Brown!

Thursday January 17th

I have hired a portable colour television, so I can watch the Gulf War in bed.

Friday January 18th

The spokesperson for the USA military is a man who calls himself 'Colon Powell'. Every time I see him, I think of intestines and the lower bowel. It detracts from the gravity of the War.

Saturday January 19th

Bert Baxter rang me up at the office today. (I will kill whoever gave him the number.) He wanted to know 'when you and my favourite gal are comin' to see me?' His 'favourite gal' is Pandora. Why doesn't Bert just *die* like other pensioners? His quality of life can't be up to much. He is nothing but a burden to others (me).

He was entirely ungrateful when I dug a grave for his dog, Sabre, last year, though I challenge anyone to dig a neater hole in compacted soil with a rusty garden trowel. If I'd had a decent spade at my disposal, then, *naturellement*, the grave would have been neater. The truth is that I hated and feared Sabre. The day the wretched Alsatian died was a day of rejoicing for me. No more smelling its noxious breath. No more forcing Bob Martin's conditioning tablets between its horrible vicious teeth.

Bert burbled on about the war for a while, and then asked me if I had heard my old enemy Barry Kent on *Stop the Week* this morning. Apparently, Kent was publicizing his first novel, *Dork's Diary*. I am now utterly convinced there cannot be a God. It was me that encouraged Kent to write poetry, and now I find out that the ex-skinhead, frozen peabrain has written a novel, *and got it published!!!*

Pandora told me this evening that Kent made Ned Sherrin, A. S. Byatt, Jonathan Miller and Victoria

Mather laugh almost continuously. Apparently the phone lines at the BBC were jammed with listeners asking when *Dork's Diary* will be published (Monday). This is absolutely and totally the last straw. My sanity hangs by a fragile thread.

Sunday January 20th

I was passing Waterstone's bookshop when I saw what appeared to be Barry Kent standing in the window. I lifted my hand in greeting and said, 'Hello, Baz,' then realized that the smirking skinhead was only a cardboard cut-out. Copies of *Dork's Diary* filled the window. I'm not ashamed to say that curses sprang from my lips.

As I flicked through the pages of the slim volume, my eye was caught not only by the many obscenities with which the book is littered, but by the name – 'Aiden Vole' – given to one of the characters. This 'Aiden Vole' is obsessed with matters anal. He is jingoistic, deeply conservative and a failure with women. 'Aiden Vole' is an outrageous caricature of me, without a doubt. I have been slandered. I shall see my solicitor in the morning. I shall instruct him or her (I haven't actually got a solicitor yet) to demand hundreds of thousands of pounds in damages. I couldn't bring myself actually to buy a copy of the book. Why should I add to Kent's royalties? But I noticed as I left the shop that Kent is giving a reading from *Dork's Diary*

on Tuesday evening at 7 p.m. I will be in the audience.
Kent will leave Waterstone's a broken man when I have
finished with him.

Monday January 21st

The Cubicle, DOE

Just listened to Kent on *Start the Week* on my portable
radio. He has certainly extended his vocabulary.
Melvyn Bragg said that the Aiden Vole character was
'wonderfully funny' and asked if he was based on
anybody real. Kent laughed and said, 'You're a writer,
Melv; you know what it's like. Vole is an amalgam of
fact and fantasy. Vole stands for everything I hate most
in this country, after the new five-pence piece, that is.'
The other guests – Ken Follett, Roy Hattersley, Brenda
Maddox and Edward Pearce – laughed like drains.

Spent the rest of the morning looking through
the Yellow Pages for a solicitor with a name I can
trust. Chose and rang 'Churchman, Churchman,
Churchman and Luther'. I am seeing a Mr Luther at
11.30 a.m. on Thursday. I am supposed to be visiting
the Newport Pagnell newts on Thursday morning with
Brown, but he will just have to face them alone. My
reputation and my future as a serious novelist are at
stake.

Alfred Wainwright, who wrote guides to the fells of
the Lake District, died today. I once used Mr Wainwright's maps when I attempted to do the 'coast to

coast' walk with the 'Off the Streets' Youth Club. Unfortunately, I developed hypothermia within half an hour of leaving the Youth Hostel at Grimsby and my record-breaking attempt had to be abandoned.

Tuesday January 22nd

Review of *Dork's Diary* in the *Guardian*:

'A coruscating account of *fin de siècle* provincial life. Brilliant. Dark. Hilarious. Buy it!' Robert Elms

Box Room 10 p.m.
Couldn't get in to see Kent; all the tickets were sold. Tried to speak to him as he entered the shop, but couldn't get near to him. He was surrounded by press and publicity people. He was wearing sunglasses. In January.

Wednesday January 23rd

Beard coming along nicely. Two spots on left shoulder blade. A slight pain in anus, but otherwise I am in superb physical condition.

Read long interview in the *Independent* with Barry Kent. He told lies from start to finish. He even lied about the reason for his being sent to prison, claiming he was sentenced to eighteen months for various acts

of violence, when I know very well that he got four
months for criminal damage to a privet hedge. I have
faxed the *Independent*, putting the record straight. It
gave me no pleasure to do this, but without the Truth
we are no better than dogs. Truth is the most important
thing in my life. Without Truth we are lost.

Thursday January 24th

Lied on the phone to Brown this morning and told
him that I could not visit the Newport Pagnell newt
habitat on account of a severe migraine. Brown ranted
on about how he had 'never taken a day off work in
twenty-two years'. He went on to brag that he had
'even passed several massive kidney stones into the
lavatory at work'. Perhaps that explains why the lavatory basin is cracked.

I was late for my appointment with Mr Luther, the
solicitor, though I left the flat in plenty of time –
another time warp or memory-loss – a mystery,
anyway. As I told Luther (in great detail) about Kent's
slander of me, I noticed him yawning several times. I
expect he was up late; he looks the dissolute type. He
was wearing braces covered in pictures of Marilyn
Monroe.

Eventually he raised his hand and said, 'Enough,
I've heard enough,' in an irritable sort of way. Then
he leaned across his desk and said, 'Are you vastly
rich?'

'No,' I replied, 'not vastly.'

He then asked, 'Are you desperately poor?'

'Not desperately. That's why I . . .'

Luther interrupted before I could finish my sentence, 'Because unless you are vastly rich, or desperately poor, you can't possibly afford to go to court. You don't qualify for Legal Aid and you can't afford to pay a barrister a thousand pounds a day, can you?'

'*A thousand pounds a day?*' I said, absolutely aghast.

Luther smiled, revealing a gold back molar.

I remembered my grandma's advice, 'Never trust a man with a gold tooth.' I thanked Mr Luther politely but coldly and left his office. So much for English justice. It is the worst in the world. As I passed the waiting room, I noticed a copy of *Dork's Diary* on the coffee table, next to copies of *Amnesty* and *The Republican*.

Got home to find a note from Leonora De Witt informing me that she is unable to keep our appointment tomorrow. Why? Is she having her hair done? Is double-glazing being installed in her consulting room? Have her parents been found dead in bed? Am I so unimportant that my time is a mere plaything to Ms De Witt? She suggested a new appointment: Thursday 31st January at 5 p.m. I left a message on her Ansafone, agreeing to the new arrangement, but announcing my displeasure.

Saturday January 26th

I was awake all last night, watching 'Operation Desert Storm'. I feel it's the least I can do – after all, it is costing HM Government thirty million pounds a day to keep Kuwait a democracy.

Sunday January 27th

According to the *Observer* today, Kuwait is not and has never been a democracy. It is ruled by the Kuwaiti Royal Family.

Bluebeard laughed when I told him. 'It's all to do with *oil*, Adrian,' he said. 'Do you think the Yanks would be in there if Kuwait's main product was *turnips*?'

Pandora bent down and kissed the back of his withered neck. How she could allow her young, vibrant flesh to come into contact with his ancient, wrinkled skin, I'll never know. I had to go into the bathroom and take deep breaths and control the urge to vomit. Why slobber over *him* when she could have *me*?

My mother rang at 4 p.m. I could hear my young stepfather, Martin Muffet, hammering in the background. 'Martin's putting some shelves up for my knick-knacks,' she shouted over the row. Then she asked me if I had read the extracts from *Dork's Diary* in the *Observer*. I was able to answer truthfully. 'No,' I said. 'You should,' said my mother. 'It's totally brilliant. When you next see Baz, will you ask him for a free copy, signed to Pauline and Martin?'

I said, 'It is highly unlikely that I will see Kent. I do not move in the same illustrious circles as him.'

'Which illustrious circles *do* you move in, then?' asked my mother.

'None,' I answered truthfully. Then I put the phone down and went to bed and pulled the duvet over my head.

Monday January 28th

Britain's Jo Durie and Jeremy Bates won the mixed doubles in Melbourne. This surely points to a renaissance in British tennis.

> *Pandora's Little Pussy*
> I love her little Pussy
> Her coat is so warm
> But if I should stroke her
> She'll call the police and identify me in
> A line-up
> And do me some harm

Wednesday January 30th

Shocked to hear on Radio Four that King Olav the Fifth of Norway was buried today. His contribution to the continuing success of the Norwegian leather industry is something that is little appreciated by the vast majority of the Great British Public. Prince Charles was England's graveside representative.

Borrowed *Scenes from Provincial Life* by William Cooper from the library. I only had time to choose one book, because a 'suspicious package' was found in the Romantic Fiction section and the library was evacuated.

Sink blocked again. Plunged for the duration of *The Archers*, but to no avail.

Thursday January 31st

I didn't arrive at the consulting room on Thames Street until 5.15 p.m. Leonora De Witt was not pleased.

'I'll have to charge you for the full hour, Mr Mole,' she said, seating herself in an armchair which was covered in old bits of carpet. 'Where would you like to sit?' she asked. There were many chairs in the room. I chose a dining chair which was standing against a wall.

When I was seated, I said, 'I was under the impression that our sessions were to be under the auspices of the National Health Service.'

'Then you were gravely mistaken,' said Ms De Witt. 'I charge thirty pounds an hour – under the auspices of the private enterprise system.'

'*Thirty pounds an hour!* How many sessions will I need?' I asked.

She explained that she couldn't possibly predict, that she knew nothing about me. That it depended on the cause of my unhappiness.

'How do you feel at the moment?' she asked.

'Apart from a slight headache, I feel fine,' I replied.

'What are you doing with your hands?' she said quietly.

'Wringing them,' I replied.

'What is that on your brow?' she asked.

'Sweat,' I answered, taking out my handkerchief.

'Are your buttocks clenched, Mr Mole?' she pressed.

'I suppose they are,' I said.

'Now answer my first question again, please. How do you feel at this moment?'

Her large brown eyes locked into mine. I couldn't avert my gaze.

'I feel totally miserable,' I said. 'And I lied about the headache.'

She talked at length about the *Gestalt* technique. She explained that it was possible to teach me 'coping mechanisms'. Apart from Pandora, she is probably the loveliest woman I have ever spoken to. I found it hard to take my eyes off her black-stockinged feet, which were slipped into black suede shoes with high heels. Was she wearing tights or stockings?

'So, Mr Mole, do you think we can work together?' she said.

She looked at her watch and stood up. Her hair looked like a midnight river pouring down her back. I eagerly affirmed that I would like to see her once a week. Then I gave her thirty pounds and left.

Friday February 1st

Just returned from Newport Pagnell. My nerves are shot to pieces. Brown drove like a man possessed. At no time did he exceed the speed limit, but he drove onto the kerb, scraped against hedgerows and on the motorway section of our journey he left only a six-inch gap between our fragile Ford Escort and the monolithic juggernaut in front of us.

'It saves precious fuel if you can stay in the lorry's slipstream,' he said by way of explanation. The man is an environmental fanatic. He spent last Christmas Day classifying seaweed at Dungeness. I rest my case. Thank God for the weekend. Or *le weekend*, as our fellow Europeans say.

Saturday February 2nd

Viscount Althorp, Princess Diana's brother, has confessed to his thin wife and the rest of the world that he had an affair in Paris. Prince Charles and Princess Diana must have been horrified to find out that there was an adulterer in the family. He should be stripped of his title immediately. The Royal Family and their close connections should be above such brutish instincts. The country looks to them to set the moral standard.

Had bath, shampooed beard, cut fingernails and toenails. Put hot oil on hair to nourish it and give it shine and the outward illusion of health.

11.45 p.m. Bert Baxter has just telephoned. He sounded pathetic. Pandora was out and in a moment of weakness I agreed to go and visit him in Leicester tomorrow. Wrote a note to Pandora, left it on her pillow.

Pandora,

Baxter rang in considerable distress, something about killing himself – I intend to visit him tomorrow. He intimated to me that he wished to see you too. I plan to rise at 8.30 to catch the train, or, should you wish to accompany me, my alternative *modus operandi* will be to rise at nine and be driven by you in your motor car, thus arriving in Leicester at approximately 11 a.m. Would you please inform me of your decision by the method of slipping a note under my door? Please do not disturb me tonight with the sounds of your wild love-making. The walls of my box room are very thin and I am sick of sleeping with my Sony Walkman on.

Adrian

Sunday February 3rd

At 2.10 a.m., Pandora burst into my box room and hurled abuse at me. She flung my note to her into my face and screamed, 'You pompous *nerd*, you pathetic *dork*! "*Modus operandi*"! 'Be driven by you in your motor car"! I want you out of this box room and out of my life, *tomorrow*!'

Bluebeard came in and led her away and I lay in bed and listened to them murmuring together in the kitchen. What brought on such an unprovoked outburst?

At 3.30 a.m. they went into Pandora's bedroom. At 3.45 a.m. I put Dire Straits into my Sony and turned the volume up to full.

Didn't wake until midday. Phoned Bert and said I was unable to visit him owing to being awake all night with intestinal pains. I could tell Bert didn't believe me. He said, 'You're a bleedin' liar. I've just spoken to my gal Pandora. She rang me on her car phone. She looked in your room before she set out for Leicester and she said you were sleepin' like a newborn.'

'Why didn't she wake me then?' I asked.

''Cos she 'ates the bleedin' sight of you,' said the diplomatic one.

Monday February 4th

Inexplicably late for work by twenty-three minutes. Brown was practically frothing at the mouth. Also accused me of stealing postage stamps. He said, 'Every penny is needed by the DOE if our wildlife is to be preserved.' As if! Are the badgers and foxes and tadpoles and lousy, stinking newts going to pop their clogs because I, Adrian Mole, made use of two second-class postage stamps paid for out of my taxes in the first place? No, Brown. I don't think so.

Tuesday February 5th

Pandora still in Leicester. Trimmed beard around mouth. Swallowed clippings. One lodged at back of throat; annoying.

Wednesday February 6th

Brown came into my cubicle today and demanded to see my 'A' level certificates! He had heard on the office grapevine that I had failed 'A' level Biology three times.

The only person in Oxford – apart from Pandora – who knows about my triple failure is Megan Harris, Brown's secretary. I confessed to her whilst in a drunken and emotional state at the DOE Christmas Party last year. She alone knows that my job as a Scientific Officer Grade One was granted to me under false pretences. Has Megan blabbed? I must know.

I told Leonora De Witt my family history tonight. It's a tragic story of rejection and alienation, but Leonora simply sat and picked balls of fluff from her sweater, which drew my attention to the shape of her comely breasts. It was obvious that she was not wearing a bra. I wanted to leave my chair and sink my head into her bosom. I went into some detail about my parents' deviant behaviour, but the only time she showed obvious interest was when I mentioned my dead grandfather, Albert Mole, whom I have to thank for my middle name.

'Did you see his dead body?' she asked.

'No,' I replied. 'The Co-op undertaker had screwed the coffin lid down and nobody could find the screwdriver at Grandma's house, so . . .'

'Continue,' ordered Leonora. So I did. Through fat, hot tears. I told about my feeling of exclusion from 'normal' life; of how I long to join my fellow human beings, to share their sorrows, their joys, their sing-songs in pubs.

Leonora said, 'People sing awful songs in pubs. Why do you feel a need to join in singing those mawkish lyrics and banal tunes?'

'I stood outside such pubs as a child,' I said. 'Every-body sounded so happy.'

Then the alarm went off on her watch and it was time to cough up thirty quid and leave.

On my way home I went into a pub and had a drink. I also initiated a conversation about the weather with an old man. There was no singing, so I went home.

Thursday February 7th

I asked Megan outright this morning. I approached her in the corridor as she was being scalded by the Autovent tea/coffee/oxtail soup machine. She ad-mitted that she had let it 'slip out' that I was totally unqualified for my position. Then she swore me to secrecy and informed me that she and Brown have been having an affair since 1977! Brown and the lovely Megan! Why do women throw themselves at worn-out old gits like Brown and Cavendish, and ignore young, virile, bearded men like me? It defies logic.

Megan was eager to talk about her affair with Brown. Apparently he had sworn to leave Mrs Brown in 1980, but has not yet done so. I feel sorry for Mrs Brown every time she comes into the office. It is not her fault that she looks like she does. Some women have got good dress sense and some women haven't. Mrs Brown obviously does not know that pop socks should only be worn under trousers or long skirts. Also, somebody should tell her that warts can be cured nowadays.

Friday February 8th

Pandora is back in Oxford, but not speaking to me much, apart from the bare facts that Bert is no longer suicidal. She bought him a kitten and also installed a cat flap in his back door. Brown asked me again for my Biology 'A' level certificate. I looked at him enigmatically and said, 'I think you'll find that Megan has the information you require.' God, blackmail is an ugly word. I hope Brown doesn't force me to use it.

I have thrown my condom away. It had exceeded its 'best before' date.

Monday February 11th

Megan came into my cubicle today, sobbing. Apparently Brown forgot her birthday, which was yesterday. Alack, alas! It looks as if I am cast into the role of Megan's only confidant. I put my arms around her and kissed her. She felt lovely and soft and squashy. She pulled away quite soon, however, and said, 'Your beard is scratchy and horrible.'

But was my beard the *real* reason?

Does my breath stink? Does my body stink?

Who can I trust to tell me the truth?

I can certainly see what Brown sees in Megan, but I will never in a billion years see what she sees in him. He is forty-two, thin, and wears atrocious clothes from 'Man at C&A'. Megan says he is good in bed. Who is she trying to kid? Good at what in bed? Doing jigsaws? Sleeping? Perhaps she means that he is unselfish with the duvet? If Brown is good in bed, then I am a tractor wheel.

Tuesday February 12th

Tried to visit newt habitat in Northamptonshire, but 'wrong kind of snow' caused Class 317 engine to fail. Was forced to sit in freezing carriage whilst buffet bar attendant gave out continuous announcements in annoying adenoidal voice. Was pleased when buffet car ran out of all supplies and closed. Got back to Oxford at 10.30 p.m., to find message from Megan. Rang her to find out that she and Brown had had a row; their affair is over. I was distraught. This means I no longer have a hold over Brown. It could signal the end of my career with the DOE.

Wednesday February 13th

Brown/Megan affair is on again. Apparently Brown cycled round to Megan's flat in the early hours, after telling Mrs Brown he was going bat-watching. Their reconciliation was very passionate.

I cannot imagine anything in the world more distasteful than seeing Brown in a state of orgasmic pleasure. Apart from *being* with Brown in a state of orgasmic pleasure.

Bought new condom – spearmint flavoured.

Also bought bunch of bananas. Megan says they are very good for those, like me, who suffer from an irritable bowel.

Thursday February 14th

Valentine's Day card from my mother as usual. Megan in tears again. Brown forgot. Bought economy box of tissues at lunchtime for Megan's sole use. I can't afford to keep wasting Kleenex on her. Bluebeard has sent Pandora a disgracefully extravagant bouquet (it is disgusting when people are starving), and at seven o'clock this evening he called with champagne, an Art Nouveau brooch and a pair of satin pyjamas. Then, as if that wasn't enough, he took her out for dinner in a hired car with uniformed driver! Most unacademic behaviour.

Cavendish behaves more like a pools winner than a professor of Linguistics at an ancient seat of learning.

Left to myself, I ate a simple meal of bread, tuna and cucumber and went to bed early. I am reading *English Love Poems*, edited by John Betjeman. Valen-

tine's Day is a ridiculous charade, the ignorant masses
are manipulated by the greetings card companies into
forking out millions – and for what? For the illusion
of being loved.

Friday February 15th

A Valentine's Day card! Signed 'A Secret Admirer'! I
sang in my bath. I walked to work without touching
the pavement! Who is she? The signature told me that
she is educated and uses a felt-tip pen, like me.

Leonora had her hair pinned up today; she was
wearing silver earrings so long that they brushed her
slim shoulders. She was wearing a scooped-neck black
top. A bra strap was visible. Black lace. She occasionally
pushed it back inside her top. Every time she did so
her sparkling bracelet fell down her arm towards her
elbow. I am not in love with Leonora De Witt. But I
am obsessed with her. She invades my dreams. She
made me talk to an empty chair and pretend that it
was my mother. I told the chair that it drank too much
and wore its skirts too short.

Saturday February 16th

I finally took my library books back today: *A Single
Man* by Christopher Isherwood, *English Love Poems* by
John Betjeman, *Scenes from Provincial Life* by William

Cooper and *Notes from the Underground* by Dosto-evsky. I owed seven pounds, eighty pence in fines. My least favourite librarian was on duty at the desk. I don't know her name, but she is the Welsh one with the extroverted spectacles.

After I'd written out my cheque and handed it to her, she said, 'Do you have a cheque card?'

'Yes,' I replied. 'But it's at home.'

'Then I'm afraid I cannot accept this cheque,' she said.

'But you know me,' I said. 'I've been coming here once a week for eighteen months.'

'I'm afraid that I don't recognize you at all,' she said and handed me my cheque back.

'This beard is quite recent,' I said coldly. 'Perhaps you could try to visualize my face without it.'

'I don't have time for visualization,' she said. 'Not since the cuts.'

I showed her a small photograph of myself that I carry in my wallet. It was taken pre-beard.

'No,' she said, after giving it a cursory glance. 'I don't recognize that man.'

'But that man is *me*!' I shouted. A queue of people had built up behind me and they were listening avidly to the exchange. The librarian's spectacles flashed in anger.

'I have been doing the job of three people since the cuts began,' she said. 'And you are making my job even more difficult. Please go home and find your cheque card.'

'It is now 5.25 p.m. and the library closes in five minutes,' I said. 'Even Superman couldn't fly back in time to pay the fines, choose four books and leave before the doors close.'

Somebody behind me in the queue muttered, 'Get a bleedin' move on, Superman.'

So I said to the spectacled one, 'I'll be back tomorrow.'

'Oh no you won't,' she said, with a tiny smile. 'Due to the cuts this library doesn't open again until Wednesday.'

On my way home I railed internally against a government that is depriving me of new reading matter. Pandora has forbidden me to touch her books ever since I left a Jaffa cake inside her Folio Society edition of *Nicholas Nickleby*; Julian's books are in Chinese and I'm finding the last hundred pages of *War and Peace* heavy going. There is no way I can afford to buy a new book. Even a paperback costs at least a fiver.

I have to cough up thirty pounds a week for Leonora. I have even had to cut down on my consumption of bananas. I am down to one a day.

I have been forced to read my old diaries. Some of the entries are incredibly perceptive. And the poems have stood the test of time.

Sunday February 17th

Pandora spoke to me today. She said, 'I want you to leave. You stultify me. We had a childhood romance, but we are both adults now: we have grown in different directions and the time has come to part.' Then she added, cruelly, I thought, 'And that bloody beard makes you look absolutely ridiculous. For God's sake, shave it off.' I went to bed shattered. Read page 977 of *War and Peace*, then lay awake staring into the darkness.

Monday February 18th

I looked into the newsagent's on my way to work. I saw the following advertisement, written in a reasonably educated hand, on a Conqueror postcard:

Large sunny room to let – in family house.
Fire sign preferred. Use of W machine/dryer.
£75pw inclusive to N/S male professional. Ring Mrs Hedge.

I rang Mrs Hedge as soon as I got to my cubicle. She asked for my date of birth. I told her it was April 2nd, which excited the response, 'Aries, good. I'm Sagittarius.'

I went to see her at 7 p.m. and inspected the room. 'It's not very sunny,' I said.

She said, 'No, but would you expect it to be on an evening in February?'

I like the cut of her jib. She is oldish (thirty-five to thirty-seven, I would guess), but has not got a bad figure, although it's hard to tell with the clothes women wear nowadays. Her hair is lovely; treacle-coloured, like Pandora's used to be before she started mucking about with Colour-Glo. She was wearing quite a bit of make-up and her mascara had smudged. I hope this is not a sign of sluttishness. She was recently divorced and needs to let the room in order to continue paying the mortgage. Apparently the Building Society (my own, coincidentally) has turned nasty.

She invited me to test the bed. I did so and had a sudden vision of myself and Mrs Hedge engaging in vigorous sexual intercourse. I said aloud, 'I'm sorry.'

Naturally Mrs Hedge was completely in the dark as to the reason for my apology and said, '"Sorry"? Does that mean you don't like the bed?'

'No, no,' I gibbered. 'I love you; I mean, I love the bed.'

I was concerned that I hadn't made a good impression, so I rang Mrs Hedge when I got home (in an effort to impress her) and informed her that I was a writer; would the scratching of my pen in the small hours bother her?

'Not at all,' she replied. 'I am visited by the Muse myself in the night occasionally.'

You can't walk on the pavement in Oxford without bumping into a published or unpublished writer. It's no wonder that the owner of the stationery shop where I buy my supplies goes to the Canary Islands twice a year and drives a Mercedes. (He drives a Mercedes in *Oxford*, not the Canary Islands, though of course it is perfectly feasible that he has the use of a Mercedes *in* the Canary Islands as well. But I doubt, given the comparative infrequency of his visits, if he actually *owns* a Mercedes in the Canary Islands though I suppose it could be leased.) I don't know why I felt the need to explain the Canary Islands/Mercedes confusion. I suppose it may be another example of what Leonora calls my 'childish pedantry'.

Tuesday February 19th

My mother rang in a panic at 11.00 p.m., to ask if Martin Muffet, my young stepfather, had turned up at the flat. Quite frankly, I laughed out loud. Why would Muffet want to visit *me*? He knows I disapprove of my mother's foolhardy second marriage. Apart from the age difference (which is as wide as the mouth of the Amazon), they are physically and mentally incompatible.

Muffet is a six foot six bag of bones, who thinks the Queen works hard and that Paddy Ashdown is incapable of telling a lie. My mother is five foot five and squeezes herself into clothes two sizes too small for her and thinks that Britain should be a republic and that our first president should be Ken Livingstone, the well-known newt lover. On my last visit, I noticed that young Mr Muffet was far less attentive to my mother than of late. I expect he is regretting his mad rush into matrimony.

My mother said, 'He went to London this morning, to visit the Lloyd's building for his Engineering course.'

My mother's grasp of the geographical layout of the British Isles has always been minimal. I informed her of the distance from the Lloyd's building in the City of London to that of my box room in Oxford.

She said in a pathetic voice, 'I thought he might have popped in on his way back to Leicester.'

She phoned back at 2 a.m. Muffet was trapped in an underground train in a tunnel for six hours, or so he said.

Thursday February 21st

This time Leonora invited me to imagine that the chair was my father. She gave me an African stick and I beat the chair until I lay limp and exhausted and physically unable to lift the stick again.

'He's not a bad bloke, my dad,' I said. 'I don't know why I went so berserk.'

Leonora said, 'Don't talk to me, talk to him. Talk to the chair. The chair is your father.'

I felt stupid addressing the empty chair again, but I wanted to please Leonora, so I forced myself to look the upholstery in the eye and said, 'Why didn't you buy me an anglepoise lamp when I was revising for my GCSEs?'

Leonora said, 'Good, good, take it further, Adrian.'

'I hate your Country and Western cassettes,' I said.

'No,' Leonora whispered. 'Deeper, darker, an earlier memory.'

'I remember when I was three,' I said. 'You came into the bedroom, yanked my dummy out of my mouth and said, "*Real* boys don't need a dummy."'

I then grabbed the stick from where it was lying on the floor and once again began to beat the chair. Dust flew.

Leonora said, 'Good, good. How do you *feel*?'

I said, 'I feel terrible. I've wrenched my shoulder beating that chair.'

'No, no,' she said, irritably. 'How do you feel *inside*?'

I cottoned on.

'Oh, at peace with myself,' I lied. I got up, gave my therapeutic dominatrix the thirty quid and left. I needed to buy some Nurofen before the late-night chemist closed. I was in agony with my shoulder.

Friday February 22nd

Another split in the Newport Pagnell newts. There are now three separate habitats. Something fishy is happening in the newt world. Brown is phoning newt experts worldwide, droning on about this phenomenon.

Mrs Hedge has interviewed other potential tenants, but has chosen me! I was racked all night by erotic dreams, concerning me, Brown, Megan and Mrs Hedge. I am ashamed, but what can I do? I can't control my subconscious, can I? I was forced to go to the launderette, though it is not my usual day.

Saturday February 23rd

Norman Schwarzkopf was on television tonight, pointing a stick at an incomprehensible map. Why he was dressed in army camouflage is a mystery to me:

a) there are no trees in the desert
b) there were no trees in the briefing room
c) he is obviously too important to go anywhere near the enemy; he could go around dressed like Coco the Clown and still not be shot at

Tuesday February 26th

Visited Mrs Hedge today, to finalize arrangements for renting the room and to discuss our tenancy agreement. She had a picture of the charred head of an Iraqi soldier who was found dead in a vehicle held against her fridge by a Mickey Mouse magnet. I averted my eyes and asked her for a drink of water.

Wednesday February 27th

Yesterday evening I informed Pandora that I am moving out of the flat at the weekend. I had hoped that she would fall on my neck and beg me to stay, but she didn't. At 1 a.m. I was woken by the sound of a champagne cork popping, glasses clinking and wild, unrestrained laughter from Pandora, Cavendish and Julian. The Infernal Triangle.

Thursday February 28th

Leonora did most of the talking tonight. She told me that I expect too much of myself, that I have impossibly high standards. She told me to be kind to myself and made me draw up a list of ten things I enjoy doing. Every time I banish a negative thought about myself, I am allowed to treat myself.

She asked if I can afford the occasional self-indulgence. I confessed that I have savings in the Market Harborough Building Society. She gave me a piece of paper and a child's crayon and told me to write down ten treats.

Treats
  1) Reading novels
  2) Writing novels
  3) Sexual intercourse

4) Looking at women
5) Buying stationery
6) Eating bananas
7) Crab paste sandwiches
8) Watching boxing on television
9) Listening to Tchaikovsky
10) Walking in the countryside

I asked Leonora what her treats were.

She said in a husky low voice, 'We're not here to talk about me.' Then she smiled and showed her beautifully white teeth and said, 'We have a few things in common, Adrian.'

I felt a throb of sexual desire surge through me.

'I too like to watch the boxing on television,' she said. 'I'm a Bruno fan.'

Friday March 1st

At breakfast this morning, I asked Cavendish if he would help me to move my things to Mrs Hedge's. He has got a big Volvo estate. He said, 'Can't think of anything I'd rather do, Aidy.' He offered to move me immediately, but I said, 'Tomorrow morning will do. Some of us have to *work*.'

He laughed and said, 'So you think teaching Linguistics is a soft option, do you, Aidy?'

I said, 'Yes, as a matter of fact, I do. I doubt if *work* is a four-letter word to you.'

'Speaking as a professor of Linguistics,' he snarled, 'I can assure you that work is indeed a four-letter word.' As he reached for the ashtray, his dressing gown fell open, revealing withered nipples and grey matted chest hair. I was almost physically sick. I could hardly swallow my Bran Flakes.

Took the portable TV back to the shop. On my return, I wrote a poem to Pandora and slipped it under her door. It was my last-ditch attempt to seduce her away from Cavendish.

> *Pandora! Let Me! by A. Mole*
> Let me stroke your inner thighs
> Let me hear your breathy sighs
> Let me feel your silky skin
> Let me make your senses spin
> Let me touch your soft white breast
> Let us stop and have a rest.
> Let me join our beating hearts
> Let me forge our private parts
> Let me delve and make you mine
> Let me give you food and wine
> Let me lick you with my tongue
> Let me do whatever's wrong
> Let me watch you take your pleasure
> Let me dress you in black leather
> Let me fit you like a glove
> Let me consummate our love.

At 1 a.m. Pandora pushed a note under my door.

Adrian,
   If you continue to send such filth to me, I will, in future, pass it on to the police.
   Pandora

Saturday March 2nd

As I packed my belongings, I reflected that I have not acquired much in my life. A basic wardrobe of clothes. A few hundred books. A Sony Walkman. A dozen or so cassettes. My own mug, cup, bowl and plate. A poster by Munch, a cactus, a magnifying mirror on a stand, a bowl for bananas, and a lamp. It is not much to show for a year and a half of toil at the DOE. True, I have got £2,579 saved in the Market Harborough Building Society, and £197.39 in Nat West, but even so.

   I found the blue plastic comb I have been searching for since last year. It was on top of the wardrobe. Why? How did it get there? I have never climbed on the wardrobe to comb my hair. I suspect Julian. He is a big fan of Jeremy Beadle's.

11 p.m. Too tired to write much, just to put it on the record that I am lying in Mrs Hedge's bed. It is very comfortable. My new address is now:

8 Sitwell Villas
Summertown
Oxford.

Sunday March 3rd

I didn't know where I was when I woke up, then I remembered. I smelt bacon cooking, but I didn't go downstairs. I felt like an intruder. I got up, tiptoed to the bathroom, got dressed, made my bed, then sat on the bed listening to sounds from below. Eventually, driven by hunger, I went downstairs. Mrs Hedge was not there. The breakfast plates were still on the kitchen table. The kitchen pedal bin was overflowing. There were eggshells on the floor. The cupboard under the sink was full of filthy yellow dusters. The fridge was full of little saucers containing mouldy leftovers. The grill pan was unwashed. The *Observer* was speckled with tinned tomato juice.

It is as I feared: Mrs Hedge is a slut. The phone rang non-stop. Took messages: 'Ted phoned.' 'Ian rang.' 'Martin called.' 'Call Kingsley back.' 'Julian rang: Are you going to the launch on Tuesday?'

I was mopping the kitchen floor when Mrs Hedge returned. She was carrying a large shrub and four tins of Carlsberg.

'Christ,' she said. 'It looks like I've struck lucky. Do you like housework, Mr Mole?'

'I find it difficult to tolerate disorder,' I said.

She went out into the garden to plant the shrub, then sat on the patio on an iron chair, swigging Carlsberg out of the tin. She didn't seem to notice the cold. When it started to rain, she came into the house, got a golfing umbrella from the jar in the hall, and went back out again. I went up to my room to work on my novel, *Lo! The Flat Hills of My Homeland.*

When I next went downstairs, there was no sign of Mrs Hedge. I was pleased to see three tins of Carlsberg still left in the fridge. She may be a slut and an eccentric, but, thank God, she is not yet an alcoholic.

Monday March 4th

Mrs Hedge was still in bed when I got back from work. The kitchen was a disgrace. The Carlsberg was gone from the fridge. She must have drunk them in bed! It is the only conclusion.

Wednesday March 6th

Went to Pandora's to pick up my post. Nothing exciting. Letters from the Market Harborough Building Society, *Reader's Digest* and Plumbs, a firm promoting stretch covers. How did Plumbs get hold of my name and address? I have never shown the slightest interest in soft furnishings. Pandora has turned my box room into a study. I opened a file on her desk marked, 'Lecture Notes'. Didn't understand a word. They were written in what was probably Serbo-Croat.

Thursday March 7th

I walked into the bathroom tonight without knocking. Mrs Hedge was in the bath, shaving her legs. I will buy a bolt for the door tomorrow. I'd guess she is at least 38C.

Friday March 8th

Mrs Hedge said, 'Feel free to invite your friends round, Mr Mole.' I told her that I hadn't got any friends. I walk alone.

When I told Leonora the same thing, she said, 'Before our next session, please try to speak to a stranger; smile and initiate a conversation; and make a new female friend.'

Saturday March 9th

There was a stranger in the kitchen when I came down. He was eating Marmite on toast. He said, 'Hi. I'm Gerry.'

I smiled and said, 'Good morning. I'm Adrian Mole.'

That was the extent of our social intercourse. I found it difficult to initiate a conversation with a man wearing a woman's negligee and nothing else.

I made myself a cup of tea and left.

I wish I was back in my box room.

Monday March 11th

Mr Major on the news. He said, 'I want us to be where we belong, at the very heart of Europe, working with our partners in building the future.'

A peculiar thing: Mr Major cannot say the word 'want' to rhyme with 'font', which is the correct English pronunciation. For some reason, he says '*went*'. I suspect that this disability stems from childhood. When little John lisped, 'I want some sweeties,' etc., etc. Did his father leap down from his trapeze and shout, 'I'll give you *want*!'? Or shout, 'Say *want* again and I'll beat you black and blue,' thus leaving little John sobbing into the sawdust of the Big Top and unable to pronounce that little English word?

My heart goes out to him. He is obviously in urgent need of therapy. It seems to me that we have both suffered for having embarrassing fathers. I will bring the subject up when I next see Leonora.

Tuesday March 12th

Brown slipped down a grassy bank and bruised his coccyx at the weekend. He was collecting owl droppings. He has been incapacitated and is lying on a plank on his bedroom floor. Ha! Ha! Ha! Ho! Ho! Ho! Three cheers!

Wednesday March 13th

Brown's deputy, Gordon Goffe, is throwing his weight (twenty stone) about. He is conducting an enquiry into 'postage stamp pilfering'. This is just my luck. I was about to send the opening chapters of my novel *Lo! The Flat Hills of My Homeland* off to Faber and Faber today. I shall have to fork out for the stamps myself. Once they have read these chapters, they will be panting for the rest.

Thursday March 14th

The Birmingham Six have been released from prison.

Gordon Goffe is lumbering around the offices, carrying out spot checks on our drawers. Megan was found to have an illicit box of DOE ballpoints. She has received an oral warning. No session with Leonora this week. She is attending a conference in Sacramento.

Friday March 15th

Barry Kent was on *Kaleidoscope* reading from *Dork's Diary*. The little I heard was nihilistic rubbish. Goffe barged into my cubicle and said that I was not allowed to listen to Radio Four during office hours. I pointed out that Mr Brown had never objected.

Goffe said, 'I am not Mr Brown,' a statement so stupid that I was lost for an answer. I've got an answer now, at three minutes past midnight, but it is obviously too late.

Saturday March 16th

Called round to Pandora's flat for my letters. Nothing of interest: circular for thermal underwear; *Reader's Digest* competition entry form – prize: a gold bar; Plumbs catalogue, offering discount on mock velvet curtains. I am twenty-four next month and I must confess, dear journal, that I had expected by now to be in correspondence with interesting and fascinating people. Instead, the world seems to think of me as a person who gets up in the morning, puts on his thermal underwear, draws his mock velvet curtains and settles down to read his new copy of *Reader's Digest*.

The cat looked thin, but was pleased to see me. I gave it a whole tin of cat food. Pandora was out, so

I had a good look around the flat. Her underwear drawer is full of disgusting sex aids. Bluebeard is obviously not up to it.

Sunday March 17th

Had an interesting talk about the Russian elections with the girl in the local newsagent's this morning. Then, as she handed me my *Sunday Times*, she remarked (joking, I presume), 'It's very heavy. Would you like me to help you carry it home?'

'No,' I jocularly replied. 'I think I can just about manage.' Though, as I took it, I pretended to buckle under its weight. How we laughed.

She is quite pleasant-looking in a sort of unassuming sort of way.

6.00 p.m. On rereading the above, I think I have been unfair to the girl in the newsagent's. A gingham nylon overall is not the most flattering of garments. And I didn't see her legs, as they were behind the counter at all times.

I have just read the *Sunday Times* books section and was appalled, astonished and disgusted to see that *Dork's Diary* is at number ten in the hardback bestseller list today!

Monday March 18th

Called in at the newsagent's for a packet of Polos on the way to work. The girl joked that I was paying for fresh air, i.e. the hole! This hadn't occurred to me before, so I handed the Polos back to her and said, 'Okay, I'll have Trebor Mints instead.' Again, we laughed uproariously. She has certainly got a good sense of humour. Legs still behind the counter. Brown still malingering at home. Goffe still rampaging in the office. Leonora will be pleased to hear about the girl in the newsagent's.

Tuesday March 19th

A letter from Pandora, my first at Sitwell Villas:

Sunday, March 17th

Adrian,

I have asked you many times to return the front door key to this flat. You have not yet done so. I'm afraid I must give you an ultimatum. Either the key is in my possession by 7 p.m. on Tuesday night, or I call out a locksmith, have the lock changed and send the bill to you. The choice is yours. I will no longer tolerate you:

a) interfering in the cat's feeding pattern;

b) snooping in my underwear drawer; or

   c) helping yourself to food from the refrigerator when I
      am not there.

As I have said, I will continue to redirect your post (such
as it is) and relay any messages that I consider to be urgent.

At 6.59 p.m., I pushed an envelope containing the key,
a ten-pence piece and a terse note under the door of
Pandora's flat. The note said:

Pandora,

a) In my opinion, the cat is too thin and appears to be
    lacking in energy;

b) I vividly remember you saying that 'Suspenders, etc.
    are symbols of women's enslavement to men's lust.'
    Ditto vibrators;

c) The pot of crab paste in the refrigerator was *mine*. I
    purchased it on February 20th this year. I have the
    receipt to prove it. I admit that I did help myself to a
    slice of bread. I enclose, as you cannot fail to see,
    a ten-pence coin, as remuneration for the slice of
    granary.

Wednesday March 20th

How do I get the legs out from behind the counter?

Thursday March 21st

Her name is Bianca. A strange name for somebody working in a newsagent's. They are usually called Joyce. I saw her carrying boxes of crisps from a delivery lorry into the shop. Legs okay, but ankles a bit bony, so, on a scale of one to ten, only five.

9.00 p.m. Leonora was in a strange mood tonight. She was annoyed because I was fifteen minutes late. I pointed out to her that she would be paid for the full hour.

She said, 'That's not the point, Adrian. Our sessions together are carefully structured. I insist that you are punctual in future.'

I replied, 'My chronic unpunctuality is one of my many problems. Shouldn't you be addressing it?'

She crossed her shapely legs under her black silk skirt and I saw a flash of white. From that point on I was helpless and could only nod or shake my head in answer to her questions. Speech was beyond me. I felt that if I opened my mouth I would utter crude inarticulate protestations of lust, which would frighten her and signal the end of our time together.

Ten minutes before the end of our session she said, 'You are displaying typically regressive behaviour at the moment, shall we take advantage of it?'

I nodded and she encouraged me to talk about my earliest memories. I remembered being bitten by a dog and my grandma applying iodine to the wound. I also remember my (now dead) grandad kicking the dog round the kitchen.

Then it was time to fork out £30 and leave.

Saturday March 23rd

Mrs Hedge asked me if she should marry Gerry, sell up and move to Cardiff. I advised against it. I have only just settled in, found out how to work the grill pan, etc. I can't face looking for alternative accommodation. Anyway, why ask me? I've only spoken to the ugly brute a few times.

Sunday March 24th

The lavatory seat was up, so I guessed that Gerry was *in situ*. I went to buy my newspaper from Bianca and, on my return, sure enough, Gerry and Mrs Hedge were in the kitchen eating eggs and bacon. Mrs Hedge didn't look pleased to see me. I threw a few Rice Krispies into a bowl and took them up to my room. But, by the time I'd got upstairs, they had stopped snapping and crackling and popping, which annoyed me considerably. I loathe soggy cereals.

Monday March 25th

Gerry is now a fixture. I am like a cuckoo in the nest. A gooseberry in the strawberry patch. A piranha in the goldfish bowl. Conversation stops when I enter the kitchen or sitting room and they are there. I wanted to watch the Oscar ceremony on television tonight, but Gerry snatched the remote control and kept it on his lap, thus denying me the pleasure of *seeing* that gifted and modest actor Jeremy Irons win an Oscar for Britain. I had to hear this wonderful news on Radio Four and visualize Mr Irons's delight myself. Whoever said that the 'pictures are better on the radio' was completely wrong.

Tuesday March 26th

I have asked Bianca to give me prior warning, should a suitable-sounding postcard arrive at the shop offering accommodation. She agreed. I think she finds me personable. Haste has changed the meaning of the above sentence: postcards cannot walk into a news-agent's and talk suitably. Leonora cancelled tonight's appointment. 'An emergency,' she said.

Am I not an emergency? My sanity hangs by a gossamer thread. Leonora is the only barrier between me and the public ward in a lunatic asylum. How will she live with herself if I am admitted foaming at the mouth and struggling inside a straitjacket?

Wednesday March 27th

Mr David Icke, who is a famous Leicester person, has revealed that he is a 'channel for the Christ spirit'. He went on television and told the goggling press that his wife and daughter were 'incarnations of the archangel Michael'. He blamed the planet Sirus for bringing earthquakes and pestilence to the world. Gerry and Mrs Hedge mocked him and said he is barmy, but I'm not so sure. We Leicester people are known for our level heads. Perhaps Mr Icke knows something that we ordinary mortals cannot even guess at.

Thursday March 28th

Bianca studied Astronomy in the sixth form. She said this morning, 'There is no such planet as Sirus.' But, as I pointed out to her, 'David Icke did say that Sirus was *undiscovered*, so naturally no reference *would* be found to it in the books, would it?'

A queue formed, so we were forced to break off our discussion. I called in on my way home from work, but Bianca was busy – some old git was complaining about his newspaper bill.

Friday March 29th

The more I think about David Icke's predictions, i.e. that the world will end unless it 'purges itself of evil', the more it makes sense. He is a successful man, who was employed by the BBC, no less! He was also a professional goalkeeper for Hereford City. We should not be too quick to scoff. Columbus was once mocked for remarking that the world was round. Something that was verified by the first US astronauts.

My mother rang tonight to ask me what I want for my birthday next week. I told her to get me the usual, a book token. She went on to say that Leicester was agog about David Icke, and that 'there has been a run on turquoise track suits' (worn by Mr Icke's followers). She said she felt sorry for his mother. Apparently, Mr Icke claimed he was born on the planet Sirus, whereas his mother said in the *Leicester Mercury* that she distinctly remembers giving birth to him in the Leicester General Maternity Hospital.

I ran out of bananas tonight. I had to walk to the outer suburbs before finding an off-licence that stocked them.

Saturday March 30th

Posted two birthday cards to myself. I put second-class stamps on, so they should get here by Tuesday morning.

Spring

Monday April 1st

A man with a Glaswegian accent rang me in my cubicle this morning and said, 'I have just finished reading the opening chapters of your novel *Lo! The Flat Hills of My Homeland* and I want to publish it next year. Would an advance of £50,000 be acceptable?'

I stammered out, 'Yes,' and asked to whom I was speaking.

'*A. Fool!*' laughed the imposter, and slammed the phone down.

How cruel can you get? For fifteen seconds, I had achieved my ambition. I was a professional writer living in my own house. I'd learned to drive. I had a car in the garage. I had a Rolex watch and a Mont Blanc pen. There was an air ticket to the USA in the pocket of my cashmere coat. Fan letters bristled inside my leather briefcase. Invitations to literary events were stacked on the mantelpiece. Then my dream was shattered by the hoaxer and I went back to being simple Adrian Mole, who was halfway through writing a report on newt movements, in a cubicle in a DOE building in Oxford. I suspect Goffe.

Tuesday April 2nd

Birthday cards from Mother, Rosie, Father, Grandma, Mrs Hedge and Megan. Six cards in all. Not bad, I needn't have posted two to myself.

Presents
1) Ten pound book token from mother.
2) W. H. Smith voucher from father (fiver).
3) 2 pairs of socks from Mrs Hedge (white).
4) Cactus plant from Megan (obscene).

No surprise party. No candles to blow out. No singing. No Leonora until Thursday.

Wednesday April 3rd

I am twenty-four and one day old. *Question*: What have I done with my life? *Answer*: Nothing.

Graham Greene died today. I wrote to him four years ago, pointing out a grammatical error in his book *The Human Factor*. He didn't reply.

Thursday April 4th

I trimmed my beard this morning. Mrs Hedge screamed when I came out of the bathroom. When she recovered, she said, 'Christ, you look like the Yorkshire Ripper.'

I had a terrible session with Leonora. I went into her room with the self-esteem of an anorexic aphid and came out feeling worse.

My low self-esteem on entering Leonora's room was due to an acrimonious phone conversation I'd had with my mother earlier. She had rung the office to ask me if I would like to go to a party given by Barry Kent to celebrate the success of *Dork's Diary*. The venue is the North East Leicester Working Men's Club, and half of Leicester has been invited.

I said to my mother, 'I would sooner wash a corpse.'

My mother accused me of petty jealousy, and then had a tantrum and recited my faults: arrogance, overweening pride, snobbery, pretension, phoney intellectualism, wimpishness, etc., etc.

I recited this to Leonora who said, 'I suggest that you take on board what your mother is saying. I also suggest that you *go to the party*.' She said that she had bought five copies of *Dork's Diary*: for her husband, Fergus; for her best friend, Susan Strachan; for her therapist, Simon; for her supervisor, Alison; and for herself. I was totally gobsmacked. When Leonora said that it was time to go, I refused to leave my chair.

I said, 'I can't bear the thought of you enjoying Barry Kent's work.'

Leonora said, 'Tough, give me thirty pounds and leave.'

I said, 'No, I am totally sexually obsessed by you.

I think about you constantly. I have revealed my innermost feelings to you.'

Leonora said, 'Yours is a standard reaction. You'll get over it.'

I said, 'Leonora, I feel betrayed. I refuse to be treated like an example from a text book.'

Leonora stood up and tossed her magnificent head and said, 'Ours is a professional relationship, Mr Mole. It could never be anything else. Come and see me next Thursday.'

'Okay,' I said. 'Take your thirty pieces of silver.'

I flung a Market Harborough Building Society cheque made out for thirty pounds onto the desk and left, slamming the door.

If my father had allowed me to abandon that dummy in my own time, I'm convinced I would now be enjoying perfect mental health.

Saturday April 6th

Am I the only person in Britain who has an open mind re the David Icke sensation? Bianca described him as a 'barmpot' this morning – but as I pointed out to her, Jesus himself was reviled in his day. The press were against him and the money-lenders slagged him off to all and sundry. Also, Jesus was a bit of an eccentric as regards clothes. He would not have won a 'Best Dressed Palestinian of the Year Award'. But, had track suits been around in Christ's day, he would almost certainly have opted for the comfort and wash-ability of such garments.

Sunday April 7th

Dork's Diary is now at number eight. Glanced through my *Illustrated Bible Stories* tonight and was startled to find on page 33 (Raising Lazarus) that Jesus is wearing turquoise robes!!!

Monday April 8th

Brown is back, but he is wearing a noisy surgical corset, which is quite useful (the noise, not the corset), because Megan is seeing Bill Blane (Badger Dept) on the side. I like Bill. He and I discussed David Icke at the Autovent today. Bill agrees with me that Sirus could have been overlooked by the astronomers. It could well have been hidden behind another, bigger planet.

The emir of Kuwait has promised to hold parliamentary elections next year. He has announced that women will be allowed to vote. Good for you, Sir!

Tuesday April 9th

John Major has been cross-examined by the press about his 'O' levels. I hope this won't remind Brown about my own, non-existent, Biology 'A' level. Why, oh why, couldn't I have been born an American? College students there are given multiple choice type exams. All the dumbos have to do is put a tick against what they think is the right answer.

> *Example:*   Question: Who discovered America?
> Was it: a) Columbus?
> b) Mickey Mouse?
> c) Rambo?

Wednesday April 10th

Bill Blane has asked me to go for a drink after work tomorrow. This could be the start of a new friendship.

Thursday April 11th

Bill wanted to talk about Megan. In fact, he talked about her all night. I couldn't get a word in edgeways, apart from saying, 'Same again?' when it was my turn to buy a round. I drank far too much (three pints) and in my muddled state started walking back to

Pandora's flat before realizing my mistake and turning my steps towards the Hedge household.

Friday April 12th

Worked on *Lo! The Flat Hills of My Homeland* tonight. Started Chapter Eleven:

As he skirted the top of the hill, he looked east and saw the city of Leicester glowing in the dying embers of the setting sun. The tower blocks reflected the scarlet rays and bounced them against the factory chimneys and the Royal Infirmary multi-storey car park. He sighed with the glorious anticipation of knowing that he would soon be tramping the reconstituted concrete streets of his home town. He could have entered the city by a more discreet route – turned off the motorway at Junction 23 – but he preferred this, the route of the sheep drovers, and anyway, he hadn't got a car.

He had been away too long, he thought. He had grown tired of the world and its attractions. Leicester was where his heart was. He strode down the hill, his eyes were wet. The wind, perhaps? Or the pain of absence? He would never know. The sun slipped away behind the grand edifice of the Alliance and Leicester Building Society headquarters and he felt the stealthy black fingers of night collect around him. Soon it was dark. Still he descended. Down. Down.

Not many people know that Leicester lies in a basin, he ruminated. No wonder it is the bronchitis centre of the world, he thought. Before long, he had descended the hill and he was on flat ground.

I think this is probably the best writing I have ever done. It is magnificent. I hope I can maintain this standard throughout the novel.

Saturday April 13th

Notes on *Lo!*:

a) Should I give my hero a name? Or should I continue to call him '*he*', '*him*', etc.?
b) Should the narrative be stronger? At the moment, not much happens. *He* leaves Leicester, then comes back to Leicester. Should the reader know what *he* does in between?
c) Should *he* have sex, or go shopping? Most modern novels are full of references to one or the other – the reading public obviously relishes such activities.

Descriptions (to be slotted in somewhere):

The tree bent in the wind, like a pensioner at Land's End.

The fried egg spluttered in the frying pan like an old man having a tubercular coughing fit in a 1930s National Health Service hospital.

Her breasts were as full as hot air balloons. Her face was infused with anger, her eyes flashed like a manic lighthouse whose wick needed cleaning.

The tea was welcome. *He* sipped it gratefully, like an African elephant which has previously found its waterhole to be dry, but then remembered, and walked to, another.

From now on, I shall write down these thoughts and ideas as they come to me. They are far too good to waste. Publication looks to be within my grasp.

Sunday April 14th

Woke at 8.30, had breakfast: cornflakes, toast, brown sauce, two cups of tea. Collected *Sunday Times* and *Observer*. Bianca not there. *Dork's Diary* has gone to number seven. Changed into blazer. Walked round Outer Ring Road, came back. Brushed and hung up blazer. Lay on bed. Slept. Woke up, put on blazer, went out, had pizza in Pizza Hut. Came back, lay on bed, slept. Woke, had bath, changed into pyjamas and dressing gown. Cut toenails, trimmed beard, inspected skin. Tidied tapes into alphabetical order, Abba to Warsaw Concerto. Went downstairs. Mrs Hedge in kitchen, in tears at kitchen table. 'I've got nobody to confide in,' she cried. Made crab paste sandwiches. Went to bed. Wrote up journal.

I can't go on like this; I'd have more of a social life in prison.

Monday April 15th

Went to see DOE doctor, Dr Abrahams. I told him I was depressed. He told me he was depressed. I told him that my life was meaningless, that my ambitions remained unrealized. He told me that his dream was to become the Queen's gynaecologist by the age of 44. I asked him how old he was. He told me that he was 45. Poor old git. He gave me a prescription for my depression. I asked the chemist if there were any side effects.

She said, 'Well, there's lack of concentration. Your physical movement may be reduced. You'll notice an increase in heart rate. There'll possibly be sweating and tremors, constipation and perhaps difficulty in urinating. Bit depressing, really, isn't it?'

I agreed with her and tore the prescription into pieces.

Wednesday April 17th

Rocky gave me a lift to work this morning in his limo. We discussed Pandora, how arrogant she is, etc. Rocky said, 'But, y'know, Aid, I'll always love the girl, she's, y'know, kinda like *unique*.'

I congratulated Rocky on his use of the word 'unique'.

Rocky told me that Carly Pick, his girl friend, is teaching him new words.

I said, 'So, she's extending your vocabulary, is she?' But he looked at me blankly, from which I inferred that she hadn't been at it for long.

When the car drew up outside the DOE, I was pleased to see that Brown was looking out of his office window. He ducked out of sight, but he couldn't have failed to see me exiting from the limousine. It won't hurt Brown to know that I mingle with the rich and powerful.

Robert Maxwell has saved the *Mirror*. He is a saint!

Thursday April 18th

The Newport Pagnell newts seem to have settled down, thank God. The road plans are finalized and construction is due to start next month.

Mrs Brown came to the office today. She had lost her handbag in the Ashmolean Museum. Brown was entirely unsympathetic. Before he closed his office door, I heard him say, 'That's the second time this year, you stupid cow.' He would not have spoken to Megan like that. Mrs Brown is very pretty. It's just that her clothes are horrible. It's as though there is a lunatic living in her wardrobe who orders her what to wear every morning. She can get away with looking ridiculous in Oxford. People probably assume that she is just another barmy professor, but she would be a laughing stock in Leicester.

Saturday April 20th

Mrs Hedge crying again this morning. I must away from this Vale of Tears. I need cheerful people around me.

Bianca handed me a card this morning. It said, in mad handwriting:

ROOM TO LET
Academic household willing to let room free to tolerant person of either gender, in return for light household duties/babysitting/cat-sitting. Would suit working person with most evenings free. Please ring Dr Palmer.

I rang immediately from the phone box outside the newsagent's. A bloke answered.

DR PALMER: Christian Palmer speaking.
ME: Dr Palmer, my name is Adrian Mole. I've just seen your postcard in the newsagent's.
DR P: When can you start?
ME: Start what?
DR P: Looking after the bloody kids.
ME: But you don't know me.
DR P: You sound okay and you've already proved you can

use a telephone. So you can't be a total simpleton.

Have you got all your faculties: four limbs, eyesight?

ME: Yes.

DR P: Ever been done for molesting kiddie-winkies?

ME: No.

DR P: Got any particularly nasty personal habits?

ME: No.

DR P: Good. So when can you start? I'm on my own here. My wife's in the States.

The telephone receiver was dropped. Suddenly I heard Palmer shout, 'Tamsin, put the top back on that bottle of bleach! Now!'

He came back on the phone and gave me his address in Banbury Road.

I went into the newsagent's and asked Bianca what newspapers and magazines Palmer read. This is a sure sign of character. It was a baffling list:

Newspapers: the *Observer*, the *Daily Telegraph*, the *Sun*, the *Washington Post*, the *Oxford Mail*, the *Independent*, the *Sunday Times*, *Today*.

Magazines: *Time Out*, *Private Eye*, *Just Seventeen*, *Vogue*, *Brides*, *Forum*, *Computer Weekly*, *Woman's Own*, *Paris Match*, *Gardening Today*, *Hello!*, the *Spectator*, the *Literary Review*, *Socialist Outpost*, the *Beano*, *Angler's Weekly*, *Canoeist*, *Viz*, *Interiors*, *Goal!*

I stopped her and said, 'Palmer's newspaper bill must be enormous. How does he pay it?'

'Infrequently,' she replied.

Sunday April 21st

Dr Palmer is tall and thin and wears his hair like Elvis Presley did during his silver-cloaks-in-Los-Angeles phase. His first words to me were, 'On your way to a fancy dress party?' He laughed and fingered the lapels of my blazer.

I mumbled something neutral and he asked, 'Is that beard *real*?'

I assured him that I had grown it myself and he said, 'How old are you?'

I answered, 'Twenty-four,' and he laughed a strange laugh, like a dog's bark, and said, '*Twenty-four*: so why the hell do you want to walk round looking like bloody Jack Hawkins?'

'Who's Jack Hawkins?' I asked.

'He's a film star,' he replied. 'Everybody's heard of Jack Hawkins.' He looked annoyed for some reason. Then he said, 'Well, unless you're twenty-four, that is.'

We were still standing on the doorstep of his decrepit house. A line of dirty, unrinsed milk bottles stood on the step. A little kid of unknown sex ran up the hall and tugged at Palmer's trousers. 'I've done a great big one! Come and look, Daddy!' it said.

We all three went into a gigantic room which seemed to be a kitchen, living-room and study combined. In the middle of the floor stood a potty in the shape of an elephant. Dr Palmer looked in the potty and exclaimed, 'Tamsin, that is a truly wonderful piece of shit.'

I averted my eyes as he carried the potty out of the room. Then I heard him shouting, 'Alpha! Griffith! Come and see what Tamsin's done!' There was a thundering on the stairs. I looked into the hall and saw two other androgynous children looking into the potty, saying, 'Wow!' and 'Mega shit!'

I adjusted my blazer in the mirror over the large fireplace and thought that the Dr Palmer household was unsuited to one of my temperament. I do not like to hear little children swear and I prefer them to be dressed in proper clothes and to have hairstyles which give a clue to their sexual orientation. However, when Dr Palmer came back from emptying the potty, I was pleased to see that he was drying his hands, which indicated to me that he knew the fundamentals of hygiene. I agreed to inspect the free room. We climbed the stairs, followed by Tamsin, Griffith and Alpha, who spoke to each other in a language I was not familiar with.

'Is it Welsh they're speaking?' I asked.

'No,' Palmer laughed. 'It's Oombagoomba. It's their own language. They're wearing their Oombagoomba clothes.'

I looked at the rags and bits of cloth and shawls, etc. with which the kids were festooned and was relieved to find out that it was not their usual mode of dress. I too used to have my own made-up language (Ikbak), until my father beat it out of me during a long car journey to Skegness.

The 'free room' turned out to be the whole of the attic floor. It had a kitchen at one end, and a private bathroom at the other. There was a proper desk. I could imagine reading the proofs of *Lo!* at that desk.

'You can do what you like up here,' said Palmer, 'apart from serial killing.'

'Are you a teacher?' I ventured.

'No,' he said. 'I'm leading a research project on popular culture. We are trying to establish why people go out to pubs, discos, bingo sessions, to the cinema, that sort of thing.'

'It's to enjoy themselves, isn't it?' I said.

Palmer laughed again. 'Yeah, but I've got to stretch that very simplistic answer into a three-year study and a seven-hundred page book.'

As we went down the stairs, I mentioned to Dr Palmer that as well as being an excellent tenant, I am also a novelist and a poet.

He groaned and said, 'So long as you *never* ask me to look at your manuscripts, we'll stay the best of friends.'

He made me a cup of coffee after grinding up some beans and he told me a bit about his wife, Cassandra, who is in Los Angeles directing a film about mutilation. She sounds horrific, although he claims to miss her. I am too tired and confused to write more. Dr Palmer has told me he must know by Wednesday if I want the room. He's got to go out on Friday to a darts competition.

Monday April 22nd

Should I go, or should I stay?

Can I stand babysitting for three children, four nights a week?

I could save £75 a week. In a year, that is . . .? As usual, when faced with mental, or even physical, arithmetic, my brain has just left my body and walked out of the room.

Thank God for calculators. Nine hundred pounds! It's not as if I would be sacrificing my social life. I haven't got one and, with a bit of luck, Mrs Palmer will stay in America, or fall over Niagara Falls, or something.

Thursday April 25th

Rang Palmer from the office and told him that I would be moving in tonight. Rang Pandora; asked if Cavendish would help me to move.

'Moving?' she said. 'Again?' Then, 'You make more moves than a tiddlywink.'

Rang Mrs Hedge, asked her to take my Y-fronts out of the washer and hang them on my bedroom radiator to dry. Mentioned that I would be moving on.

She said, 'Everybody does, eventually.'

*

Rang my mother and gave her my new address in case of a family tragedy. She yakked on for half an hour about President Gorbachev's threat to resign and predicted that the USSR was in danger of collapse. I cut in eventually and said, 'I no longer take an interest in world events. There is nothing I can do to influence them, so why bother?'

Rang Grandma, in Leicester. Had a long chat about Princess Diana. Grandma doesn't think she's been looking happy lately. I voiced my own concern. Diana is too thin.

Rang Market Harborough Building Society to notify change of address.

Rang Waterstone's. Pretended to be irate reader; threatened to sue them for selling pornography, i.e. *Dork's Diary*.

Rang Megan. Pretended to be Brown. Said, 'God, I love you, Megan,' in his horrible squeaky voice.

Eventually, Brown burst in and demanded that I get off the phone. I sincerely hope he hasn't been listening outside the door.

I had a compulsion to visit Leonora again. She agreed to see me immediately. She was wearing a white dress. She looked like a sacrificial virgin. I wanted to deflower her, but I found myself talking about Bianca.

Leonora leant forward in her chair, displaying her dark cleavage. I found myself saying that I was quite interested in Bianca, although I found her lack of cleavage disappointing.

Leonora said, 'But could you love Bianca?'

I said, 'The idea is ridiculous. The thought of *her* doesn't keep me awake at night, but the thought of *you* does.'

Leonora sighed and said, 'I suggest you cultivate this friendship with Bianca. I am a married woman, Adrian. Your obsession with me is typical of a therapist/client relationship. It is called transference. You must face the truth about your feelings.'

I said, 'The truth about my feelings is that I don't love you. I just want to go to bed with you.'

Leonora said, 'Thirty pounds please.'

I felt like a client paying a whore.

Friday April 26th
Moving Day

Cavendish and Palmer are old friends. When they saw each other, they did that arms-clasped-on-each-other's-shoulders, then grin-and-shake, which so many men in Oxford seem to go in for these days. As I removed my possessions from the back of the Volvo and tried to stop Tamsin, Griffith and Alpha from interfering, I heard Cavendish and Palmer laughing like madmen in the living-room. I'm not sure, but I think I heard the word 'blazer' mentioned. The children spoke Oombagoomba all night until their father returned at 11.30 p.m. They flatly refused to go to bed, or to converse with me in English. Instead, they lay under the massive pine table on a pile of cushions and jabbered away in that made-up lingo. It was like being abroad; if you closed your eyes.

Saturday April 27th

Bought *The White Hotel* by D. M. Thomas this morning. If it is even half as good as *The Great Babylon Hotel* by Arnold Bennett I will be more than satisfied. When Christian saw me take it out of the carrier bag, he raised his eyebrows and said, 'Don't leave it lying around. Alpha's got a reading age of thirteen.'

I said, 'You should encourage your child to read.'

Christian snapped, '*The White Hotel* is a bit heavy for a kid who still believes that fairies live at the bottom of the garden.'

I must say this surprised me. I went down to the bottom of the garden yesterday. It is covered in rusting toys and stinking garden rubbish. It is hardly Fairyland.

At 11.30 p.m., I opened *The White Hotel*, read for ten minutes, then got out of bed and bolted the door. It must never fall into Alpha's hands.

Monday April 29th

Babysat. Christian is at the semi-final of a darts competition with his dictaphone and clipboard. Do the big-bellied darts players realize that they are taking part in a research project? I doubt it. They all seem to have tunnel vision, which I suppose is an advantage if you play darts for a living.

Christian told me today that Bianca was enquiring about me, asking if I'd settled in. He told her that the kids like me. I wish he'd told me. Christian asked me why I don't ask Bianca for a date. I answered nonchalantly that I was too busy. But, dear journal, the truth is that I'm afraid *she might refuse*. My ego is but a frail and fragile thing and furthermore am I sure I want to commit myself to a person who works in a newsagent's shop?

Notes on Bianca:

Negative

1. She is pleasant-looking but certainly not a head-turner, unlike Leonora, who is capable of stopping the traffic.
2. When I mentioned that my walk to work was 'pleasantly Chekhovian', largely due to the blossoming cherry trees, she looked at me blankly and asked me what 'Chekhovian' meant.
3. Her hips do not look capable of bearing a child.
4. She wears Doc Marten boots.

5. She is a Guns 'n' Roses fan.

Positive
1. She is kind, especially to the children who linger over the sweets section in the newsagent's.
2. I seem to be able to make her laugh.
3. Her skin looks like white silk. I have a strange desire to stroke her face whenever I am close to her.

Tuesday April 30th

I'm glad April is over. It is a bitter-sweet month. The blossom is out, but the wind still swells around and flaps the bottoms of your trousers unless you tuck them into your socks.

Beard bushy now. Food gets caught in it. Brown pointed out a piece of egg white at 9.30 a.m. I ate my boiled egg at 7.39 this morning. Since that time, I have spoken to, or been seen by, at least thirty people. Why did no one else point out that I had egg white in my beard? It is not as if it was a *small* piece. As egg white goes, it was quite a large piece, and as such, impossible to overlook. I will have to buy a small hand mirror and check my beard regularly after meals. I cannot risk such social embarrassment happening again.

Wednesday May 1st

Babysat. Griffith asked me to help him with his model of a Scud missile, which he is making out of a toilet roll tube and cut-up bits of washing-up liquid bottle. I pointed out to him that I am a pacifist.

Griffith (six) said, 'If your sister was being threatened by a gang of vicious thugs, would you stand by and do nothing?'

I said, 'Yes.' Griffith doesn't know my sister Rosie. She is quite capable of seeing off a gang of vicious thugs.

Christian was back from his karaoke evening by 11 p.m. Apparently, he'd been forced to sing 'Love is a Many Splendoured Thing' in order to keep his cover. So his research project *is* an undercover operation. That explains why Christian changes out of his ragged denims and into his Sta-Pressed polyesters before joining his unsuspecting fellow low-culture vultures.

Thursday May 2nd

Read through the whole of *Lo! The Flat Hills of My Homeland* manuscript so far. It is crap from start to finish.

Friday May 3rd

Perhaps I was too harsh last night. *Lo!* has passages of sheer brilliance. About five.

Saturday May 4th

Left *Lo!* on kitchen table overnight. No comment from Christian this morning, though Alpha said, 'You've spelt "success" wrong on page four. It's got two c's and two s's.' Christian didn't even look up from his *Sun*.

If there's one thing I can't bear, it's a precocious child. It's completely unnatural. I was tempted to tell Alpha that any fairy living in the Hell Hole at the bottom of her garden should have a tetanus jab, but I didn't.

I received the new Plumbs catalogue this morning, offering me four tapestry-look cushions with frilled edges at the bargain price of £27.99. How did they track me down? The envelope came direct from Plumbs to the Banbury Road. Are they watching me?

Sunday May 5th

Put blazer on and went for my customary Sunday walk around the Outer Ring Road at 2 p.m. Some old git in a Morris Minor stopped and asked me for directions to the Oxford Bowling Club. As if I'd know! Returned to find house full of Christian's friends having what he described as a 'fondue party'. They were dipping raw vegetables into a stinking pot of what looked like yellow emulsion paint. I declined to join them.

Monday May 6th

Bianca was passing as I left for work this morning, so we walked part of the way together. As we crossed at the lights, her hand brushed mine. An electric shock passed through me. I apologized and put my hand in my raincoat pocket to prevent another such occurrence. She took off her Sony headset and invited me to listen to her Guns 'n' Roses tape. After five minutes I handed it back to her. I couldn't stand the din.

Tuesday May 7th

Bianca was there again outside the house this morning. I don't know why she keeps coming down this road. It's not on her route to work.

Babysat. The kids went to bed at 9.30 p.m., after I'd read them the first three chapters of *Lo!* For once, they seemed quite tired, yawning, etc.

Wednesday May 8th

Bianca there yet again, tying the laces on her Docs.
She told me that she gets bored in the evenings – she
hasn't got that many friends in Oxford. She misses the
cinema especially, but she is fed up with going on her
own. She went on and on about Al Pacino. She has
seen *Sea of Love* eleven times. I haven't seen it once.
Personally, I can't stand the man. I told her that I too
haven't seen a film in ages. When she left me and
went into the newsagent's, she looked irritable. Pre-
menstrual, probably.

Thursday May 9th

Babysat. At 7.30 p.m. I offered to read more of *Lo!* to
the kids, but they said, as one, that they were very
tired and wanted to go to bed! I had a peaceful night
washing my working wardrobe and shampooing my
beard. Christian got back at 1 a.m. after observing a
fight in an Indian restaurant. I advised him to put his
trousers in cold water to soak overnight. Turmeric is
one of the most stubborn stains known to man. It is a
pig to shift once it has gained a hold.

Monday May 13th

A terrible scandal at lunchtime today! Megan Harris
and Bill Blane were caught in the act of photocopying
their private parts! They would have got away with it,
had the machine not jammed. They have both been
suspended on full pay, pending an internal enquiry. I
am quite pleased. It has saved me from having to
photocopy two hundred pages of Newport Pagnell
newt drivel.

Tuesday May 14th

It is totally unfair. Because of Bill's suspension, I
have been given responsibility for the entire Badger
Department. Brown threw the badger case histories
on my desk and said, 'You're a friend of Bill's. Sort
this out.'

   Just because Brown was the one to force the photocopy room door open yesterday, there's no need to
take it out on me. He may have lost a mistress and a
secretary, but he must remember what he learned on
his managerial training course and keep his head.

Wednesday May 15th

Up at dawn to catch taxi to badger set. I must learn to drive. On the return journey, the taxi driver kept complaining about the smell. I had the fresh badger droppings in a sealed DOE jar, so how the aroma came in contact with the taxi driver's nose is a mystery to me. Personally, I found the fresh air 'pine tree' hanging from the roof of his taxi to be much more olfactorily offensive.

Friday May 17th

I am already up to my ears in newts and badgers, and now Brown is hinting that I may also be given responsibility for *natterjack toads*! He is obviously trying to force me into resigning or having a nervous breakdown due to overwork.

Photocopies of Megan's and Bill's private parts are being passed around the office. I think this is absolutely disgusting – a total invasion of their private lives, not to mention their private parts. Anyway the copies are so blurred that it is impossible to tell which is Bill's and which is Megan's. That photocopier never did work properly.

Bianca came round with Palmer's newspaper bill tonight. I answered the door and would have invited her in, but I didn't want her to think that sexual intercourse was on my mind – though, of course, it was. It's never off my mind. She had obviously gone to some trouble with her clothes, for a change. She was wearing tight denim jeans, high-heeled ankle boots and a white shirt which was tucked into a brown leather belt. She had recently washed her hair. I could smell Wash 'n' Go – the shampoo I use myself. It was on the tip of my tongue to ask her if she would come in for coffee, but something held me back.

She didn't seem to want to move off the doorstep – she kept talking about how fed up she was with having nothing to do in the evening. I was forced to stand in a cold wind, wearing only a shirt and trousers. This could result in a severe chill. I must check my temperature over the next few days.

Sunday May 19th

As predicted, I woke up yesterday feeling feverish, so I had three tablespoons of Night Nurse (though it was only 8.30 in the morning) and went back to sleep. Today, Christian knocked on my door at 12.30 p.m. and asked if I could watch the kids for three hours while he attended a 'Stag Strip' at a Working Men's Club. I reluctantly agreed and dragged myself out of bed.

I myself, personally, have never watched a strip show. I wouldn't know how to arrange my facial features. Would I watch with studied indifference like

TV detectives when they are forced to interview scumbag low-life in strip joints? Would I smile and laugh as though *amused* by the sight of a young woman taking her clothes off? Or would I swallow frequently, pant and goggle my eyes and reveal to onlookers that I am sexually excited? I fear the latter.

When Christian returned, he went upstairs. The shower was running for at least three quarters of an hour. I suspect he was symbolically cleansing himself.

Today was an Oombagoomba day, so I didn't – indeed, *couldn't* – talk to the kids.

The Chancellor, Norman Lamont, is going to sue a sex therapist for damages. But *how* did she damage you, Lamont? The British people should be told.

A letter from *Reader's Digest* arrived on Saturday, informing me that my name has been shortlisted out of many hundreds of thousands to receive a huge cash prize! All I have to do is agree to subscribe to the *Reader's Digest* magazine! It is easy to sneer at *Reader's Digest*, but it has to be said that they are an extremely handy way for busy bibliophiles to keep abreast of matters literary.

Plumbs have also written to me, offering to supply a lace circular tablecloth, plus a plywood circular table, should I not already have one. I must say I was quite tempted by both.

Thursday May 23rd

Christian held a drinks party last night and Cavendish and Pandora came round. I tried to engage Pan in conversation, but every time I did, I could see her eyes looking past me over my shoulder. Am I such boring company?

At 8 o'clock, Bianca turned up in a shiny, tight black dress. I introduced her to Pandora. Pandora said to her, 'That's a great dress, Bianca. God, don't you love lycra? What did we do without it?' They then yakked on about lycra for half an hour. In my opinion, Pandora's expensive education has been entirely wasted.

There must have been at least fifty people in the living-room/kitchen/study at one point. The majority of them were graduates, but you would never have known it from their conversation. The main topics were, in order:

1) *The Archers*
2) Football (Gazza)
3) Lycra
4) University cuts
5) Princess Diana
6) Alcoholism
7) The Oxford murder
8) Oats
9) Rajiv Gandhi being burnt
10) The Gossard Wonderbra

Call themselves intellectuals! My efforts to talk about my book, *Lo! The Flat Hills of My Homeland*, were met with cool indifference. Yes! The so-called 'best brains' in the land listened to me for a few minutes, then made feeble excuses to leave my company. At one point, just as I was telling him about my hero's apprenticeship to a cobbler in Chapter Eleven, a man called Professor Goodchild moved away, saying: 'Please spare me the sodding details.'

Yet only minutes later, I overheard him talking about his fish tank and how best to clean it.

Bianca left at 11.30 in the company of a dubious-looking type in a black leather jacket. He is something big in astrophysics, apparently, though in my opinion he looked like the type of moron who wouldn't know which end of a telescope to put his eye to.

As we were cleaning up after the party, Christian said, 'Adrian, take a tip from me, throw that bloody blazer away. Buy yourself some fashionable, young man's clothes!'

I replied (quite wittily, I thought), 'Lycra doesn't suit me.' He looked puzzled for a moment, then continued to wash the glasses.

Pandora also commented unfavourably, saying, 'That fucking awful blazer: give it to Oxfam, for Christ's sake.'

Perhaps I will.

I lay awake for hours imagining Bianca and the astrophysicist gazing at the stars together. Would he trust her with his telescope?

Friday May 24th

A household on my route to work has acquired an American pit bull terrier. On the surface, it seems to be a friendly beast. All it does is stand and grin through the fence. But in future I will take a different route to work. This is a considerable inconvenience to me, but I cannot risk facial disfigurement. I would like the photograph on the back of the jacket of my book to show my face as it is today, not hideously scarred. I know that plastic surgeons can work miracles, but from now on I am taking no chances.

Brown was in a foul mood today. He has had a letter from Megan's solicitor. She is threatening to sue him for defamation of character, unless she is reinstated immediately. I hope Brown caves in. Megan's replacement, Ms Julia Stone, is one of those superior types who never lose their money in chocolate machines in railway stations.

Saturday May 25th

Oxford is full of sightseers riding on the top deck of the tourist buses and walking along the streets gazing upwards. It is extremely annoying to us residents to be asked the way by foreigners every five minutes. Perhaps it is petty of me, but I quite enjoy sending them in the wrong direction.

I have just remembered! When I gave my blazer to the Oxfam shop yesterday, my condom was in the top pocket. This means that, should a sexual opportunity arise today, I will be unprepared. It also means that I can no longer go into the Oxfam shop – at least, not until Mrs Whitlow, the volunteer helper I gave it to, dies or retires. Mrs Whitlow has often congratulated me on being a 'decent, clean-living young man', though I have given her absolutely no grounds for thinking so.

Monday May 27th

Why do the banks have to close just because it is a Bank Holiday? It is a day when people want to *spend* money, isn't it? Borrowed £5 from Christian for Durex and bananas.

Tuesday May 28th

I have just finished Chapter Twelve of *Lo! The Flat Hills of My Homeland*, 'The Dog It Had To Die':

He closed the front door of his mother's house with a sigh. He had left her slumped on the kitchen table surrounded by brimming ashtrays and empty Pilsner cans. Upstairs, his father was injecting heroin into his collapsed veins. The family pet, an American pit bull terrier, looked out from the front window of the squalid terraced house and growled, showing its fearsome jaws. He walked down the street and tossed off greetings to the stunted neighbours. A couple fornicated in an alley, their eyes dead, their motions automatic. He wept internally. Anguish gripped his soul. He rued the day he had been born. Then, suddenly, a shaft of sunlight fell across his path. He stood, mesmerized. Was it a sign, a portent, that his life would improve from now?

He turned and went back to the house. He opened the front door. The dog, Butcher, growled at him, so he strangled it until the dog lay dead at his feet. He felt Evil, but at the same time strangely Good. The dog had been nothing but a nuisance and nobody ever took it for a walk. His conscience was clear.

Wow! Powerful writing, or what? I believe Dostoevsky would be proud of me. Canine murder is surely a first in English fiction. I expect I'll get a few letters from English dog lovers when *Lo! The Flat Hills of My Homeland* is published, but I shall write back and point out that I am an artist and must go where my pen takes me.

Wednesday May 29th

Julia Stone and I had a brief conversation at the Autovent machine today, while my oxtail soup was pouring into my plastic cup. She asked me not to use the ladies' lavatory again. I pointed out to her that the men's lavatory had run out of toilet paper, but she said if I continued to 'invade female space', she would report me for sexual harassment. She also said that she had checked the post book and that I used more postage stamps than any other member of staff.

I told her in cold tones – though not as cold as my oxtail soup – that I wrote more letters, therefore I needed more stamps. But I fear I have made an enemy.

Ms Julia Stone is a daunting woman. My throat constricts whenever I have to talk to her. Lipstick might help. Her, not me.

Christian returned from the Golden Gate nightclub with a black eye. His crime was to look at a yob. Yes, the yob accused Christian of 'looking' at him. This is a frightening example of the disintegration of British society. Yobs used to *enjoy* people looking at them. From now on, I shall avert my eyes whenever I see a yobbish person approaching me.

After Christian had stopped fussing with his eye and gone to bed, I sat at the kitchen table and tried to get some sex into *Lo! The Flat Hills of My Homeland*.

Chapter Thirteen: Deflowering

He lay in bed in his Parisian bedroom. Fifi began to remove her lycra dress. His breathing rate increased. She stood revealed before him, her chest strained beneath her Gossard Wonderbra, her knickers were clean and nicely ironed. He reached out for her, but she said to him in her French accent, 'No, no, *mon amour*, I am thinking you must wait.'

His ardour increased as he noticed that her bottom was smooth and had no pimples. He groaned and . . .

It's no good. I can't write about sex. Not even French sex in Paris.

Saturday June 1st

Two letters, one from Plumbs, offering me a set of matching towels with my personal monogram embroidered on the hems; the other from Sharon Bott.

Dear Adrian,

I hope you are well   long time no see   I saw your mum in town and we had a talk   she said how much Glenn looked like you   I said yes and she said is he our Adrians Sharon I must know   she just came out with it like that   I din't know what to say   I have got to confess I was seeing someone else at the time as I was seeing you I din't want to double time you Adrian but you was sometimes moody and I wanted some laffs I was only young. Glenn is going to school now and is a big boy. My mum says you should pay some money but I said no mum it would not be fair cause I dont no if Glenn is Adrians or not   Your mum gave me this address to write to you   I hope they're is not to many spelling mistakes and that but I never write anything now since I left school their is no need I saw Baz on the telly did you   He has done alright for himself I have not got a bloke now sinse Daryl run off with the video and

£35 I had saved for the gas   I have put a bit of wait on but I am going to go to Waitwatchers and get it off   You mum said she would babysit   she is so good to me.

Cheers,

Sharon

Sunday June 2nd

I spoke to my mother this morning and ordered her to keep her nose out of my affairs. She said, 'Glenn is the *result* of one of your affairs,' and put the phone down. From then on, I got the engaged signal.

I was enraged by my mother's interference. How dare *she* pontificate about *anybody*'s morals? I know for a fact that she was not a virgin on her wedding night. Grandma told me.

And anyway, my mother should not have spoken in the plural. I have not had *affairs*. I have had *an* affair. In the singular. With Sharon Bott, a simpleton who cannot differentiate between 'they're', 'there' and 'their' and is a virtual stranger to the comma and full stop. She probably thinks that a semi-colon is a partial removal of the intestines.

Memo to self: Is the kid mine? Blood test? Letter of denial?

2 a.m. Wrote to Sharon.

3 a.m. Destroyed the letter. (My reply to her must be carefully crafted. I need time to read up on the law relating to paternity.)

Tuesday June 4th

Thank God, Prince William has made a full recovery after being bashed on the head by a golf club. When I think how close we came to losing our future King, my heart stands still. Well, not literally *still*, it doesn't *stop*, but I'm glad the kid is better. I phoned Grandma in Leicester. She wanted to know why Prince Charles didn't pick his son up from the hospital. She said, 'Doesn't he know that it is traditional in our English culture?' She thinks that the monarchy is losing touch with the common herd and she complained bitterly that the Royal Yacht *Britannia* costs thirty-five thousand pounds a week to run.

5.00 p.m. The *Oxford Mail* has just informed me that the emir of Kuwait has yet to announce the date for democratic elections to be held in his country. Puzzling, considering all the trouble and expense the allies went to only recently. Get a move on, emir! I'm also informed by the *Oxford Mail* that the Royal Yacht *Britannia* costs thirty-five thousand pounds *a day*! *A day*! I phoned Grandma immediately and put her right. She was disgusted.

Query: Why does the emir of Kuwait spell his name with a small 'e'?

Friday June 7th

I spent the morning writing a report on a projection of newt births and the early afternoon on a report on the distribution of badgers. But I fear some of the paperwork has got mixed up. As I was photocopying the reports, I noticed that I had muddled a few facts. However, Brown was shouting down the corridor for the reports, so what could I do? His management meeting was due to start at 4 p.m., so I had no choice but to hand him the papers.

Saturday June 8th

Wrote to Sharon:

Dear Sharon,

How very nice to hear from you after all this time.

I'm afraid that there is no chance at all that I can be the father of your child, Glenn.

I have recently had my sperm counted and I was informed by the Consultant Spermatologist that my sperms are too weak to transform themselves into a child. This is a personal tragedy to me, as I had planned on having at least six children.

You mention in your letter that you were double-timing me. I was most upset to read this – our relationship was not ideal, I know; we came from different backgrounds: me: upper working/lower middle; you: lower working/ underclass. And, of course, our educational attainments are worlds apart, not to mention our cultural interests. But despite these differences, I had thought that we rubbed along quite well sexually. I see absolutely no reason why you should have betrayed me and sought out another sexual partner. I confess that I am devastated by your revelation. I feel cheap and used. I would be most obliged to you if you would stop seeing my mother. She is addicted to human dramas of any kind. She thinks of herself as a character in a soap opera. I suggest that you should go to Weight-watchers (not *Wait*watchers, by the way), and hire yourself a competent child-minder. My mother is not to be trusted with young children: she dropped me on my head at the age of six months, whilst taking a boiled egg out of a saucepan.

Anyway, Sharon, it was very nice to hear from you.

Regards,

Adrian

PS. Who were you double-timing me with? Not that it matters, of course. I have had a constant stream of lovers since our relationship ended. It is simple curiosity on my part. But I would like to know the youth's name, though it is not in the least important. Don't feel obliged to let me know. I just think it may help you to get it off your chest. Guilt can eat away at you, can't it? So would you please write to me and let me know the youth's name? I think you would feel better about yourself.

Sunday June 9th

I spent the day quietly, working on Chapter Fourteen of my novel.

He looked at the young boy, who was poking a stick at a natterjack toad. 'Stop!' he cried. 'It is one of an endangered species. You must be kind to it.' The young child stopped poking at the toad and came to hold his hand.

'Who are you?' lisped the child. He longed to shout, 'I am your *father*, boy!' but it was impossible. He looked at Sharon Slagg, the boy's mother, who weighed twenty-one stone and had numerous split ends. How could he have once enjoyed sexual congress with her?

He let go of the boy's hand and said, 'I am nobody, boy. I am a stranger to you. I am simply a person who loves the planet we live on – including the dumb creatures that we share our planet with.'

With that, he walked away from his son. The boy exclaimed, 'Please, stranger, don't go.' But he knew he must, before Sharon Slagg looked up from *Damage*, the book she was reading on the park bench. The boy said, 'I wish you were my father, stranger, then I too would have a daddy to come to parents' evenings.'

He thought his heart would break. Sobbingly, he walked

away across the grass until the boy was the size of an ant in the distance.

I don't mind admitting that this piece of writing had me wiping my eyes. God, I'm clever. I can tug at the heart strings like no other writer I know. I do feel that my book is now vastly improved by these additions. It still lacks narrative thrust (or does it?), but nobody can say that it doesn't engage the reader's emotions.

Thursday June 20th

Bianca came round tonight to borrow a cup of Basmati rice. She has stopped going out with the Stargazer: she said his breath smelled constantly of kiwi fruit.

She is a nicely spoken girl, with quite an extensive vocabulary. I asked her why she was serving in a newsagent's. She said, 'There are no jobs for qualified engineers.'

I was totally gobsmacked to learn that Bianca has an upper second degree in Hydraulic Engineering – from Edinburgh University. Before she left with the rice, I asked her to mend the leaking shower in my room. She said she would be pleased to come round tomorrow night and see to it for me. She asked if she should bring a bottle of wine with her. I said there was no need. She looked disappointed. I sincerely hope she is not an alcoholic or a heavy drinker who needs a 'nip' before she can do a job of work.

I am making good progress on the novel. I took out my epic poem *The Restless Tadpole* tonight. It is amazingly good, but I can't spare the time to finish it. The novel has to come first. There is no money in poetry. Our Poet Laureate, Ted Hughes, has been wearing the same jacket in his photograph for the past twenty years.

Friday June 21st

Bianca came round *avec* tool box, but *sans* wine. She hung about after she'd fixed the shower and talked about how lonely she is and how she longs to have a regular boy friend. She asked me if I have a regular girl friend. I replied in the negative. I sat in the armchair under the window and she lay on my bed in what an old-fashioned kind of man could have interpreted as a provocative pose.

I wanted to join her on the bed, but I wasn't sure how she would react. Would she welcome me with open arms and legs? Or would she run downstairs screaming and ask Christian to call the police? Women are a complete mystery to me. One minute they are flapping their eyelashes, the next they are calling you a sexist pig.

While I tried to work it out, a silence fell between us, so I started to talk about the revisions I am making to my book. After about twenty minutes, she fell into a deep sleep. It was a most awkward situation to be in.

Eventually, I went downstairs and asked Christian to come and wake her up. He sneered and said, 'You're unbelievably stupid at times.' What did he mean? Was he referring to my inability to fix my own shower head, or to my timidity regarding sex?

When Bianca woke up she looked like a sad child. I wanted to put my arms round her but before I could she had grabbed her tool box and run down the stairs without saying goodnight.

Saturday June 22nd

Had a most satisfactory shower this morning. The force of the water has improved considerably.

2.00 p.m. Worked on Chapter Fifteen. I have sent *him* to China.

11.30 p.m. I have brought *him* back from China. Can't be bothered to do all that tedious research. I just got him walking along the Great Wall, then flying back to East Midlands Airport. I went down to the kitchen to make myself a cup of hot chocolate and told Christian about my hero's trip to China. Christian said, 'But you told me that he is a pauper. Where would he get the money for his air ticket?' God, how I hate pedants!

1.00 a.m. Insert for Chapter Fifteen:

What was this on the mat? He bent down and picked up a letter from the *Reader's Digest*. On the front of the expensively papered envelope was written 'OPEN AT ONCE'. He obeyed. Inside was a letter and a cheque for one million pounds! He was fabulously rich! 'How shall I spend it all?' he asked the cat. The female cat looked back at him inscrutably. 'China?' he said. 'I'll have a day trip to China!'

I hope this satisfies my pedantic landlord and my most critical of readers.

Sunday June 23rd

At breakfast, I told Christian how my hero got the money to go to China. He now wants to know what my hero does with the *remaining* money. There is no pleasing him.

12 noon

Chapter Sixteen: A Gratuitous Act
The beggar outside Leicester bus station stared in disbelief as £999,000 showered down onto his head. *He* walked away, a pauper once again.

5.00 p.m. Saw Bianca walking towards me as I was returning from my perambulations around the Outer

Ring Road this afternoon. She was wearing shorts and a T-shirt: her legs, apart from the ankles, looked superb, long and slim. I hurried towards her. To my astonishment, she crossed over the road and ignored me. So much for Christian telling me that she fancies me! It's certainly a good job I didn't join her on the bed the other night. I could be in prison now, on a sexual assault charge.

The next time I go to the library I will try to find a book that explains to the intelligent layman how women's brains work.

Summer

Wednesday July 3rd

Brown reminded me today that I have two weeks' holiday entitlement which I will lose unless I take it within the next two months.

Rang my travel agent. Told her I want two weeks in Europe in a four star hotel with half board, but for no more than £300. She promised to ring back if anything turned up in Albania. I said, 'Not Albania, I hear the food is inaudible.' After I'd put the phone down, I remembered that the word for bad food is, of course, 'inedible'. I hope I'm not suffering from an early onset of senile dementia. Word-loss is an early signal.

Friday July 5th

The travel agent rang today. Unfortunately, the call was put through to Brown's office, where I was being reprimanded because of a mix-up over the newt and badger reports. The Department of Transport had received the erroneous intelligence that a family of badgers had appeared on the route of the projected Newport Pagnell bypass. Naturally, I was constrained by Brown's presence, so I was unable to concentrate on what the travel agent was saying.

I said that I would ring her back, but she said, 'You must book it *now* if you want it.'

I said, 'Book what?'

She said, 'Your holiday. A week on the Russian lakes and rivers, and a week in Moscow. A fortnight for £299.99, full board.'

'Go ahead,' I said.

Saturday July 6th

Rang 'Easy-pass' Driving School and booked a free lesson as advertised in the *Oxford Mail*. I take to the road on Thursday, July 18th.

I have taken driving lessons before, but have been badly let down by my previous instructors. They were all incompetent.

Sunday July 7th

Babysat while Christian went to bingo. He won £7.50 and was near to winning the area prize of £14,000. He only needed two fat ladies.

Monday July 8th

Worked on *Lo*! Shall I give *him* a name? If so, what shall it be? It needs to express his sensitivity, his courage, his individualism, his intellectual vigour, his success with women, his affinity with nature, his proletarian roots.

Tuesday July 9th

How about Jake Westmorland?

Wednesday July 10th

Maurice Pritchard?

Thursday July 11th

Oscar Brimmington?

Friday July 12th

Jake Pritchard?

Saturday July 13th

Maurice Brimmington?

Sunday July 14th

A decision will have to be made soon. I can't move on with my book until it has. Christian prefers 'Jake Westmorland'. However, the man in the greengrocer's likes the sound of 'Oscar Brimmington'. Whereas a bus conductor, whose opinion I sought, was very keen on 'Maurice Westmorland'.

Monday July 15th

Spent the day babysitting. I got the kids to test me on the Highway Code. Somebody kept ringing the house tonight. A woman. All she said was, 'Hello.' But when I asked who was calling she put the phone down. It sounded like Bianca, but why should she behave in such a childish manner?

Tuesday July 16th

Brown had to have his surgical corset adjusted at the Radcliffe Hospital this morning, so I took the

opportunity to go into his office and look at my file:
'MOLE – ADRIAN.'

FORESIGHT – NONE

PUNCTUALITY – POOR

INITIATIVE – NONE

RELIABILITY – QUITE GOOD

HONESTY – SUSPECTED OF PILFERING POSTAGE
  STAMPS

ACCEPTANCE OF RESPONSIBILITY – POOR

RELATIONS WITH OTHERS – QUITE GOOD

I believe his 'A' level Biology qualification to be
  bogus.

Wednesday July 17th

Dear Mr Brown,

It is with great regret that I write to inform you of
my intention to resign from the Department of the
Environment. I will of course serve out my statutory two
months' notice. I have been unhappy for some time now
with how the department is run. I feel that my talents
have been wasted. Collecting badger faeces was not in my
original job description.

Also, in my opinion, the protection of animals has
reached ludicrous levels. The beasts have more rights than
I do. Take bats. If I were to hang upside down and defecate
in a church, I would be taken away to an institution. Yet
bats are *encouraged* by conservationists such as yourself,

Mr Brown. It's no wonder that our churches are empty of parishioners.

I remain, sir,
   Adrian Mole

At 10.00 a.m. I wrote the above letter, put it into an envelope and wrote 'FOR THE ATTENTION OF MR BROWN'.

At 11.00 a.m., after staring down at the envelope for a full hour, I put it under my blotting pad. Thinking perhaps that I could brazen it out regarding the bogus 'A' level.

At midday, while I was at the Autovent, the envelope disappeared. I searched my cubicle but found nothing, apart from my little blue comb.

At 1.00 p.m., I was summoned to Brown's office and told to clear my desk and leave the premises immediately. He gave me an envelope which contained a cheque for £676.31 = two months' pay plus holiday money less tax and National Insurance.

Who delivered my resignation letter? I suspect the Sexually Harassed One.

So, like three and a half million of my fellow citizens, I am without work.

1 a.m. Christian got me drunk tonight. I had two and a half glasses of Vouvray and a pint of draught Guinness in a can.

Thursday July 18th
Driving Lesson

Stayed in bed until 2 p.m. My driving instructor is a woman called Fiona. She is old (47) and has got lots of loose skin around her neck, which she pulls at in times of crisis. I did *tell* her that it is over a year since I was behind the wheel. I did *ask* if I could practise first on Tesco's Megastore out-of-town car park, but Fiona refused and forced me to drive on real roads with real traffic. So what happened at the roundabout was not my fault. Fiona should have been quicker with the dual controls.

Friday July 19th

A letter from Faber and Faber:

Dear Mr Mole,

I am afraid that I am returning your manuscript, *Lo! The Flat Hills of My Homeland.*

It is a most amusing parody of the English *naïf* school of fiction.

However, we do not have a place for such a book on our list at the moment.

Yours sincerely,

Matthew Evans

After reading the letter six times, I tore it in pieces. Mr Evans will be sorry one day. When my work is being auctioned in hotel rooms, I will instruct my agent to disqualify Mr Evans from the bidding.

There was no reason to get up, so I stayed in bed all day, wondering if there was any point in going on. Pandora despises me, I am out of work and I am incapable of driving a car in a straight line. At 7 p.m. I got out of my bed and rang Leonora. A man answered the phone: 'De Witt.'

'It's Adrian Mole,' I said. 'Could I speak to Leonora?'

'My wife's dressing,' he said; which threw me for a while. Images of Leonora in various lingerie outfits flashed into my mind.

'It's an emergency,' I managed to croak out. I heard him put the receiver down with a crack and shout, 'Darling, it's for you. Something about moles.'

There was a muttered oath, and then Leonora came on the phone.

'Yes?'

'Leonora, I'm in despair. Can I come round and see you?'

'When?'

'Now.'

'No, I'm giving a dinner party at eight and the first course is an asparagus soufflé.'

I wondered why she would think I was remotely interested in her menu.

'I need to talk to you,' I said. 'I've lost my job, my

novel's been rejected and I crashed the driving school car yesterday.'

'They are all life experiences,' she said. 'You will come out of this a stronger man.'

I heard her husband shouting something in the background. Then she said, 'I have to go. Why don't you talk to that girl, Bianca? Goodbye.'

I did as I was told. I went and stood outside Bianca's house and looked up at her flat. Nobody went in or came out.

After watching for an hour I went home and got back into bed. I hope the De Witts and their guests all choked on their asparagus soufflé.

Saturday July 20th

Cassandra Palmer turned up on the doorstep this afternoon. Christian's face turned white when he saw his wife. The children greeted her politely, but without much enthusiasm, I noticed. She looks as though she wrestles in mud for a living. I loathed her on sight. I cannot stand big women who shave their heads. I prefer them with hair.

Her first words to me were, 'Oh, so *you*'re the cuckoo in the nest.'

Sunday July 21st

The dictatorship of Cassandra started this morning. Our household is not allowed to drink tap water, coffee, tea or alcohol, nor to eat eggs, cheese, chocolate, fruit yoghurt, Marks & Spencer's lemon slices . . . etc., etc. The list goes on forever. There are also things we mustn't say. I happened to mention that Bianca's boss, the newsagent, is a fat man. Cassandra snapped, 'He's not fat, he's dimensionally challenged.'

I laughed, thinking this was a good joke, but Cassandra's mouth turned into a grim slit and with horror I realized she was serious.

Christian remarked to his wife over lunch that he was losing his hair, 'going bald' were his words. Once again, Cassandra snapped into action.

'You're a little follicularly disadvantaged, that's all,' she said, as she inspected the top of her husband's head.

I cannot share this house with that woman, or *her* language. It is not as though she is pleasant to look at. She is as ugly as sin, or, as she might put it, she is facially impaired.

Monday July 22nd

I asked Bianca if she would keep a lookout for suitable accommodation. She agreed, though there is nothing to keep me here in Oxford any more, apart from my unrequited love for Dr Pandora Braithwaite.

Tuesday July 23rd

> *Dr Braithwaite*
> Since you gained your Ph.D.
> You have had no time for me.
> You loved me once, you could again.
> Pandora, give up other men!
> You swore to love me for all time.
> As long as Moon and June would rhyme.
> Please marry me and be my wife.
> For you I'll sacrifice my life.
> I'll stay at home, I'll cook and clean
> In the background, never seen.
> When you return from brainy toil,
> I'll have the kettle on the boil.
> While you translate from Serbo-Croat,
> I will shake our coco doormat.
> I'll gladly wash your duvet cover,
> If only I can be your lover.

I put the poem through Pandora's door at 4 a.m. This is my last-ditch attempt to sound out Pandora's true feelings for me. Leonora has said that I must move on emotionally. What will Pandora's reaction be?

Wednesday July 24th

I found this letter on the doormat.

Dear Adrian,

You woke me at 4 a.m. with your clumsy manipulation of my letter box. Your poem caused my lover and me much merriment. I hope, for your sake, that it was *meant* to be funny. If it was *not*, then I urge you to seek further psychiatric advice from Leonora. She told me that you have stopped seeing her regularly. Is it the cost?

I *know* you can afford £30 a week. You don't drink, or smoke, or wear decent clothes. You cut your own hair, you don't run a car. You don't gamble or take drugs. You live rent-free. Withdraw some money from your precious Building Society and *get help*.

Regards,
Pandora

PS. Incidentally, I am *not* a Ph.D., as you state in your poem. I am a D. Phil. A subtle but important difference here in Oxford.

So that's it. If Pandora came to me tomorrow, begging to be Mrs A. A. Mole, I would have to turn her down. I have moved on. It's Leonora I must see. Must.

Thursday July 25th

5.15 p.m. I have just phoned Leonora and insisted that she gives me an emergency appointment. I said I had something momentous to tell her. She agreed reluctantly.

5.30 p.m. I burst into Leonora's room this evening and found her with another client, a middle-aged man who was sobbing into a Kleenex (woman trouble, I suppose). I was ten minutes early and Leonora was furious and ordered me to wait outside. At 6.30 p.m. precisely, I knocked on her door and she shouted, 'Come.' She was still in a bad mood and so I tried to make conversation and asked her what had upset the sobbing middle-aged man. This angered her even more. 'What is said to me in this room remains confidential,' she said. 'How would *you* feel if I talked about *your* problems to my other clients?'

'I don't like to think about you having other clients,' I confessed.

She sighed deeply and curled a hank of black hair around her finger. 'So what's the momentous happening?' she said eventually.

'I've moved on from Pandora Braithwaite,' I said, and I told her about the poem and Pandora's reaction to it and my reaction to Pandora's reaction. At that moment, a tall, dark man wearing a suede shirt came in. He looked surprised to see me.

'Sorry, darling. I can't find the small grater, for the parmesan.'

'Second drawer down, darling, next to the Aga,' she said, looking up at him in rapt adoration.

'Terribly sorry,' he said.

When he'd gone out, I stood up and said, 'How dare your husband interrupt my consultation with his petty domestic enquiries?'

Leonora said, 'My husband didn't know you were here. I squeezed you in, if you remember.' Her tone was carefully measured, but I noticed that a vein was pulsating on the side of her temple and that she was wringing her hands.

'You should learn to express your anger, Leonora. It's no good for you to bottle it up,' I said.

She then said, 'Mr Mole, you are not making progress with me. I suggest you try another analyst.'

'No,' I said. 'It's you I want to see. You're my reason for living.'

'So,' she said. 'Think what you're saying. Are you saying that without me you would commit suicide?'

I hesitated. Noises of pans banging and glasses tinkling came up from the basement, as did a delicious smell that made my mouth water. For some reason I blurted out, 'Could I stay to dinner?'

'No. I never socialize with my clients,' she said, looking at her slim, gold watch.

I sat down and asked, 'How mad am I, on a scale of one to ten?'

'You're not mad at all,' she said. 'As Freud said, "It

is impossible for a therapist to treat either the mad or those in love."'

'But I *am* in love. With you,' I added.

Leonora sighed very deeply. Her breasts rose and fell under her embroidered sweater.

'That is why I think that seeing another therapist would be a good idea. I have a friend, Reinhard Kowolski, who has a superb reputation . . .'

I didn't wait to hear any more about Herr Kowolski. I left her room and put three ten pound notes on the hall table, next to the laughing Buddha and walked out into the street.

I felt angry, so I decided to express my anger and I kicked an empty Diet Coke can all the way home.

When I got to the attic, I laid out all my job-searching clothes ready for the morning. Then I lay on my bed with the *Oxford Mail* and ringed all the likely looking jobs in the situations vacant columns.

There was nothing that required one 'A' level in English.

Friday July 26th

Went to the Job Centre, but the queue was too long, so returned to find Cassandra in the kitchen, examining the children's books, pen in hand. She picked one up and changed *Winnie the Pooh* to *Winnie the Shit*. 'I hate ambiguity,' she explained, as she snapped the cap back on her Magic Marker.

Saturday July 27th

Saw Brown in W. H. Smith's, buying the current wild-life magazines. He smiled and said, 'Enjoying your life of leisure, Mole?'

I forced a smile to my lips and said, 'On the contrary, Brown, I am working as hard as ever. I am a middle manager at the Book Trust in Cambridge, at £25,000 a year, plus car. I got the position thanks to my having English Literature at "A" level.' Brown stormed off, forgetting to pay for his magazines. He was stopped on the pavement by a security guard. I didn't hang around to watch Brown's humiliation.

Sunday July 28th

Stayed in room all day, out of Cassandra's way. She is insisting that everyone in the house meditates for half an hour each morning. Christian has stopped doing his research into popular culture. Cassandra objected to the smell of cigarette smoke on his clothes when he returned from his low-class haunts. If she is not careful, she will wreck his academic career.

I am living on my savings, but I cannot continue to do so. The State will have to keep me – after all, I didn't ask to be born, did I? And one day the State will be glad it supported me. When I am a high-rate taxpayer.

However, before I throw myself on its mercy, I am going to tramp the streets of Oxford tomorrow and look for a job, any job that doesn't involve driving or working with animals.

Next year, I will have lived for a quarter of a century and as yet I have made no mark on the world – apart from winning a *Leicester Mercury* literary prize when I was seventeen.

If I died tomorrow, what would be written on my tombstone?

> Adrian Albert Mole
> Unpublished novelist
> and pedestrian
>
> Mourned by few
> Scorned by many
> Winner of the *Leicester Mercury*
> 'Clean Up Leicester' Essay Prize

Tuesday July 30th

Why do beggars *always* want money for a cup of tea? Don't any of them drink coffee?

Wednesday July 31st

Why didn't palace flunkies arrange for Princess Diana to be kept dry at the open-air Pavarotti concert last night? If she develops pneumonia and dies, the country will be plunged into crisis and Charles will be devastated with grief. He obviously adores her. Somebody's head should roll.

Thursday August 1st

Dear Adrian,
   I was sorry to read about your poor cwallity seed   the person I was seeing on the side was barry kent   I feel better now it is off my chest.
   Yours sinserely,
      Sharon

Barry Kent! I should have known! He is an amoral, talentless turd! He is lower than a cesspit. He has the prose style of a *Daily Sport* leader writer. He wouldn't know what a semi-colon was if it fell into his beer. The little I have read of *Dork's Diary* forced me to the conclusion that Kent should be arrested and charged with criminal assault on the English language. He deserves to burn in everlasting hell with a catherine wheel tied to his cheating penis.

Friday August 2nd

Dear Sharon,

Many thanks for your commiserations regarding my 'seed', as you put it. May I suggest that you get in touch with Barry Kent (who, as you know, is now both *rich* and famous) and ask him to contribute to Glenn's upbringing? The least Kent can do is to send Glenn to a private school, thus giving his child an excellent start in life.

I remain,

Yours,

Adrian

PS. I am absolutely sure that Barry will be thrilled to hear that he has a child.

PPS. Eton is quite a good private public school.

Sunday August 4th

Cassandra announced at breakfast that she has taken the locks off the bathroom and lavatory doors. 'Inhibitions about nakedness and bodily functions are the reason why the English are no good at sex,' she said. She looked pointedly at her husband, who blushed and rubbed the side of his nose.

The Queen Mother is 91 today. I suppose she doesn't think it is worth getting her teeth seen to now. I can see her point.

Monday August 5th

Contacted Foreign Parts, the travel agents, about my Russian cruise and explained that I have been made redundant and would like to cancel and have my money back. The travel agent told me that it was impossible and told me to refer to the small print on my documents. I peered in vain and eventually went to Boots and bought a pair of 'off the peg' reading spectacles for £7.99. The travel agent was right; I will have to go.

Tuesday August 6th

Christian told me (shamefaced) that Cassandra requires my attic room. She is opening a reincarnation centre where people can get in touch with their former selves. She wants me out of the attic by mid-September. I couldn't help myself. I burst out, 'Your wife is a cow!' Christian said, 'I know, but she used to be a kitten.'

So, no job and, when I get back from the Russian cruise, nowhere to live.

Thursday August 8th

Dear John Tydeman,

The last time I wrote to you, it was to apologize for clogging up the BBC's fax machines with my 700-page novel, *Lo! The Flat Hills of My Homeland*. You sent it back to me (eventually) and said, and I quote: 'Your manuscript is awash with consonants, but vowels are very thin on the ground, thin to the point of non-existence.'

You will, I am sure, be delighted to hear that I have now reinstated the vowels and have spent this year rewriting the first sixteen chapters, and I would value your comments on them. They are enclosed with this letter. I know you are busy, but it wouldn't take you long. You can read them in the BBC's coffee lounge during your coffee breaks, etc.

I remain, Sir,

Yours,

Adrian Mole

10.30 p.m. I have seen Leonora for the last time. She has dismissed me from my post as her client. I over-played my hand and declared my love for her. In fact, it wasn't so much a declaration, it was more of a proclamation. It was probably heard all over Oxford. Her husband heard it because he came into the room with a tea towel and a little blue jug in his hand and asked Leonora if she was all right.

'Thank you, Fergus, darling,' she said. 'Mr Mole will be leaving soon.'

'I'll be outside if you need me,' he said, and left, leaving the door slightly open.

Leonora said, 'Mr Mole, I am calling a halt to our professional relationship, but before you leave I would like to reassure you that your problems are capable of being solved.

'You expect too much of yourself,' she said, leaning forward sympathetically. 'Let yourself off the hook. Be *kind* to yourself. You've expressed your worries about world famine, the ozone layer, homelessness, the Aids epidemic, many times. These are not only your problems. They are shared by sensitive people all over the world. You can have no control over these sad situations – apart from donating money. However, over your personal worries, lack of success with your novel, problems with women, you do have a certain amount of control.' Here she stopped and she looked as though she wanted to take my hand, but she didn't.

'You are an attractive, healthy young man,' she said. 'I have not read your manuscript, so I can't comment on your literary talent or otherwise, but what I do know is that there is somebody out there who is going to make you happy.'

I turned on my dining chair and looked out of the window. 'Not literally out there, of course,' she snapped, following my glance. She stood up, shook my hand and said, 'There will be no charge for this session.'

I said, 'It isn't transference: it's true love.'

'I've heard that at least twenty times,' she said, softly. She rose to her feet. Her rings sparkled under the light and she shook my hand. As I left, I passed her husband, who was still drying the little blue jug twenty minutes later. A suitable case for treatment if ever I saw one.

'I intend to marry your wife one day,' I said, before closing the front door.

'Yes, that's what they all say. Cheerio.' He smiled and went towards Leonora and I closed the door on a painful – and expensive – period of my life.

Friday August 9th

Adrian,

What the fuck are you playing at, getting Sharon Bott to write to me and ask for money to send her sprog to fucking Eton? I'm down here at Jeanette Winterson's place, trying to finish my second novel and I can do without all this fucking rubbish.

Baz

Saturday August 10th

I looked in the Job Centre window today. There were three vacancies in the window. One for a 'mobile cleansing operative' (road sweeper?), one for a 'peripatetic catering assistant' (pizza delivery?) and one for a 'part-time clowns enabler' (!). I didn't exactly reach excitedly for the Basildon Bond on my return to Stalag Cassandra.

Sunday August 11th

Went to the newsagent's. Bianca is back from Greece. She has got a fantastic tan. She was wearing a low-cut white tee shirt, which displayed her breasts. They looked like small, ripe, russet apples. I asked her facetiously if she had had a holiday romance. She laughed and admitted that she had – with a fisherman who had never heard of Chekhov. I asked if she was going to continue the romance. She gave me a strange look and said: 'How would you *feel* about it if I did, Adrian?'

I was about to reply when a member of the underclass thrust a *Sunday Sport* into her hands, so the moment was lost.

10.00 p.m. How do I feel about Bianca's holiday romance? I'm always pleased to see her, but I can't stop comparing her to the lovely Leonora: Bianca is a Malteser: Leonora is an Elizabeth Shaw gold-wrapped after dinner mint.

Tuesday August 13th

I leave for Russia on Thursday. I bought myself a new toiletry bag – it's time I treated myself. I hope there are some decent women of childbearing age aboard.

I spent the evening packing. I decided not to take any books. I expect there will be a library on the ship, well stocked with the classics of Russian literature in good translations. I hope my fellow passengers are cultured people. It would be intolerable to have to share the dining room and decks with English lager louts. I decided to include a huge bunch of semi-ripe bananas amongst my luggage. I am used to eating a banana a day and I have heard they are in short supply in Russia.

Saturday August 17th

River camp – Russia
It is 7.30 p.m. There is no cruise ship. There are no passengers. Each member of our party is paddling their own canoe. I am crouched inside a two-man tent. Outside are swarms of huge, black mosquitoes. They are waiting for me to emerge. I can hear the river throwing itself over the rapids. With a bit of luck, I will die in my sleep.

The man I have been sharing my tent with, Leonard Clifton, is out chopping trees down with a machete, borrowed from Boris, one of our river guides. I sincerely hope that one of Clifton's trees falls on his horrible bald head. I cannot stand another night listening to his interminable anecdotes about the Church Army.

I told Boris earlier today that I would give him all my roubles if he would arrange for me to be airlifted to Moscow. He paused from repairing the hole in my canoe and said, 'But you must paddle now to the river's end, Mister Mole; there is no inhabitations, peoples or telephonings here.'

On my return to civilization, I will sue Foreign Parts for every penny they've got. At no time did they mention that I would be paddling a canoe, sleeping in a tent, or drinking water from the river. The worst privation of all is that *I have got nothing to read.* Clifton lent me his Bible, but it fell overboard at the last rapids. As I watched it sink, I shouted 'My God, my God, why hast thou forsaken me?' To the bewilderment of the rest of the group and of myself, I must admit.

Monica and Stella Brightways, the twins from Barnstaple, are outside leading the singing of 'Ten Green Bottles'. Leonard and the rest of the gang are joining in lustily.

10.00 p.m. Tent. I have just returned from the forest, where I was forced to urinate into the darkness. I stood with the others round the fire for a moment, drinking black tea.

Monica Brightways had a serious argument with

the scoutmaster from Hull. She claimed she saw him take two slices of black bread from the sack at lunchtime. He denied it vehemently and accused her of hogging the camp fire. Everyone took sides, apart from me, who loathes them both equally.

Capsized eleven times earlier today. The rest of the hearties were furious with me for holding them up. It is all right for them. They are all members of the British Canoe Union. I am a complete novice and crossing a lake in a force-nine gale is something out of my worst nightmare. The Waves! The Wind! The Water! The lowering black Russian sky! The Danger! The Fear!

I pray to God we may soon come to our journey's end. I long for Moscow. Though I will have to stay in my hotel room; the mosquitoes have attacked my face unmercifully. I look like the Elephant Man on acid.

Midnight The drinking of vodka is now taking place. From my tent I can hear every word. The Russians are maudlin. Every time they talk about 'our souls', the English snigger. I crave sleep. I also crave hot water and a flushing lavatory.

Moscow! Moscow! Moscow!

Wednesday August 21st

Moscow train
The lavatory on the train defies description. However, I'll try. After all, I am a novelist.

Imagine that twenty buffalo with loose bowels have been trapped inside the lavatory for two weeks. Then try to imagine that an open sewer runs across the floor. Add an IRA prisoner on dirty protest. Then concoct a smell by digging up a few decomposed corpses, add a couple of healthy young skunks and you come quite near to what the lavatory looks and smells like.

Leonard Clifton is writing to President Gorbachev to complain.

I said, 'I think Gorbachev has other things on his mind at the moment, such as preventing civil war and feeding his fellow citizens.'

A harmless remark, you might think, but Clifton went mad. He screamed, 'You have ruined my holiday, Mole, with your pathetic whingeing and nasty, cynical comments.'

I was totally gobsmacked. Nobody in the group came to my defence – apart from the Brightways twins, who had already informed the group at frequent intervals that they 'loved all living things'. So anything they had to say was irrelevant. They no doubt equate my life with that of a lugworm.

Thursday August 22nd

Hotel room – Moscow

I am staying in the 'Ukraina', near the Moskva River. It looks like a hypodermic syringe from outside. Inside, it is full of bewildered guests of all nationalities. Their bewilderment stems from the hotel staff's reluctance to pass on any information.

For instance, hardly anybody knows *where* meals are being served, or even *if* meals are being served.

For breakfast this morning I had a piece of black bread, four slices of beetroot, a sprig of fresh coriander and a cup of cold, black tea.

An American woman in the queue behind me wailed to her husband, 'Norm, I gotta have juice.'

Norm left the queue and went up to a group of loitering waiters.

I watched him mime an orange, first on the tree and then off the tree. The waiters watched him impassively, then turned their backs on him and huddled around a portable radio. Norm returned to the queue. His wife shot him a contemptuous look.

She said, 'I just gotta have some fruit in the morning. You *know* that, Norm. You know how my system seizes up.'

Norm pulled a face indicating that he remembered *exactly* what happened to his wife's system when it seized up. I thought fondly about the bunch of bananas upstairs in my room.

They were worth their weight in gold.

At nine-thirty, most of our group gathered in the foyer of the hotel ready to start our visit to Red Square. I lurked behind a pillar, dabbing TCP onto the fourteen mosquito bites which disfigured my face.

The Barnstaple twins, Monica and Stella Brightways,

kept us waiting for ten minutes, claiming that they had to wait for the lift to ascend to where their room was on the nineteenth floor. Eventually we set off in a bus which seemed to have an interior exhaust pipe next to my seat at the back. I coughed and choked on the diesel fumes and made a futile attempt to open the window. The coach driver was wearing a Gorbachev badge and seemed to be in a bad mood. Our coach parked on the edge of Red Square and we got out and gathered around our Intourist guide, Natasha. She held up a red and white umbrella, and we followed behind like moronic sheep. When we got to the Square, it became obvious that something was happening, a protest march or a demonstration of some kind was taking place. I lost sight of the red and white umbrella and became lost in the crowd. I heard an ominous rumbling behind me, but was unable to move.

An old lady in a headscarf shook her fist towards the noise. She screamed something in Russian. Spittle flew out of her mouth and landed on my clean sweater. Then the crowd parted and the rumbling grew nearer and the tracks of a Russian army tank clanked past an inch away from my right shoe. The tank stopped and a young man clambered aboard and began to wave a flag. It was the hammer and sickle flag I'd been used to seeing everywhere. The crowd roared its approval. What was happening? Had Moscow Dynamo won at football? No, something more important was taking place.

A young woman who wore too much blue eye-shadow said to me, 'Englishman, today you have witnessed the end of Communism.'

'I nearly got run over by a tank,' I said.

'A proud death,' she said. I reached into my pocket for a banana to boost my blood-sugar level. I started to peel it. The young woman's eyes filled with tears. I offered her a bite, but she misinterpreted my gesture and shouted something in Russian. The crowd roared and cheered. She then turned and told me she was shouting 'Bananas for all under Yeltsin!' The crowd began to chant. Then the young woman ate my banana.

'A symbolic gesture, of course,' she said.

When I returned to my room, I found a hefty young Russian woman sitting on a chair outside the door. She was wearing a low-cut brown lamé minidress.

She said, 'Ah, Mr Mole, I am Lara. I come to your room, to sleep, of course.'

I said, 'Is this part of the Intourist programme?'

Lara said, 'No. I am, of course, in love with you.'

She followed me into my room and went to the bunch of bananas on the bedside table. She looked down at them with lust in her eyes and I understood. It wasn't me she wanted: it was the bananas. I gave her two. She went away. Intercourse with her might have done me some harm. She had thighs like Californian redwoods.

Friday August 23rd

I lay awake most of the night, scratching at my mosquito bites and regretting my hasty decision and wondering how news about my bananas had spread. The next day the streets were full of rioting Muscovites and we were confined to the hotel.

After lunch (black bread, beetroot soup, a wizened piece of meat, one cold potato), I returned to my room to find that my bananas had gone. I was outraged.

I complained to Natasha, but she only said, 'You had *ten* bananas?' She looked misty-eyed and then snapped, 'You should, of course, have put them in the hotel safe. They will be changing hands on the black market by now.'

I found Leonard Clifton in the gloomy basement bar. There had been a coup against Gorbachev and then a counter-coup by Boris Yeltsin.

'This is bad news for Soviet Communism,' he said, 'but good news for Jesus.'

England! England! England!

I long for my attic room.

Monday September 2nd

Oxford

I am in bed, exhausted and hideously deformed. Why do mosquitoes exist? Why? Cassandra said they are 'a

vital component of the food chain'. Well, I Adrian
Mole, would gladly *pull* the chain on them. And, if
the food chain collapses and the world starves, so be
it.

I have written to Foreign Parts, threatening to report
them to ABTA unless I receive *all* my money back,
plus compensation for the double trauma suffered
from the mosquitoes and the revolution.

Tuesday September 3rd

Christian passed by Foreign Parts today. He said it
looked deserted. There was a pile of unopened letters
on the doormat inside the shop.

Thursday September 5th

A reply from John Tydeman, Head of Drama, BBC
Radio.

Dear Adrian,

To be perfectly honest, Adrian, my heart sank when I
returned from holiday and saw that your manuscript, *Lo!
The Flat Hills of My Homeland* had landed on my desk yet
again. You say in your letter, 'I expect you are busy'. Yes, I
damned well *am* busy, incredibly so.

What exactly is a 'coffee break'? I've never had a 'coffee
break' during the whole of my long career with the BBC.

I drink coffee at my desk. I do not go to a 'coffee break' lounge where I loll about on a sofa and read handwritten manuscripts, 473 pages long. My advice to you (without reading your wretched MS) is to:

1) Learn to type
2) Cut it by at least half
3) Supply a SAE and postage. The BBC is suffering from a cash crisis. It certainly cannot afford to subsidize your literary outpourings.
4) Find yourself a *publisher*. I am *not* a publisher. I am the Head of Radio Drama. Though sometimes I wonder if I am Marjorie Proops.

I am sorry to have to write to you in such terms, but in my experience it is best to be frank with young writers.

Yours, with best wishes,

John Tydeman

Poor old Tydeman! He has obviously gone mad. 'Sometimes I wonder if I am Marjorie Proops' (!) – perhaps the Director General should be told that his Head of Radio Drama is suffering from the delusion that he is an agony aunt.

And he admitted that he hadn't even read the re-edited *Lo! What do we licence-payers pay for*?

Dear Mr Tydeman,

I would appreciate it if you could send my MS back, ASAP. I do not want it circulating around the corridors of the BBC and being purloined by a disaffected freelance producer, anxious to make his or her mark on the world of broadcasting.

    Adrian Mole

PS. Allow me to inform you, sir, that you are *not* Marjorie Proops.

Saturday September 7th

Spent most of the day in a futile search for a reasonably priced room. As I made my weary way back home, I passed Foreign Parts. There was a note on the door:

This business is closed. All enquiries to Churchman, Churchman, Churchman and Luther, Solicitors.

I didn't take down the telephone number. It was already in my filofax, under 'S'. A middle-aged couple *were* taking the number down, though. They were due to depart tomorrow on a cycling holiday in 'Peter Mayle Country', Provence. They were facing the awful realization that they were not going to see the famous table on the infamous terrace, and possibly take tea with Pierre Mayle plus *femme*.

    As the couple walked away, I heard her say to him: 'Cheer up, Derek, there's always the caravan at Ingoldmells.' A fine woman, indomitable in the face of disaster. Mr Mayle has been cheated of meeting a true Brit.

Sunday September 8th

I have decided to go with Jake Westmorland.

Chapter Seventeen: Jake – A Hero of Our Time
Jake stood on top of the tank in Red Square. What a good job I took Russian at school, instead of French, he thought. Then, quieting the multitudes by a small gesture of his hand, he spoke.

'I am Jake Westmorland,' he shouted. The revolutionary hordes bellowed their grateful recognition. A sea of banners waved joyously. The sultry Russian sunlight glinted on the dome of St Basil's Cathedral as Jake tried to quieten the crowds and begin his speech. The speech that he hoped would prevent the disintegration of the Soviet Union . . .

Monday September 9th

I have written eleven speeches for Jake and thrown them all in the bin. None of them was capable of changing the course of world history.

. . . But before Jake could make the speech that would almost certainly have saved the Soviet Union, a shot rang out and Jake fell off the tank and into the arms of Natasha, his Russian mistress. She threw Jake over her shoulder and the silent crowd parted to let them through.

Thursday September 12th

Cassandra has ordered me to be out of the house by noon on Saturday! The lousy, stinking undergraduates have hogged all the private rented accommodation. I had no choice but to throw myself on the mercy of Oxford Council. But the Council official I spoke to today maintained that I am 'intentionally homeless' and refused to help me. I have started collecting cardboard boxes. Either to pack my belongings in, or to sleep in – who knows?

Friday September 13th

Christian has taken the children to see his mother in Wigan. He is a spineless coward. The hideous Cassandra is walking around the house in her absurd clothes, singing her ludicrous rapping songs. I asked her tonight if I could store my books in the attic until I've found a place of my own. She replied, 'Books?' as though she'd never heard the word before.

I said, 'Yes, *books*. You know, those things with cardboard covers stuffed with paper. People read them, for pleasure.'

Cassandra snorted contemptuously. 'Books belong in the past, together with stiletto heels and Gerry and the Pacemakers. This is the nineties, Adrian. It's the age of technology.'

She went to her word processor and pressed a button. A series of little green men wearing Viking helmets filled the screen and began to fight with little red men wearing baseball caps, who came out of a cave. Cassandra leaned eagerly towards the screen. I sensed that our conversation was over and left the room.

Query: Is the world going mad, or is it me?

Saturday September 14th

8.30 a.m.

Options

1) Pandora (no chance)
2) Bianca (possible)
3) Mother (last resort)
4) Bed and breakfast (expensive)
5) Hostel (fleas, violence)
6) Streets

11.30 a.m.

1) Pandora turned me down flat. She is a true *Belle Dame sans Merci*.
2) Bianca is away attending a Guns 'n' Roses convention in Wolverhampton. Left note at newsagent's.
3) My mother is out gawping at a new crop circle just outside Kettering.

4) The cheapest B&B is £15.99 a *night*!
5) There is nothing under 'Hostel' in the phone book.
6) I hit the road at high noon.

11.35 p.m. Leicester. Bert Baxter's house
So, it has come to this. I am reduced to sleeping on a Put-U-Up in a pensioner's living-room, which stinks of cats. Baxter is charging me £5 for tonight, plus £2.50 for bacon and eggs. My mother's house is locked and dark, and the key is not in its usual place under the drain cover. In normal circumstances I would have broken the small pantry window and climbed in, but my mother has had a security system installed. Delusions of grandeur, or what?

My father, supposedly penniless, is on holiday in Florida with a rich divorcee called Belinda Bellingham. I know I could go to my grandma's but I can't bear her to find out that I am unemployed and homeless. The shock could kill her. She has my GCSE certificates framed on the hall wall. My 'A' level English certificate is in a silver frame on the mantelpiece in her front room. Why give such anguish to an elderly diabetic?

Monday September 16th

1.35 a.m. I am now trying to sleep on the sofa-bed in my mother's living-room. As I write, the television in my mother's bedroom is blaring. The washing machine is on its spin cycle. The dishwasher is shrieking and somebody is taking a shower. Subsequently, the water pipes are banging all over the house. My stepfather, Martin Muffet, has just gone upstairs with his DIY toolbox. Does nobody sleep in this house?

Tuesday September 17th

My grandma knows all. My mother has told her everything. She is disgusted. I hope she never finds out that Bert Baxter gave me a bed for the night.

Wednesday September 18th

G knows about B&B at BB's. She saw BB in C&A.

Friday September 20th

A postcard of Clifton Suspension Bridge came this morning.

Dear Adrian,

I've only just got your message! Sorry I didn't see you before you left. That Cassandra is a sad woman all right!

I've never been to Leicester. Is it nice? Hope so for your sake!

There's a floor here for you if you fancy coming back to Oxford! I know where I can borrow a double mattress.

Let me know soon, please!
Love,
B.

The exclamation marks gave me some pain. Could I share a floor with a woman who was so profligate with them? And what would the sleeping arrangements be? This 'double mattress' she mentioned. Was it for me only? If so, why a double? I presume she has an adequate bed of her own. I decided to write an ambiguous reply, keeping my options open, but committing myself to nothing. My mother, who had brought the postcard to me in bed, wanted to know *everything* about 'B'. Height, weight, build, colouring, education, class, accent, clothes, shoes. 'Is she nice?' Have I 'slept with her'? 'Why not?' The Spanish Inquisition would be nothing compared to my mother. Nothing.

Dear Bianca,

It was most kind of you to write to me and offer the use of a double mattress and your floor.

I confess to you that when I asked you for your help in solving my temporary difficulty regarding my lack of accommodation, I was in somewhat of a panic.

I am surprised that you responded as you did. Ours has not been a long acquaintanceship. For all you know, I could have severe character faults or a psychotic personality.

I would urge caution in the future. I would not like to see you taken advantage of. I am not sure about my future plans. Leicester has a certain *je ne sais quoi*: it is quite pleasant in the autumn, when the fallen leaves give the pavements a little colour.

Yours,

   Best wishes,

     Adrian

Sunday September 22nd

I was looking forward to a traditional Sunday dinner with Yorkshire pudding and gravy, etc. But my mother informed me at 1.00 p.m. that she doesn't *do* Sunday dinner any more. Instead, we were driven four miles in Muffet's car to a 'Carvery' where we paid £4.99 a head to be served with slices of cardboard and dried up vegetables by a moronic youth in a chef's that. My sister Rosie spilt Muffet's half pint of Ruddles all over our table. I tried to come to the rescue with half a dozen beer mats – but the beer mats refused to soak up any beer. They repelled all liquid. In the end, the moronic one threw us a stinking dishcloth.

Query: What is the purpose of modern beer mats? Are they now merely symbolic, like the crucifix?

6.00 p.m. My mother has informed me that I have got to pay her board of 'a minimum of thirty-five pounds a week, or you're out on your ear'. Does blood count for nothing in 1991?

Tuesday September 24th

My grandma has said I can move in with her, rent free, providing I cut the grass, wind the clocks and fetch the shopping. I agreed immediately.

Wednesday September 25th

I read the first three chapters of *Lo!* aloud to Grandma tonight. She thinks it is the best thing she has ever heard. She thinks that the publishers who rejected it are barmy. And she has got nothing but contempt for Mr John Tydeman. She recently wrote to him to complain about the sex in *The Archers*. She claims that he didn't reply personally. Apparently he got a machine to do it for him.

Sunday September 29th

Archers omnibus. Egg, bacon, fried bread, the *People*. Roast beef, roast potatoes, mashed potatoes, cabbage, carrots, peas, Yorkshire pudding, gravy. Apple crumble, custard, cup of tea, extra strong mints, *News of the World*. Tinned salmon sandwiches, mandarin oranges and jelly, sultana cake, cup of tea.

Monday September 30th

Chapter Eighteen: Back to the Wolds
Jake settled back in the rocking chair and watched his grandmother making the corn dolly. Her apple cheeks glowed in the flames from the black leaded range. The copper kettle sang. The canary in the cage by the window trilled along with it. Jake sighed a deep, contented sigh. It was good to be back from Russia and all that unpleasantness with Natasha. Here, he could truly relax, in his grandma's cottage on the Wolds.

Autumn

Tuesday October 1st

My father brought Mrs Belinda Bellingham round to meet me at Grandma's house tonight. I was totally gobsmacked; she is a posh person! My father has started to pronounce his aitches religiously and to say 'barth' instead of 'bath'. And he has also discovered manners: every time my grandma came into the room, he leapt out of his chair.

Eventually she snapped, 'Sit *down*, George. You're up and down like a window cleaner's ladder.'

Mrs Bellingham is blonde and pretty, with those cheekbones that denote centuries of wise breeding. I thought she was very pale, considering she had just spent two weeks in the sun. Later in the evening, I found out that she lives in fear of skin cancer. Apparently she spent her holiday running from one patch of shade to another. Mrs Bellingham is the managing director of 'Bell Safe' – a burglar alarm company. My father starts work next Monday as Mrs Bellingham's sales director. They tried to persuade my grandma to allow them to install a burglar alarm at cost price, but she refused, saying, 'No, thank you. If I have to go out, I turn the volume up on Radio Four and leave my front door open.'

Mrs Bellingham and my father exchanged scandalized glances. Grandma continued, 'And I've never been burgled in sixty years, and anyroad up, if I had an alarm on the front of the house, folks'd know I've got something valuable, wouldn't they?'

There was an awkward pause, then my father said, 'Well, Belinda, I'll see you home, shall I?'

He fetched her coat and held it out while she put it on. He has obviously been having lessons in social etiquette. When they'd gone, my grandma shocked me by saying, 'Your dad's turned into a right brown-nosing bugger, hasn't he?'

Perhaps she is suffering from the early symptoms of senile dementia. I have never heard her swear before.

Sir Alan Green, the Director of Public Prosecutions, has been caught talking to a prostitute and has resigned. Under the 1985 Sexual Offences Act, a man seen approaching a woman more than once can be stopped by the police. This is news to me. I shall certainly be more careful whom I approach in the street from now on.

Friday October 4th

Grandma and I have scoured the house from top to bottom today. Grandma has a fixation about germs. She is convinced that they are lying in wait for her, ready to pounce and bring her down. I blame the television advertisement for a lavatory cleaner which depicts 'germs' the size of gremlins, who lurk about in the 'S' bend, chuckling malevolently. Although I've seen this advertisement hundreds of times, I simply can't remember what the product is called.

Query: Is television advertising effective?

Later, Grandma sat down and watched the Labour Party singing 'We Are the Champions' as the finale to their conference in Brighton. Not many of the shadow cabinet knew the words. I hope Freddie Mercury wasn't watching – it would have stuck in his teeth, not to mention his craw.

Sunday October 6th

Turning the pages of my *Observer* today, I saw Barry Kent's ugly face staring out at me. Apparently he is a new member of a place called the Groucho Club. I read the accompanying article avidly. It is exactly the sort of place I would like to be a member of. Should I ever reach that goal, I shall tell the manager (Liam) the truth about Kent's past and have him blackballed.

Elizabeth Taylor has married a bricklayer with a bad perm. He is called Larry Fortensky. Michael Jackson's ape, Bubbles, was the best man.

Chapter Nineteen: Time to Move On
Jake slipped out of the cottage as the village church struck

midnight. He ran stealthily down the lane and towards the minicab which was waiting, as instructed, by the post office. As he threw his rucksack into the back of the car and climbed in after it, he sighed with relief. He never again wanted to see the apple cheeks of his grandmother and he vowed to burn the next corn dolly he came across.

'Put your foot down!' Jake barked to the minicab driver. 'Take me to the nearest urban conurbation.'

The minicab driver's brow was furrowed. 'What's an urban conurbation when it's at 'ome?' he said.

Jake snapped, 'Okay, dolt! You want specifics, take me to the Groucho Club.'

At the mention of the magic words, the cab driver's shoulders straightened. The dandruff stayed on his scalp. He had waited years to hear the words, 'Take me to the Groucho Club'. He looked at Jake with a new respect and he did as he was told. He put his foot down on the clutch and the minicab sped away from the Wolds and towards the great metropolis where, in the Groucho, the Great were no doubt quaffing the house wine and exchanging witticisms. Jake hoped Belinda would be there, at the bar, showing her legs and laughing hysterically at one of Jeffrey Bernard's jokes.

Monday October 7th

Barry Kent is making a film for BBC2 about his 'roots'. The television cameras were in the Co-op, blocking the aisles. I couldn't get to the cat food, so I complained to the manager (who, incidentally, didn't look a day older than seventeen). He replied, 'Barry Kent's comin' here in person this afternoon.' It was as though he were talking about royalty.

I said, 'I don't give a toss. I want three tins of Whiskas, *now*!' The boy manager went off and, in crawling tones, asked the cameraman to pass him three tins of cat food. With what I thought was ill grace, the cameraman obliged and, after paying the starstruck child, I left the shop.

Tuesday October 8th

My mother has been persuaded to give a talk to camera about 'the Barry Kent she once knew'. I urged her to tell the truth, about the bullying, lying, scruffy, thick youth we knew and despised.

But my mother said, 'I always found Barry to be a sensitive child.' The director made her stand by her overflowing wheelie bin in the side yard.

My mother said, 'Shouldn't I be made-up, by a proper make-up artist?' Nick, the director, said, 'No, Mrs Mole, we're going for actuality.' My mother touched the cold sore on her lip and said, 'I'd counted on a bit of camouflage to hide this.' A strong light was turned on her, which showed every line, wrinkle and bag on my mother's face.

Then the director shouted, 'Go!' and my mother went. To pieces. After seventeen attempts, BBC2 gave up, packed their gear and went off. My mother ran upstairs and threw herself on the bed. There is nothing so pitiful as a failed interviewee.

Saturday October 12th

Kent is still poncing around the neighbourhood. I saw him being filmed walking up our street. He was wearing a floor-length overcoat, cowboy boots and dark glasses. I ducked out of sight. I have no wish to be publicly identified as the dork in *Dork's Diary*.

I took the dog for a walk to the field where Pandora used to ride Blossom, her pony. It tired very quickly. I had to carry it back.

I saw Mrs Kent, Barry's mother, on the way home. She was walking her pit bull terrier. I asked her if she had registered the beast yet (as required by law).

She said, 'Butcher wouldn't hurt a fly.'

I said, 'It's not flies I'm worried about. It's the tender flesh of small children.'

She changed the subject and told me that Barry had bought her the council house she now lives in. This made me laugh quite a lot. The Kents' house is a byword for squalor in our neighbourhood. They chop the internal doors up for firewood every winter.

Sunday October 13th

Finished Chapter Nineteen tonight.

Jake was sick of being interviewed. He ordered the journalists to leave the Groucho Club and leave him alone. He turned to Lenny Henry and said, 'Let's have a drink, Len.' Lenny smiled his thanks and Jake snapped his fingers. A waiter came running immediately and bent deferentially towards Jake. 'A bottle of champagne – a big one – and make that three glasses,' for Jake had just seen one of his best friends, Richard Ingrams, of *News Quiz* fame, come through the hallowed swing doors. 'Hey, Rich, over here!' shouted Jake. There was a sound of scuffling coming from the reception area. Jake turned his head round to see Liam, the manager, throwing Kent Barry, the failed writer, out of the club and into the gutter.

Monday October 14th

Dear Bianca,

After further reflection, can I take you up on your offer? It would be most convenient for me to spend a few days sleeping on your floor in Oxford. Quite honestly, I cannot tolerate another moment living with my family. It isn't just the noise level and the constant bickering; it's the small things – the encrusted neck of the HP Sauce bottle; the slimy soap dish; the dog hairs in the butter.

You can telephone me on the above number, any time, night or day. Nobody sleeps in this house.

All my very best wishes,
Adrian Mole

Tuesday October 15th

My sister Rosie told me that she hated me this morning. Her outburst came after I suggested that she comb her hair before going to school. My mother got out of bed and came downstairs. She lit her second cigarette of the day (she smokes the first in bed) and immediately took Rosie's side. She said, 'Leave the kid alone.'

I said, 'Somebody has to maintain standards in this house.'

My mother said, 'You can talk. That beard looks like a ferret's nest. I don't know how you can bear to have it so near to your mouth. A public health inspector would close it down.'

During the ensuing row, nasty things were said on both sides, which I now regret. I accused her of being a neglectful mother, with loose morals. She counter-attacked by describing me as 'a fungus-faced dork'. She said she had secretly read my *Lo!* manuscript and thought it was 'crap from start to finish'. She said, 'in the unlikely event of it being published, I hope you will use a pseudonym, because, to be honest, Adrian, I couldn't stand the public shame.'

I put my head on the kitchen table and wept.

My mother then put her arm around me and said, 'There, there, Adrian. Don't cry. I didn't mean it, I think *Lo! The Flat Hills of My Homeland* is a very interesting first attempt.'

But it was no good. I wept until dehydration set in.

10.00 p.m. Why hasn't Bianca phoned? I used a first class stamp.

Thursday October 17th

Drew more money out of the Market Harborough Building Society. My dream of being an owner-occupier has receded even further into the realms of fantasy.

I have received a postcard of the Forth Bridge, with no address but posted in London.

Dear Adrian,

I'm going to London to try for a proper job. I've got an interview with British Rail. In a rush. Please reply c/o my friend Lucy:

Lucy Clay
Flat 10
Dexter House
Coghill Street
Oxford

She has promised to pass on any messages.

I hope you are well and happy. I miss you!
  Love,
   B.
PS. How about a London floor when I find one?

Friday October 18th

Chapter Twenty: The Reckoning
Jake pushed the earth wire out of the lawnmower plug, then screwed the plug together again. He could hear his mother on the telephone to her new lover (a schoolboy called Craig).

He waited for her to finish cooing her endearments down the phone and re-emerge on the terrace. 'I've cut half the lawn, mother,' he shouted, 'but I've got to go to the barber's now.'

His mother frowned and dropped ash all down her cashmere dress. 'But Jake, darling,' she remonstrated. 'You know I hate to see a job half done.' She went towards the lawnmower.

Jake chuckled inwardly. He had banked on this trait of his mother's. As he passed through the french windows, he heard the hover-mower whir into life, to be followed immediately by the high-pitched scream.

Jake immediately felt guilty, then comforted himself by thinking that he had advised his mother time after time to install a circuit breaker; advice she had foolishly chosen to ignore.

Sunday October 20th

It was my father's access day today. He came to take Rosie out to McDonald's as usual. While she looked for her shoes, my father and I talked man to man about my mother. We agreed that she was an impossible person to live with. We had a good laugh about Martin Muffet, who was in the back garden building a lean-to conservatory with the assistance of his Black and Decker work bench. We agreed that, since marrying my mother, Muffet has aged ten years.

I congratulated my father on capturing Mrs Belinda Bellingham, and confessed that I didn't have much luck with women. My father said, 'Tell them what they want to hear, son, and buy them a bunch of flowers once a fortnight. That's all there is to it.'

I asked him if he intended to marry Mrs Bellingham, but before he could answer, my mother staggered into the room carrying a large cardboard box which contained the swag she'd bought from a car boot sale. She'd bought a painting of Christ on the cross; an ashtray with two scottie dogs painted on it; an aluminium toast rack; twenty-seven bent candles; a chenille tablecloth; a Tom Jones LP; six cooking apples; and a steering wheel. As she excitedly unpacked the junk onto the kitchen table, I saw my father looking at her with what I can only describe as lovelight in his eyes.

Monday October 21st

Bianca rang, but I was out cutting Bert Baxter's disgusting toenails. My mother wrote down a telephone number where I could contact Bianca, but then lost it almost immediately. We searched the house, but failed to find the scrap of paper. I expect the dog ate it. It has recently taken to scoffing whole pages of the *Leicester Mercury*, a sign of its increasing neurosis or a vitamin deficiency – who knows? Nobody can afford to take it to the vet to find out.

Tuesday October 22nd

I sent a postcard of Leicester Bus Station to Bianca c/o Lucy Clay:

Dear Bianca,

Thank you for your postcard of the Forth Bridge.

I was most surprised to hear that you were leaving Oxford and going to the 'Smoke', as the cockneys say.

I wish you luck in your search for a 'proper' job. Keep me posted. I have had no luck yet, but I keep trying.

It is very difficult living here with my family. There is a total clash of lifestyles. I strive to be tolerant of the noise and disorder, but it is hard, very hard.

Yours,

With very best wishes,

Adrian

Mrs Bellingham has offered me a job selling security devices. It is evening work. I have to call on nervous householders after dark and put the fear of God into them until they sign up for a burglar alarm or security lights. I said I would think about it.

Mrs Bellingham said in her careful voice, 'There are three million unemployed. Why do you need to think about it?'

I said I hoped that beggars could still be choosers.

She is offering me £3.14 an hour. No commission, no insurance stamp, no contract of employment – cash in hand. I asked her if she objected to my belonging to a union. Her face went whiter than ever and she said, 'Yes, I'm afraid I do. Mrs Thatcher's greatest achievement was to tame the unions.' My father is a Thatcherite's lackey!

Thursday October 24th

I despise myself. I have only been working for two nights, but I have already sold a whole house security system, six car alarms, four peepholes and half a dozen bike locks. My method is simple. I get into the house and show the householders the portfolio that Mrs Bellingham has assembled. It consists of lurid stories cut out of the tabloid newspapers and police press releases. After leafing through this alarming document, it would take great insouciance for the householder to deny that more security in the home is a desirable thing.

Mrs Bellingham has instructed me to ask the question, 'Don't you think your family deserves more protection from the dark forces of evil that are at large in our community?'

So far only one person has said, 'No,' and he was the defeated-looking father of six teenage boys.

Monday October 28th

Shaved beard off. Mrs Bellingham said it made me look untrustworthy. I am completely in her power. If she ordered me to go to work wearing a Batman outfit, I would have to obey her. I have no legal rights of employment.

Thursday October 31st

At last! The economic recovery is on its way! The Confederation of British Industry has reported that they expect outputs and exports to increase in the years ahead. According to the CBI, manufacturers are expecting huge new orders. I broke this good news to my mother. She said, 'Yes, and the dog is getting married on Saturday and I'm its Matron of Honour.' Then she and Martin Muffet went off into one of their mad laughing fits.

Ken Barlow of *Coronation Street* fame has been on

trial for being boring. He was found 'Not Guilty' and awarded £50,000.

My mother has got a job as a security guard in the new shopping centre that has just opened in Leicester city centre. She looks like a New York City police-woman in her uniform. She told the security firm, 'Group Five', that she was *thirty-five years old*! She is now living in fear that her true age, forty-seven, will be revealed. Is everybody partially sighted at Group Five? Did her interview take place in a candlelit office? I asked her these questions.

She said, 'I bunged on rather a lot of Max Factor's pan-stick and sat with my back to the window.'

Friday November 1st

In view of my continuing success in flogging her security paraphernalia, Mrs Bellingham has raised my hourly rate from £3.14 to the heady sum of £3.25! Gee whiz! Fire a cannon! Release the balloons! Open the Bollinger! Issue a press release! Inform the Red Arrows!

Saturday November 2nd

Jake used his Swiss Army knife to dismantle the burglar alarm and in a matter of moments he had circumnavigated the padlocks, bolts and chains on the front door and was standing in the front hall of Bellingham Towers.

Upstairs, sleeping after an hour of arduous lovemaking, were the owners of the historic country house, Sir George and Lady Belinda, and their daughter, the Honourable Rosemary. Jake chuckled as he stuffed silver and *objets d'art* into a black plastic bag. He felt no guilt. He was robbing the filthy rich to feed the filthy poor. He was the Robin Hood of Leicestershire.

My mother claims that I look exactly like John Major, especially when I am wearing my reading glasses. This is total rubbish: unlike Mr Major, I have got lips. They may be on the thin side, but they are distinctly there. If I were Major, I'd have a lip transplant. Mick Jagger could be the donor.

Tuesday November 5th

Robert Maxwell, the mogul, has fallen overboard from his yacht, the *Lady Ghislaine*.

Went to Age Concern Community Bonfire Party. Pushed Bert Baxter there in his wheelchair. Baxter was asked to leave after half an hour because he was seen (and certainly heard) to throw an Indian firecracker into the bonfire. The organizer, Mrs Plumbstead, said apologetically, 'Safety has to be paramount.'

Baxter said scornfully, 'There were no such thing as *safety* when I were a lad.'

I pushed him home in silence. I was furious. Because of him, I missed the baked potatoes, sausages and soup. I had to wait for an hour for the district nurse to come and put him to bed.

Thursday November 7th

Kevin Maxwell has denied that his deceased father's businesses have financial problems.

Query: Would our banks lend £2.5 billion to a man with money problems?

Answer: Of course not! Our banks are respected financial institutions.

Sunday November 10th

To Grandma's for the Remembrance Day poppy-laying ceremony. I am proud of my dead grandfather, Albert Mole. He fought valiantly in the First World War so that I would not have to live under the tyranny of a foreign oppressor.

I cannot let the above sentence lie. The truth is that my poor, dead grandfather fought in the Great War because he was ordered to. He always did what he was told. I take after him in that respect.

Monday November 11th

A gang of Leicester yobs shouted out, 'Hey, John Major, how's Norma?' tonight, as I came out of the cinema. I looked around, thinking that perhaps the Prime Minister was visiting the Leicester Chamber of Commerce, or something, but there was no sign of him. I then realized, to my horror, that they were addressing their yobbish remarks to me.

Wednesday November 13th

A letter from Bianca.

Dear Adrian,

Thank you for your letter, which Lucy forwarded to me. As you can see from my address, I am living in London. I am renting a small room in Soho at the moment, but it is costing £110 per week, so I won't be here long!

I've got a job as a waitress in a restaurant called 'Savages'. The owner is a bit strange, but the staff are very nice. It would be lovely to see you when you're next in London. My day off is Monday. How is the novel going? Have you finished your revisions? I can't wait to read it in full!

Love,

Bianca (Dartington)

Thursday November 14th

Dear Bianca,

Many thanks for your letter of the 11th. I must confess that I was rather surprised to hear from you. I am hardly ever in London, but I may drop in and see you on my next visit. Isn't Soho a dangerous place in which to live? Please take care as you walk the streets. Personally, I am ossifying in this provincial hell.

Lo! is going very well. I have called my hero Jake Westmorland. What do you think?

Please write back.

Yours as ever,

Adrian

Friday November 15th

The New York Stock Exchange collapsed today. I hope this won't affect the interest rates of the Market Harborough Building Society.

Saturday November 16th

No reply from B.

Sunday November 17th

Why isn't there a Sunday delivery in this country? I expect it is because of objections from the established Church. Do the clergy imagine that God gives a toss if humans receive letters or not on a Sunday?

Monday November 18th

By second post. A postcard of Holborn Viaduct.

Dear Adrian,
    No. Soho is not dangerous. I *love* Jake Westmorland. When are you coming to London?
    Lots of love,
        Bianca

Tuesday November 19th

I sent Bianca a postcard of the Clock Tower, Leicester.

Dear Bianca,
    As it happens, I shall be in London next Monday. Would you like to have lunch? Please write or ring to confirm.
    Very warm wishes,
        Adrian

PS. I have shaved my beard off. It was the television pictures of Terry Waite that decided me.

Wednesday November 20th

Grandma's Christmas card arrived. The shops are full of Santa Clauses ringing bells and getting in the way of legitimate shoppers. My mother said that whilst on duty she saw an old lady shoplifting a Cadbury's Selection Box. I asked her what action she'd taken. She said, 'I turned and walked the other way.'

There is a rush on for burglar alarms. Everybody wants them fitted before Christmas when they fill their homes with consumer durables and Nintendo games.

Saturday November 23rd

A postcard from Bianca, of the original Crystal Palace.

Dear Adrian,

I have got to work on Monday. The office party season has started, but come down anyway. I will get off early. I look forward to seeing you. Come to 'Savages', Dean Street, at 2.30 p.m.

Love,

Bianca

Sunday November 24th

Freddie Mercury has died of Aids. There was no time for me to mourn, but I put 'Bohemian Rhapsody', which is one of my favourite records, on the record player.

I laid my wardrobe on my bed (or rather, the *contents* of my wardrobe) and tried to decide what to wear for my trip to London. I do not wish to be marked out as a provincial day-tripper by sneering metropolitans. Decided on the black shirt, black trousers and Oxfam tweed jacket. My grey slip-on shoes will have to do. Set my alarm for 8.30 a.m. I catch the 12.30 p.m. train.

Monday November 25th

Soho
I am in love with Bianca Dartington. Hopelessly, help-lessly, mindlessly, gloriously, magnificently.

Tuesday November 26th

I am still here, in Soho, in Bianca's room above Brenda's Patisserie in Old Compton Street. I have hardly seen daylight since 3.30 p.m. on Monday.

Wednesday November 27th

Poem to Bianca Dartington:

> Gentle face,
> Night black hair,
> Natural grace,
> Love I swear.
> Marry me, be my wife,
> Make me happy, share my life.

Thursday November 28th

Phoned my mother and asked her to send my books to Old Compton Street. Informed her that I am now living in London, with Bianca. She asked for the address, but I wasn't falling for that. I hung up.

Friday November 29th

God, I love her! I love her! I love her! Every minute she is away, working at 'Savages', is torture for me.

Query: Why didn't I *know* that the human body is capable of such exquisite pleasure?

Answer: Because, Mole, you had not made love to Bianca Dartington – somebody who loves you body and soul – before.

Saturday November 30th

What did I ever see in Pandora Braithwaite? She is an opinionated, arrogant ball-breaker. An all-round nasty piece of work. Compared to Bianca, she is nothing, nothing. And as for Leonora De Witt, I can hardly remember her face.

I never want to leave this room. I want to live the whole of my life within these four walls (with occasional trips to the bathroom, which we have to share with a fire-eater called Norman).

The walls are painted lavender blue and Bianca has stuck stars and moons on the ceiling which glow in the dark. There is a poster of Sydney Harbour Bridge on the wall between the windows. There is a double bed with an Indian bedspread covered in cushions; a chest of drawers that Bianca has painted white; an old armchair covered in a large tablecloth. A wonky table, half painted in gold, and two pine chairs. Instead of a bedhead, we have got a blown-up photograph on the wall of Isambard Kingdom Brunel, Bianca's hero.

Every morning when I wake up, I can't believe that the slim girl with the long legs who is lying next to me is mine! I always get out of bed first and put the kettle on the Baby Belling cooker. I then put two slices of toast under the grill and serve my love with her breakfast in bed. I won't allow her to get out of bed until the gas fire has warmed the room. She catches cold easily.

I want to please her more than I want to please myself.

This morning, 'Stand By Me', sung by Ben E. King, was playing on Capital Radio.

I said, 'I love this song. My father used to play it.'

Bianca said, 'So do I.'

We danced to it, me in my boxer shorts and Bianca in her pink knickers with the flowers on.

'Stand By Me' is now our song.

Sunday December 1st

Went to the National Gallery today. We walked around the Sainsbury Wing like Siamese twins, fused together. We cannot bear to be apart for even a moment. The renaissance pictures glowed like jewels and inflamed our passion. Our mutual genitalia are a bit sore and bruised, but it didn't stop us making love as soon as we got back to the room. Norman next door banged on the wall and nearly put us off, but we managed to ignore him.

Monday December 2nd

I was putting my socks and shoes on this morning, when I noticed a strange expression on Bianca's face.

I said, 'What is it, darling?'

After a lot of cajoling, Bianca confessed that she

adored everything about me except my grey slip-on shoes and white towelling socks. As a mark of my love for her, I opened the window and hurled my only pair of socks and shoes into Old Compton Street. I was unable to go out all day as a consequence. I was a barefoot prisoner of love.

Late that afternoon, Bianca bought me three pairs of socks from Sock Shop, and one pair of dark brogues from Bally. They all fitted perfectly. The shoes are *serious*. I felt like a grown-up in them as I walked around the room. I then walked to the Nat West Bank in Wardour Street and removed £100 from the Rapid Cash machine. This is the most I have ever withdrawn in one go. I paid Bianca for the shoes (£59.99), which is also the most I have ever paid for a pair of shoes. Incidentally, it is now late evening and the grey slip-ons are still in the gutter. I *did* see a tramp try them on, but he scowled and took them off immediately, though they looked a good fit.

Wednesday December 4th

I telephoned my mother today and asked her why she hadn't sent my books on as I had asked.

She screamed, 'Mainly because you refused to give me your address, you stupid sod.' She then went on to say that she had asked our postman, Courtney Elliot, for an estimate of the cost of sending the books by Parcel Post. Apparently, he 'guestimated' (her word, not mine) that it would cost about a hundred quid! She said that my father is driving to London on Friday to attend a conference on Home Security. She said she would ask him to drop the books, and the rest of my worldly goods, off. I agreed reluctantly and gave her the address.

When Bianca had gone to work, I walked to Oxford Street and bought a dustpan and brush, a packet of yellow dusters, Mr Sheen, a floor cloth, some liquid Flash, a bottle of Windolene and a pair of white satin knickers from Knickerbox.

Bianca was thrilled when she returned at 3.00 p.m. to find our room cleaned and sparkling. Almost as thrilled as I was at 1.00 a.m. when she put the satin knickers on.

Friday December 6th

My father was in a foul temper when he got here tonight. The conference was in Watford, so he had to go considerably out of his way (backwards) in order to deliver my stuff. When he eventually found Old Compton Street, it was 9.30 p.m.

He parked outside on double yellow lines, with his hazard lights flashing. Together, we lugged the boxes of books and plastic bags of clothes four floors up to the room. When we'd finished, my father collapsed on the bed. His bald patch was glistening with sweat. I was glad that Bianca was at work. When he'd recovered, I went down to see him off. Mrs Bellingham had ordered him to be home at a reasonable time. He is obviously afraid of her. As we walked to the car, my father stopped, pointed to the gutter and shouted, 'What the bleeding hell is that?'

His Montego had been wheel-clamped. I thought he was going to break down and cry in the street, but instead he went berserk and kicked at the yellow clamp and shouted obscenities. It was highly amusing to the posing idiots who were drinking cappuccino in the cold wind on the opposite pavement.

I offered to go with him to the outer reaches of London, to start the long, bureaucratic process of declamping the car, but my father snarled, 'Oh, bugger off back upstairs to your cowing love nest.' He hailed a black cab and jumped in. As it turned into Wardour Street, I could tell that it wouldn't be long before my father was whining to the cab driver about his bad luck, his ungrateful son, his fearsome mistress and his feckless ex-wife.

Saturday December 7th

Spent a pleasant day cataloguing and then arranging my books on the bookshelves I constructed from three planks and nine old bricks I found in a skip in Greek Street. Cost? Nil. In the same skip, I found *Moral Thinking* by John Wilson. It was printed in 1970, before sex came into *The Archers*, however, so I suppose the morality may be out of date.

Bianca came home at lunchtime and asked if I wanted a job as a part-time washer-up in 'Savages'. It is cash in hand, off the books. I said, 'Yes.'

We went to see the Thames Barrier and talked about our future. We pledged that we would not let riches and fame divide us.

I start washing up on Monday.

Monday December 9th

Peter Savage, the owner of 'Savages', is certainly aptly named. I have never known a man with such a bad temper. He is rude to everybody, staff and customers. The customers think he is amusingly eccentric. The staff hate him and spend their meal breaks fantasizing about killing him. He is a tall, fat man with a face like a beef tomato. He dresses like Bertie Wooster and talks like Bob Hoskins of *Roger Rabbit* fame. He wears a CND tiepin on his Garrick Club tie.

Culturally, he is all over the place.

Tuesday December 10th

Savage was drunk at 10 a.m. At 12 noon he vomited into the yukka plant in the corner of the restaurant.

At 1 p.m. his wife came, abused him verbally and then carried him out to her car, helped by Luigi, the head waiter.

I am reading *The Complete Plain Words* by Sir Ernest Gowers. I am on page 143: *Clichés*. Far be it from me to say so, but I'm sure my writing style will improve by leaps and bounds.

Bianca startled me this evening by suddenly shouting, 'Please, Adrian, can't you stop that perpetual sniffing. Use a handkerchief!'

Wednesday December 11th

I toil over greasy pots and pans for £3.90 an hour, and the customers fork out £17 for a monkfish and £18 for a bottle of wine! Savage is obviously not as stupid as he looks.

Fogle, Fogle, Brimmington and Hayes, the advertising firm, held their Christmas party in 'Savages' at lunchtime. The restaurant was closed to ordinary customers. Bianca said that the managing director, Piers Fogle, told her that they were in a celebratory mood because they had just won a contract worth £500,000 on the strength of a slogan for an advertising campaign for condoms.

'What the well-dressed man is wearing' is to appear on billboards all over the country.

Their bill came to over £700. They gave Bianca and the other waitresses £5 each. I, the serf in the kitchen, got nothing, of course. Luigi put two fingers up to Fogle's back as he staggered out of the restaurant.

Saturday December 14th

We haven't made love for over twenty-four hours. Bianca has got cystitis.

Sunday December 15th

Bought *The Joy of Sex* in the Charing Cross Road. Cystitis is called 'The Honeymooners' Illness'. It can be caused by vigorous, frequent sex. Poor Bianca is in the toilet every ten minutes. Why is there *always* a price to pay for pleasure?

Monday December 16th

Savage was in court this morning, charged with assaulting a customer last April. He was fined £500 and ordered to pay costs and damages totalling my wages for five years. He came back to the restaurant with Mrs Savage and his lawyer to celebrate the fact that he hadn't been sent to prison, but after the champagne had been drunk and the tagliatelle consumed, Savage spotted a group of Channel Four executives on table eight and began to abuse them because they didn't show enough tobogganing on their sports programmes.

According to Bianca, Mrs Savage said, 'Darling, do be quiet, you're starting to get a little tedious.'

Savage shouted, 'Shut your mouth, you fat cow!'

She shouted, 'I'm a size *ten*, you callous bastard!'

The lawyer tried to conciliate, but Savage tipped the table up and Luigi ended up throwing his boss out of his own restaurant.

Personally, I would be happy to see Savage chained up in prison, on bread and water, with rats gnawing at his feet – and I'm a supporter of prison reform.

Tuesday December 17th

Experimented with making very gentle love. I was the passive partner.

Later, we had our first argument. Where are we spending Christmas Day and Boxing Day? In our room? At her parents'? At my parents'? Or with Luigi, who has invited us to his house in Harrow? We didn't shout at each other, but there was (and still is) a distinct lack of seasonal goodwill. Bianca turned her back on me in bed tonight.

Thursday December 19th

We woke up tangled together, as usual. Christmas wasn't mentioned, but love, passion and marriage were. We are going to spend Christmas with her parents in Richmond. Her father is going to pick us up on Christmas Eve. It will save me having to buy presents for my family.

Saturday December 21st

Tonight, Savage promenaded around the restaurant with a miniature Christmas tree on his head, complete with twinkling lights. He kissed all the women and blew cigar smoke at all the men. Luigi led him into the kitchen and propped him up against the sink. Savage then proceeded to tell me that his mother had never loved him and that his father had run away with an alcoholic nurse when he was eight. (When Savage *junior* was eight.) He broke down and wept, but I was too busy to comfort him. The cook was screaming for side plates.

Sunday December 22nd

Bianca stayed in bed today, tired out, poor kid, which gave me a chance to work on chapter twenty-one of *Lo! The Flat Hills of My Homeland.*

Jake ran his fingers down the length of her back. Her skin felt like the finest silk, even to his fingers, roughened by years of immersion in washing-up water. She sighed and squirmed into the flannelette sheet. 'Don't stop,' she said, her voice cracking like a whip. 'Don't ever stop, Jake . . .'

Tuesday December 24th
Christmas Eve

I braved the maddening crowds today and went out to buy Bianca's Christmas present. After tramping the streets for two hours, I ended up in Knickerbox and bought her a purple suspender belt, scarlet knickers, and a black lace bra. When the saleswoman asked me about size, I confessed I didn't know. I said, 'She's not Rubenesque, but she's not Naomi Campbell.'

The woman rolled her eyes and said, 'Okay, she's medium, yeah?'

I said, 'She looks a bit like Paula Yates, but with black hair.'

The woman sighed and said, 'Paula Yates breast-feeding or not breastfeeding?'

I said, 'Not breastfeeding,' and she snatched some stuff off the racks and gift-wrapped it for me.

I agonized in Burger King over whether or not to buy her parents presents. At four-thirty, I decided that, yes, I would ingratiate myself with them and bought her mother some peach-based pot-pourri. I phoned Bianca at 'Savages' and asked what I should get for her father. She said her father was fond of poetry, so I went and bought him a book of poems by John Hegley, called *Can I Come Down Now Dad?* which has a picture of Jesus on the cross on its cover. I also managed to track down a copy of *The Railway Heritage of Britain* by Gordon Biddle and O. S. Nock for Bianca.

Thursday December 26th
Boxing Day

Richmond

Bianca's mother is allergic to peaches; and her father, the Reverend Dartington, thought that the John Hegley book was in extremely bad taste. Also, I hate Bianca's brother and sister. How my sweet, darling Bianca could have come from such a vile family is a mystery to me. We slept in separate beds in separate rooms. We had to go to a wooden hut of a church on Christmas Day and listen to her father rant on about the commercialization of Christmas. Bianca and I were the only people to buy presents. Everyone else had given money to the Sudanese Drought Fund. Bianca bought me a Swatch watch and the *Chronicle of the Twentieth Century*, which will be an invaluable work of reference to me. I was very pleased. She was pleased with the Biddle and Nock.

Her brother, Derek, and her sister, Mary, obviously disapprove of our love affair. They are both unmarried and still live at home. Derek is thirty-five and Mary is twenty-seven. Mrs Dartington was forty-eight when Bianca was born.

There was no turkey, no drink and no celebration. It made me long for my own family's vulgarity.

This afternoon, we had to go for a walk alongside the river. Little kids were out in force, wobbling on new bikes and pushing prams with new-looking dolls inside. Derek has now taken a shine to me. He thought I was a fellow trainspotter; I quickly put him right. Bianca and I managed a quick embrace in the kitchen tonight before being interrupted by Mary, who came in looking for her constipation chocolate.

Mrs Dartington had a convenient 'turn' just before dinner and took to her bed. Bianca and I cooked the meal. We had salad, corned beef and baked potatoes. I cannot wait to get back to our room. I need Bianca. I need onions. I need garlic. I need Soho. I need Savage. I need air. I need freedom from the Dartingtons.

There are four beige car coats hanging up in the downstairs cloakroom.

Friday December 27th

The Reverend Dartington drove us back to Soho in martyred silence. Every time he stopped at a red light or pedestrian crossing, he drummed his fingers on the steering wheel impatiently.

Two days with her family have had a deleterious

effect on Bianca: she seems to have shrunk physically and regressed mentally. As soon as she got back into the room she burst into tears and shouted, 'Why didn't they *tell* me they were giving their Christmas presents to the Sudanese?'

I said, 'Because they wanted to claim the moral high ground and make you feel foolish. It's obviously a punishment because you are living in sin, in Soho, with a lowly washer-upper.'

An hour later, Bianca had sprung back in size and mental capacity. We made love for one hour, ten minutes. Our longest yet. It is quite useful having a stopwatch facility on my new Swatch.

Sunday December 29th

We went to Camden Lock today to buy Bianca a pair of boots. The whole area was thronging with young people who were both buying and selling. I said to Bianca, 'Isn't it nice to see the young out and about and enjoying themselves?'

She looked at me in a funny way and said, 'But *you* are young. You're only twenty-four, though sometimes I find it hard to believe.'

She was right, of course. I am young, officially, but I have never felt young. My mother said I was thirty-five on the day I fought my way out of her womb.

The cystitis is back. Bianca has reluctantly put the

satin knickers back in her underwear drawer and gone back to the cotton gussets.

I am reading a play, *A Streetcar Named Desire* by Tennessee Williams. Poor Blanche Dubois!

Winter

Wednesday January 1st 1992

'Savages' was closed last night, so we went to Trafalgar Square at 11.30 p.m. to see the New Year in. The crowd was like a drunken field of corn rippling and swaying in a storm. For over two hours I lost myself and went with the flow. It was frightening, but also exhilarating to find myself in a line doing the conga up St Martin's Lane. Unfortunately, the person in front of me had extremely fat buttocks. It was not an attractive sight.

When Big Ben struck twelve, I found myself kissing and being kissed by strangers, including foreigners. I tried to get to Bianca, but she was surrounded by a party of extrovert Australian persons who were all over seven foot tall. But finally, at 12.03 a.m. on the 1st of January, we kissed and pledged our troth. I can't believe I've got such a wonderful woman. Why does she love me? I live in fear that one day she will wake up and ask herself the same question.

We went to Tower Bridge today. It left me cold, but Bianca was enraptured by the structural design of the thing. I practically had to drag her away.

Thursday January 2nd

Got up at 3.30 a.m. and joined the queue outside Next in Oxford Street. The sale started at 9.00 a.m. I got into conversation with a man who had his eye on a double-breasted navy suit, marked down from £225 to £90. He is getting married to a parachute packer, called Melanie, next Saturday.

In my new black leather jacket, white T-shirt and blue jeans, I look like every other young man in London, New York and Tokyo. Or Leicester, come to think of it. For Leicester is at the very epicentre of the Next empire.

Bianca wanted to visit Battersea Power Station today and asked me to go with her, but I pointed out to her that *Lo!* was about to develop in a revolutionary direction and that I needed to work on Chapter Twenty-two.

She left the flat without saying a word, but her back looked very angry.

Jake pulled the collar of his Next black leather jacket up against the cruel wind that blew across the Thames. He stared down into the ebbing water. It was time he did something with his life other than help with famine relief in Sudan. He knew what it was. It was something he had fought against – God knows how he had fought! But the compulsion was overwhelming now. He had to do it. He had to write a novel . . .

Wednesday January 8th

President Bush vomited into the lap of the Japanese Ambassador at an official banquet in Tokyo tonight. We watched it on the portable television in the kitchen at 'Savages'. Mrs Bush shoved her husband under the table, then left the room. She didn't look too pleased. The television news showed the whole incident in slow motion. It was sickening. The Japanese people looked horrified. They are sticklers for protocol.

Savage has fired little Carlos for smoking a joint in the yard at the back of the restaurant. Savage then drank half a bottle of brandy, three bottles of Sol, stole various drinks from customers' tables and ended up fighting with the palm tree at the bar after accusing it of having an affair with his wife. Alcohol is certainly a dangerous drug in the wrong hands.

Wednesday January 15th

Jake sat in front of his state of the art Amstrad and pressed the glittery knobs. The title of his novel appeared on the screen.

SPARG FROM KRONK
Chapter One: Sparg Returns
Sparg stood on the hilltop and looked down on Kronk, the settlement of his birth. He grunted to his woman,

Barf, and she grunted back wordlessly, for the words had not yet been found.

They ran down the hill. Sparg's mother, Krun, watched her son and his woman come towards the fire. She grunted to Sparg's father, Lunt, and he came to the door of the hut. His eyes narrowed. He hated Sparg.

Krun threw more roots into the fire: she had not expected guests for dinner. It was typical of her son, she thought, to arrive unexpectedly and with a woman with a swollen belly. She hoped there would be enough roots to go round.

She was glad the words had not been found. She hated making small talk.

Sparg was here, in front of her. She sniffed his armpit, as was the custom when a Kronkite returned from a long journey. Barf hung back and watched the greeting ceremony. Her mouth salivated. The smell of the burning roots inflamed her hunger.

Because the words had not been found no news could be exchanged between mother and son.

Jake fell back from his computer terminal with a contented sigh. It was good, he thought, damned good. The time was right for another prehistoric novel without dialogue.

Tuesday January 21st

A letter from Bert Baxter. Almost illegible.

Dear Lad,

It seems a long time since I saw you. When are you coming to Leicester? I've got a few jobs that need doing. Sorry about the writing. I've got the shakes.

Yours,

Bertram Baxter

PS. Bring your toenail scissors.

Had a serious row with Bianca tonight. She accused me of:

a) Never wanting to go out
b) Excessive reading
c) Excessive writing
d) Contempt for Britain's industrial heritage
e) Farting in bed

Monday January 27th

At last reconciled, we went to the National Film Theatre tonight and saw a film about a Japanese woman who cuts her lover's penis off. During the rest of the film, I sat with my legs tightly crossed and at intervals looked nervously across at Bianca, who was staring up at the screen and smiling.

My hair is almost long enough for a pony tail. *The Face* tells me that pony tails are becoming passé. But it may be my last chance to try one. So I am going for it. Savage has been boasting that he has had his for five years.

Bianca has bought a secondhand electric typewriter and is typing *Lo!* She has already presented me with seventy-eight beautifully laid-out pages. It is amazing how much a novel is improved by being typed. I should have taken Mr John Tydeman's advice years ago.

Wednesday January 29th

UK heterosexual Aids cases rose by fifty per cent last year. I gave this information to Bianca as we walked to 'Savages' early this evening. She went very quiet.

I had to wait ages outside the bathroom tonight to clean my teeth. Eventually Norman came out and apologized for the new scorch marks on the frame of the mirror. He has been *told* not to practise in there.

When I got back to our room, I found Bianca reading a pamphlet written by the Terrence Higgins Trust.

I said flippantly, 'Who's Terrence Higgins when he's at home?'

'He's dead,' she said, softly. The pamphlet was about Aids.

Bianca broke down and confessed that in 1990 she had had an affair with a man called Brian Boxer, who in turn confessed to her that in 1979 he'd had an affair with a bisexual woman called Diane Tripp. I shall ring the Terrence Higgins Trust Helpline in the morning and ask for help.

Saturday February 1st

The first twenty-two chapters of *Lo! The Flat Hills of My Homeland* are now a pile of 197 pages of neat typescript. I keep picking it up and walking round the room with it in my arms. I can't afford to get it photocopied, not at ten pence a page. Who do I know in London who has access to a photocopier?

Flat 6

Brenda's Patisserie

Old Compton Street

London

Dear John,

I have taken your advice and revised *Lo! The Flat Hills of My Homeland*. I have also employed the services of a professional typist and you will be pleased to see that my manuscript now consists of twenty-two chapters in typewritten form. I consider that, when completed, *Lo! The Flat Hills of My Homeland* will be eminently suitable for being read aloud on the radio, possibly as part of your Classic Serials series.

As you can see, I have enclosed my MS and entrust it into your care. However, I still need to make several minor changes. Would it be too much trouble for you to photocopy the hundred and ninety-seven pages and send a copy to me at the above address?

Thanking you in advance,

Yours as ever,

Adrian Mole

Tuesday February 4th

I walked to Broadcasting House this morning. As I struggled to push the big metal doors open, a gaggle of autograph hunters rushed towards me. I reached inside my jacket for my felt tip, but before I could extract it, I saw them surrounding Alan Freeman, the aged DJ. I pushed through them and entered the hallowed reception area of the British Broadcasting Corporation, watched by the stern-looking security staff. I walked up to the reception desk and joined the short queue.

In the space of four minutes, I saw famous people galore: Delia Smith, Robert Robinson, Ian Hislop, Bob Geldof, Annie Lennox, Roy Hattersley, etc., etc. Most of them were being seen off the premises by young women called Caroline.

Eventually the blonde receptionist said, 'Can I help you?' And I said, 'Yes. Could you please make sure that Mr John Tydeman receives this parcel? It is most urgent.'

She scribbled something on the jiffy bag which contained my letter and the manuscript of *Lo! The*

Flat Hills of My Homeland and threw it into a wire basket.

I thanked her, turned to go and bumped into Victor Meldrew, who plays the grumpy bloke in *One Foot in the Grave*! I apologized and he said, 'How kind.' He is much taller than he looks on television. When I got back to the room I told Bianca that I had been chatting to Victor Meldrew. I think she was quite impressed.

Wednesday February 5th

We both woke early this morning, but we didn't make love as usual. We had a shower and got dressed in silence. We went downstairs and had croissants and cappuccino in Brenda's Patisserie and listened to the gossip about the demise of the British film industry. Then, at 10.45 a.m., we paid our bill and walked to the clinic in Neal Street. (We forked out one pound, forty pence to the various beggars who met us on the way.)

We were counselled separately by a very empathetic woman called Judith. She pointed out that, should our tests prove positive, it wouldn't necessarily mean that we would develop full-blown Aids. After seeing Judith, we went for a drink in a pub in Carnaby Street to discuss our options:

a) Have the test and know the worst
b) Not have the test and suspect the worst

We decided to sleep on it.

Thursday February 6th

We have both decided to have the test and have pledged to care for each other until the day we die. Whatever the outcome.

Saturday February 8th

Mr Britten, the greengrocer who supplies 'Savages' with fruit and vegetables, came into the kitchen today and told us that he is going out of business next week. He said that Savage owes him seven hundred pounds in unpaid bills. I was outraged, but Mr Britten said defeatedly that Savage is only one of his many bad debtors. He said, 'If the Bank'd give me another two weeks I'd be all right, but the bastards won't.'

I made him a cup of tea and listened to him ranting on about interest charges and Norman Lamont. I think he felt slightly better by the time he left to make his next delivery.

I rang my mother to tell her about my conversation with Victor Meldrew and found that she has also been seeing a counsellor. A debt counsellor. I have been wondering for some time now how she has been paying her mortgage. Now I know. She hasn't. She has received a legal notice from the Building Society, informing her that the house where I spent my childhood is to be repossessed on March 16th. She begged me not to tell the other members of the family. She is hoping that something will turn up to avert disaster.

I didn't tell her that I have got one thousand, one hundred and eleven pounds in the Market Harborough Building Society. But I did say that Bianca and I would come to Leicester tomorrow. She sounded pathetically grateful.

Sunday February 9th

When we got to St Pancras Station, Bianca told me to look up.

'You are looking at one of the largest unsupported arch structures in the whole world,' she said. 'Isn't it beautiful?'

'Quite honestly, Bianca,' I said, 'all I can see is a dirty, scruffy roof covered in pigeon shit.'

'It was stupid of me to ask you to look at something further than your own nose,' she said, and stormed onto the train, leaving me to carry our overnight bags.

I'm always forgetting that Bianca is a qualified engineer. She doesn't look like one and since I've known her, she's only ever worked as a shop assistant and a waitress. She applies for at least two engineering jobs a week, but has yet to be called for an interview. She is considering calling herself 'Brian Dartington' on her cv.

The ticket inspector forgot to punch our three-monthly returns, so our journey to Leicester cost us nothing. But any feelings of happy triumph vanished as we got into the house. My mother was putting on a brave front, but I could tell she was inwardly distraught – at one point, she had one cigarette in her mouth, another in the ashtray and another burning on the edge of the kitchen window sill. I asked her how she'd got into such terrible debt.

She whispered, 'Martin needed the fees to finish his degree course. I borrowed a thousand pounds from a finance company, at an interest rate of twenty-four point seven per cent. Two weeks later, I lost my job with Group Five – somebody grassed on me and told them I was forty-eight.' I asked her to tell me the full extent of her indebtedness. She brought out unpaid bills of every description and colour. I urged her to tell Muffet the true nature of their financial situation, but she became almost hysterical and said, 'No, no, he *must* finish his engineering degree.'

I seem to be surrounded by engineers. Bianca informed my mother that she too was a qualified engineer.

I said jokingly, 'Yes, but she has not built so much as a Lego tower since she left university.'

To my amazement, Bianca took great exception to my harmless joke and left the room, looking tearful.

My mother said, 'You tactless sod!' and followed her into the garden.

I sat at the kitchen table, braced myself, and wrote three cheques: to Fat Eddie's Loan Co. (two hundred and seventy-one pounds); to the Co-op Dairy (thirty-six pounds, forty-nine pence); to Cherry's Newsagent (seventy-four pounds, eighty-one pence). I know it does not solve my mother's housing problem, but at least she can answer her front door now without being hounded by local creditors.

When Martin came back from Grandma's (where he is in the middle of replacing her two-pin sockets with three-pin ones), I introduced him to Bianca. Within seconds, they were bonded. They talked non-stop about St Pancras Station and unsupported arch structures. It is some time since I saw Bianca so animated. They sat next to each other at the dinner table and volunteered to wash and dry afterwards.

I helped Rosie with her English homework essay, 'A Day in the Life of a Dolphin'. I then went into the kitchen and found Bianca and Muffet droning on about the St Pancras Station Hotel and its architect, Sir George Gilbert Scott.

I interrupted them and informed Bianca that I was going to bed. She hardly looked up; just muttered, 'Okay, I'll be up soon.'

The spare bedroom was full of Rosie's hideous, fluorescent My Little Pony models.

Monday February 10th

I have no idea what time Bianca came up last night. She must have got into bed beside me without waking me up. All I know is that Muffet and my mother are not speaking and that I am utterly miserable.

11.30 p.m. Worked on *Chapter Twenty-Three: Conundrum.*

Jake sat in Alma's, the patisserie favoured by the intelligentsia, and scribbled on his A4 pad. Night and day, he worked on his novel. He was already on Chapter Four.

Chapter Four: Rocks
Sparg crept through the lush undergrowth. He knew they were there. He heard them before he saw them. They were grunting about their mutual interest in rocks.

Sparg parted a yukka plant and they were there in front of him: Moff and Barf, bathed in sunlight, tangled together. Their limbs were entwined in an intimate manner.

Sparg stifled a jealous grunt and crept back towards Kronk, the settlement of his birth.

Tuesday February 11th

We get our results tomorrow. I should be agonizing and reflecting on mortality, etc. But all I can think about is the way that Muffet looked at Bianca and the way that Bianca looked at Muffet when they said goodbye on Monday morning at Leicester station.

Wednesday February 12th

Judith told us that our tests are negative! We are not HIV positive! We are not going to die of Aids!

However, I feel that I may well die of a broken heart. Bianca has suggested another day trip to Leicester. She claims that she is tired of London. A feeble excuse. How could anyone be tired of London? I am with Dr Johnson on this one.

Thursday February 13th

A letter has arrived from the BBC.

Dear Adrian,

When my secretary handed me your letter and your manuscript of *Lo! The Flat Hills of My Homeland* yet again, I thought I must be hallucinating.

You have more cheek than a Samurai wrestler, more neck than a giraffe. The BBC does not run a free photocopying service. As to your laughable suggestion that your novel be read as one of our classic serials . . . The writers of such texts are usually dead, their work having outlived them. I doubt if your work will outlive you. I am returning the manuscript immediately. Owing to an administrative error, a photocopy *was* taken. I am sending this on to you, though with great reluctance. You really must not bother me again.

John Tydeman

Friday February 14th
St Valentine's Day

A disappointingly small card from Bianca. Mine to her was a thing of splendour. Large, padded, expensive, and in a box tied with a ribbon.

Savage is in a clinic for drug and alcohol abuse. Luigi went to see him on Sunday and said that Savage was playing ping-pong with a fifteen-year-old crack addict from Leeds.

Saturday February 15th

Bianca is going to Leicester for the day on Monday, to see my mother. I wish I could go with her, but I am now working a sixteen-hour day, seven days a week. Somebody has to keep my mother out of prison, and I am now the only person in our family who has a proper job.

My duties at 'Savages' now include the preparation of vegetables. It is tedious work, made more difficult by the obsessive attitude of Roberto, the chef. He insists on uniformity of vegetable length and width. I have to keep a tape measure in my apron pocket.

Sunday February 16th

It is now seven days and nights since Bianca and I made love. It is not only the sex I miss. It isn't the sex. It really isn't only the sex. I miss holding her and smelling her hair and stroking her skin. I wish that I could talk to her about how I feel. But I can't, I just can't. I really can't. I've tried, but I just can't. I held her hand in bed tonight, but it didn't count. She was asleep.

Monday February 17th

Before I went to work at 6.30 a.m., I wrote a note and left it propped against the bowl of hyacinths on the table.

Darling Bianca,
Please talk to me about our relationship. I am unable to initiate a discussion. All I can say to you is that I love you. I know something is wrong between us, but I don't know how to address it.
Love, for ever,
Adrian

Bianca was very kind to me early this evening. She assured me that nothing has changed regarding her feelings towards me. But she was talking to me on the telephone from Leicester. She has arranged to stay another day, to help my mother.

When I got home from work at 11.30 p.m., I re-read the note, which was still on the table, and then tore it up and threw it down the lavatory. It took three full flushes before it disappeared completely.

Tuesday February 18th

I was very tired last night, but was unable to sleep, so I got out of bed, got dressed, and went for a walk. Soho never sleeps. It exists for people like me: the lonely, the lovesick, the outsiders. When I got home I read Dostoevsky's *The Humiliated and Insulted*.

Wednesday February 19th

The gods are not exactly smiling on our family. Mrs Bellingham has sacked my father and kicked him out of her bed. She was outraged to find out that my father had been selling her security lights for half price in low-life pubs. He is back living with Grandma. I only know this because Grandma rang me at work, complaining that my mother owes her fifty pounds from last December. Grandma needs the money because she is going to Egypt with Age Concern in June and needs to pay the deposit next week.

I pointed out to Grandma that she has got substantial savings in a high interest bank account. Couldn't she withdraw fifty pounds? Grandma pointed out that the bank requires a month's notice of withdrawal. She said, 'I'm not prepared to lose the interest.'

I casually asked Grandma if she had seen anything of Bianca. She casually answered that she had seen Bianca and Muffet on the top deck of a number twenty-nine bus, heading towards the town. She threw in a few details. They were laughing. Bianca was holding a bunch of freesias (her favourite flowers). And Muffet looked 'happier than I've ever seen him'. There was a twanging noise as she leaned back in her chair by the telephone and said, 'It doesn't take an Einstein to work that one out, does it, lad?'

Thanks, Grandma, Leicester's answer to Miss sodding Marple.

Thursday February 20th

I fear the worst. Bianca is still in Leicester. I received a brochure this morning from an organization called the Faxos Institute. They were offering me a holistic holiday on the Greek island of Faxos, complete with courses in creative writing, dream workshops, finding your voice and stress management. One photograph in the brochure showed happy, tanned holidaymakers scoffing green foodstuffs at long tables under blue skies. Close examination with a magnifying glass showed the foodstuffs to be made up of lettuce and courgettes with a bit of what looked like cheese thrown in. There were bottles of retsina on the tables, vases of flowers and rough-hewn loaves of bread.

Another photograph showed a beach and a pine forest and the bamboo hut accommodation spread over a hillside. It looked truly idyllic. I turned a page and saw that Angela Hacker, the novelist, playwright and television personality, was 'facilitating' the writing course for the first two weeks in April. I have not read her books or seen her plays, but I have seen her on the television programme *Through the Keyhole*. She has certainly got a gracious home, though I remember being struck at the time by the amazing amount of alcohol in evidence. There were bottles in every room. Loyd Grossman made a quip about it at the time, something about 'sauce for the goose'. The studio audience laughed itself stupid.

I closed the brochure with a sigh. Two weeks on Faxos talking about my novel with Angela Hacker would be paradise, but I can't possibly afford it. My Building Society reserves are running low. I'm down to my last thousand.

Saturday February 22nd

Bianca rang the restaurant at lunchtime and said that she would be catching the 7.30 a.m. train from Leicester tomorrow and would be arriving at St Pancras at around 9.00 a.m. Her voice sounded strange. I asked her if she'd got a sore throat. She replied that she'd been 'doing a lot of talking'. Every fibre of me longs for her, especially the bits around my loins.

Sunday February 23rd

I was on the platform when the train came in and saw Bianca jump onto the platform. I ran towards her, holding a bunch of daffodils I'd bought from a stall outside the Underground on Oxford Street. Then, to my surprise, I saw Martin Muffet step down from the train, carrying two large suitcases. He put them down on the platform and put his arm around Bianca's slim shoulders.

Bianca said, 'I'm sorry, Adrian.'

Muffet said, 'So am I.'

To be quite honest, I didn't know what to say.

I turned away, leaving the two engineers under the engineering miracle of St Pancras Station and made my way back to Old Compton Street on foot. I don't know what happened to the daffodils, but I hadn't got them when I arrived home.

Monday February 24th

Chapter Twenty-Four: Oblivion
Jake slipped the hose over the exhaust pipe and checked

that it was properly connected. Then he put the other end of the hose through the side window of the car. He took a long, last look at the glorious vista of the Lake District panorama spread beneath him. 'How glorious life is,' he said, aloud, to the wind. All around him the daffodils nodded their agreement. Jake took his portable electric razor from his toiletry bag and proceeded to shave. He had always been vain and he was particularly keen to look good as a corpse. His bristles flew into the wind and became as one with the earth. Jake splashed on Obsession, his favourite after-shave lotion. Then, his toilette completed, he climbed into the car and switched on the engine.

As the fumes filled the inside of the car, Jake ruminated on his life. He had visited four continents and bedded some of the world's most beautiful women. He had recovered the Ashes for England. He had climbed Everest backwards, and found the definitive source of the Nile. Nobody could say that his life had been without interest. But, without Regina, the girl he loved, he did not want to live. As Jake slipped into oblivion, the needle on the petrol gauge turned to 'E'. Which would run out first, Jake's oxygen supply, or Jake's petrol . . .?

Tuesday February 25th

Got the courage up to ring my mother. My father answered. He said that he has moved back to live with my mother 'on a temporary basis' until she has recovered from the immediate shock of the Bianca/

Muffet affair. Apparently, she is too ill to leave her bed and look after Rosie.

He asked how I had taken it.

I said, 'Oh me, I'm fine,' and then big, fat tears rolled down my cheeks and into the electronic workings of the telephone handset. My father kept saying, down the phone, 'There, there, lad. There, there, don't cry, lad,' in a tender voice that I don't remember him using before.

Roberto the chef came and stood at my side and wiped the tears away with his apron. Eventually, after promising to keep in touch, I said goodbye to my father. For years I have thought of him as a feckless fool, but I now see that I have misjudged him.

When I got back to the room, I found that Bianca had taken all her personal belongings, including the photograph of Isambard Kingdom Brunel.

Wednesday February 26th

I went to a place called Ed's Diner at lunchtime today and had a hot dog, fries, a Becks beer and a mug of filter coffee. I asked for a glass for my beer and then noticed that the other men of my age were swigging it from the bottle, so I pushed my glass away surreptitiously and did as they did. I sat at a high stool at the counter in front of a mini-jukebox. Each selection cost five pence. I selected only one record, but I played it three times.

I used to be able to recite the lyric of 'Stand by Me' off by heart. Bianca and I used to sing along with Ben E. King when we cooked Sunday breakfast together. Our percussion instruments included: a box of household matches, a spatula, and a tin of dried lentils.

In Ed's Diner I tried to sing the words under my breath but I couldn't remember a word.

At the end of the song I was in tears. Why couldn't she have stood by me?

A man sitting on the next stool asked if there was anything he could do. I tried to compose myself, but to my absolute horror I began to sob loudly and without restraint. There were tears; there was snot; there were undignified gulpings and heavings of the shoulders. The stranger put his arm around my shoulders and asked, 'Have you had a relationship gone wrong?'

I nodded, then managed to say, in between sobs, 'Finished.'

'Same here,' he said. Then 'My name's Alan.' Alan told me that he was 'devastated' because his partner, Christopher, had fallen for another man. I ordered two more beers and then I told Alan the whole story about Bianca and Martin Muffet. Alan confessed himself to be shocked and was thoughtful enough to enquire as to my mother's feelings. I told him that I'd phoned her last night and that she'd told me that her life was over.

Alan and I have arranged to meet for a drink at

8.00 p.m. tonight. Am I now, like Blanche Dubois, dependent on the kindness of strangers?

Midnight Alan didn't turn up. I sat in the 'Coach and Horses' for over an hour, waiting for him. Perhaps he met another stranger with a more original tragic story.

I miss her. I miss her. I miss her.

Thursday February 27th

Roberto stood over me this evening and made me eat a plate of tagliatelle with hare sauce. He said, 'A woman issa woman, but food issa food.'

Perhaps it has more meaning in the original Italian.

Jake handed the envelope containing the money to the sinister man.

'Quick and clean,' he said. 'They mustn't know what hit them.'

The man grunted and left the Soho drinking den. Jake looked around him, at the tawdry, painted girls, at the bestial faces of the late night drinkers. Was it only yesterday he was in the Lake District attempting suicide? As he rose to his feet, a young prostitute attempted to procure him. He pushed her away irritably, saying, 'Get lost, baby, I've known and lost the only woman I'll ever want.'

He strode out into the vibrant Soho night, his cowboy boots tapping strangely on the murky pavement. I must get them soled and heeled tomorrow, he thought. As he passed down Old Compton Street, he looked up at the window of the flat above Alma's Patisserie. The light was still burning but he knew that by now all human life had been extinguished. He was a murderer by proxy.

Tears poured inside his heart, but his face was as it always was, hard and unforgiving and without God's blessing.

Saturday February 29th

I have informed Mr Andropolosis, the landlord, that I have taken over the tenancy, and paid him a month's rent in advance, so the room is now mine. Thank God for the end of this month. It has surely been the worst since time began.

To complete our catalogue of family misery, Grandma was admitted to hospital during the early hours of this morning with abdominal pains. I rang the hospital this afternoon and was told by the ward sister that Grandma was 'comfortable'. If this is true, then she is the only member of the family who is – the rest of us are in total misery.

Sunday March 1st

I joined my mother, father and Rosie at Grandma's hospital bedside this afternoon. It was the first time I had seen Grandma without her teeth. I was shocked at how *old* she looked.

My mother has lost weight and her eyes looked sore, as though she has been weeping constantly since Muffet upped and left her. After visiting time was over and we were trooping down the ward, my mother said bitterly: 'They're in Hounslow, staying with his brother, Andrew.'

I said, 'I don't want to know, Mum.'

My father said, 'Let it drop, Pauline.'

Rosie said, 'I'm glad he's gone. I hope he never comes back.' She held her hand up and my father took it and steered her through the big double doors at the end of the ward. As we walked alongside the hospital tower blocks, the litter swirled around our feet and I had a premonition of doom.

I almost turned back to say a proper goodbye to Grandma, but I didn't want to keep the others hanging around in the potholed car park, so I didn't. Instead, we went home and had a Marks & Spencer's roast beef dinner each. Mine was quite nice, but it wasn't a patch on the real thing cooked by my grandma. As I was compressing the dirty tin foil trays into the kitchen pedal bin, the telephone rang. It was the hospital, telling us that 'Mrs Edna May Mole passed away at 5.15 p.m.'

I tried to remember where I was *exactly* at 5.15 p.m. I worked out that I was in a BP petrol station, helping my father to check the pressure in his car tyres.

I haven't shed a single tear for her yet. I'm dried up inside. My heart feels like a peach stone.

Monday March 2nd

It is a well-known fact that Grandma and my mother never got on, so nobody was prepared for the positively Mediterranean grief my mother is displaying over her mother-in-law's death: copious tears, breast-beating, etc. This morning she was lamenting, 'I owed her fifty quid' over and over again.

My father continues to astonish me with his maturity. He has dealt with all the death paperwork and haggled over the cost of the funeral with commendable efficiency.

Tuesday March 3rd

At 10.00 p.m. I rang 'Savages' to tell them that I am staying in Leicester for the funeral on Friday afternoon. Roberto said, 'I'm glad you ring, Adrian. Your flat has been called on by burglars.' He made it sound as though burglars had been invited to tea, brought flowers and left a visiting card. There's nothing I can do tonight. The police have employed the services of a locksmith. The new key is at 'Savages'. I feel strangely calm.

Wednesday March 4th

Train to Leicester 8.40 p.m.
They have taken everything, apart from my books,
boxer shorts and an old pair of polyester trousers.
How they got the bed down the stairs will probably
always remain a mystery. The policeman I spoke to
on the phone said, in answer to my question about
the likelihood of their finding the culprits: 'You
know what chance a snowball has in hell? Well, halve
that. Then halve it again.' He asked if I had insurance.

I laughed scornfully and said, 'Of course not. This
is Adrian Mole you're speaking to.'

I am now a man without possessions.

Thursday March 5th

I went into Grandma's home this morning. Everything
was the same as ever. My GCE certificates were still
there, framed on the wall. My dead grandad Albert's
photograph was on the mantelpiece. The clock was
still ticking. Upstairs, the linen lay folded in the cupboard and in the garden the bulbs pushed through
the earth. The biscuit barrel was full of fig rolls and
her second best slippers stood by her bed. Inside a
kitchen cupboard, I found her Yorkshire pudding tin.
She had used it for over forty years. Stupid to weep

over a Yorkshire pudding tin, but I did. I then wiped it dry and replaced it in the cupboard, as she would have liked.

Friday March 6th
Grandma's Funeral

My mother and father, Rosie and I worked together as a team today and managed to give Grandma a good send-off. There was a respectable turnout in the church, which surprised me, because Grandma didn't encourage people to call on her. She preferred the company of Radio Four. She had been known to turn people away from her doorstep, should they be inconsiderate enough to call during the Afternoon Play.

The hymns were 'Amazing Grace' and 'Onward Christian Soldiers'. Bert Baxter sang out loudly, almost drowning the others in the congregation. For an atheist, he certainly enjoys singing in church. As I watched him, I couldn't help thinking wistfully that it should have been him who died instead of Grandma. The vicar said a lot of incredibly stupid things about Grandma being born into sin and dying in sin.

Anybody who knew Grandma knew that she was incapable of sin. She couldn't even tell a lie. When I asked her once if my spots were clearing up (I must have been about fifteen), she answered, 'No, you've still got a face like a ladybird's arse.' She occasionally used such mild profanities, but she was certainly not a sinner.

I don't like to think of her lying under the earth, alone and cold. Still, at least she was never burgled or mugged. She is safe from all that now.

The funeral tea was held at our house. My mother had been up most of the previous night, cleaning and polishing and trying to get the stains out of the lounge carpet.

My father replaced the missing light bulbs and mended the ballcock so that the lavatory flushed properly.

Tania Braithwaite came round to give her commiserations and kindly offered to defrost some vegetarian quiches she had in the freezer. She told us that Pandora had cancelled a lecture and was intending to come to the funeral tea and would be bringing six bottles of Marks & Spencer's champagne with her.

She said, 'Pandora believes in celebrating death. She sees it as a new adventure, as opposed to a rather boring ending.'

Bert Baxter had phoned to ask what time the service started, which reminded my mother that there was no beetroot in the house. So Rosie was given a personal safety alarm and sent round to the corner shop to buy a jar from Mr Patel's shop.

At midnight, I watched my parents spreading a white tablecloth over the dining-room table, which had had its leaves fully extended. As they flapped and adjusted the cloth, one at either end, I had a sudden sense of being a member of the family.

Rosie had arranged some daffodils and freesias nicely in a vase and was praised by everyone. Even the dog behaved itself. When we finally went to bed, the house looked perfect; everything was in its place and we Moles could hold our heads high. Grandma would have been proud of us.

After the funeral service, Rosie and I ran ahead of the other mourners to take the clingfilm off the sandwiches and sausage rolls.

Pandora was waiting outside the house in her car. We filled the bath with cold water and put the bottles of champagne into it to chill.

Pandora looked beautifully severe in a black tailored suit. However, I no longer felt in awe of her, so we were able to talk to each other as friends and equals. She complimented me on how well I was looking and she even praised my clothes. She fingered the lapel of my navy blue unstructured Next suit and said, 'Welcome to the nineties.'

The house soon filled up with mourners and I was kept busy circulating with glasses of champagne on a tray. At first, everyone stood around, not knowing what to say, nervous of enjoying themselves for fear of being thought disrespectful to the dead. Then Pandora broke the ice by proposing a toast to Grandma.

'To Edna Mole,' she said, lifting her glass of champagne high, 'a woman of the highest principles.'

Everyone clinked glasses and swigged back the champagne and it wasn't long before laughter broke out and I was fishing the bottles out of the bath.

My mother rummaged in the sideboard and brought out the photograph albums. I was astonished to see a photograph of my grandma at the age of twenty-four. She looked very dashing, dark-haired, with a lovely figure, and was laughing and pushing a bicycle up a hill. There was a man next to her wearing a flat cap. He had a big moustache and his eyes were crinkled against the sun. It was my grandad. Everybody remarked that I looked like him.

My father took the photograph out of the album and went into the garden and sat on Rosie's swing. After a while, I followed him out. He handed me the photograph and said, 'I'm an orphan, son.'

I put my hand on his shoulder, then went back inside to find that the funeral tea had turned into a party. People were laughing hysterically at the photographs in the album. Me at the seaside, falling off a donkey. Me in a secondhand cub's uniform three sizes too big. Me at six months, lying naked on a half moon-shaped rug in front of a gas fire. Me two days old with my grinning, young-looking parents in the maternity hospital. On the back was written, in my mother's handwriting, 'Our darling baby, two days old'.

There was a photograph I don't remember seeing before. It was my mother and father and my grandma and grandad. They were sitting in deckchairs, watching me, aged about three, playing in the sand. On the back was written: 'Yarmouth, Bank Holiday Monday'.

Rosie said, 'Why aren't I in the photo?'

Bert Baxter said, 'Cos you 'adn't been bleedin' born, that's why.'

At seven o'clock, Ivan Braithwaite offered to escort some of my grandma's elderly neighbours back to their pensioners' bungalows while they and he could still walk.

The rest of us carried on until eleven o'clock. Tania Braithwaite, who has been vegetarian for nine years, cracked and ate a sausage roll and then another.

My mother and father danced together to 'You've Lost That Loving Feeling'. You couldn't have slid a ruler between them.

Pandora and I watched them dancing. She said, 'So they're back together again, are they?'

'I hope so,' I said, looking at Rosie.

As I said before, it was a good send-off.

Monday March 9th

Old Compton Street

I am back in my room with only my books and boxer shorts for company. I have given the trousers away to a young man selling *The Big Issue*. I made a pillow out of my underwear and slept on the floor. I have often wondered what it would be like to be a celibate monk in a bare cell. Now, thanks to burglary and desertion, I know.

I went into 'Savages' to help clean the kitchen. Savage himself was there, released from the alcohol abuse unit and looking fit and athletic and sipping on a glass of mineral water. He commiserated with me on my various losses and said that there was some old furniture in the attic above the restaurant that I could have.

'Just help yourself, kid,' he said.

I can't get used to this new, kind, philanthropic Savage. I keep thinking he must be Savage's long lost twin brother, recently returned from a missionary station in Amazonia.

My room is now furnished with rococo style banquettes and fag-stained *faux* marble tables. Stuff that was obviously thrown upstairs when Savage took over the restaurant. I now sleep on two banquettes pushed together. I have angels at my head and cherubs at my feet. Roberto gave me some cutlery and crockery and kitchen utensils. Most of my fellow workers brought something to work with them this morning, to donate to the Adrian Mole Disaster Fund. I cook on a ring fuelled by a gas canister and I read by a mock chandelier, both donated by Luigi.

Wednesday March 11th

I rang home this morning. My father is still there, living in sin with my mother. My mother told me that Bianca and Muffet are intending to set up an engineering partnership called 'Dartington and Muffet'.

I cannot bear the thought of Muffet's bony fingers touching Bianca's lovely pale skin.

I cannot bear it.

Thursday March 12th

Chapter Twenty-Five: Resurgence
Jake sat down at the *faux* marble table and began to write another chapter of his novel, *Sparg from Kronk*.

Chapter Five: Green Shoots
Sparg missed his woman, Barf. There was a part of him that would never be reconciled to her loss.

It was springtime. Green shoots showed through the earth. Sparg left his hut and went outside. He was glad to be outside, for the hut was damp and the damp was rising fast.

Sparg needed a woman, but the only woman in sight was Krun, his mother. Though her face was wrinkled, her thighs were inviting. But it was forbidden by Kronkian law to take your own mother, even if she agreed.

Sparg walked aimlessly up a small hill and then walked aimlessly down. He was bored. There was firewood to collect, but he was sick of collecting firewood. It did not challenge his intellect. He grunted in despair and wished it were possible to communicate with his fellow Kronkians. It was just his luck, he thought, to be born in prehistoric times.

If only there was *language*, grunted Sparg internally . . .

to be continued

Jake fell back. The intensity of the writing had left him drained and pale. He left his room and walked to Wilde's, his favourite restaurant, where he was greeted by Mario.

'Longa tima noa see, Mr Westmorland.'

'Hi, Mario. My usual table, please, and my usual bottle, well chilled, and I'll have my usual starter, usual main course and usual pudding.'

'And for your aperitif, Mr Westmorland?' purred Mario.

'The usual,' barked Jake.

I've got to finish *Lo! The Flat Hills of My Homeland* soon, but I can't do that until Jake has finished writing *Sparg from Kronk*. I wish he would hurry up.

Friday March 13th

More businesses are closing around us. Every day, the boards go up at shop and restaurant windows. Every night, I pray that 'Savages' stays financially viable. I need my job. I'm aware that I'm being exploited, but at least I have a reason to get up in the morning, unlike three and a half million of my fellow citizens.

Grandma left my father three thousand and ninety pounds in her will, so my mother is not going to have her house repossessed. This is truly joyous news. It means that I won't have to break into my Building Society savings. I couldn't have seen her thrown onto the street. At least, I don't think I could.

Saturday March 14th

I received the following message when I got to work this morning. It was written on the back of a paper napkin. 'Forgot G. Left 500.' Nobody knew what it meant or who had taken the message.

Monday March 16th

Received another brochure from the Faxos Institute. Why are they mailing me so assiduously? Who has put them on to me? I don't know any holistic types. I'm not even a vegetarian and I swear by paracetamol.

I went to the National Gallery today, but it brought back painful memories of B., so I went back to Soho and paid two pounds to watch a fat girl with spots remove her bra and knickers through a peephole. I *watched* her through a peephole. She didn't remove her underclothes through a peephole.

Query: Are there night classes in syntax?

Tuesday March 17th

I ran out of toilet paper last night and reached for the Faxos Institute brochure to help me out of my emergency, when something about Angela Hacker's face made me pause. It seemed to say, 'Come to me, Adrian.' Her face is nothing to write home about, in fact it's nothing to write *anywhere* about.

I put the brochure down and picked up the *Evening Standard* instead. It has far better absorbency qualities.

11.45 p.m. Can't sleep for St Patrick's Day revellers, so have idly filled in the booking form for the first two weeks in April at the Faxos Institute in Greece.

Thursday March 19th

Idly filled in a cheque made out to 'Faxos Institute', but I was only trying out a new pen. I couldn't possibly afford the time off work, or the money.

10.00 p.m. The full message was: 'Forgot to tell you Grandma has left you five hundred pounds, love, Dad.' Luigi, who had been away from the restaurant with food poisoning, returned today and congratulated me on 'Alla money ya got'. Naturally, I looked at him blankly. Confusion abounded for some minutes and then came the glorious realization, which we celebrated with a bottle of corked Frascati.

Saturday March 21st

The newly benign Savage has agreed to give me two weeks' leave (without pay). I posted my booking form this morning and this afternoon I bought some swimming trunks from a shop that was closing down in the Charing Cross Road. I can't wait to feel the warm Aegean sea on my body.

Worked on *Lo!* with Angela Hacker in mind.

Jake opened his manuscript book. The ivory handmade paper looked enticing. He took his Mont Blanc pen in his hand and began to write.

'Sorry, darling,' he said to the glorious example of English womanhood who sprawled opposite him, showing her knickers, 'but the Muse is upon me.'

Then he lowered his handsome head and was at once in Kronk, the home of his hero, Sparg.

Sparg grunted, recognizing the hated form of his father in the darkness. His father grunted back. Sparg threw a pebble from one hand to the other. Why hadn't something been invented to pass the hours of darkness before bed, he wondered. Something like a game such as cards, he wondered. He went back into his hut and pushed the animal skins listlessly around on his bed. He was cold at night without a woman. He determined that he would get up early the next morning and find one and bring her home to Kronk.

Thursday March 26th

I bought a short-sleeved shirt and a pair of Bermuda shorts from a stall in Berwick Street market. I have never worn shorts since reaching adulthood.

A new Adrian Mole is emerging from the ashes.

Savage turned up drunk and disorderly at the restaurant and proceeded to fire Luigi, Roberto and the whole of the kitchen staff apart from me. He said, 'You can stay, Adrian. You're a fucking loser, like me.'

He has promoted me to *Maître d'*, a position I do not want and cannot do.

Luigi and Roberto sat in the kitchen, smoking and talking in Italian. They didn't seem too concerned. Meanwhile, dressed in Luigi's suit, I was forced to fawn over customers, show them to their seats and pretend to be interested in their requirements. Savage sat at the bar, shouting out the biographical details of his customers as they came in. As one respectable-looking middle-aged couple entered, he yelled: 'Well, if it isn't Mr and Mrs Wellington. He's wearing a toupée and she's paid three thousand pounds for those perky looking titties.'

Instead of going straight back out, or thumping him on the side of his drunken head, Mr and Mrs Wellington grinned and allowed me to show them to table number six. Perhaps they are proud of their artificial attributes. As my recently dead grandma would say, 'There's nowt so strange as folk, especially London folk.'

Poor Grandma. She never went to London in her life.

For the past four days, I have been unable to write a word. The thought of Angela Hacker reading my manuscript has totally inhibited me. However, tonight I achieved a breakthrough.

He had writer's block. For over five hours he stared down at the mockingly empty page. His publisher was calling hourly. The printing presses were waiting, but still he could not finish his book. Jake looked out of the window, hoping for inspiration. The New York skyline stretched away into infinity . . .

'Infinity!' shouted Jake, excitedly, and he began to work on his novel, *Sparg from Kronk*.

Sparg had wandered far from Kronk and was standing on a high headland, looking in wonderment at a strange watery mass and a blue line ahead of him. Without knowing it (because there was no language), Sparg was marvelling over the sea and the far distant horizon. Sparg growled and began to descend the headland. He would walk to the far blue line, he thought. It would be something to do. Sparg thought this because there was as yet no swimming ...

Received confirmation from Faxos Institute that I have a place on the Writers' Course. I am terrified.

Friday March 27th

Luigi has been reinstated and I am safely back in the kitchen, thank God. Roberto has been allowing me to watch him at work. For most of my life, I have been denied a proper food education. There was never anything to learn from my mother; she stopped cooking real food soon after reading *The Female Eunuch*. Though, ironically, the author of that seminal tome, Ms Germaine Greer, is a renowned cook and dinner party giver.

Thanks to Roberto's kindness, I can now cook pasta '*al dente*' and make a basic sponge cake and I've almost cracked making watercress soup. I now spring from my double banquettes in the morning, eager to get to work.

Plane tickets arrived today.

A new girl started work as a waitress at 'Savages' this evening. Her name is Jo Jo and she is from Nigeria. She is studying Art at St Martin's. She is taller than anybody else in the restaurant. Her hair is braided with hundreds of tiny beads. She rattles when she walks. Her mother is something big in the Nigerian tractor industry.

Saturday March 28th

Made a *tower* of profiteroles today. Roberto said: 'Congratulations, Adriana! The chocolate icing issa perfection.'

Jo Jo tasted the first one and pronounced it to be 'delectable'. Luigi happened to have his polaroid camera with him, so he photographed me and the tower and Jo Jo. I have pinned the photograph on my wall. I look quite handsome.

Sunday March 29th

I was still in bed at midday when there was a knock on the door. I never have visitors, so I was a little alarmed. I put my ear to the door, but all I could hear was a peculiar rattling noise. I eventually opened the door, but I kept the security chain on. I was delighted to see Jo Jo through the crack.

She smiled at me and said that she was going to the Tate Gallery.

'Do you want to come?' she asked.

I slipped the chain off and invited her in. She walked around the room and commented on how tidy it was.

She stopped at the table where my manuscript lay in its transparent folder and said, 'So this is your book.'

She touched it reverently. 'I would like to read it one day.'

'When it's finished,' I said.

I made her a cup of Nescafé and then excused myself and went into the bathroom to wash and change.

I looked at myself in the washbasin mirror. Something had happened to my face. I no longer looked like John Major.

Jo Jo likes walking, so we walked to the Tate. I was proud to be seen with such a stunning looking woman. I asked her about Nigeria and she spoke about her country with obvious love. She is a Yoruba and comes from Abeokuta.

She asked me about my family and I told her about the tangled web of relationships, the break-ups and the reconciliations.

She laughed and said, 'To work out the relationships in my family, you would need an extremely sophisticated computer.'

I had never been to the Tate, but Jo Jo knew it well. She guided me round and made me look at a few of her favourite paintings – all depicting people, I noticed. We looked at paintings by Paula Rego, Vanessa Bell and Matisse, and a piece of sculpture by Ghisha Koenig called 'The Machine Minders', and then she insisted that we leave before we got bored and our feet started to ache.

As we were going down the steps, Jo Jo asked if I would like to have tea at her flat in Battersea.

I said, 'I'd love to.' We crossed the road and stood at the bus stop, but then, on impulse, I flagged down a black cab and we rode to her flat in style.

She lives on the top floor of a mansion block. Every room is full of her paintings. Many of the paintings are nude self-portraits, in which she has depicted herself in many colours, including green, pink, purple, blue and yellow.

I asked her if she was making a statement about her colour. 'No,' she laughed. 'But I would get bored only using blacks and browns.'

We ate scones and drank Earl Grey tea and talked non-stop: about 'Savages'; Nigerian politics; cats; one of her art teachers, who is going mad; Cecil Parkinson; the price of paint brushes; Vivaldi; our star signs – she is Leo (but on the cusp of Cancer); and her girls' boarding school in Surrey, where she lived from the age of eleven until she got expelled at sixteen for climbing on the roof of the chapel in a protest against the lousy food.

Over a glass of cheap wine, we discussed trees; Matisse; Moscow; Russian politics; our favourite cakes; the use of umbrellas; cabbage; and the Royal Family. She is a republican, she said.

Over a final glass of wine and a plate of bread and cheese, I talked to her about my grandmother, my mother, Pandora, Sharon, Megan, Leonora, Cassandra and Bianca. 'You're carrying a lot of baggage,' Jo Jo said.

We parted at 10.30 p.m. with a friendly handshake. Before she closed the door, I asked how old she was. 'Twenty-four,' she said. 'Goodnight.'

Monday March 30th

I ran out of 'Savages' during my break time and bought Ambre Solaire (Factor 8), espadrilles, sleeveless tee shirts, three more pairs of shorts and sixteen thousand drachmas.

I worked on the book late into the night. I am nervous about Angela Hacker's opinion. Added more descriptive words to *Lo! The Flat Hills of My Homeland* and took out more descriptive words from *Sparg from Kronk*.

Tuesday March 31st

The staff arranged a small *bon voyage* party in the kitchen after the restaurant closed at lunchtime. I was very touched. Roberto cooked kebabs and arranged an authentic Greek salad in my honour. Jo Jo bought two bottles of retsina earlier in the day and we all clinked glasses and swore eternal friendship. Then Savage came in, complaining that Luigi had forgotten to add VAT to somebody's bill, so the party broke up. Jo Jo is good at packing, she said. She offered to come and help me.

I laid my clothes, toiletry bag and manuscript out on my bed before proceeding to pack, and then realized that the burglars had taken my suitcase.

Jo Jo ran to Berwick Street market and bought one of those man-made fibre striped bags, the type that refugees have on the television news. Once I was packed, I debated with Jo Jo on whether or not to take a warm coat with me. She said I ought to, but I decided not to. Instead, I slung a cotton sweater around my shoulders. Everybody has said that Greece is warm in April. My legs look very white at the moment in my shorts, but by the time I return, they will be gloriously tanned.

Spring

Dear Jo Jo,

For the first time in my life, there is nobody to wish me a Happy Birthday. I am now twenty-five years old. Which is a millstone in anybody's life. Do I still qualify to be called a 'Young British Novelist'? I hope so.

Other participants in the Faxos Institute course are swirling around downstairs in the hotel lobby, chatting easily to each other. I fled back into the lift when I saw them, and went up to the roof terrace, but Angela Hacker was up there, smoking a cigarette and looking moodily at the Acropolis in the far distance. She is skinny and dresses in white clothes. She was weighed down by ethnic silver jewellery.

I don't know when the photograph of her in the brochure was taken, but in life she looks at least forty-eight. Obviously past it, sexually and artistically.

I didn't thank you properly for that afternoon in the Tate. I keep thinking about the pictures. I particularly liked those painted by that Portuguese woman, Paula something.

    All best wishes,
      Adrian

                      Ferry
                Friday April 3rd

Dear Mum and Dad,

    I am writing this on the first ferry, which is taking us to where we catch the second ferry to Faxos. Angela Hacker and most of the twelve members of the writers' group are already in the bar. The majority of them smoke. You would probably get along famously with them, Mum. The other, more holistic, holidaymakers are looking over the side of the ship, taking photographs or swapping aromatherapy recipes. I am keeping to myself. I don't want to lumber myself with a hastily-made 'friend' and spend the next fortnight getting rid of him or her. It has just started to rain. I will have to stop now and go inside.

    Love from your son,
      Adrian

                      Ferry
                Friday April 3rd
                    4.00 p.m.

Dear Jo Jo,

    There has been torrential rain for the whole of the three-hour crossing. I am wearing my cotton sweater, but am still cold. I now wish I'd followed your advice and brought a coat with me.

Angela Hacker has been falling down in the bar. The sea *is* choppy, but I think her lack of balance is due more to the copious amounts of retsina she is throwing down her neck. My fellow writers have been laughing non-stop since boarding the ferry. Some private joke, no doubt. I have not yet introduced myself to them.

Bamboo Hut Number Six
8.00 p.m.

The wind is whistling through the slats of my hut. Outside, the sky is grey and dotted with storm clouds. Supper was eaten in the open air, under a 'roof' of palm fronds. Not surprisingly, the ratatouille was cold.

I can hear Angela Hacker coughing from here, though her hut is at least two hundred yards further down the rocky hill.

There was a community meeting at eight o'clock, where the permanent staff and the facilitators introduced themselves and their work. The meeting was held in what they call here the 'Magic Ring', which is on the very top of the hill. The Magic Ring is a concrete base, surrounded by a low wall and covered in the usual palm frond and bamboo roof. There is nothing magical looking about it.

I was most concerned to hear Ms Hacker describe her course as 'Writing for Pleasure'. I get no pleasure from writing. Writing is a serious business, like painting.

There is a man here who wears his hair like yours. I saw him on the headland, looking out to sea. From a distance he looked like you. My heart did a backflip.

My hut is next to the hen-coop. A goat has just put its

head inside my hut and a donkey is braying somewhere in the pine woods. If Noah's Ark was washed up on the beach, I wouldn't be surprised.

Best wishes,
Adrian

Faxos
Sunday April 5th

Dear Pan,

You asked me to let you know how the Faxos course was, so I'll tell you about the first day.

The writers collected on the terrace at 11.15 a.m. I sat upwind, away from the cigarette smoke. At 11.30 a.m. Angela Hacker had still not appeared, so a man called Clive, who had seven boils on his neck, was sent to her hut. She eventually showed up at noon and apologized for having overslept. She then rambled on for an hour and fifteen minutes about 'Truth' and 'Narrative thrust' and 'developing an original voice'.

At 1.15 p.m. she sprang to her feet and said, 'Okay, that's it for the day. Write a poem including the word "Greece". Be prepared to read it aloud at 11.15 tomorrow morning.' She then headed for the bamboo bar, where she stayed for most of the day. When I'd written my poem, I went in for a cup of tea and heard her talking about your college in Oxford.

I asked her if she knew you and she said she had met you at Jack Cavendish's house a few times, 'before Jack left his third wife,' she said.

I said, 'It's a small world.'

'Try not to use clichés, darling,' she said.

She's a strange woman.

All the best from,

Adrian

Faxos

Monday April 6th

Dear Rosie,

I hope you like this postcard of the cheerful donkey. There is something about its daft expression that reminds me of the dog.

I have sent you a poem I was forced to write about Greece. It's time you started to take an interest in cultural matters. There is more to life than Nintendo games.

Love from your brother,

Adrian

Oh Greece, ancient cultured land
You wrap around my heart just like
An old elastic band.
Your hag-like women pensioners
Clad in clothes of black,
Are they unaware of all the services they lack?
Will they be content to watch
The donkey with its load?
Won't they want a vehicle to
Drive along the road?

Faxos
Tuesday April 7th

Dear Baz,

I am here on Faxos with Angela Hacker, whom I under-stand you know quite well. She and I hit it off immediately and she has invited me to stay at her place in Gloucestershire when we get back. I may be able to make the odd weekend, but I am currently doing research in a restaurant kitchen in Soho for my next book, *The Chopper*, so will not be able to stay for a couple of weeks, as she would like.

The reason I am writing is to say that I hope there are no hard feelings any more over the Sharon Bott affair, because we are likely to be moving in the same circles soon and I would rather there were no acrimonious feelings between us.

Congratulations on finally getting to number one!

Cheers,

Your old friend,

Adrian Mole

Faxos
Wednesday April 8th

Dear John Tydeman,

As you cannot fail to see, if you have noticed the post-mark, I am on the Greek island of Faxos. I am a member of a writers' course being facilitated by Angela Hacker (she sends you her love).

She asked us to write the first scene of a radio play, which is something I have never attempted to do before.

I thought you might be interested to read what I have written. I would be more than willing to finish it, if you thought it had merit.

I shall be back in London at 3.00 p.m. on the 15th April, if you would like to talk to me face to face.

On second thoughts, the 16th would be more convenient for me. I shall probably need to rest after my journey.

Here is how the play opens:

The Cucumber Sandwich
A Play for Radio by Adrian Mole

A room in a wealthy house. A game of tennis can be heard through the french windows. Tea is poured. A spoon rattles in a cup.

LADY ELEANOR: A cucumber sandwich, Edwin?

EDWIN: Don't try to fob me off with your bourgeois ideas of gentility. I know the truth!

LADY ELEANOR (*gasps*): No! Surely not! You don't know the secret I have kept for forty years!

EDWIN (*contemptuously*): Yes, I do. The servant girl, Millie, told me.

A bell rings.

MILLIE: You rang, mum? Sorry to keep you, only I was 'elpin' cook with Master Edwin's twenty-first birthday cake.

LADY ELEANOR: You are dismissed, Millie. You have blabbed my secret.

MILLIE: What secret? Oh! The one about your being born a man?

To be continued

I do not wish to prejudice you in any way, but after I had finished reading this text, there was a stunned silence from my fellow writers. Angela's only comment was, 'You should have spun the secret out until the last scene of the play.'

Good advice, I think.

Anyway, I hope you enjoy *The Cucumber Sandwich*.

Yours,

With best wishes,

    Adrian Mole

Faxos
Thursday April 9th

Dear Jo Jo,

The sun has shone for two days now and has turned Faxos into Paradise. The colours are breathtaking: the sea is peacock blue, the grass is peppermint green and the wild flowers are scattered on the hillside like living confetti.

Something has happened to my body. It feels looser, as though it has broken free and is floating.

I have been going to dream workshops at 7.00 a.m. The facilitator is a nice American woman dream therapist called Clara. I told her about a recurring dream I have that I am trying to pick up the last pea on my dinner plate by stabbing it with a fork. Try as I may, I cannot get the prongs of the fork to stab into the flesh of the pea.

For years I have woken up feeling frustrated and hungry after dreaming my pea dream.

Clara advised me to look at the dream from the *pea's*

point of view. I did try hard to do this and, by discussing it with Clara later, I understood that I, Adrian Mole, was the pea and that the fork represented DEATH.

Clara said that my pea dream showed that I am afraid to die.

But who is *looking forward* to death? I don't know anybody who is cock-a-hoop at the prospect.

Clara explained that I am *morbidly* afraid of death.

How do you feel about death, Jo Jo?

I have made friends with the bloke with the beaded plaits like yours. His name is Sean Washington. His mother is Irish; his father is from St Kitts. He is here taking the stress management course, but he hangs out with the writers' group on the bar terrace.

We were both on vegetable chopping duties today and I was complimented by him and others on my expertise. I think I would like to be a chef. I may ask Savage if he'll give me a trial when I get back.

Angela Hacker has forbidden her writers' group to use clichés, but she will not be reading this letter, so I'll sign off by saying:

Wish you were here,

Adrian

Saturday April 11th

My first fax! It was addressed to 'Adrian Mole, Faxos Institute', and arrived at the travel agent's shop in the town. It was then conveyed to the Faxos Institute by greengrocer's van and delivered to me on the bar terrace by Julian, the handsome bald-headed administrator. It caused a sensation.

Dear Adrian,

Thank you for your letters. I wish I were there with you. It sounds idyllic.

I'm so glad that you feel at ease. When I first saw you in Savage's kitchen, I thought: that man is in *pain*. I wanted to touch you and comfort you there and then, but of course one does not do such a thing – not in England.

I think you have it in your power to become a happy man, providing you can let go of the past. Why not try to live in the present and leave all that baggage behind on Faxos when you return?

I couldn't wait to tell you that I have been offered a shared exhibition of 'Young Contemporaries' in September. Will you come to the opening? Please say you will.

Roberto is complaining that the man Savage has hired to take your place for a fortnight is massacring the vegetables and he now regrets letting you go on holiday.

Everybody at 'Savages' sends their best wishes. Roberto asks if you will bring a bottle of ouzo back for him.

I miss you.

I send you my best wishes as well,

Jo Jo

Hut Number Six
Faxos Institute
Faxos
Sunday April 12th

Dear Jo Jo,

What fantastic news about the exhibition! Of course I will come to the opening. September seems a long way off, though. The spring is so glorious here. I've never seen such colours before.

At our meeting yesterday morning Angela Hacker asked the writers' group to write the first page of a novel.

I wanted to run up the hill to my hut immediately and present her with the whole manuscript of *Lo! The Flat Hills of My Homeland*, but I restrained myself. The book was only a few pages short of completion. Why spoil the ship for a ha'p'orth of tar? (Since being forbidden to use clichés, I find myself using them all the time.)

I worked all day and most of the night on *Lo!* And I think that now the book is finished. This is how it ends:

Jake got up from his computer terminal and paced around his study. He adjusted the painting of a stately African woman that he had recently bought in an exhibition.

He then stared moodily out of the window and watched a child dragging a stick along the ground.

Jake was desperate to finish *Sparg from Kronk*. He could hear the printer banging on his door, demanding the finished manuscript. His publisher had been admitted to hospital the night before with nervous strain, but the ending of his book continued to elude him.

The child outside the window stopped to scratch the stick into the dry earth of drought-hit London.

'Goddit!' shouted Jake, and he leaped into his state-of-the-art typing chair and began to write the end of his book.

Sparg wrestled with Krun, his father, for possession of the stick. He wondered why they were fighting over this particular stick. There were plenty of others lying around.

He looked at his father's old face, now disfigured by anger, and thought: why are we *doing* this? He let go of the stick and allowed his father to take it away.

Sparg sat on the baked earth and thought, if only there was *language*, we wouldn't have to be so damned *physical*.

He poked his finger into the dust. He drew it along. In a few minutes, he had made marks and symbols.

Before the sun had gone down, he had written the first page of his novel. He hoped it wouldn't rain in the night and obliterate his work.

Tomorrow, he would continue his work inside a cave, he thought. What should he call his novel? He grunted to himself and tried out several titles. Finally, he settled on one and hurried to the big cave to scratch it on the wall before he forgot:

A BOOK WITH NO LANGUAGE

Yes, that was it. And he picked up a stick and began to gnaw the end of it into a point.

Jake could hardly wait for the electronic printer to spew out the typewritten page.

'At last,' he jubilated, 'I have finished *Sparg from Kronk*!'

Please let me know what you think, Jo Jo. I really value your opinion.

I gave the completed manuscript to Angela Hacker this morning. She took it from me and groaned, 'Sodding hell. I only asked for one page!' Then she put it into the blue raffia bag that she carries everywhere with her and continued her conversation with Clara about a dream she'd had of being chased by a giant cockroach.

At 11.00 p.m., after spending the evening with my friends, singing on the bar terrace, I got back to my hut to find that the following note had been slipped under my door:

Adrian,

I've skipped through *Lo! The Flat Hills of My Homeland*. I won't waste words. It's typical juvenilia and has no merit at all. *Sparg from Kronk* has been done a million times, dearest boy. But *A Book With No Language* – Sparg's novel – is a truly brilliant concept.

I would like you to come and see me when we get back to London. I'd like to introduce you to my agent, Sir Gordon Giles. I think your originality will appeal to him.

Congratulations! You are a writer.

Angela Hacker

I may be a writer, Jo Jo, but I can't find the words to express my happiness.

My plane gets into Gatwick on Wednesday at 3.00 p.m.

Love from,
   Adrian

Tuesday April 14th

Angela Hacker announced this morning that the writers' group's last meeting was to be held on 'Bare Bum Beach'. My penis shrivelled at the thought. I have never appeared in the nude in public before. 'Bare Bum Beach' is where the extrovert and confident desport themselves. I am neither of these things. However, after three glasses of retsina at lunchtime I found myself slithering over the rocks, heading for the nudist beach.

I was astounded by the ridiculous blue of the sea. The rocks shone pink as I stumbled towards the beach which was the colour of custard. It seemed the most natural thing in the world to shrug my shorts off and embrace the sand. For twelve long years I have worried about the size of my penis. Now, at last, by glancing at my fellow male writers I could see that I am made as other men. I easily fell within the 'normal' range.

At half past six in the evening I turned over and exposed myself to the sun. Nothing terrible happened.

There was no thunderbolt. Men and women did not run away, shrieking in horror at the sight of my full frontal nakedness.

I walked into the sea and swam towards the blood-red sunset. I allowed myself to float and to drift. It was almost dark when I swam back to the beach. I did not use my towel. I let the water dry on my body.

I walked back to the Institute in pale moonlight. I took a short cut through the woods. The floor was covered in pine needle debris, every footstep was a crackling aromatic delight.

I walked ankle deep through a glade of soft grass and wild flowers. Then I smelled honeysuckle and felt a tendril brush across my face. I reached the headland and stood for a moment, looking down at the Institute. The kitchen door was open. Out of it spilled bright light, laughter and the delicious smell of grilling meat.

Wednesday April 15th

10.00 p.m. I saw Jo Jo waiting beyond the barrier. I threw all my baggage down and ran towards her.

...a

...a equin *nce Mather comes to life on the movie screen*

starring

KEIR DULLEA · SUSAN PENHALIGON

Leopard in the Snow

Guest Stars

KENNETH MORE · BILLIE WHITELAW

featuring GORDON THOMSON as MICHAEL
and JEREMY KEMP as BOLT

Produced by JOHN QUESTED and CHRIS HARROP
Screenplay by ANNE MATHER and JILL HYEM
Directed by GERRY O'HARA

An Anglo-Canadian Co-Production

OTHER
Harlequin Romances
by JANE CORRIE

Many of these titles are available at your local bookseller
or through the Harlequin Reader Service.

For a free catalogue listing all available Harlequin Romances,
send your name and address to:

HARLEQUIN READER SERVICE,
M.P.O. Box 707, Niagara Falls, N.Y. 14302
Canadian address: Stratford, Ontario, Canada N5A 6W2

or use order coupon at back of book.

Patterson's Island

by

JANE CORRIE

Harlequin Books

TORONTO • LONDON • NEW YORK • AMSTERDAM • SYDNEY

Original hardcover edition published in 1977
by Mills & Boon Limited

ISBN 0-373-02167-4

Harlequin edition published May 1978

Printed in U.S.A.

CHAPTER ONE

BETH KNIGHT climbed stiffly out of the ancient taxi she had been lucky enough to secure at the island's small airport, and had barely had time to pay her fare before she was engulfed by what felt like a small tornado, but was actually her sister Janice.

'How on earth did you manage it?' demanded Janice, and hardly giving Beth time to draw breath, dragged her into the house, holding on to her as if she feared she might vanish into thin air. They had got as far as the hallway before she remembered Beth's luggage, and shouted for someone called Johnny to collect it.

Still holding tightly on to Beth's arm, Janice drew her into a room to the right of the well-carpeted hallway, and thrusting her into an armchair, stood looking at her with a smile on her face but tear-dimmed eyes. 'I just can't believe it!' she said happily. 'I only got your cablegram an hour ago. You should have sent it to Chartways, and I could have arranged for someone to meet you.'

Beth, still recovering from her sister's exuberant welcome, grinned back at her, although the smile was tremulous, for she was dangerously close to tears herself. It had been almost two years since she had seen her sister, but felt more like five, for they were very fond of each other, and were the only survivors of what had once been a reasonable sized close-knit family, until a motor accident had robbed them of their parents and an older brother in one fell swoop.

Hastily swallowing a lump in her throat, Janice grinned weakly at Beth. 'Howdy, Paleface!' she said shakily, raising a hand in mock salute.

'Don't rub it in,' Beth said ruefully. 'It's April back home, remember. As for you—put a white flower in your hair, and you'd pass for a native of the Isles!' she commented, studying Janice and noticing how her golden tan was accentuated by the white dress she wore. Her long dark hair hung loose and gently curled at the ends, in a pageboy style.

The sisters were not much alike; Janice, tall and dark, had taken after her father, but had the gentle nature of her mother; whereas Beth had inherited her mother's fairer colouring, and grey-green eyes, but there the resemblance ended, for she had been endowed with her father's blunt Scots temperament, adored an argument, and would go to extraordinary lengths to prove her point.

Janice was twenty-six, and three years older than Beth, but to see them together, the gap looked much wider, for Janice's five feet nine, against Beth's demure five feet four, made Beth appear very much the little sister, but those well acquainted with the sisters never made the mistake of referring to this. What Beth lacked in inches, she made up for in character.

'You haven't answered my question,' prompted Janice. 'How did you manage it? I've been consumed with curiosity since I got the cablegram.'

'I made a run for it while the going was good,' replied Beth a shade defiantly, her chin held high.

Janice stared at her. 'You mean Nicholas didn't know you were coming?' she asked incredulously, adding quickly, 'Well, that explains a lot. When do we start the countdown?' she tacked on dryly.

'We don't. It's over—finished!' answered Beth, and held her hand out for Janice to see the empty space on her third finger, that still felt curiously light after supporting the large ring for almost a year.

Janice's fascinated eyes lingered on the unadorned hand still held out for her inspection, then burst into tears. 'I'm so happy,' she sobbed, fumbling in her dress pocket for a handkerchief she failed to locate.

Calmly handing her one of her tissues, Beth waited while her sister carried out a hasty repair job, and sniffed a couple of times before going on. 'I knew you'd come to your senses one day,' she said shakily, taking a deep breath. 'But I was so afraid it would be too late when you did.' She gave Beth a watery smile. 'If only you knew how worried I've been about you!' She drew another deep breath. 'He was all wrong for you; I didn't see much of you on that flying visit home, did I? He saw to that! He was terrified I'd whisk you back with me—which I would have done given half a chance!' She swallowed. 'Because that was the original plan, wasn't it? I wouldn't have left otherwise; it was knowing that you would join me when you'd got through the secretarial course, that made me go at all.'

Beth remembered, and sat silent, knowing her sister's thoughts, like hers, were on the past. She recalled a tearful Janice waving goodbye on the plane's runway; the plane that was to take her to the island they were now on; Patterson's Island; one of a small cluster of islands in the Caribbean, on the other side of the world, and it had certainly felt that far away to Beth at the time. Even now she could recall the utter loneliness that had engulfed her as she had watched the plane circling above her, then dwindling away into the distance. Gone was the bravado she had determinedly shown whenever Janice had tried to back out of the fabulous job she had landed in one of the world's playgrounds; for there were times when one could carry the big sister act too far, and Beth had felt that this would have been one of them.

Home, as they had known it, no longer existed. It was just a house full of memories; one day there had been laughter, life, and expectation—the next, nothing. Only an awful stillness; Beth, at least, had been able to escape to the hostel in London, where she had had to stay in order to attend the secretarial course, but Janice had no such escape, for she had worked in an accountants' office in the small town near their home.

When Janice had applied for the advertised job on Patterson's Island, it had caused much apprehension in the family, for both Mr and Mrs Knight had not been at all keen on their lovely daughter straying that far from the fold. However, it was considered highly unlikely that she would be successful, for the salary alone had guaranteed an overwhelming response, let alone the locality; and to be strictly honest, Beth had had doubts that Janice, should she have been successful, would have gone through with it, for although she might dream of faraway places, she was really a home-loving girl and very attached to her parents.

Confirmation that she had been successful came just two days after the tragedy, and it was the best thing that could have happened to her at that time. Beth gave herself a mental shake. That was all in the past, this was the future. She looked back at Janice, who sat watching her, her large brown eyes now showing concern.

Seeing that she had caught Beth's attention, she jumped up quickly. 'What am I thinking of? You must be longing for a drink! All this way, and her loving sister doesn't even offer her a drink! What will it be, love?' Then before Beth could answer, she added, 'I think we need something stronger than tea or coffee—we're celebrating!'

While Janice busied herself with the drinks, Beth looked about her. For a 'Cottage' as Janice had continually called her home, the lounge they sat in was a large room, and hardly what Beth had imagined Janice's home to look like, for she had somehow got the idea of a small cottage dwelling on the outskirts of Janice's employer's land, and had expected to find just that; but as she gazed around at the expensive lounge, not to mention the luxurious fittings, where old-world furniture blended harmoniously with modern pieces—the cocktail cabinet Janice was now standing by, for one thing—Beth found herself slightly bewildered, and wondered how Janice had managed to furnish it so lavishly.

It did occur to her that perhaps Janice had spent

her half of their inheritance on the trappings she had
surrounded herself with, for the girls were not short
of money—their father's building business had been
in a healthy state before his premature demise—but
even so, the contents of this room alone would have
rapidly depleted such resources, Beth mused, as her
eyes lingered on the thick carpeting her feet had
sunk into, and went on to take in the handsome velvet
curtains that hung either side of the french windows
opposite her. She looked across at Janice busily mix-
ing the drinks, and frowning in concentration. 'Are
you still solvent, darling?' she asked dryly.

Picking up the drinks and carrying them over towards Beth, Janice was too immersed in her thoughts
to hear the question. 'How you ever got engaged to
him in the first place was beyond me,' she commented,
handing Beth her drink, and subjecting her to a quick
appraisal.

Beth accepted the drink and gave a wry grimace in
answer then said almost apologetically, 'I can't say I
actually remember him asking me. It was taken for
granted, it seems.'

Janice gave a loud sniff. 'Yes, that would be like
him. Not the type to let the grass grow under his feet,
is he? He frightened me to death—so domineering!'
She gave Beth a straight look. 'You barely spoke, and
when you did, he finished the sentence for you!
What did he do—brainwash you?' she demanded,
then went on before Beth could answer, 'Now that
type would have found me a pushover, but you ...'
she frowned. 'How on earth you could have let someone make a——' she groped for the word she wanted.

'Zombie?' replied Beth helpfully.

'Exactly!' cried Janice triumphantly. 'Oh, I'll grant you he's good-looking, and if his home's anything to go by, disgustingly rich, but looks and wealth do not make for happiness.' She shook her head bewilderedly. 'How could you be happy with a man like that? It was "Yes, Nicholas" or "No, Nicholas" —I'd never thought I'd live to see the day someone could do that to you.'

Beth knew what she meant; although she was only just beginning to understand it herself. 'I can only plead temporary insanity!' she said softly. 'What did John think of him?'

'The same as I,' answered Janice, smiling in recollection. 'Poor darling, I gave him a rough passage back. At first, I didn't want to come back. I had some mad idea of staying on and trying to persuade you to break off the engagement—or at least, make certain that you really knew what you were doing.' She gave a rueful grin. 'But John was right; he said you were over twenty-one, and could please yourself.' She brushed a stray hair off her forehead. 'I was so cross with him at the time; he didn't really know you, and had no idea how much you'd changed——' she broke off abruptly and dabbed her eyes quickly. 'Oh, dear,' she gave a strangled chuckle, 'do you remember the scrapes I had to get you out of when we were young? How you had a nasty habit of picking an argument with someone twice your size, and how I'd have to finish it for you? and then to find you like that—afraid to say boo to a goose . . .' She couldn't go on, and swallowed hastily.

Beth grinned weakly at her. 'Guilty, me lud, but insane,' she intoned.

'I couldn't,' went on Janice, after taking a quick sip at her drink, 'get it out of my head that it was all my fault,' and at Beth's raised brows at this statement, she went on quickly, 'Yes, it was,' she insisted. 'I should never have left you. We were both in a state of shock, and goodness knows how long it takes to wear off. Thank heaven, in my case, I had John. Gavin sent him to meet me when I first arrived here, and since then he's always been around.' She blushed rosily. 'He said it was love at first sight, but he didn't crowd me. Somehow he sensed I needed help, and between them, Gavin and John pulled me round.'

'Gavin?' queried Beth, not recalling having heard Janice mention the name before.

'Mr Patterson,' said Janice. 'My boss, and a nicer man I've yet to meet—excluding my John, of course!' she smiled. 'Honestly, love, I've been so lucky. I love my job, and—oh, everything!' She broke off, frowning. 'At least, I was happy, until we paid that flying visit home when John and I became engaged.' She sighed. 'And I'd so much wanted to meet your Nicholas—not that you'd said much about him—and no wonder! It's a marvel he didn't insist on vetting your mail, out as well as in!' Her fingers clenched round the damp tissue she still held. 'If Nicholas Harbin had had half of my John's sensitivity, I wouldn't have been so worried, but that type of man sees only what he wants to see, and heaven help anyone who gets in their way!'

She grinned shamefully at Beth who sat watching

her with a hint of amusement in her eyes, thinking
that although Janice had only been in Nicholas's
presence twice for what could have been not much
longer than an hour, she had correctly assessed him,
and again wondered how she could ever have con-
templated marrying him.

Holding her hand out for Beth's empty glass, Janice
carried them back for a refill, but before doing so she
walked over to the french windows and drew the
curtains, for it was now dusk, and Beth, noting this,
felt a spurt of surprise, for she had arrived in broad
daylight, but she recalled Janice telling her that night
fell suddenly in that corner of the world. It was going
to take some getting used to, she thought tiredly—
that, and her liberation from Nicholas's dominant
presence.

Janice walked back to the cocktail cabinet, and
continued her theme with, 'John said that if you had
any sense you'd wake up to what was happening to
you.' She gave Beth a lopsided grin. 'He also said
there were some women who actually liked being
dominated.' Her cheeks flooded with colour at the
recollection. 'I'm one of them, I'm afraid,' she confessed. 'I don't think I could love a man who lets
himself be ruled by a woman. Mind you, that's me,
not you; and there's a difference in John's dominance
of me—at least he lets me think I'm getting my own
way, when really I'm not—but I don't realise it until it's too late!'

Beth chuckled; she had formed the same opinion
of John herself. The tall solid-looking blond man,
with the twinkling blue eyes, and quiet unassuming

nature, had given the impression of an easy-going man, yet underneath Beth had sensed a very determined character, and had been so happy for Janice, and so grateful for that flying visit they had paid her as soon as they had got engaged.

Ever since John's name had first cropped up in Janice's letters, it was easy to see which way the wind blew. As Mr Patterson's estate manager, he was in constant contact with Janice, a situation which suited both parties admirably. Thinking back, Beth recalled how she had tried to persuade Nicholas to take her out there for a holiday, but he always found a perfectly valid excuse as to why such a journey was out of the question, at the particular time she had suggested. It had never occurred to her that he might be jealous of Janice's influence on her. She took a sip of the drink Janice had just handed her, absently noticing how refreshing it was, but her thoughts were far away. If it hadn't been for Janice and John's visit, she might still be living in cloud cuckoo land, for there wasn't any other way she could describe her state of mind at that time.

It was the way they had looked at each other, as if some invisible thread held them together, and for the first time, Beth looked at her relationship with Nicholas. And it was Nicholas, she thought sadly, not Nick—one would never entertain calling him Nick. There was something about him that definitely discouraged such familiarity. It had never occurred to her before to wonder why, perhaps because he was too proud, not to mention arrogant. She sighed inwardly. Perhaps if he'd had a sense of humour it might have helped, but he hadn't, at least, not at the small, but human frailties of life. He would never ever laugh at himself, or admit defeat in any sphere. Surrounded by wealth and a doting mother, he had never known what it was like to have to go without, in fact the word 'no' didn't exist in his vocabulary!

'Darling?' Janice broke into her musings quietly with, 'Do you mind if I vanish for a second or two? Mabel will be waiting to know what time to serve dinner.'

A slightly bewildered Beth shook her head, and her bemused eyes followed Janice as she left the room. Servants too! She had known Janice was getting an extremely good salary, but didn't think it went that far! The help might, of course, come with house, and if so, it appeared Janice had certainly fallen on her feet. She gave herself a mental shake; all this Janice would tell her later. She closed her eyes. She felt extremely tired, mentally exhausted as well as physically, and still not quite able to believe she was actually here, and able to live as a person in her own right—to be able to make her own decisions, she shuddered, and never ever allow herself to become enmeshed again.

'Beth, don't you dare fall asleep!' Janice's voice broke through her consciousness and made her start guiltily and blink her eyes in an effort to dispel the urge to close them again. 'Mabel's surpassed herself —come on, I'm starving! I usually eat as soon as I get home,' Janice said gaily, as she pulled Beth out of her chair and towards the door, and through the hall again to a room at the end of the passage.

As Beth sat at a table that would have comfortably
seated four, she saw that there was no cramping here
either, and no lack of essentials. The room was small,
yet ample for its purpose, and somehow elegant. Her
glance roamed over an old, beautifully carved sideboard, that held an array of silverware, as highly
polished as the sideboard it was displayed on, and it
suddenly dawned on her that while Janice might own
some of the furniture, she definitely did not own that
sideboard, let alone the silver it displayed. Quite
apart from the fact that Janice's taste was more on the
modern side, the cost alone would have been way
above her resources. Nicholas would have been able
to name the exact cost had such a piece come on the
market, for he was an avid collector of antiques, and
having the money to indulge in his hobby, possessed
an impressive collection.

At this point they were joined by a plump, homely-
looking West Indian woman, with twinkling black
eyes and an orange overall, one corner of which she
had used as an oven glove to enable her to hold the
huge steaming silver dish she placed on a mat in the
middle of the table, and from which emanated a
mouthwatering smell not unlike an English stew.
Her wide grin and slightly lisped, 'Howdy!' at Beth,
owing to a missing front tooth, made her grin in-
fectious, and Beth grinned back as she returned her
greeting.

Within a short space of time the table was loaded
with beautifully decorated dishes, and Beth wondered
how she was going to do full justice to Mabel's obvious slavery on her behalf, particularly as she hadn't

had all that much notice of an extra place at dinner —although one would never have known it from the way she had served the food, and her apparent willingness to please. On this alone Beth was determined to do her best in helping to demolish the feast prepared for them, although to be honest, she had little appetite.

Many of the dishes were new to Beth, and Janice gave her a little of each as samplers for a start, explaining that many of the dishes were made up of various kinds of fish, but although Beth made a valiant effort, she was beaten long before the sweet arrived, and had to be coaxed into trying a sample of what looked like a huge cream cake, but was in fact layers of ice cream interspersed with a kind of sponge cake.

When the meal was over, Janice suggested they take their coffee in the lounge, and when Mabel brought the tray in to them a short time later, Beth took the opportunity to thank her for the meal, which was received by a delighted grin from Mabel. 'I see my sister has been very well looked after,' she commented smilingly, and this produced an even wider grin from Mabel and a lisped, 'Thank you, missy,' before she bustled back to the kitchen with an air of having accomplished a great feat, and highly satisfied with the result.

While Janice poured the coffee, Beth leaned back in the deep armchair, wishing fervently that she could close her eyes and relax completely, but she knew if she did she would fall asleep, and knowing that Janice was longing to know the whys and wherefores, she hadn't the heart to ask her to wait until she had had a good night's sleep.

'How did Nicholas take it?' asked Janice, as she handed Beth her coffee, making no secret of the fact she was still having some difficulty in believing Beth's statement that it was all over.

Beth took a sip of her coffee before replying sardonically, 'He didn't.'

Janice nodded thoughtfully. 'Refused to believe you?' she asked with a twinkle in her eyes.

Beth's eyebrows raised. 'You learnt quite a lot about him during that visit, didn't you?' she said quietly.

'Enough,' replied Janice. 'I told you he scared me half to death. I'm proud of you for standing up to him at last. I presume you're back to normal,' she added dryly. 'I only wish I'd been there,' she tacked on wistfully.

Beth shook her head slowly, 'I'm afraid it wasn't quite as you imagine, dear. I don't rate a medal for bravery. You see, I didn't exactly stand up to him—it's so difficult to explain ...' She ran a hand distractedly through her hair. 'It was as if everything blew up in my face.' She broke off hesitantly, and stared down into her cup as if marshalling her thoughts, then began again, this time more slowly, almost as if trying to explain her actions to herself as well as to Janice. 'We'd been down to Kent for the weekend, and Nicholas and his mother had been discussing the wedding——' She broke off suddenly and gave Janice an apologetic look. 'It was fixed for May, you know. I would have written and told you, of course,' she added quickly, then gave a sigh, and continued with her narration. 'It was as if I wasn't there; I can't explain it. It was when Mrs Harbin started to talk about the trousseau, and how she intended to accompany me when I bought it, making sure, as it were, that I didn't let the side down and buy something quite out of keeping with their station in life ... and ... and the way Nicholas just stood by listening, and nodding his approval of her decision—because that's what it was—not a suggestion, a decision. I ... I just couldn't go through with it. I felt as if I was being slowly suffocated ...' She broke off and hastily swallowed the remains of her coffee, in an action that said more than words, needing some sort of action to erase the memory of her feelings at that time.

Janice held her breath. She longed to rush over to her and comfort her, but felt it wasn't the right time, for the Beth she knew hated any outward show of affection, so she held herself in check and gave her time to compose herself, noticing with a stab of sorrow the dark smudges under her eyes that gave them a translucent look. She's too pale, she thought, even for England in winter, and felt a rush of rage against the man who had brought her once lively sister to this level—as for the mother! Just let them try and get her back, that's all! She told herself grimly.

'I told him last night——' continued Beth in a slow halting voice, then broke off and stared at her sister in a half-surprised way. 'Was it only last night?' she murmured in wonderment, then gave a tiny shake of her head. 'What I mean is, I tried to tell him. He kept saying I was tired, and that I'd be all right in the morning. That it was talking about the wedding that had given me stage fright,' she swallowed. 'He said I was not to worry, and that it was natural for me to feel like that.' She stared at Janice. 'He just wouldn't listen; I knew it was hopeless, and that I'd have to do something to make him understand that I wasn't going to marry him—I didn't know what. I remember going back into the hostel, and there was your letter in the rack—I knew then what I had to do.'

Janice's eyes grew wide as she pictured the scene that must have taken place at the airport. She just couldn't see Nicholas waving Beth goodbye, and said as much, adding, 'He must have tried to stop you.'

Beth gave a wry smile at this; all too well could she imagine the scene Janice had in mind. 'I have to disappoint you again, dear. There were no dramatics; I simply took advantage of a business trip Nicholas was paying to Scotland. It really couldn't have happened at a better time. I was in such a state that it was ages after I'd made up my mind to come to you that I realised I had a clear run.' She sighed softly. 'I suppose it was cowardly of me, but I had no choice; I left him a letter—one he couldn't possibly misconstrue,' she darted a mischievous glance at Janice that echoed her innermost feelings. 'So I'm free, my love, although it's going to take me some time to really believe it!'

Catching a glimpse of the old Beth, Janice felt a surge of relief. It wouldn't take too long for her to readjust back to the happy carefree girl she had once been, but to be honest, she still had doubts of Nicholas's reaction to the letter Beth had left. No matter how she tried, she just couldn't see him accepting it. He wasn't that kind of man. She cast a quick look back at Beth, now replacing her coffee cup back on the small side table. She looked so fragile, Janice could well see why Nicholas had been drawn to her—he was a collector of objects of art, and her unique pocket-Venus style beauty would have magnetised him from the start. In a way, she thought, he did love her, but there was a difference in loving someone and completely annihilating them—which, in Janice's opinion, Nicholas had set out to do. To make her his conception of perfect beauty, in other words, a robot, and this was the state she had found her in on her visit home, and one that had constantly haunted her ever since. But that was all over now, she thought happily.

'Well, he can't make you marry him, love. And if he dares to follow you here, my John will stand up to him,' she announced proudly.

Beth gave a low chuckle. 'Poor Nicholas! He really did impress you, didn't he? I'm beginning to feel a tiny bit sorry for him.'

'Sorry for him!' squeaked Janice in indignation. 'Sorry for that pompous, overstuffed apology for a tailor's dummy! Why, he's ...' she searched for the right definition to convey her contempt of the man who had very nearly succeeded in breaking Beth's spirit.

Beth grinned at her sister's vehemence, and added

fuel to fire by observing provocatively, 'Most girls thought him handsome. He's considered quite a catch!' and had to duck hastily to miss the cushion hurled at her by an irate Janice.

Later that night, in the cosy guest room Janice had had prepared for her, Beth lay longing for sleep. That, considering how tired she had been earlier in the evening, was a little unusual, for she had been certain she would fall asleep the minute her head touched the pillow, but here she was, tossing and turning, and going over the events of the past twenty-four hours. It was going over everything with Janice that had brought the memories she had wanted to forget, back into sharp focus.

You could run so far, she thought sadly, but no further. She had no regrets where Nicholas was concerned, and even in her half-awakened state she was able to see how completely he had overshadowed her, moulding her into perfection for the role she was to play as his wife. She shuddered at what might have been had not Janice and John suddenly appeared on the scene. Their kind of love was the true conception of what love should be. Of giving and taking, of understanding one another's faults and accepting each other for what they were—not what they wanted to make them into.

She turned restlessly. Even Nicholas's kisses weren't given, not in the sense they ought to have been given; they were imposed as a seal of ownership on her. Inexperienced as she was, at first they had thrilled her, pushing all her doubts aside as they tried to rise to the surface. And later still they had been used as a weapon to stem any argument or protest she might have voiced about the way her life had been taken over. Beth wondered whether he had sensed she was coming out of the cocoon of bewilderment she had existed in for so long, and was almost sure he had. He was extremely astute; but even knowing this, it wouldn't have stopped him. He knew what he wanted, and would have swept her into marriage without considering her feelings in the matter.

When Beth had told Janice that she hadn't been responsible for her actions and her subsequent engagement to a man like Nicholas Harbin, she had been telling the truth, for Nicholas had 'found' her working temporarily in an antique dealer's shop, one that he frequently visited in his quest for collector's items. She had taken the job on shortly after Janice had left the country, for she had soon found that she wasn't quite as tough as she had thought she was, and came to dread the weekends, and the painful memories solitude brought in its wake. There was no home now for her to go to, and the few friends she did have in the hostel always took off at the weekends, as she herself used to do before fate had struck its terrible blow. In sheer desperation, she had found herself work that wouldn't interfere with her studies, for she was determined to join Janice at the earliest given opportunity. It was not the need for money that drove her on, but the necessity to keep the past at bay until she was better able to cope with it. In this she had been fortunate, for one of the students recommended her to an uncle of hers who kept an antique shop situated reasonably near the hostel, and Beth was subsequently employed for Saturdays.

A very quiet and much subdued Beth, still partially under shock from the sudden loss of her family, found herself receiving the attention of Nicholas, who, after his first visit to the shop after her arrival, became a very determined suitor, and was waiting for her to finish work that same day, and carried her off for a meal. Not only was Beth's loneliness over, but her freedom as well. Without knowing quite how it had happened, she would find her weekends being spent at Nicholas's home in Kent, and being fussed over by not only Nicholas, but his mother as well. Mrs Harbin simply adored her son, and if Beth was what Nicholas wanted, then Beth he must have. The quiet, unassuming girl would be no problem to lick into shape as the wife of her distinguished son, and between them, the mother and son set about remoulding Beth's life.

The wealth of the Harbins came from a chain of fashionable gift shops that ran the length of the country, and Nicholas presided over the board of directors, so it was not surprising that Beth found herself working at head office, under Nicholas's direction, when she had qualified, and was given no chance of choosing her own employment.

None of this meant anything at the time to Beth; she had stopped thinking for herself by then, so complete had been the takeover by Nicholas. It was as if she had been lost, found, and re-pigeonholed.

All these thoughts went through her tired brain, and she gave a drowsy thank-you to the powers that be that she had had the strength and the opportunity to free herself. It would be a very long time indeed before she allowed herself to get involved again. Once bitten, twice shy, she muttered just before she fell asleep.

CHAPTER TWO

BETH awoke to a brilliant sunny morning. At first she was bewildered, wondering what she was doing in this strange room, then her drowsy glance rested on the pale blue carpet that covered the floor, and drifted on to take in the white matching furniture, the pale blue walls, a shade deeper than the carpet, and rested finally on the frothy white organza curtains that fluttered gently as the breeze caught them. The room was entirely feminine, and Beth decided she liked it; it wasn't unlike Janice's room in their old home. Janice! Beth sat up with a jerk—she was with Janice!

A wonderful feeling came over her as her eyes gazed once more over the room, this time wide awake. It wasn't a dream. She had broken free of Nicholas at last. Now she could go anywhere—do anything—without his continual presence. She jumped out of bed and ran to the window. Still with that sense of wonderment she stared out at the scene before her. Why, it was like being in a great park—there were trees, some with blossom on, and others with great spreading leaves of a satiny olive colour; flowers too, that seen at a distance looked like a huge patchwork quilt sown on a green background.

At this point Beth wasn't too sure that she wasn't dreaming, but was afraid to pinch herself in case she was. She breathed a sigh of utter contentment. She could even paint if she wanted to—there was no Nicholas to discourage her; he had not encouraged her to do anything that did not warrant his personal supervision, and as Beth had not the strength of will to oppose him, she had weakly accepted it. That had been another thing that had horrified Janice on that visit of hers, to find that Beth had stopped painting, for she had been a very promising student, and although she might not have produced a masterpiece her work was good enough to have earned her a modest living, apart from the pleasure it had given her.

With her eyes still on the landscape in front of her, Beth sadly conceded the fact that Nicholas had done his best to stamp out all artistic inclination on that front. Her timid request to join a local art club in order to later exhibit some of her work was met with bland incredulity. Nicholas did not approve of art students, and Beth was very quickly made aware of this fact. Because painting meant so much to her, it was the one and only time she had stood up to Nicholas, and actually gone ahead and joined the group, but Nicholas was not so easily beaten. He would escort her to the weekly evening sessions with the air of a martyr—not only that, but actually stay during each session keeping a caustic eye on any student, particularly male, who had the effrontery to take an interest in Beth's work; and that went for the teacher too! It soon became obvious that this state of affairs could not go on. As Nicholas had had the foresight to pay a subscription fee, he had every right to attend the classes, but his presence, and none too flattering remarks on some of the work produced, soon brought about the desired reaction on Beth's part, and for the good of the group, not to mention peace, she gave up the course.

There was a tap on the door, and Janice appeared carrying a tray. 'Oh, you're awake, dear. No need to ask if you slept well—this is the third time I've come up!'

'Is it late?' asked Beth guiltily, knowing Janice had to be at work later, and approvingly stared at her crisp blue and white dress, that looked efficient yet very feminine. 'I'm afraid I didn't wind my watch— I was dead beat,' she confessed.

'Why should you?' grinned Janice. 'You're taking things easy now. No, darling,' she went on, in answer to Beth's earlier question, 'it's not late. About ten to nine, and I've a few minutes to spare. As yet I haven't been able to arrange any time off—not knowing you were coming, that is!—and I must go in today. Gavin's giving a garden party tomorrow, and I have to attend to last-minute chores, but I'll be back for lunch around oneish.'

She poured Beth's tea out for her, and waited while she sipped it, watching her with an indulgent expression. 'There's something I want to show you before I go,' she said, with a hint of mystery in her voice, and as soon as Beth had finished her tea, Janice caught her hand and led her from the bedroom to a small box room at the end of the passage.

A very mystified Beth found herself staring at an array of packing cases and odd bits of furniture that had been pushed aside until a use could be found for them, and wondered if Janice was going to show her what she had so far collected for the home she would soon be sharing with John, until Janice drew her attention to something propped up against the wall in a far corner.

In spite of the cloth that covered the article and partially concealed its shape, Beth had no trouble identifying the object; it was an artist's easel, the type that could easily be folded and carried around on outdoor excursions. Janice, watching her reaction, gave a delighted grin at Beth's puzzlement at seeing such treasure there. 'And that's not all,' she told her slightly bemused sister, and opened up a large box standing next to the easel.

Beth let out a gasp of pure delight as her eyes alighted on the contents of the box. There was a profusion of oil paints, canvases, and fine well-kept brushes. With shining eyes she looked from the box to Janice. 'Have you started painting?' she asked delightedly.

Janice chuckled. 'No, dear; you're the only painter in the family. They belonged to Gavin's mother, she used to use the place as a studio until her illness forced her to give it up. She died shortly after I came here, and Gavin told me to get rid of them, or find someone to give them to.' Her smile was tremulous now. 'Of course, I kept them for you—even though it looked as if you'd never be around to use them—but something made me hang on to them.'

Beth gave her a brief hug, too full for words, and gave her attention to the box that in her eyes repre-

sented all that Aladdin's cave might hold for someone like her. With her eyes still on the well-stocked
paintbox, she asked, 'Are there any of Mrs Patterson's paintings in the house?'

'Here, you mean?' Janice answered, and at Beth's
nod, said, 'No, but there are several up at Chartways.
If you feel like a stroll later, come up there, and I'll
show you round. They're quite good.' Her eyes twinkled. 'I'm rather biased, though, I think you're better!'

Beth's brows raised at this compliment, and she
sketched her a little curtsy in acknowledgement, to
which Janice gave a grin, and murmured, 'You're
welcome,' and would have said something else, but a
swift glance at her watch put whatever she would
have said out of her mind as she exclaimed, 'Goodness, I must fly,' and rushed to the door. 'See you
later, love, at lunch,' she called as she flew down the
stairs.

Later, Beth enjoyed a solitary breakfast, and planned what she would do that morning, feeling a surge
of happiness flow through her at the thought of painting again, when and where she wanted, and she had
to curb a desire to gather everything up and rush out
to find a suitable subject to paint—not that she en-
visaged having any difficulty in that direction; the
problem would be which to paint first, for she had
seen enough from her bedroom window to ascertain
this at least.

She had not forgotten Janice's suggestion that she
should take a stroll up to her employer's house, but
decided against this. She had no wish to take up any
of Janice's time during working hours, and she had

said she would be busy arranging a garden party. Very nice, mused Beth, and another surge of happiness went through her as she thought of how lucky her sister had been, not only in finding John, but having a considerate employer as well, especially when she recalled what Janice had said about the help that had been given her when she had so badly needed it on her arrival on the island. Beth's silent gratitude went out to Gavin Patterson, and she promised herself that she would take the first opportunity of personally thanking him for the kindness he had shown to her sister.

When she had finished breakfast she decided to go on a tour of the house, for as yet, apart from the first floor, she had only seen the lounge and dining room. When Mabel appeared to clear the table a short time later, Beth asked her if she might look around the house, and Mabel shyly offered to show her round.

The house was, as Beth had suspected, much larger than Janice's letters had intimated. Across the corridor from the dining room was another room that appeared to be a smaller version of the lounge she had seen the previous evening, except for the colour scheme, that was predominantly blue. The walls were the same delicate shade as in her bedroom, and deep blue velvet curtains hung either side of the window bay. Beth saw that although the room was well furnished, it lacked the personal touch, and no ornaments could be seen. The only ornamentation of the room was a large bowl of brilliant blue flowers placed on a beautifully engraved escritoire near the window. The room, though peaceful, had a forlorn air about it.

'Mrs Patterson's room,' lisped Mabel. 'Nobody much come in now.'

She sounded sad, and Beth felt that Mrs Patterson had been a very nice person. Mabel obviously missed her, and so, she felt, did this room.

The remaining room to be seen was an office, and Beth was surprised to find it there, for she knew Janice worked at her employer's house, and wondered if she was ever expected to work at home, but Mabel soon enlightened her. 'Mr Gavin's office,' she explained. 'If he don't want to be pestered, he come along here.' She bent to straighten the desk blotter. 'He don't come now Miss Janice here. Miss Janice right good secretary. He no worries now.'

Beth smiled at this accolade to her sister's work, glad she appeared to be earning the fabulous salary she received.

There were some maps on the walls, presumably of the island, and Beth looked at them; some were very old, and others looked reasonably up to date. Looking down on it as the plane made its descent, it had appeared very small indeed, but now she saw it wasn't quite so small. Distances, she thought, could be deceptive, and she tried to work out how long the taxi ride had been from the airport, which she had gathered was just outside the main township. In the end she gave it up and asked, 'How far is the town, Mabel?'

Mabel's brow wrinkled in concentration. ' 'Bout five miles, I reckon,' she said slowly, and looked expectantly at Beth. 'You maybe want to go there?' she queried.

Beth considered this for a moment or two, then said, 'Well, there are a few things I need. I did pack in rather a hurry,' not to say panic, she thought wryly.

Without further ado Mabel went to the telephone on the office desk and started dialling. After a moment Beth heard her say, 'That you, Johnny? Miss Beth want to go to town. You take her, hey?' and turning to the slightly stunned Beth, she asked, 'What time you want, Miss Beth?'

'Oh, dear,' answered a flustered Beth. 'I didn't want to bother anyone—couldn't I get a bus or something?'

Mabel giggled. 'Bus once a day; take folk to town at eight, back at six. Johnny take you, it's okay, Miss Janice arrange.'

Miss Janice, thought Beth, appeared to have quite a lot of authority, and hoped her request to be taken to town at such short notice wouldn't impose on it. So she asked if Johnny could collect her in an hour's time.

Johnny was a thin wiry West Indian, and like Mabel, had a wide and welcoming grin, making Beth abandon any thought of apologising to him for being called out at short notice, for again, like Mabel, his attitude clearly showed a wish to please, and as he settled her in the car Beth had an absurd feeling that royalty couldn't have been given better treatment. It was no wonder, she thought, that Janice was happy, for if Mabel and Johnny represented the local inhabitants, she couldn't have been anything else. No sour looks, or grumbles, just smiles all along the way, and the wonderful feeling that nothing really mattered unless you wanted it to.

As the car cruised along the well maintained roads, Johnny passed out information on local points of interest, and as they passed a stretch of land that looked like open country to Beth, he drew her attention to a dirt track that led up to a distant hill and seemed to disappear into thin air. 'That leads to the caves,' he told her.

'Crystal caves?' asked Beth eagerly; she had heard that some of the islands possessed them, but his answer disappointed her.

'Smugglers' caves,' he said, with a hint of pride in his voice. 'We traded with pirates for centuries.' He shook his head regretfully. 'My granddaddy used to tell us kids about them days, and he had it from his granddad.'

Beth didn't share his regret, and said so. 'They weren't good times, Johnny, to live in,' she replied gravely, and with an air of a teacher giving a pupil a history lesson, she added, 'For instance, you might have been made a slave, and goodness knows, they had a lean enough time of it. But you're happy, and well fed, and have a kind employer—what more could you ask for? Just think, if Mr Patterson hadn't come along and bought this island ...' She was halted by a shout of delighted laughter from Johnny.

Wiping his streaming eyes with one hand, while keeping a steady hand on the wheel, he gave the astonished Beth a sideways look that showed the whites of his eyes. 'Mr Gavin's a pirate,' he said

solemnly, trying hard to keep his face straight, and
gave up the struggle at the sight of Beth's startled
reaction to the news.

With wide eyes she gave him a searching look.
'Are you having me on, Johnny?' she asked uncer-
tainly.

His grin widened as he shook his head emphatic-
ally. 'The Patterson's were pirates, that's how they
come by the island. Been handed down to the eldest
sons through the centuries.'

Beth was stunned, and it took her a little while to
digest this astounding fact. The island was called
Patterson's Island, wasn't it? Why she should have
imagined some wealthy person had just happened
along and bought it, simply because the island had
his name, was not a very intelligent deduction on her
part, but just the sort Nicholas would have expected
her to make. It was just as well, she mused, that she
hadn't known this before Janice had left, or she
might have tried to dissuade her from taking the
position. However, after giving the matter due consideration, she came to the undeniable conclusion
that Gavin Patterson could hardly be held responsible for the past; that he was nothing like his pre-
decessors was obvious by his treatment of not only
her sister, but all his employees. 'I don't suppose Mr
Patterson likes to be reminded of the past,' she murmured half to herself. 'It's not a thing to be terribly
proud of, is it?' she added abstractedly.

Johnny grinned again. 'Got a big picture in the
house. You see it when you go there.'

By now they were on the outskirts of the town, and

Johnny took up the role of guide again, pointing out buildings that had been built by either Gavin Patterson or his father, and although Beth was curious to hear more on the piratical doings of the Pattersons, she was content to let the matter drop, for the time being anyway. Janice would no doubt fill her in later.

The town was not a large one, and within a few minutes Johnny was parking the car near the quaint old harbour, beside a notice that clearly stated 'Space reserved', and as Beth caught several indignant glances from tourists, slowly driving past in the hope of finding a parking space in the crowded area, she found herself thinking there was something to be said for pirates after all!

After arranging to meet Johnny later, in time to be taken back to join Janice for lunch, Beth was free to wander off in search of the items she required. It was mainly summer wear, such as jeans and cotton tops, for the clothing she had brought with her consisted mainly of dresses and several woollen jumpers. Sandals too, were a must, and as she gazed into the shop window of a fashionable boutique, she could scarcely believe that she was actually on the island, and thought that it was a marvel that she had had the foresight to pack as much as she had, for she had received a slight shock when she had rung the airlines requesting the first available seat on the Caribbean route, and was rung back within the hour and told of a cancellation she could take that same day. As her passport was in order, and all other necessary qualifications for foreign travel also in order, it only remained for her to pack and leave a letter for Nicholas to find on his return from Scotland.

Going into the boutique, it did not take long for Beth to buy what she required, and as the weather was so marvellous, she slipped out of the dress she had worn and changed into the jeans and cotton top before she left the boutique. With her dress in a folder, she left the shop and set about finding a shop that sold sandals, and did not have far to look. Everything, it appeared, was catered for in the town's one main street. Tourism would demand such service, Beth mused, as she threaded her way past the throngs of people obviously bent on sightseeing tours.

By snatches of conversation caught as she passed, she gathered they were mostly Americans—the men with bright-checked shirts, and cotton shorts, the women with floral patterned trouser suits, and nearly all clutching the inevitable camera held at the ready should any unusual sight appear before them.

Now, wearing her sandals, her shoes having joined her dress in the folder, Beth wandered happily past the shops, and saw with delight at least two art shops. She would have no trouble in replenishing supplies, she noticed, as she entered one of the shops to take note of their stock, and to purchase a block of drawing paper and several pencils. The island would attract artists like bees to honey, for already Beth felt the old urge to capture a scene and make it come to life with a few deft strokes of the brush. Take the harbour, she mused, if only she could catch something of its antiquity, for despite the milling crowds, the up-to-date and sometimes garish clothes worn by all and sundry, the old stone walls stood proud and somehow isolated from the gum-chewing, lollipop-licking crowds that surged past them.

She took a breath of sheer pleasure as she decided to make the harbour her first picture of the island, and made her way back towards it. It would take many sketches at first, she knew, and her fingers itched to begin committing the scenes to paper.

On reaching the harbour, she gave a little sigh of exasperation, for there were even more tourists there— and more to come, she thought wryly as she spotted a graceful liner anchored out in the bay, bringing in boatloads of passengers.

Her disappointment at not being able to sit down in a place of her choosing and start sketching was soon overridden by the fact that she could at least choose her times for work. The majority of tourists were, it seemed, day trippers, and those who were staying on the island would have set times for meals. All she had to do was bide her time—and she had all the time in the world, she told herself with a spurt of happiness, and contented herself with just gazing at the scene in front of her.

Taking everything down with the eye of a painter, Beth looked at the weathered buildings that stood either side of the entrance to the harbour. The flower sellers, natives of the islands, with their bright-coloured sarongs, intent on weaving leis of exotic frangipani blossoms, the traditional welcome to the Caribbean; the fruit stalls, overflowing with tropical fruit, the expectancy—the gaiety—all this Beth saw and felt, and she longed to capture it. In her mind's eye she had already begun her picture, and was mentally miles away when she felt herself jostled and hemmed in by a small crowd of tourists.

Coming out of her abstraction, she saw they were all craning their necks upwards towards the hills at the back of the harbour, and winced as a small freckled-faced boy stood on her foot. At her gasped 'Ouch!' he swung round and apologised quickly.

'What's everybody staring at?' she asked bewilderedly.

'It's a cannon!' the small boy answered excitedly, then stared towards the hills again. 'I'm not tall enough,' he complained after a moment or so. 'I wanted to get a shot of it,' he added despondently.

'Well, I can't see it,' replied Beth, squinting a little as she gazed at the hill.

'Over there,' pointed the boy, and following his direction, Beth caught sight of a very businesslike weapon situated in a strategic position on the top of the hill. It was also extremely old, and in all probability dated back to the days of piracy. 'Pirate Patterson's welcome to unwanted visitors,' she murmured half to herself.

'What did you say?' queried her new-found friend.

'Oh, nothing,' laughed Beth. 'Come on, let's see if I can give you a lift up.'

The boy looked doubtfully at her. 'You're not very tall, are you?' he commented frankly.

'No, but I can give you a few inches,' replied the amused Beth. 'Got your camera ready?'

He still wasn't too sure he ought to impose on her generous offer, so Beth settled the matter by lifting him up, and holding on to him while he prepared to take a shot of the cannon.

She was coping nicely, for the boy was no weight at all, when there was a sudden surge forward as more tourists joined the crowd, and she found herself pushed back hard against the harbour wall, and only just managed to keep her grip on the boy, who was forced to drop one hand on to her shoulder in order to keep his balance, but lost his camera, and instantly wriggled out of her grasp. 'My camera!' he wailed as he peered over the harbour wall.

Beth, following his gaze, was just in time to see the camera slowly sinking down beneath the clear blue water, and looking back at the boy was dismayed to see tears welling up in his eyes. 'It's my dad's camera,' he gulped. 'I didn't tell him I was borrowing it—what'll I tell him?' he asked pleadingly.

Beth's gaze went back to where the camera had disappeared. The water was so clear she could just discern the shape of it lying on the sandy bottom of the sea. 'What's your name?' she asked the boy.

'Jim—Jimmy,' he got out.

'Well, Jimmy, shall we see if we can find someone to fish it out for us?' she asked brightly, hoping to take that stricken look from his face, but before he could answer, a portly man in a loud checked shirt called across to them, 'There you are! We've been looking for you for ages. Come on, we're having an early lunch today.'

Jimmy replied, 'Just coming, Dad,' and flung Beth a look of desperation.

'Can you come back after lunch?' she asked him quickly.

Another shout from his father decided him. 'Be back as soon as I can,' he whispered before darting off.

CHAPTER THREE

BETH waited until Jimmy and his father had left the harbour before going in search of someone who could rescue the camera for her, and idly noticed that an early lunch appeared the order of the day, as the harbour was now practically deserted.

She stared down at the camera again trying to gauge how far out it was from the beach, and decided it wasn't too far out. What she needed, she thought, was someone with a boat, and gave a little nod of satisfaction when her gaze fell on a small clutch of boats further up the beach. Hoping to find someone willing to help in the rescue operation, she made her way down the harbour's ancient stone steps to the beach. But to her disappointment, when she reached the boats, she found the area completely deserted. The boats were obviously fishing boats, and their owners would not apparently make themselves visible until the next fishing excursion out to sea.

For a moment or so Beth was tempted to give it up, for she couldn't see how else the camera could be retrieved, but the thought of the small boy's distress nagged her conscience, and she knew she couldn't leave him in the lurch. For one thing, it was quite probable that Jimmy's family was only spending the day there, and in that case, it wouldn't be too long before his father discovered the loss of the camera;

and for a second, he wouldn't have lost the camera if she hadn't offered to give him a lift up.

Now that her mind was made up, it didn't take her long to decide on her next move, and she slipped her sandals off before wading out into the water, thinking how fortunate it was that she wore jeans and cotton shirt, neither of which would take long to dry in that heat. She had no fear of getting out of her depth, as she was a strong swimmer, and as soon as she reached the deeper water, she struck out with a strong crawl stroke towards the harbour.

It took her a little while to get to the exact position she wanted, and as soon as she felt she was within range of the spot the camera had gone in, she dived. In all, it took three dives to locate the camera, as it had sunk a little further into the shifting sand, and with a feeling of having unearthed treasure, she rose triumphantly to the surface clutching the camera by its strap.

On breaking to the surface, she was somewhat disconcerted to find herself gazing into a pair of not very cordial blue eyes.

'What the devil do you think you're doing?' demanded the man glaring at her.

Beth took a moment or two to recover from the shock of the encounter, then she grinned at the man and clung to the side of his motorboat. 'Sorry if I startled you,' she apologised, 'You see, the camera fell in ...' she began to explain, but found he wasn't interested in her explanation, for he cut it short with an abrupt, 'Get in!'

It wasn't a request but an order, and Beth was

immediately on the defensive. She hadn't liked being spoken to like that at all! She looked back towards the beach. 'Thank you,' she replied stiffly, 'It's not very far to the beach, and I'm a good ...'

Again she was interrupted in the middle of a sentence, and to her utter fury found herself unceremoniously hauled into the boat and plonked into the middle of it—just as if she had been a fish! she thought furiously, and glared at the man now starting the engine of the boat. For two pins she would ... The man looked up just then and caught her glowering at him, and there was something in his eyes that quelled any further thought of resistance on her part, and Beth found herself both angry and puzzled by him.

As he took the wheel of the boat, she studied him coolly, wondering what it was about him that she so resented—apart from the way he had treated her—although, she conceded, trying to be absolutely fair about it, she must have given him quite a shock at her sudden appearance like that, for he could have run her down—even so, she mused, most men would have said something on those lines, and offered—yes, offered, to run her back to the beach.

Perhaps it was the way he had utterly ignored her apologies that had so riled her? Her back unconsciously stiffened as she acknowledged the cause of her resentment. The man reminded her of Nicholas—which was odd, for he was nothing like Nicholas to look at; he was fair, for one thing, whereas Nicholas was dark. Her brows contracted slightly as she tried to pinpoint the likeness. Both men, in their individual ways, were handsome, although this man was deeply tanned, as if he had lived in the climate for many years. Her gaze lingered on the haughty stare that had made her feel like something that had been dredged up from the bottom of the sea, and that he didn't like the look of—so that was it! Nicholas had the same look when something or someone displeased him!

She took in the navy blue blazer he wore, and the white sweater with navy blue slacks. Authority was written all over him she thought, and catching the strength in his impassive features as he looked ahead while guiding the boat towards the harbour, she had an absurd urge to get as far away from him as possible, which under the circumstances, was ridiculous, and she roundly scolded herself for such innate cowardice. The wretched man was only giving her a ride back to the harbour, after all.

'Which hotel are you staying at?' he asked abruptly.

It was on the tip of her tongue to ask him what business it was of his, when a tiny voice inside her whispered caution. He must have some authority, Beth decided, harbour police in all probability, and Janice wouldn't thank her for getting embroiled with the force on her first day. She swallowed her resentment and tried to remember the name of an impressive hotel she had passed on her shopping expedition. Was it the Carlton?—or the Savoy? All she could remember was that it bore the name of one of London's large hotels. 'The Savoy,' she replied promptly.

His grim expression told her that she had made a bad guess. 'Try again,' he said curtly.

Sparks flew from Beth's eyes as she made an effort

to stem the tide of a few well-chosen words to put this tinpot god in his place. She could, of course, explain that she was Janice's sister and watch him start squirming and worrying about his job, but she decided against this, for the time being anyway. If they did meet again, she would enjoy every minute of his embarrassment.

'I've forgotten,' she answered in an offhand way.

It was clear he was not used to this kind of response, for his lips tightened as he replied caustically, 'You seem to be somewhat lacking in manners, young lady. If I'd the time, I'd give you what it appears your father omitted to give you a few years ago.'

Beth's eyes opened wide in astonishment. For goodness' sake, how old did he think she was? However, there was no time to take him up on this somewhat misguided comment, for they were now drawing alongside the harbour, and Beth saw no point in prolonging the interlude. As soon as he cut the motor she was off the boat and heading for the harbour steps. Her bag and shoes she would collect later, when she had got a certain infuriating individual's presence out of her vicinity.

She was so intent in putting as much distance between her and the man in the boat, she did not see the two people coming down the steps to meet her, and before she knew it she had cannoned into them. Looking up to offer her apologies, she found herself accepting the hand of the man who had earlier called to Jimmy, and who was obviously his father; Jimmy was with him.

'That sure was a fine thing you did for Jimmy,'

beamed the man, vigorously pumping Beth's hand.

'We watched you from the top,' broke in Jimmy. 'I bet Dad you'd get it the third time, and you did!'

'Have you,' queried a cold voice at Beth's elbow, 'any idea of the risk she took? The harbour is a dangerous place for swimming at any time. With the tide coming in, it's suicidal.'

Beth took a deep breath, she might have known she wouldn't get away quite so easily, and was about to expound on the fact that as she had come to no harm, wasn't it time the subject was closed, when Jimmy's father, recovering from the sudden on-slaught, started to explain. His attempt received the same treatment as Beth's had—in other words, he was cut off in mid stream, and Beth felt her hackles rising at the way the man swept aside all explanation, showing no interest whatsoever in another's point of view, except his own! Her furious musings were cut short when the man demanded to know which hotel they were staying at, and her brows lifted as he added, 'Your daughter appears to have conveniently forgotten it.'

The look these words produced on Jimmy's father was almost too much for her, and she choked back the laughter that threatened to make things worse; looking at Jimmy didn't help much either, for he had his mouth open in dumb amazement. Beth closed her eyes. Things were going from the ridiculous to the sublime!

Jimmy's father made a belated recovery. 'Now look here——' he began.

'Just the name of the hotel, if you please,' persisted the man icily.

Beth did a rapid calculation. He must be the har-bourmaster—at least!

'The Astoria, but I don't see ...' argued the harassed father.

'Thank you!' replied the man with an air of successfully completing his interrogation. 'It appears they are neglecting to inform their guests of the island's rules. I shall make it my business to see that incidents of this nature are not repeated. Good afternoon!'

In stupefied silence Beth and her companions watched the tall arrogant figure as he strode on his way up the steps, and out of sight.

'Phew, we seem to have upset the Admiral!' gasped Jimmy's father.

Beth gave way to her feelings. All anger now gone, she started to chuckle, her mirth set Jimmy laughing too, and his father's rueful expression soon gave way to one of amusement. 'Seems I've acquired a daughter,' he commented dryly. 'I guess I'd better introduce myself. The name's Jackson, Lee. We hail from Iowa.'

Still chuckling, Beth held out her hand to him. 'I'm Beth Knight. Nice to meet you, Mr Jackson. I'm sorry I brought the wrath of the gods down on you,' she added, as she handed him the camera. 'I hope you're able to save some of the films.'

Taking the camera from her, Mr Jackson commented dryly, 'If I'd known the risks you were taking——' He shook his head slowly. 'And to think I stood by and watched!'

'Nonsense!' interrupted Beth. 'I'm a very strong swimmer, Mr Jackson, I wouldn't have made the attempt otherwise. I think our pompous friend overdid the danger theme.'

Mr Jackson was not convinced of the truth of this. 'He looks the sort of man who knows what he's talking about,' he replied slowly.

Beth grimaced, and found herself hoping Mr Jackson was wrong in his assessment, for if he were right, the man had probably saved her life, and she didn't care for this thought at all. 'If he hadn't been so overbearing, I might have thanked him,' she muttered darkly. 'But I'm not sure I share your opinion,' she added.

Her comments on the man's attitude met a kindling spark in Mr Jackson, and he grinned at her, taking in her slim boyish figure, and the way her damp hair clung to her head. She didn't look much more than sixteen, at that, he thought. 'Shouldn't you get those wet things off?' he demanded. 'Our hotel's just across the way. Would you like to come back with us and get dried out?' he offered kindly, adding for good measure, 'I do believe Mrs Jackson ought to meet her daughter, don't you?' he teased.

Beth wasn't too sure how much time she had left before her rendezvous with Johnny, and at that moment she saw him coming towards them, and knew she would have to decline the invitation, explaining that she was staying with her sister, and that her transport had arrived to take her back.

Mr Jackson was clearly disappointed, but suggested that as they were spending the week there, perhaps they would meet up with her again, and thanking her again for rescuing the camera for them, they left her with Johnny.

'Bin swimming, Miss Beth?' asked Johnny with a wide grin, when they were alone.

Beth bit back a smile. 'Now don't you start!' she retorted smartly. 'I know it's the fashion to wear a costume, but it's a long story. I'll tell you about it on the way back, but first I have to collect my bag and sandals. I won't be a minute,' she called as she ran back down the harbour steps.

On the way back to the house, she related some of the morning's events to Johnny, not giving any specific details of the man who had so enraged her, for she had decided not to mention it to Janice, working on the principle of what she didn't know wouldn't harm her—or what was more to the point, worry her, for Janice was apt to worry over any hint of dissension.

One point did emerge from her conversation with Johnny, and it didn't help to soothe Beth's slightly ruffled aplomb, for it appeared that the insufferable man had been perfectly right about the dangers of the harbour, and Johnny related several incidents in the past, that had brought in the strict measures now enforced on swimming there.

A rather crestfallen Beth consoled herself with the thought that if they did meet again she would make an attempt to apologise—if he recognised her, that was, and she devoutly hoped to avoid both eventualities!

CHAPTER FOUR

IT was a scramble, but Beth just managed to get changed in time for lunch with Janice, and the only sign of her morning dip was in her still slightly damp hair. Janice, however, made no comment on this, and chatted happily on her morning's work.

'Do you usually have to organise these do's?' Beth asked interestedly. 'Isn't it a bit much on top of your usual work?'

Janice laughed. 'It's part and parcel of the job, dear, and I love it. Mind you,' she added, as she handed Beth some salad dressing, 'it did give me qualms at first, particularly as I was expected to act as hostess as well at the dinner parties Gavin gave. He's a bachelor, you see, and it saves him the embarrassment of having to delegate the task elsewhere. His mother used to officiate for him before.'

Beth hadn't thought much about Mr Patterson until now, apart, that was, from feeling grateful for his kindness to Janice, and now, thinking about him, she felt a stab of pity for him. It was sad that he had to pay someone to act as hostess for him in his own home. It didn't sound as if he had many friends, and she saw him as an elderly, shy man, and found herself looking forward to meeting him.

When Janice enquired how her morning had gone, Beth told her about the camera, and how she had

fished it out—not mentioning the exact location, or
the resulting consequences; time enough for that if
there was any comeback, but she couldn't see how
there could be. Even if she did meet that insufferable
man again, she couldn't see him admitting that he
had mistaken her for a teenager—he was far more
likely to want to forget the whole incident!

The story amused Janice, who suggested Beth
wore her swimming costume under her clothes the
next time she went for a walk on the island.

The lunch hour passed swiftly, and Janice was on
her way back to work, when she paused in the door-
way. 'I nearly forgot!' she exclaimed, and walked
back to Beth. 'Mrs Harris rang this morning. I don't
know whether I mentioned it in my letters, but I
stayed with them when I first came here, before
Gavin had me settled in here, and they're longing to
meet you.' She glanced doubtfully at Beth. 'I hope
you don't mind, love, but I felt I couldn't refuse
when she offered to take you out to dinner tonight.
I had planned to take you with us, we're going to look
at a house that's just come on the market. In fact it
was Mrs Harris who told us about it, and knew that
we'd arranged to see it tonight, so I suppose she
thought you'd be at a loose end—but you're still
welcome to come with us, dear, if you'd rather,' she
added quickly.

Beth thought about this for a moment or two. To
be honest, she would welcome an evening completely
on her own, for being alone was still a novelty to her,
but she sighed inwardly as she thought that neither
Janice nor Mrs Harris would understand her feelings

in this, and she had no wish to hurt anyone's feelings. She smiled at her sister. 'Thank you for the invitation, dear, but I'll accept your Mrs Harris's offer. Trailing behind two moonstruck lovers is definitely not on my agenda. I'm recuperating, remember? The very mention of wedding bells is likely to bring on a relapse!'

Janice chuckled at this, remarking gaily as she left, 'You won't feel like that when you meet the right man, just you wait and see!'

Beth's soft mouth twisted at this; she wasn't going to 'wait and see'. Once was enough for her.

She spent a lazy afternoon lapping up the warm rays of the sun on the patio adjoining the dining room. Although she had her sketchbook beside her, she made no attempt to try to capture the idyllic scene in front of her, for the scent of the flowers, and the lazy humming of numerous insects as they buzzed around the flora display, lulled her into tranquillity —a state Beth had almost forgotten existed. It was like being reborn again, she thought sleepily, and she wasn't going to waste a minute of her new-found freedom.

It seemed no time at all before Janice was back again, and the girls had a light tea to keep them going until their respective dinner dates. John, Janice said, would arrange for them to eat later, after they had seen the house, and Beth, watching the way Janice's eyes lit up when she mentioned the house they were going to see, hoped it came up to expectation, but even if it didn't, she told herself, Janice was too much in love to let anything cloud her happiness. As long as she was with her beloved John, a mud hut would serve just as well.

'What are you smiling at?' asked Janice, breaking into her thoughts.

Beth grinned at her. 'I was just thinking you'd be happy in a mud hut,' she commented teasingly. 'As long as your John was there, of course!'

Janice laughed at this, then her expression sobered for a moment. 'Now perhaps you know what I meant when I said Nicholas wasn't the right man for you,' she scolded her affectionately. 'Can you see Nicholas in a mud hut?'

Beth's grin widened. 'Not exactly,' she admitted. 'Not unless someone was selling antiques there, and then he'd demand the place was fumigated before he entered!'

'I couldn't have put it better myself,' agreed Janice enthusiastically. 'He would, wouldn't he?'

At this point, Beth felt a stab of conscience on Nicholas's behalf. He couldn't help being as he was, and in his own rather autocratic way, he had loved her—no, not her, she corrected herself quickly, what he'd wanted to make her. He would certainly have to make a big adjustment to his previous ideas if he wanted her back again. She pulled herself up short on this thought. She wasn't going back—she couldn't! The very idea frightened her, and to stem these thoughts that were beginning to bring the dreadful feeling of claustrophobia on her again, she changed the subject quickly. 'Ought I to wear evening dress to-night?' she asked Janice.

Janice nodded, 'I think you'd better,' she said. 'I'm

pretty sure they'll take you to the Falcon.'

'What's that? A pub?' queried Beth.

'Don't let Gavin hear you say that!' laughed Janice. 'The Falcon, my love, is the island night spot. It's a sort of night club, and although it's not the only one the island has, it is the most exclusive. If you do go there, take the opportunity of looking at the swimming pool. It's the latest addition, and Gavin plans to hold swimming parties there later on in the year.' She looked at Beth as if a thought had suddenly struck her. 'You do have an evening gown, don't you, pet?' she asked.

'I have two, actually,' replied an amused Beth. 'I won't let you down. Would you like to inspect them?' she asked teasingly.

To her astonishment Janice took her up on her offer, and deciding to humour her, Beth showed her both the gowns. One was a pale green chiffon, with floating skirt and high kimono-style collar, that Nicholas had instantly approved of, for even her dresses had come under his strict scrutiny in the past. The second gown was a white silk, cut on more severe lines, that clung to her slim figure, and was plain, but very sophisticated.

Janice pointed to the green dress. 'Wear that one,' she ordered.

'Very well,' agreed Beth obediently, still amused at Janice's determination to show her off at her best.

When Janice left her to get herself ready for her date with John, Beth gave a little sigh; there was not much doubt that Janice was hoping to marry her off to one of the island's bachelors; that way she could be absolutely certain of keeping her near her, and while she understood her motives, she also knew that she was in for a big disappointment.

Mr and Mrs Harris arrived on the stroke of eight, and were duly introduced to Beth. It was obvious that they had expected to meet a younger edition of Janice, by the almost comical surprise registered on their faces as they gazed from Janice's dark hair and slender height, to Beth's long fair hair and diminutive figure.

Taking full note of their bewilderment, Janice chuckled. 'I didn't give you the family history, did I?' she said. 'Well, I'll enlighten you now. I take after my father—the Scots side of the family; Beth takes after our mother, who was Norwegian.'

Mr Harris, a plump, goodnatured man, gave his wife a knowing look as he commented, 'All I can say is, they must have been an exceptionally good-looking couple. My, my,' he grinned, 'if half the island's bachelor's aren't running round in circles by this time tomorrow, I'll buy Winifred that summer house she's always on about!'

His wife, a short, matronly woman with grey-streaked hair and a warm disposition, threw up her hands in mock horror. 'Now I'll never get it,' she complained sadly.

A short while later they were on their way, Beth sitting in between her hosts on the front seat of the spacious American car. They kept up a lively flow of conversation in order to make her feel at ease, for which Beth was grateful. They told her how fond they were of Janice, and how happy they had been when they had heard about John. 'We couldn't have wished for a better husband for her,' confided Mrs Harris to Beth, who didn't need any assurance on this matter, for she felt the same about John herself. 'And now that you've come, dear—well, I shouldn't think there's anything else she could possibly want.' She patted Beth's hand. 'You must stay, now that you're here. After all, there are only the two of you now, aren't there? And she really did miss you in those first few months. It was always, "When Beth comes ..."' She was silent for a moment, then added hastily, 'Well, you're here now, and as I've said, I do hope you'll stay.'

Mr Harris's gaze left the road ahead for a split second as he gave Beth a teasing look. 'It's my guess she'll have no choice in the matter. The young men these days don't wait for visiting cards—look at the way John homed in on Janice. She didn't know it at the time, but he took one look at her, and that was that.'

Beth knew a slight sense of irritation, in spite of their well-meant teasing, and wished they would change the conversation; she was soon rewarded by Mrs Harris's, 'That's the harbour down there,' and Beth, following her gaze, saw the twinkling lights some way below them and realised with a start that they must have been climbing steadily up a hillside, although she couldn't remember seeing any hills on her short excursion with Johnny that morning. Then she recalled the hills behind the harbour. 'Is this where the cannon is?' she asked.

'Yes,' replied Mrs Harris, a little surprised that

Beth knew about the cannon, and Beth explained how she had come to see it. 'It's quite a tourist attraction,' commented Mrs Harris. 'Gavin's very proud of it. It dates back to the days of his forefathers. On the odd special occasion, it's fired; all shipping warned, of course,' she chuckled.

Minutes later, they were gliding into a large parking space beside a well-lit ranch-style building. 'This is the Falcon,' Mr Harris remarked as he drew up beside an elegant Daimler, and as he courteously assisted Beth and his wife out of the car, he commented idly. 'Not so busy as usual,' looking at the empty spaces in the parking area.

'It's the yacht club do tonight,' Mrs Harris reminded him as they walked towards the entrance of the club. 'I expect they'll be over later,' she added.

'Do you sail, Beth?' Mr Harris asked, as he escorted them into the foyer of the club.

Beth admitted that she was a very bad sailor. Nicholas had tried to get her to take an interest in the sport, as he had been a keen sailor, but the results had not been successful.

'Oh, well,' sympathised Winifred Harris, 'there're lots of other interests here. I'm sure you won't get bored.'

They had by now reached the dining section of the club, and were greeted by several patrons already at dinner. Beth felt the curious looks that followed her as they made their way to a table that had been reserved for them, stopping once or twice to introduce her to particular friends of theirs. As they moved away from one table, a young man dining with his parents gave a nervous gesture of straightening his tie, and this did not go unnoticed by either of Beth's hosts, and she caught Mrs Harris giving her husband an outrageous wink as they moved on.

When they were settled at their table, Beth took in her surroundings while Mr and Mrs Harris concentrated on the menu. Her glance took in the muted lighting, the carpet into which her feet had sunk, that in itself must have cost a small fortune, let alone the fabulous decor and the exotic arrangements of the numerous flowers the island boasted. In a far corner of the dining room, set on a small dais, was a Hawaiian band, to whose music several couples were dancing on a space immediately adjoining the dining area.

The meal consisted mainly of various seafood specialities, and Beth was amazed at the variety offered, and managed to eat enough to satisfy her anxious hosts, but had to smilingly refuse the tempting-looking rum babas offered for the sweet.

Lulled by good food and a liberal amount of wine, she found herself beginning to feel sleepy; the soft lilting music took on the role of a lullaby, and she had to blink hard in order to stay awake, and when Mr Harris had to repeat a question twice Mrs Harris became aware of Beth's tiredness.

'You poor child!' she exclaimed. 'All that travelling! You must be worn out—I didn't think about that at all.' She turned to her husband. 'We must take her home, John.'

At John Harris's goodnatured, 'Sure—ready when you are,' Beth felt guilty. The evening had barely begun and here she was, falling asleep on them.

'I do apologise,' she said hastily. 'I'm sure if I slip out and freshen up a bit——' adding quickly as she saw the doubt on Mrs Harris's face. 'A drop of cold water works wonders, you know.'

Not quite convinced, her hostess said doubtfully, 'Well, we'll see.'

Beth excused herself and slipped out to the powder room; she was determined not to spoil the evening for the Harrises. The powder room lay to the right of the reception area, and passing through the dining room, she noted absently that the place had now filled up and there was hardly a vacant table. As she went through reception, a neon sign pointing the way to the swimming pool caught her eye, and remembering Janice's comments, she decided to take a look at it. Fresh air, she thought, would be more beneficial than a dab of cold water on the face.

Once outside, the air was fresh without being cold, and Beth caught her breath when she saw the pool, now completely isolated, although tables and chairs had been placed on the gleaming mosaic tiles that surrounded it. Of course, a swimming pool was a swimming pool, but Beth had never seen anything like this. It reminded her of fables from the Arabian Nights. Small coloured lanterns hung in the dense shrubbery that screened the pool, giving it a fairy tale effect, and as she wandered along the sides of the pool, intrigued by the reflection of the softly coloured lights in the still water, the fragrant scent of the flowers drifted past her and she gave a sigh of pure contentment. She would have dearly loved to be able to stay in that place of enchantment.

As she looked up at the brilliant sky, seeing how even the stars were reflected in the water, her peace was suddenly shattered by an American voice somewhere behind her. 'How about joining a lonely sailor for a drink, honey?'

Beth turned to locate the owner of the voice, and saw that the man was sitting at one of the tables close up to the shrubbery, and partially in shadow. Judging by the slurred voice, she deduced the man was drunk, and she politely declined the offer, feeling a stab of annoyance at the way her peaceful interlude had been shattered. Then she made her way back towards the club entrance.

She had not got far when her arm was caught in a vicelike grip. 'Come on, honey. I've enough in the bottle for two,' he cajoled.

The man was, as Beth had thought, very much the worse for drink, and even though she was completely alone with him, it did not occur to her to be afraid. She had the sense to know that losing her temper with him would only make matters worse, so she tried the rational approach. 'I'm with some friends,' she explained, 'and they'll be waiting for me to join them. Would you mind letting go of my arm?' she requested politely.

To her relief he complied, but only to clasp her round the waist instead, and Beth almost reeled from the smell of whisky on his breath. 'If you're lonely, why not come back and meet my friends?' she asked, mentally patting herself on the back for such a brilliant solution to the problem.

He laughed, and she winced as she caught the full

blast of the whisky fumes, then still keeping a firm hold on her waist, he waggled an accusing finger towards the entrance of the club. 'They won't let me in, see? Not got a monkey suit, see?' he mumbled.

Beth was not so easily beaten. 'Shall I bring my friends out here?' she asked hopefully.

The only response was an uncomfortable tightening of the arm around her waist. 'Nope. Just you and me, honey,' he answered, crushing Beth's last hope.

She sighed inwardly; from now on she'd have to play it by ear. If she could just get him to release his grip on her ... 'All right, then,' she replied airily, 'just one drink, then I must go.'

As they turned towards his table, he released his grip on her, as she had hoped he would, and when they were about level with the entrance to the club she made her dash for freedom, but there were several tables to negotiate first, and she collided with one of them as her floating skirt caught the edge of another, making her stop to untangle it.

'Got you!' cried the triumphant sailor as he hauled her back to him, quite obviously enjoying himself hugely.

Unfortunately Beth was in no good mood to humour him. Chances were that she had ruined the dress, and a slight tearing sound coming from the skirt as the man pulled her towards him confirmed her suspicion, and she struck out at him with clenched fists. 'Will you let me go?' she demanded furiously, but vainly, as her words were having as much effect on him as her small clenched fists were.

The next minute she found herself hammering away

at thin air, and the sailor was measuring his length on the mosaic tiles in front of her. Beth stared down at him, then back at her clenched fists in wonderment, and jumped when a voice close to her said, 'When your friend sobers up, I advise you to find another club. This type of conduct is not tolerated here.'

Beth gasped, stung by the cold arrogance of the voice she had heard once before. She had no need to look at him to ascertain who he was. The harbour-master—or Admiral, as Jimmy's father had dubbed him—was a very busy bee, she thought. 'He's not my friend,' she got out stiffly, feeling a little sorry for the sailor.

She might have known that her words would have no effect on the man. They hadn't before, and they wouldn't now, she thought furiously, and what business was it of his, anyway? Was he an official chucker-out of the Falcon's exclusive premises? His next words confirmed this thought.

'I don't blame you for disowning him,' he drawled maddeningly, 'but my advice remains the same. There are plenty of places that cater for this kind of patron-age in the town.'

Beth stared up at the man beside her. 'Cater for this ...' she began indignantly, but as before, she was not allowed to finish the sentence.

'Haven't I seen you somewhere before?' demanded the man, giving her an intent look.

Grateful for the shadows, Beth moved a little way back from him. 'I don't think so,' she said quickly, purposely keeping her voice low. At the rate things were going she felt it would be better if the man did not recognise her.

It wasn't her night; for the second time that evening, she found her arm grasped and steered firmly into the light.

'I thought so!' he said acidly. 'Out to paint the town red, are you? Well, young lady, I suggest you do it elsewhere, although what the devil your parents are doing letting you wander around at this time of night is beyond me.'

Beth stared back at him, not knowing which annoyed her most; the fastidious expression on his face, or the autocratic lift of his left eyebrow. Just like Nicholas, she thought. 'As I happen to be over twenty-one, I would say it's none of your business!' she bit back scathingly, and shook off his hand on her arm as if it had been some poisonous insect. 'If you've no objection, I'll join my friends in the club,' she added meaningly, showing him that at least she had friends.

'And I would like to meet these friends of yours,' he drawled, watching her with narrowed eyes, his whole attitude suggesting that she was lying, and endearing her yet closer to him.

Her hands clenched by her side as she attempted to keep a tight rein on her temper, for the urge to rave and shout at him was sorely tempting, yet she knew it would not serve her purpose—not with this man, so she swallowed her anger and managed an icy, 'I only came out to look at the pool,' and looking back at the sailor still recovering from what must have been a knock-out punch, she went on, 'and there he was.' She favoured the man beside her with a look of hauteur. 'I thank you for your timely intervention. I am not,' she added scathingly, 'entirely devoid of manners.'

Her wide grey-green eyes, now shooting off light green sparks, met the insolent blue ones squarely, and to her fury she watched him take a cool inventory of her, from her face to her gown, and pass on slowly down the rest of her, and she repaid the doubtful compliment by doing the same thing. He was immaculately dressed in evening wear. His startlingly white shirt had a frilled front, and although Beth knew this was a quirk of fashion, she did not like them, and much preferred the plain style, and felt a mad urge to tell him so. However, she held her tongue and went on with her appraisal, at the end of which she had to admit grudgingly that in spite of the frilled shirt, he was a magnificent specimen of manhood—and he knows it, she thought bitingly.

She looked up to find him watching her, acknowledging her assessment by a slight lift of the eyebrow, and she waited, for what she felt ought to be an apology from him for his high-handed behaviour. She waited in vain, and it occurred to her after a moment's silence that he was waiting for her to lead the way back into the club—so he hadn't believed her! she thought furiously, and was about to utter a withering comment on this when the sailor decided to join the party.

Lurching to his feet, he demanded, 'What are you doing with my girl?' and without waiting for an answer, lunged at the man beside Beth.

Sidestepping neatly, the man caught the sailor

deftly by his uniform collar, and Beth saw that he had
an unfair advantage, for he was at least four inches
taller than the other man. However, she did not stop
to put her point of view for the opportunity of fading
out of the scene was too good to miss, and she sidled
gradually towards the club doors.

'You stop right where you are,' commanded her
tormentor. 'So you didn't know him, eh? Well, I
haven't finished with you yet.'

Beth felt like screaming; she couldn't win. She
would have to wait until he had dealt with the sailor,
then take him to meet Mr and Mrs Harris. She could
derive no satisfaction from this thought, for it was
certain that Janice would get to hear about the whole
wretched incident, and not only that, what had happened that morning as well. She sighed. Probably
Janice's boss as well; she could only hope he had a
sense of humour. Of all the insufferable types to
tangle with, she had had to choose this one, and she
could well imagine the report he would give of their
two meetings. It all depended, she pondered miserably, just what position he held in the island's hierarchy, and even then it would be Janice's word
against his. At this thought she brightened visibly;
the wretched man must have dulled her wits; she had
nothing to worry about. He was entirely in the wrong
on both counts—well, perhaps not both counts, she
conceded grudgingly, but certainly on this one!

Her smouldering eyes watched the man and the
sailor. The latter showed no sign of giving up the
fight, and his arms flailed wildly at the empty air. Her
eyes widened as she saw that his captor was moving
slowly but surely towards the pool.

'What are you going to do with him?' she asked, thinking it was a silly question, for it was obvious.

'Cool him off,' was the haughty reply.

'He mightn't be able to swim,' cried Beth, now very alarmed.

'We shall soon see, won't we?' drawled the man, 'In any case, he won't drown in three feet of water.'

Beth gasped, and for a second she was speechless; the sheer audacity of the man confounded her, but not for long. Her sense of fair play refused to let her just stand by and watch, and she threw herself into the battle by grabbing hold of one of the man's arms and attempting to slow up the process. 'Let him go!' she said furiously. 'This instant, do you hear?' she demanded.

'Thass right, you tell him, baby,' hiccoughed the sailor.

The man turned his attention to Beth, but still kept a firm hand on the sailor. 'I'll come to you later,' he threatened. 'Now stand aside, unless you want a little of the same treatment.'

Beth stared at him, unable to believe her ears, but he had meant every word of it, and she knew it, and was forced to do just that, but she contented herself with a fierce, 'You try, that's all. You might find that you're taking on more than you can chew!' she ground out.

In more ways than one, she told herself consolingly, for she couldn't see the kind Mr Patterson standing for this sort of treatment to visitors, be they intoxicated sailors or what have you.'

Her fury rose to fever pitch as she watched the man's elegant back bend as he lowered the sailor into

the pool. People could still drown, she told herself
furiously, in three feet of water. Her eyes narrowed as
the thought occurred to her that it might be a good
idea if the Admiral went in with him—at least he'd be
on the spot to administer a spot of life-saving! He
didn't stand a chance; it only took one push in the
middle of his back, and there was a gasp, then, 'Why,
you little . . . !' and half the pool came up to meet her.

The last thing Beth heard as she fled through the
club doors was a hiccoughed laugh from the sailor that
considerably cheered her up. At least he was all right;
as for the Admiral—well, she had no worries on that
score. All he'd be suffering from was a deflated ego—
and about time, too, she told herself happily.

CHAPTER FIVE

THE following morning Beth had a silent argument with herself about how much of the previous evening's episode she should tell Janice, and a sense of preservation to both of them won in the end, and her conscience was stifled. It stood to reason, she argued with herself, that the insufferable man was hardly likely to broadcast the fact that a mere girl had got the better of him, for his pride's sake if nothing else. No, it was best that she said nothing; she didn't intend to have Janice worried. If it did eventually come out—well, she would worry about that when it happened, and she felt sure Janice would wade in on her side. On this thought, she gave a little chuckle; just like the old days, she thought.

Apart from asking her if she had enjoyed the evening with the Harrises and receiving a favourable report, Janice's mind was on other matters, and was in fact floating on cloud nine. The house had come up to full expectation, and they had said 'yes' then and there. With eyes shining like stars, she told Beth, 'It's only two miles from the estate, so John will be practically living on the doorstep. I just can't wait to show it to you!'

It wasn't until the subject of the house and its numerous advantages had been fully expounded that she returned to the subject Beth would rather have left unexplored, and she had a few qualms when asked, 'Did you see the pool?' to which she gave a wary yes, adding quickly, 'It's lovely, isn't it?' and hoping that would be that.

'Did you meet Gavin?' persisted Janice, and Beth explained about there being something else on at the yacht club, and she presumed he was there. This satisfied Janice, and gave Beth a momentary reprieve, for it was quite possible that he had been present later, but due to her enforced sojourn at the pool she hadn't met him, for she was sure Mr and Mrs Harris would have introduced her to him had the occasion arisen, but it hadn't, for the simple reason that she had met them in the foyer on her return from the pool, and this was a relief all round, as they were beginning to get worried about her.

'Oh, well, you'll meet him this afternoon,' said Janice happily. 'I'm sure you'll like him. He's a perfect pet, and I'm certain you'll love working for him just as much as I do.'

Beth stared at her. 'W-working for him?' she asked bewilderedly.

Janice chuckled delightedly. 'It's a plot John and I have hatched up, love. You see, he doesn't want me to go on working after we're married, and I see no reason why you shouldn't take my place. It lets me out of a fix, too, because I didn't want to let Gavin down, but I knew how John felt. I also know how Gavin feels about employing a local person—not that there's any shortage of candidates. Miss Greer, for one, but she'd send Gavin crazy in a week.'

Still reeling under her sister's plans for her future, Beth queried absently, 'Miss Greer?' not that she was interested, but it held Janice's attention while she considered her proposal.

'Colonel Greer's daughter,' explained Janice. 'She's got a soft spot for Gavin, and wouldn't give him a minute's peace. That was why he advertised the position abroad. He felt that it wouldn't be a good thing to employ a local person; could have caused a lot of jealousy. It's quite a responsible post, and a lot of the work is confidential—another reason why he didn't want someone local.'

Beth's brows raised at this, and her feelings were clear to Janice, who gave her a wide grin. 'Oh, not the secret service, darling,' she chuckled, then grew serious again. 'It's just that Gavin's promoting tourism. It's the island's main income, and provides work for the local people, but some of the people who come are what's known as V.I.P.s, who wish to remain incognito, and you'd be surprised how many do come. The island's perfect as a kind of hideaway for them —it's not on the usual travel agent's itinerary, for one thing, and for another, they know from past experience that their identity will not be disclosed. If it was they wouldn't be able to take two steps without being gaped at, not to mention the rush of the social climbers to invite them to dinner.'

She gave a wry smile. 'What a few of them wouldn't give to take a peep at my season's visiting list, but only Gavin sees it, and he has the right to refuse entry to someone he feels would be an undesirable visitor. It's the same with the cruisers, only a few are allowed to call during the season, enough to ensure a good living for the inhabitants, but he has no intention of letting things get out of hand. It's his island, and he likes to keep a strict eye on all events. There's not much that goes on that he doesn't get to hear about sooner or later.'

On this remark, Beth choked on her last sip of coffee and found herself swallowing hard. It hardly sounded as if he had a sense of humour—a sense of propriety, more likely! What had she done? Well, one thing was certain, she had to tell Janice now. At least her version would reach Mr Patterson before that detestable man could put his on record.

Taking a deep breath, she was about to confess all when Janice jumped up from the table. 'Is that the time?' she wailed, as the silver chimes of the clock on the bureau struck the hour. 'I must rush, dear. See you at lunch. It'll have to be a quick one, I have to be back to supervise everything before the kick-off. Now don't wander off, will you?' she called back to Beth, who sat in dejected silence for a long time after she had gone.

By the time Janice put in her next appearance, Beth's courage had deserted her, and all she could do was hope for the best, for it had occurred to her that the man she least wanted to meet might be at the garden party—he certainly seemed to be everywhere else, to her way of thinking. Being Janice's sister, of course, might make a difference, and should she be unfortunate enough to cross his path again—well, this time she would have Janice with her, and he might, she thought hopefully, even apologise to her. She tried to imagine the scene, with her graciously forgiving him, but somehow it didn't gell, and she had to abandon it. She simply could not see him apologising to anyone, let alone someone who had flouted his authority, not to mention pushing him into the swimming pool!

After a hurried lunch the girls prepared for the garden party, and as before, Janice suggested the dress Beth should wear. It was pale blue, and had long sleeves with lace at the cuffs, and a Peter Pan-style collar, that Beth had bought in a weak moment during a shopping spree and had since wondered why, because it was very dressy, and she really preferred simplicity. 'I shall feel like Little Boy Blue,' she complained when Janice pounced on it when going through her wardrobe to find a suitable dress for her, determined she should make a good impression on whom she hoped would be her future employer.

'I don't know why I brought the wretched thing,' Beth went on. 'Just shows what a state I was in when I packed!'

Her remarks were blithely ignored by Janice, who would not hear of her wearing anything else. 'It looks adorable on you. Do wear it, love—just to please me!'

The dress wasn't the only thing she was prevailed upon to wear, for Janice provided her with a wide-brimmed straw hat, in a slightly darker blue than the dress. It was a nice hat as hats went, and Beth felt this one could go. 'I never wear hats—you know I don't,' she protested.

'I'm afraid you must today,' answered Janice firmly. 'It's an unwritten law for these occasions. I don't know what you're complaining about. It's the nicest hat I own, and it goes with the dress beautifully.'

If Janice was proud of Beth's appearance, Beth

was no less proud of her sister's. She wore a lime
green dress cut on simple lines, that clung to her slim
figure and looked elegant without being too fussy.
Her hat was a white floppy style, that with her height
she could wear so well. Hats, decided Beth, suited
Janice, but all they did for her was sap her confidence, and between the hat and the dress, she did not
envisage herself deriving much enjoyment from the
coming occasion.

The walk through the park-like scenery that led
to Chartways soon took Beth's mind off her appearance. The tall trees on either side of them, forming
an avenue to the house, were the trees she could see
from her bedroom window. 'They'll soon be coming
into flower,' remarked Janice, noticing Beth's interest.
'You've come a little early for the summer blooms,
but they're worth waiting for.' She gave Beth's hand
a squeeze. 'You won't know what to paint first,' she
teased.

Beth's first sight of Chartways rather pleased her,
for it was no different from many of the large country
houses she had seen in England, although few now
were privately owned, the upkeep alone forcing
many to sell, owing to their dwindling fortunes and
the estates were either sold off piecemeal, or snapped
up intact by oil sheiks.

The grounds were beautifully landscaped, and
pleasing to the eye. The velvet green lawns were another reminder of home to Beth, but the brilliance of
the flowers and the calendar date brought sharp re-
minders that this was a tropical world. As they
neared the house there were signs of great activity;

long trestle tables had been placed on the lawn directly fronting the house and food had been arranged on snowy white cloths. Noticing the amount catered for, it occurred to Beth that at least half the island's inhabitants were expected, and she said as much to Janice, who chuckled, and replied, 'No, dear, this is purely a get-together for the residents, plus a few extra guests that Gavin is entertaining.'

There were small groups of people standing by the open french windows, engrossed in conversation, and Janice said in a low voice, 'Oh, bother, I had hoped to be the first. Will you mind, dear, if I introduce you to a few of them and leave you to it? I promise to be back as soon as I can, but I must make sure all's well with the catering firm.'

Beth would have preferred to have gone with her sister, but had no wish to get in her way, so she answered a trifle untruthfully, 'Not a bit—but don't be long,' she added quickly.

The conversation ceased as Janice and Beth approached the first group, and Beth noticed with a spurt of pride how popular Janice was, for she was hailed from all sides as more people joined the gathering, and after introducing Beth to a few of them she excused herself and slipped away, leaving a rather nervous Beth to cope with what seemed an enormous amount of strangers.

Before long, however, she found herself chatting amicably with all and sundry. To her surprise, many of the residents had ties with England, and were hungry for news of what they still called 'home'. Quite a few, Beth found, were a little behind with the times, and one little old lady enquired whether they were still receiving food parcels, which made Beth wonder if her figure had prompted this enquiry, but she managed to answer soberly enough. This was the start of a series of questions from the same good lady. Did Beth know of a village in Surrey called Meresworth, or at least, she thought it was called Meresworth, or it might be Meresdale. Her sister had lived there for some years, and was quite well known there as a matter of fact. To this query Beth had to plead ignorance. She had never even heard of the village, let alone the sister, and she felt a spurt of relief at Janice's reappearance at this point.

When they had moved away, Beth couldn't resist relating the food parcel query to Janice, who laughed and said, 'It shows just how much interest they really take in what they fondly call home. We do get the London papers here, you know, a day or so later, it's true, but nevertheless, if they really wanted to, they could keep abreast with the times.' Her eyes rested on the vista of gardens gently sloping away from where they stood. 'I guess it's the climate, but one gets the definite feeling that time has stood still here. There's none of the bustle, you see, that you find in the big cities. I don't think I could ever go back—at least, not to stay.' She smiled at Beth. 'Soon you'll feel the same—it's catching, you know.'

But Beth did know, for she had already felt the call of the island; the horrible feeling of being slowly asphyxiated by Nicholas's personality had now receded into the past, even though it was such a recent past.

Janice's gaze went back to the guests. 'I did want

you to meet ...' her look centred on a small group a little way away. 'Oh, there he is; come along, Beth, you'll like Mr Fisher, he dabbles in watercolours. He's quite good, too, but a bit shy about talking about his work. Let's try and draw him out. He doesn't really like these occasions, and only comes to please Gavin.'

Mr Fisher turned out to be a middle-aged man Beth had seen hovering on the fringe of a few groups during her earlier introductory tour, looking as if he wished he were elsewhere, and she had felt a kindred sympathy with him. Of the few men that were there, all wore correct wear for such a function in spite of the warmth of the day, and all appeared to be reasonably comfortable, except for the man Janice was now taking her to meet. His continual jerking at his collar said more than words, and Beth knew he felt as comfortable in his collar and tie as she did in her long-sleeved dress.

As Janice had said, he was shy, but it did not take long for Beth to put him at his ease, particularly when he found he had a fellow artist beside him, and was soon advising her on the local beauty spots, promising to let her have a map some time of where they were to be located. On this pronouncement Janice's brows went up, but she held her tongue, suffice to say that Beth had scored a hit, for he was not usually so forthcoming.

They were in the middle of an interesting discussion on the merits of watercolour as against oils, when he broke off in the middle of a sentence and hurriedly excusing himself, drifted off towards another group, leaving a perplexed Beth staring after him.

Beside her, Janice gave a low chuckle, and said

softly, 'He's had to take evasive action—look ahead!'

Beth looked, and saw a matronly woman bearing down on them with a sense of purpose in her stride. Her bright pink hat, with a red rose dead centre, made Beth wince. 'Mrs Winton,' supplied Janice still in a soft voice. 'She's always trying to get Mr Fisher to join the local bridge set. He made the dreadful mistake of telling her he played, but he hates it. As long as he can keep out of her way, he's safe.'

'Ah, Janice!' exclaimed the woman as she reached them, her eyes focusing on Mr Fisher's retreating back. 'I see I've missed Mr Fisher again.' Her brown eyes held a positive gleam in them she added, 'I'll make it one day, you see if I don't!' Her attention then focused on Beth. 'So this is your sister, is it? Do you play bridge?' she asked hopefully.

Beth had the same feelings about bridge as Mr Fisher had, and happily disappointed her.

'Oh, well, we can't win them all, can we?' she remarked philosophically. 'I thought I saw Amanda somewhere——' She looked round vaguely, then spotting another quarry, excused herself and sailed off.

'She's all right really,' remarked Janice, smiling. 'Just a bit overpowering. I think Mr Fisher suspects a deeper motive in her pursuit of him. I'm afraid the women outnumber the men here, and we have quite a few of what's known as "merry widows", Mrs Winton being one of them. Mr Fisher's a bachelor, and intends to stay that way. Oh, here's Gavin,' she exclaimed brightly.

Beth turned in the direction Janice was looking,

and her welcoming smile froze on her face as she saw the person striding towards them. It couldn't be! she told herself frantically, but Janice ought to know her own boss! She swallowed; there was no mistaking that height, let alone the blond hair, blanched almost white by the sun. Janice's boss and Beth's 'Admiral' were one and the same person! A number of thoughts flashed through Beth's mind at that moment, and none of them what one would call comforting. For instance, what time was the next flight back to dear old Blighty? Janice was going to be very disappointed, but not half so miserable as she would be if her John lost his job!

By now he was almost upon them, and Beth, trying to stave off the inevitable, pushed her straw hat right over her face into a position from which she could just peep out, but leaving her features in shadow. She now wore high heels, and she fervently hoped this would help the camouflage act. Janice dug her in the ribs. 'Do something about your hat,' she muttered in an aside, as the man approaching them thrust out his hand in welcome.

As Beth's small hand was lost in the large one offered, she listened in a kind of daze as he welcomed her to the island, and hoped he would put her refusal to look him in the eye—what part of her face, that was, that he could see—down to embarrassment. By the polite way he enquired about her journey out, she knew he had not recognised her, but had a sneaking feeling he was working on it, as she felt the gaze of those searching blue eyes of his upon her.

Help came for Beth in the shape of a gorgeous redhead, who demanded his attention towards some new arrivals and practically dragged him off to meet them. Beth didn't know who the girl was, but she was devoutly grateful to her.

'What's with the hat?' demanded Janice, giving her an odd look.

'I've a headache,' lied Beth quickly. 'I'm not used to the sun yet.' Then to change the conversation, she asked hurriedly, 'Who's the lovely redhead?'

The question had the desired effect, and took Janice's mind off the subject of the hat, which relieved Beth, for it wasn't easy trying to fool Janice, who just happened to know her a little too well. 'That is Amanda, Mrs Winton's daughter,' answered Janice, glancing at her watch. 'Countdown in five minutes from now,' she said airily.

'I beg your pardon?' said Beth.

'Time to pry him loose, if he hasn't managed to do it himself,' Janice explained drily.

Beth stared at her. 'You mean he doesn't like her?' she asked, intrigued, and from under the brim of her hat she studied the tall man, now at a safe distance, and went on to take in the slim girl clinging to his arm; and clinging was the only way one could put it, she thought. Nevertheless, who in their right minds would pass up a beauty like that? She wore a twenties-style tea-gown, with floating chiffon skirt, and large picture hat to match. Tall for a woman—Beth judged her to be around the five feet ten mark—she was still a few inches shorter than the man beside her. All in all, they made a splendid pair, she thought, and her sympathies were with the girl entirely for judging by the way she kept gazing up adoringly at Gavin Patterson, she was way past redemption. Beth felt a fresh surge of dislike towards the man who had plagued her existence so early on her visit to the island. He would take such adoration as his due, much as Nicholas had done in their early association, although, she reminded herself, he had wanted to marry her, while this autocratic character was just playing the field. However, she kept these thoughts to herself. Janice only knew him as a kind boss, and Beth fervently hoped she could keep things that way.

'It's not so much a question of not liking her,' went on Janice. 'He has to be on the defensive, like Mr Fisher. She's like her mother, a very determined young woman, and like her mother, she thinks she'd make an excellent wife for Gavin. Gavin, however, thinks otherwise.'

As if feeling their eyes on him, he suddenly turned and looked straight back at them, and Beth hastily averted her eyes, terrified she had been recognised, but Janice's next words made her relax. 'To the rescue,' she said, giving Beth a swift grin as she made her way towards the group.

Beth breathed a sigh of relief, so it was Janice he was looking at, hoping to spur her into action, and like the well-trained secretary she was, she was answering the silent call. Beth wondered what she would say to break up the gathering, as she watched her sister go up to Gavin Patterson and say something to him, and the pair of them shortly headed back towards the house. Beth, glancing back at Amanda, caught a malicious look directed at Janice's back;

gone was the soft fluffy little girl act she had adopted
in Gavin Patterson's presence, she was now, as Janice
had said, a woman with a purpose. Silently, Beth
thanked the powers that be for John. Janice would
be safe from such a woman, for there was no romantic
involvement with her boss.

Left on her own, Beth accepted a cold drink from
the tray a resplendent Johnny was carrying around.
He was correctly dressed as a waiter, and it took a
minute or so for Beth to recognise him, and catching
her eye, he gave her his flashing grin, then suddenly
recollecting where he was, and his responsibilities,
he straightened up, and adopting a sober expression,
carried on with his duties.

Alone again, Beth felt a wave of sadness pass over
her. It could have been so wonderful being back with
Janice again, but there was little hope now that the
arrangement would work out. As for Janice's aspirations of her following in her footsteps—well, that
scheme was out of the question for a start. No, she
mused, she would just have to find a good excuse for
going back to England, and what that would be she
simply hadn't a clue as yet. She needed time to think,
time to work out how she could go back and somehow keep out of Nicholas's way. She bit her lower lip;
there were other places she could go—say Australia.
She could tell Janice she wanted to travel. She sighed
heavily; might as well tell her the truth and be done
with it, then she would be able to help her keep out of
the range of Gavin Patterson's eagle eye, and no
harm would be done. But not now, she thought as she
saw Janice heading her way; later, when they were

alone, just in case Janice had any conscientious notion of dragging her off to apologise to her boss.

'How did you manage that?' she asked her curiously as she joined her.

'Long-distance call,' Janice replied airily.

'That you took on the terrace, a few yards away from her, with no telephone in sight? Couldn't you do better than that?' demanded Beth, grinning.

Janice chuckled. 'It's not so crazy as it sounds. All calls are referred to me, and I decide whether they're important enough for Gavin's attention. When Amanda starts her clinging act, all calls are important!'

In spite of the ferocious look Amanda had sent Janice earlier, Beth felt a little sorry for her. Gavin Patterson, it appeared, was no easy prey to stalk.

The girls drifted off in search of food then, and the rest of the time was spent in idle conversation with various people whom Beth was introduced to. Had it not been for the likelihood of coming into contact with Janice's boss again, Beth would have enjoyed herself, but she was constantly on the lookout for the tall figure, and kept her straw hat tilted over her face to avoid the possibility of suddenly finding him in front of her.

When the guests started taking their leave shortly after five, she knew a sense of relief that she had managed to stay out of her host's orbit, and thus out of trouble. She had had one or two nasty moments when she had caught sight of him in the distance talking to some of the guests, but he was obviously keeping on the move, not risking being pinned down by the de-

termined Amanda again. Soon the terrace was deserted, and a small army of servants proceeded with
the job of clearing the buffet section. Janice, telling
Beth she wouldn't be long, slipped into the house for
a final check on everything, and Beth began walking slowly back the way they had come, thinking it
wouldn't be good policy to hang around too near the
house. She had been extremely fortunate so far, and
didn't believe in pushing her luck!

Stopping to admire a brilliant patch of shrubbery,
and studying the bright orange blooms with the eye
of an artist, she wondered how she could reproduce
their glowing translucent beauty in oils, then started
when a voice close at hand said silkily, 'Might I
recommend the swimming pool to you, Miss Knight?'

Beth straightened and swallowed hard. She didn't
have to turn round to recognise the owner of that
voice. It was no use, she thought, he had recognised
her. She swung round and looked straight at him.
He stood watching her with one eyebrow raised, and
seemed to be waiting for something, and Beth didn't
need a glass ball to know what.

'I do apologise,' she began lamely. 'It seemed a
good idea at the time ...' Heavens, she shouldn't have
said that, she thought, as she watched a certain glint
appear in his eyes.

'No doubt,' he replied ironically, 'but I shouldn't
hang around there in the near future, if I were you—
or take to swimming in the harbour.' His eyes pierced
her.

'Oh, I ... er ... no, of course not——' She broke
off confusedly, willing herself not to lose her temper,

or all would be lost. She tried another approach and gave him what she hoped was an apologetic smile. 'I didn't know about the rules, you see,' she explained blandly. 'It won't happen again.'

He didn't have to answer that, his expression told her what he was thinking. Beth felt herself flushing under his relentless gaze, and as there was nothing else to be said, she frigidly excused herself and marched off in the direction of the cottage. Janice would just have to catch her up, she told herself, after, no doubt, a few well-chosen words from her boss on the behaviour of her sister! In all probability, Beth thought scathingly, she would be asked to try and exercise some control over her, for it was obvious that he thought her a troublemaker, and it went without saying that he would be on the lookout for her in the future!

Janice caught Beth up just before she got to the cottage, and Beth steeled herself in readiness for the lecture she was sure was about to be delivered. To her surprise, however, her sister chatted on about the party, and what a success it had been, and what did Beth think about her boss—quite dishy, wasn't he? This question nearly proved her undoing, for she was about to categorically state her feelings on this point, when it occurred to her that Janice knew nothing about her two brushes with the autocratic owner of the island. It took a little while for this extraordinary fact to sink in, and finding it hard to believe, she stole a surreptitious peep at Janice who was still expounding on the merits of her boss.

'Of course,' she went on in blissful ignorance,

'we'll wait a little while before broaching the subject of you taking over from me.' She grinned at the now very wary Beth. 'Just drop a few hints here and there about you seeking work on the island. If I know Gavin, he'll take it from there. He knows the wedding's not all that far away, and when I tell him John's feelings about my giving up work—well, that will be that!'

Beth swallowed and tried to look grateful; somehow she had to disabuse Janice of this extremely unlikely idea. 'I'm not sure that I'll like the job,' she said quickly. 'It might suit you, dear, but I've a mind to branch out for myself.'

Janice, in the act of walking through the door, stopped dead and stared at Beth. 'Branch out?' she echoed with some incredulity in her voice. 'For goodness' sake, Beth—in what? You can't mean to pass up the best job on the island.' There was a hint of pleading in her voice that made Beth wince inwardly.

'Well,' answered Beth, desperately searching for the right words, without telling the truth, that was, 'your Mr Patterson didn't strike me as the kind of person to just take anyone on. I mean,' she went on a little more firmly, 'he mightn't take to me, and we'd both be in a rotten position then, wouldn't we? And,' she added for good measure, 'I haven't had as much experience as you've had. I worked for Nicholas, remember? I can take dictation and I can type, but that's as far as it goes, and there's much more than that involved here, isn't there? I haven't a clue about arranging parties—or hostessing either, come to that,' she ended lamely, her heart sinking as she watched

Janice's grin widen, telling her that she was on a losing streak.

'Neither did I, my pet,' answered Janice blithely. 'And if I can do it, I'm sure you can, too,' then seeing Beth's worried frown, and mistaking the reason, she added soothingly, 'Don't worry, dear, we've plenty of time, things will work out, you'll see.'

As Beth followed her into the house, she wished miserably that she had put Janice into the picture right from the start of her unfortunate clashes with her boss, for if she had, she wouldn't now be in this mess. If Gavin Patterson had decided to say nothing, then there was no point in worrying Janice about it now. It appeared he had decided to give her the benefit of the doubt, although Beth found this hard to believe, particularly when she recalled the look he had given her a short while ago. It wasn't so much what he had actually said, but what he had implied. Perhaps he had persuaded himself that Janice couldn't be held responsible for her troublesome sister.

She sighed. It did look as if he were really fond of her, and instead of easing things, made things worse from her point of view. There would, for instance, be an awful lot of explaining to do in the not too distant future, unless she could somehow convince Janice of her unsuitability for the post she was hoping she would take. It was either that, or prove to her boss that she wasn't the hoyden he thought her. She brightened visibly; if she could keep out of his way until things smoothed down again—well, who knows?

CHAPTER SIX

By the time John had arrived that evening, ostensibly to spend the evening with the two girls, Beth had talked herself into a happier frame of mind. With the threat of having to make an abrupt departure to unknown pastures no longer hanging over her, she began to feel quite optimistic about the future. Not that she could see herself taking over from Janice; there was just no way that either she or Gavin Patterson could compromise on this. Eventually Janice would see this, and as long as Beth stayed within visiting distance, Janice would have no cause to complain.

Now as she sat and watched Janice and John as they argued lightheartedly over the redecorating of the house they had settled for, Beth felt a surge of thankfulness for her sister. John was so obviously right for her; the fact that he adored her was touchingly patent in each glance he sent her. Although the conversation was general, and much of it directed towards her, Beth felt rather de trop, and as soon as she was able, she pleaded tiredness and went to her room.

Her ablutions over, she lay down on the bed and thought what she would do the next day. There was the harbour scene, of course, and that, in Beth's mind, was the first priority. She longed to begin work then and there, but would have to wait until she had enough sketches to complete the picture, the first of which she would get tomorrow. She sighed happily at the thought; to be able to paint again was an added bonus to her new-found freedom. No matter what, Beth knew she would never ever again lose this precious freedom. Marriage would suit Janice, but not her; if anyone was cut out to be a spinster, she was! It had only taken one near miss to prove this to her, and she planned to be two steps ahead of getting embroiled again with another man.

Her thoughts roamed on; Gavin Patterson was another Nicholas. It was partly the reason why she had acted as she had at the Falcon although she hadn't realised it at the time. A slow grin crept over her face as she recalled the immense satisfaction she had felt as she had 'persuaded' him to try the pool. What had he said? She frowned in memory, then she had it. He had advised her not to 'hang around the pool'. In other words, she thought, she was likely to receive the same treatment!

'Thanks for the warning,' she murmured drowsily, before she fell asleep.

The following morning, Beth remembered to ask Janice if Johnny could be spared to run her down to the town again, and told her about her plans to sketch the harbour. Janice agreed that it should make a fine picture, and said she would arrange for Johnny to pick her up later that morning, and suggested Beth take sandwiches with her, as knowing her of old, she knew she wouldn't be watching the time and would not be back for lunch.

When Beth collected the lunch pack later from Mabel, she had to smile at the amount of food Mabel had provided for her. 'I'm only out for the day, Mabel,' she said, smiling, 'not on safari, you know.'

Mabel replied in her soft sing-song voice, 'Maybe you get hungry, Miss Beth, then you tuck in good.'

Not wanting to upset her, Beth put the lunch pack into her satchel. There was barely room for such a bulky package, but somehow she squeezed it in alongside her sketch pads and box of pencils, even though she knew she wouldn't get through a quarter of the contents of the food parcel. Gulls, of course, could help her out, for she would have hated to have taken most of it back.

By the time Johnny turned up Beth was ready for her day out. She still felt a little guilty at using Gavin Patterson's private transport, and when they arrived at the harbour she suggested she catch the bus back. There was, according to Mabel, a bus at six o'clock, she told Johnny, and she would be on that.

It was plain that Johnny did not think this would be a good idea. The bus, he explained, was used solely by the locals, and apt to get a mite crowded. In other words, there was a distinct possibility of finding herself sitting on top of the bus—and this, gathered Beth, was hardly suitable transport for Janice's sister! As it was also plain that Johnny considered himself responsible for her well-being, Beth conceded on this point, and agreed to be picked up at six by an extremely relieved Johnny.

In her jeans and cotton top, plus sandals, Beth looked much as any tourist would, except that she did not have the inevitable camera slung round her neck, and carried a satchel instead of one of the gay plastic carrier bags many visitors favoured. Apart from these differences, she felt much like a tourist, and looked forward with great expectation to what the island had to offer. This, she thought as her eyes took in the scene before her, was only a small part of the vast wealth of material to be gathered and brought to life under the strokes of a brush; and when she thought of the places Mr Fisher had mentioned, she gave a sigh of sheer contentment. Life was wonderful!

A few minutes later she sat perched on the harbour wall, sorting out her drawing implements. From this position she had an uninterrupted view of the entrance to the harbour, and a guarantee that no one would be peering over her shoulder, a thing she hated. Many artists had learnt to take it in their stride, but she hadn't. The trouble was, they not only looked but commented as well, and were rather apt to discuss different techniques; all of which might be very interesting to them, but was hardly helpful when one was concentrating on a particular composition.

When she was ready, Beth studied her subject with narrowed eyes, and had her pencil poised in her hand ready for action. Gradually, the small area was being invaded by the islanders, all intent on arranging their wares for sale, hoping to persuade the tourists to part with some of their spending money.

One woman in particular caught Beth's eye, and in fascinated absorption, she watched as she placed her huge basket of flowers on the ground, then settled down beside them. Her bright red dress, contrasted vividly with the gorgeous pastel colours of the

flowers spilling out of her basket; but it was her hat
that compelled attention. Made of straw, it was quite
the largest hat Beth had ever seen. Its decorations,
plastic flowers and several bunches of black plastic
grapes, that emerged from all points as if they were
actually growing there, was worth a study in itself,
thought a delighted Beth, as her hand moved swiftly
over the pad in front of her.

Glancing up a few moments later, she saw with
exasperated amusement that her model, discovering
Beth's preoccupation with her, had started to pose in
a most unnatural way. A few early customers, however, soon put an end to this, and Beth was able
to continue work.

Time passed, and she happily sketched on. Several
fishermen had drifted past carrying loaded panniers
of fish. The catch had been a good one, as was evident
by their high spirits and gay laughter.

The tourists had moved on, and the flower woman,
now free of encumbrances, adopted her pose again.
The fishermen, not slow in catching on, saw no
reason why they should not be included in the picture, and when Beth next glanced up she found herself confronted by what appeared to be a small crowd
of willing models.

A slightly dismayed Beth had to abandon her
original sketch in using the flower woman as her
centrepiece, and with stoic complacency decided to
include her 'extras' in the picture. She wouldn't get
such a chance again, she told herself, and they were
only preliminary sketches.

Unfortunately it didn't stop at that, for a second
batch of fishermen arrived on the scene, and like their

compatriots, became extremely interested in the proceedings. Soon Beth's flower woman was completely eclipsed by her additional extras. A little belatedly, Beth realised she ought to have called a halt on the first appearance of the fishermen, for now things had got slightly out of hand. What had once been a peaceful harbour scene had turned into Petticoat Lane on a Sunday.

Suddenly the place was filled with tourists, and the fishermen, making full use of the occasion, started selling their catch. Somebody produced a guitar, and this sparked off an impromptu dance from the irrepressible islanders, and before long a few of the tourists joined in. An amused Beth closed her sketchbook; it was impossible now to go on working. All interest in the picture was now gone, the opportunity of selling their wares overriding all else, and Beth was more than a little relieved.

Everyone, it appeared, was thoroughly enjoying themselves, and as Beth's eyes roamed over the crowd she caught sight of her flower woman determinedly making her way towards her. Her passage had not been an easy one, if the rakish angle of her enormous straw hat was anything to go by. As her basket was empty, she had obviously done well, and Beth assumed she was on her way to finish her elected role as her original model—not that Beth could see that there was any hope of continuing her earlier theme.

'What on earth is going on?' demanded an irate voice that rang imperiously over the heads of the crowd.

Beth's fingers froze on her sketchbook, and she

wondered if she could somehow lose herself in the
crowd, but she wasn't quick enough. As if by magic,
what had once been a thriving market place reverted
back to peace. Only a few interested spectators remained, one of whom was the faithful flower seller,
who stationed herself by Beth's side, not only claiming her acquaintance but giving Beth no chance of
assuming an innocent façade in the face of the earlier
bedlamic proceedings. Of the fishermen there was no
sign; it was as if the earth had opened up and swallowed them.

Noticing the way Gavin Patterson's eyes rested on
her, Beth knew she would be blamed for the whole
affair. The mere fact that she was in the vicinity was
enough for him, she thought miserably, and she was
not at all surprised when he acknowledged her presence with a drawled, 'Good morning, Miss Knight,' in
a voice that said she hadn't heard the last of this. He
then turned to his companions, whom Beth presumed
to be some of those V.I.P.s that Janice had mentioned, since he was taking the trouble to personally
escort them. 'This part of the harbour dates back
to the sixteenth century.' Beth felt his eyes rest on
her again as he continued. 'Normally, this is a quaint
and peaceful place,' he glared at Beth again, 'and
we try to keep it so . . .'

They had now moved on towards the harbour entrance, and Beth took the chance of making herself
scarce. She would not have risked going near the
harbour had she known he was liable to put in an
appearance. It wasn't such a large place after all,
she thought, although she had grave doubts that any

place would be large enough to prevent her colliding
with that man! Beth had not been a great believer in
fate until now, but she had a nasty suspicion that
Gavin Patterson was going to play a major role in
her future on the island—which looked like being a
very short future indeed.

Making certain that the autocratic owner of the
island was safely out of her vicinity, Beth found a
secluded spot below the harbour steps and had her
lunch. What appetite she might have worked up had
now gone, and by the time she had struggled with
one crisp, salad-filled roll, she was replete, and the
gulls fought for the rest of the lunch. Only the hot
coffee received full justice, and she was grateful for
it.

Like an outflanked general, Beth had to think carefully about her next move. She couldn't risk attempting to get any more harbour sketches that day—indeed, any day, not if what had happened was liable to
be repeated! Getting out her sketchbook, she studied
her morning's handiwork. Considering everything,
she was quite pleased with what she had got. Enough
to make a start anyway, she thought happily, so her
day hadn't been entirely ruined.

There only remained the question of how to fill the
rest of the day until Johnny was due to pick her up.
She looked at her watch; as it was only just past
midday, that meant a long afternoon to contend with.
She stared moodily out to sea, thinking how happy
she had been that morning, and of the wonderful
pictures she was going to paint of this island of paradise. Her mouth twisted wryly at the thought. Of

course there just had to be one fly in the ointment, she sighed inwardly, and what a fly! With anyone else it might have been possible to make amends, an apology even—but not with this haughty individual! Apologies were things he never listened to, as Beth had good cause to know.

Her eyes rested on a distant sailing boat with bright orange sails. Nicholas wasn't the only one who had tried to smother the artistic streak in her; Gavin Patterson, it seemed, was taking up where Nicholas had left off. Her forehead wrinkled in thought; surely there was somewhere she could go without running into the wretched man? After a second's thought her brow cleared. Janice, of course! Being such a good secretary she would be bound to know her boss's movements. All she needed was an itinerary of his working day, and her problem was solved.

Her frown was soon replaced at the thought of just how she was going to get this information from Janice without certain facts coming to light. Her small chin squared; she would tell the truth—the whole truth; it was the only way to gain Janice's co-opera-tion—and not only her co-operation, she thought, unable to suppress a smile—she might well be horri-fied enough to forbid her to leave the cottage grounds!

Her amusement soon faded as she visualised Janice's reaction to the news that her boss and her sister didn't exactly see eye to eye—and that was putting it mildly! There was only one redeeming factor about the whole wretched business, and that was that she would no longer be considered a candi-

These three exciting Harlequin romance novels are yours FREE

Lucy Gillen sets this romance among the wild lochs and mountains of Scotland. **"A Wife for Andrew"** is a touching account of a young governess, her dour yet compassionate employer and the children in his care who suffer at the hands of a jealous woman.

In Betty Neels' **"Fate Is Remarkable"** Sarah's "marriage of convenience" is dramatically altered. Just as Sarah was getting ready to tell Hugo that she'd fallen in love with him, a lovely woman from Hugo's past shows up…

In **"Bitter Masquerade"** by Margery Hilton, mistaken identity is the basis of Virginia Dalmont's marriage. When Brent mistook her for her twin sister Anna, she wondered if her love was strong enough to make up for the deceit…

I n the pages of your FREE GIFT Romance Treasury Novels you'll get to know warm, true-to-life people, and you'll discover the special kind of miracle that love can be. The stories will sweep you to distant lands where intrigue, adventure and the destiny of many lives will thrill you. All three full-length novels are exquisitely bound together in a single hardcover volume that's your FREE GIFT, to introduce you to Harlequin Romance Treasury!

The most beautiful books you've ever seen!

Cover and spine of all volumes feature distinctive gilt designs. And an elegant bound-in ribbon bookmark adds a lovely feminine touch. No detail has been overlooked to make Romance Treasury books as beautiful and lasting as the stories they contain. What a delightful way to enjoy the very best and most popular Harlequin Romances again and again!

A whole world of romantic adventures!

If you are delighted with your FREE GIFT volume, you may, if you wish, receive a new Harlequin Romance Treasury volume as published every five weeks or so—delivered right to your door! The beautiful FREE GIFT VOLUME is yours to keep with no obligation to buy anything.

Fill out the coupon today to get your FREE GIFT VOLUME.

Three exciting, full-length Romance novels, in one beautiful book!

FREE GIFT!

Dear Ellen Windsor:

Name

Address

City   State   Zip

Romance Treasury

Detach and Mail Post Paid Card **TODAY!**

date for the job Janice had lined up for her—not even the most fanatical optimist could hope for that!

Beth spent the rest of that day wandering around the hills at the back of the harbour, only taking her sketchbook out when there was no likelihood of interruption, which was not often. The places she chose would be deserted one moment, but bunches of tourists would come into sight before she could really get to grips with the view she was attempting to sketch—and never being certain that one of the groups wouldn't contain her public enemy number one, she would hastily close her book and move on.

It was with a kind of relief that she set about the task of disillusioning Janice and bringing her up to date with recent events, asking casually when they had had their evening meal and were now relaxing over their coffee if she remembered the camera episode.

Janice's vague, 'Yes, dear,' told Beth she hadn't entirely got her attention, and that she was with her John, in spirit, if not in body! but she persevered anyway. 'Er ... it fell in the harbour, you know,' she continued, and went on to fill in a few very relevant facts that she had left out previously.

She was gratified a little while later to note that she now had Janice's full attention—not to say shocked reaction! In fact she had it the moment Gavin Patterson's name was mentioned.

'You mean to tell me,' said Janice in a weak voice, 'that you were swimming in the harbour, and Gavin hauled you out?'

Beth nodded, trying unsuccessfully to keep the

spark of amusement out of her eyes at the thought of
the next disclosure, particularly on seeing the result
of this very mild confession, and rather unfairly she
did not give her sister time to assimilate the news
before giving her another shock, launching straight
away into the swimming pool fiasco and subsequent
events.

Janice's brown eyes opened to their full capacity.
'You pushed him into the pool?' she squeaked.

'I didn't see any point in worrying you about it
before,' said Beth defensively, adding quickly, 'I
thought he was just some official trying to throw his
weight about.'

'Throwing his weight about,' repeated Janice in a
daze, then stared at Beth. 'You say he recognised you
at the garden party?' she asked, and frowned. 'He
didn't say anything to me,' she muttered half to herself.

'No,' answered Beth thoughtfully, 'I did wonder
about that. I was expecting him to ask you to try
and keep me in order.' The twinkle in her eye belied
her words, and for the first time since the confessions,
Janice's sense of humour came to the rescue and she
grinned at Beth.

'Of course he would do no such thing! He wouldn't
hold me responsible for my madcap sister—others
might, but he wouldn't.' There was silence for a
moment or so while Janice took stock of the situation,
and it no longer amused her. She sighed. 'Oh, dear, I
did so want you two to get along. I hoped you would
impress him.'

Beth chuckled and received an injured look from

her sister. 'But I did impress him, dear,' she said in mock solemnity. 'Only it wasn't what you had in mind.'

'Congratulations, said Janice dryly. 'Now I know you're back to normal.' Her eyes went upwards in a glance of hopeless resignation. 'Just like old times, isn't it?'

A thought suddenly struck her and she stared at Beth. 'So that's why you hid under the hat! You hoped he wouldn't recognise you.' She nodded to herself. 'That's one little mystery solved. The headache excuse didn't fool me one bit.' She lapsed into a silence that made Beth a little discomfited and want to defend herself.

'He reminds me of Nicholas,' she said abruptly.

Janice broke out of her reverie with a jolt. 'Nicholas?' she said incredulously. 'Oh, Beth, he's not a bit like him! You've got an obsession about that man—and no wonder; but for goodness' sake don't let the past sway your judgment on Gavin. For instance, Gavin has a sense of humour, and Nicholas hadn't, had he?' she demanded.

If Gavin Patterson had a sense of humour, Beth had yet to see it. It didn't stretch far, if he had, she thought, recalling the harbour scene that morning. It was only innocent fun anyway, and certainly didn't warrant such a crushing reception. He couldn't have been more infuriated had he witnessed a striptease act! Beth's mouth quirked at the corners, and she was tempted to relate these thoughts to Janice, but one look at her sister's worried expression decided her against this. She just wouldn't see the funny side of it right now. 'So you see, dear,' she said, deciding to ignore her last question, and pressing home her advantage. 'I think it might be wise if I kept out of his way for a while, don't you—at least,' she added quickly, 'until things have quietened down a bit. If you would let me know where he's likely to turn up, then I'll give the area a wide berth.' She looked hopefully at Janice.

'I do see your point,' agreed Janice resignedly, then sighed. 'Perhaps when things settle down ...' She lapsed into silence.

Beth had a sneaking suspicion that Janice hadn't given up the hope of her replacing her as Gavin Patterson's secretary, and she knew there was nothing she could do to dissuade her. If she could still nurse such a hope in spite of the recent revelations, then Beth would just be wasting her breath.

Time only would prove her point, and she felt a little guilty that she couldn't make Janice's dream come true. With anyone else it might have been possible, but as it was, the whole idea was a positive nonstarter! Beth only hoped that she wouldn't attempt to drop any of the hopeful hints that she had earlier intimated that she would do. They would not only fall on deaf ears, but very probably give her pompous boss apoplexy!

CHAPTER SEVEN

THE following week was a blissful one for Beth. Armed with Gavin Patterson's movements, she was able to plan her day with reasonable confidence that all would be well.

Mr Fisher had lived up to his promise and provided her with a map on which he had marked the island's beauty spots. The only problem was transport; some of the places were on the other side of the island, and Beth was reluctant to ask for transport more than twice a week.

After spending two days in or around the cottage, taking sketches of the building and surrounding fauna, a slightly puzzled Janice asked why she hadn't followed up Mr Fisher's suggestions for possible pictures. A little adroit questioning soon revealed Beth's reluctance to ask for Johnny's assistance.

'Honestly, Beth, it's all right,' insisted Janice, 'Gavin doesn't need Johnny in the chauffeur line, he drives himself everywhere, always has done. Besides, I told Johnny you'd be needing transport each day. I think he's afraid you've lost faith in him as a driver!' she said, smiling.

Beth smiled back at her, then sobered; she couldn't tell Janice that she had no wish to be under any sort of obligation to her boss. There was always the possibility that he might need Johnny for something or other, and would be furious when he discovered the reason for his absence. Things were going so well, Beth wanted to keep it like that; there was no such thing as taking a chance where that man was concerned. However, she kept these thoughts to herself, for there had been no mention since of her earlier exploits in that direction, and while she was grateful, Beth knew Janice preferred to keep her head in the sand like the proverbial ostrich, thus paving the way for the realisation of her dreams. Dreams that Beth knew hadn't a hope of coming true; she also knew that she had to avoid any future confrontation with her boss—for her sake and her sister's.

Janice, seeing that Beth was not entirely happy over the question of asking for transport, came up with a brilliant idea. 'You can learn to drive!' she announced triumphantly. 'Now why didn't I think of that before? Johnny can teach you,' she told the slightly stunned Beth. 'And,' she added gaily, warming to her subject, 'John's got an old banger you can use when you've learnt.' She looked at Beth. 'How's that?' she said happily. 'Just imagine, you can sling your gear in the back and just take off any time you like!'

Beth had to admit the idea was tempting. To be able to take off whenever she wanted to, and better still, be able to put a fair distance between herself and that man, should he suddenly appear on the scene, without having to wait for Johnny to collect her. The more Beth thought about it, the more the idea appealed to her. The island was an ideal place for her to learn—no traffic as such, for Johnny would

teach her to drive in the estate grounds, according
to Janice, so there was no problem there.

It was agreed that the lessons would begin the next
day, and Beth, now fired with enthusiasm, was eager
to start. It was not the first time she had had lessons,
for she had previously attempted to learn soon after
Janice had left. The fact that she was in no state at
that time to concentrate on anything was soon evident
by her complete failure to grasp even the simple
mechanics of driving. But this time things were different, she told herself confidently, while she waited
for Johnny to appear. For one thing, the car Johnny
used to take her to the town had automatic gears. It
was just a question of pressing a button, she thought
happily.

A thought then struck her that she had to be very
careful not to do any damage to the car, since it was
by no means a cheap model. Beth didn't know the
make as it was an American car, but she did know
it would be beyond Johnny's price bracket—and that
meant that it belonged to Gavin Patterson. This
thought gave her a few qualms, and it was as well
that Johnny turned up at that particular moment,
with a decidedly battered model that looked as if it
had already done the rounds of the crash circuit! But
Beth didn't care; this car would be his own property,
for by no stretch of the imagination could she see the
haughty Gavin Patterson owning to such a wreck!

When settled in the driving seat, Beth was a little
disappointed to find no automatic gearing system,
but plain ordinary gears—however, this was of little
account considering that she was in no danger of

doing anything to the car that hadn't been done before!

The ever cheerful Johnny gave her more confidence, taking time and trouble to explain what this or that lever did, and when she crashed the gears would just grin at her, and make her take her time.

That Beth had some knowledge owing to her earlier attempts was helpful, and on the first day great strides were made. Her confidence grew, Johnny's did too, and this proved to be their undoing, for disaster struck on the second day.

Having been lulled into a state of confident belief in her ability to grasp each instruction and carry it out faultlessly, Johnny became a little ambitious on her behalf and set her reversing up a steep slope. This was carried out neatly with Beth managing to keep the car on a steady course. A delighted Johnny suggested they do it just once more, which was unfortunate, for in her eagerness to take the car back down the hill again for the next attempt, Beth forgot to change the gears.

An amazed Beth and a frantic Johnny found themselves propelled back at what appeared to be around thirty miles an hour. By the time Beth had found the foot brake, it was too late. There was a jerk, then a grinding crunch as they came up against a solid object.

Beth sat recovering her breath, vaguely aware of the tinkling sound of broken glass coming from the car they had run into. A second later she was gazing into the furious eyes of Gavin Patterson, who looked fit to commit murder—hers, that was. She glanced quickly at Johnny, who seemed to have shrunk into his seat, and received the distinct impression that had there been room under the car seat, he would have got there somehow.

'And what idiot suggested you should get within ten feet of the wheel of a car?' exploded Gavin Patterson, glaring at her.

Beth took umbrage at her sister being called an idiot, but he couldn't know it was Janice, in all probability he would blame Johnny. 'It's not Johnny's fault,' she said hastily, wanting to get that straight for a start.

'I don't recall saying it was,' he replied through set teeth, and walked back to his car to inspect the damage.

Beth's eyes followed him, and she saw that the front bumper had a definite lean to the left, and one headlight was smashed in. 'I'll pay for the damage,' she said haughtily.

Not trusting himself to answer, he got into his car, reversed slightly, and swept past them without affording them another glance.

Beth looked at Johnny, who seemed to have made a remarkable recovery from the paralysis that had gripped him earlier. He gave her a grin. 'I'm sorry, Johnny,' she said. 'I hope it's not going to get you into any trouble.'

His confident answer reassured her. 'There'll be no trouble, Miss Beth. Boss mad now, but he'll get over it. You'll see.'

Beth wished she could believe him, but felt she had run the gauntlet once too often where Gavin

Patterson's patience was concerned. Any time now he would be making a few enquiries as to how long she intended staying on his island, and whether he could get her to leave while it was still intact. That he saw her as a disaster zone to be guarded against at all costs she was in no doubt. He'd probably take to hoisting a few red flags up in the area she was likely to be visiting, she thought miserably.

It was quite definitely the end of her driving aspirations; she hadn't the heart to carry on. Nothing, but nothing was going to go right for her in this part of the globe, she was now convinced. With a sigh of resignation she got out of the driving seat and indicated that Johnny should take over. Thinking she was probably suffering from after shock, Johnny willingly complied, remarking cheerfully, 'You'll be all right tomorrow, Miss Beth,' and drove her back to the cottage.

Beth hadn't the heart to disillusion him either, not right then. She'd leave it to Janice to break the news that his services as a driving instructor were no longer required. She sighed; he was going to be disappointed, but it couldn't be helped. From now on she would find her subjects within walking distance of the cottage. And that wasn't such a hardship—there were plenty of lovely scenes to be captured, she told herself consolingly. Her lips straightened; from now on the only way she could meet Gavin Patterson was if he sought her out, and the likelihood of that happening was about the same as her chances of becoming his secretary!

That evening Janice had a date with John and was meeting him straight from work, so Beth had to leave her sorry story till later, when she returned. At least she would be able to get her version in first before Janice heard it from her boss, for Beth couldn't see him holding his peace about her latest attack. There was the bill for repairs, for one thing!

After her evening meal, Beth settled down to some painting; she wanted to start on the harbour scene while it was still fresh in her mind—the peaceful scene, that was, not the subsequent events! Happily immersed in her work, she frowned when she heard a car draw up outside the cottage, and wondered why John had brought Janice back early. Going to the window of the room she was using as a studio, she frowned when her gaze alighted on an estate car, and on closer examination, she saw with a pang of dismay that it was the car she had run into that morning. Her courage nearly failed her at the thought that her arch-enemy had decided to carry the war to her doorstep, and she knew sweet relief when she saw Johnny climb out of the driving seat, and went out to meet him.

Giving her a cheeky grin, Johnny handed her an envelope. 'From the boss,' he said.

As she accepted it, Beth thought it was a bill for repairs, and stared back at the damaged car. He was rather laying it on, wasn't he? she thought. There was no need to rub it in, was there?

She thanked Johnny and prepared to go back in, and was very surprised when with a cheery wave at her, he made his way back to Chartways by foot, leaving the car sitting outside the cottage. A very indignant Beth stalked back into the cottage; Johnny had evidently been given orders to leave the evidence right there, for her to check against the repair bill no doubt, she thought furiously as she tore open the envelope and perused its contents.

It was not a bill, but a letter, and one that took her breath away. With flushed cheeks she re-read the short but concise message: 'You might as well make a good job of it. I see no point in getting repairs done until I can be assured of a safe passage through my grounds. You will no doubt find it easier to manage than Johnny's apology for a car.'

Underneath was Gavin Patterson's bold signature. Beth flung the letter down in disgust. Not only had he refused to let her pay for the damage, but he made her feel beholden to him.

Beth was still fuming when Janice got back that evening. She saw the car, of course, and when Beth told her what had happened, showing her the letter Gavin Patterson had sent her, she went off into peals of laughter, saying it was the funniest thing that had happened there for years.

This time Beth's sense of humour failed to rise to the occasion. 'I'm not driving it, Janice,' she said crossly. 'So you can take it back tomorrow.'

A more sober Janice stared at her. 'Oh, no, I'm not,' she replied firmly. 'I think it's very good of him to take it like that. I know he's got other cars to use; but it's still a nice thought,' adding coaxingly, 'He's right, you know, you will find it easier to drive than Johnny's. You should be grateful.' Beth looked anything but grateful, and seeing this, Janice went on, 'And you're not to ask Johnny to take it back either; you'll only get him into trouble.'

'Trouble?' asked Beth, frowning.

Janice nodded. 'Yes, trouble. Johnny knows why the car has been left here. If you continue to use his car, he's the one who'll get blamed for not carrying out orders—especially if there's any more trouble,' she added significantly.

On this statement Beth's lips set ominously. 'That settles it!' she said darkly. 'I'm not learning to drive. I'd more or less made my mind up earlier on this. Now I'm certain; if I can't do it my way, then I'm not doing it at all. For one thing, I'd be terrified of doing any more damage to the wretched car, so let's forget it, shall we? It goes back tomorrow.'

Janice sighed. 'Between the two of you,' she muttered, 'I'll put my money on Gavin—he's got an odd way of getting his own way.'

She left Beth to work that one out, and Beth wondered if Janice had realised what she had said, because if it were true, then at the first given opportunity Beth could expect to find herself on the next flight out!

Although Janice made one last attempt the following morning, to get Beth to change her mind and accept the use of the car, Beth remained adamant, and Janice had to leave for work, feeling very depressed about the whole situation. It wasn't the only thing that would depress her, thought a guilty Beth, knowing what was in store for her should she be rash enough to voice her ambitions for her future stay on the island.

When Johnny turned up a little later that morning, all smiles as usual, Beth concluded that Janice had not said anything to him, so it was left to her. 'I'm giving it a miss for a while, Johnny,' she said, and handed him a letter she had written to Gavin Patterson which should, she had surmised, let everybody off the hook; that way there could be no comebacks. She had stated that she had lost her nerve, thanked him for the offer of the car, and hoped he would let her have the bill for repairs in due course. 'Would you give this to Mr Patterson, Johnny?' she requested with a smile. 'It explains why you've taken the car back.'

Johnny's smile faded slowly. 'This car is better than mine, Miss Beth,' he said earnestly. 'I'll be able to teach you better.'

'It's not that, Johnny,' Beth said hastily. 'I've every confidence in you. It's just that ...' She racked her brains to try and come up with a plausible explanation that would take that injured look off his face.

'You think Mr Patterson can teach you better?' he asked while she was still floundering.

Beth stared at him; now where on earth had he got that idea from? 'There's no question of Mr Patterson teaching me,' she replied indignantly. 'No, I've just decided to leave it for a while. I promise you that if I do decide to take it up again, you'll be the one to teach me.'

Johnny's face brightened at this, but he still looked doubtful, and Beth couldn't think what was troubling him, unless it was taking the car back. She waited. 'Mr Patterson asked me how you was getting on,' he said simply. 'Wanted to know if I could teach you, and to let him know if I couldn't.'

Beth was still puzzled. 'Now why should he want

to know that?' she demanded.

Johnny grinned. 'Boss think he could teach you better,' he told the slightly stunned Beth.

'Well, Mr Patterson's wrong,' she said, when she had got her breath back. It didn't bear thinking about, she told herself quickly. So that was what Janice had meant by getting his own way. Beth wanted to drive, and he had decided to give a helping hand, whether she wanted it or not, she was going to learn to drive! With a feeling of resignation, she walked towards the car. 'All right, Johnny, where shall we go today?'

This time Johnny really grinned!

CHAPTER EIGHT

ANOTHER week passed by, and Beth felt she was going to make the grade as a driver. Her confidence had grown with each day that passed. Having the go-ahead from his boss, Johnny was able to put more time into the task allotted him. With Gavin Patterson waiting in the wings, as it were, to take over should Johnny fail, not only Beth was on her mettle, Johnny was too! There were no more incidents either, for Johnny was careful to keep the practice runs well away from the house.

On the third day of the following week Johnny announced her capable of driving herself. There were no tests as such, but some standard of driving was of course necessary when one entered the outskirts of the town, and after four trips to town in order to familiarise her with the sort of traffic she was likely to come across, he pronounced her fit and able to take her maiden run.

Beth chose the day that Janice would be hostessing an important dinner given by her boss to entertain several business colleagues of his, plus a few of the island's hierarchy to level the numbers. As Janice had taken her evening wear with her when she left that morning, Beth knew she had a completely free day, and meant to make full use of it.

Feeling that the world was her oyster, she perused

Mr Fisher's map and selected one of the marked areas as her destination, then studied the route. Soon she was on her way with her easel and stool, canvas and paints stowed in the back of the car, together with one of Mabel's 'siege' food parcels.

The journey was not a long one, and Beth met no other traffic; she might have been the only human abroad in that part of the world, and the thought lifted her spirits. There would not be a repeat of the harbour fiasco, nor crowds of tourists to contend with. It was one of the reasons she had chosen this particular site, for Mr Fisher had pencilled in a cryptic 'Peaceful. No tourists!' Beth smiled as she thought of that remark—it appeared he didn't like folk peering over his shoulder as he worked either!

To get the view she wanted, she had to station herself on a small hillock overlooking the bay, and when she had settled on the angle she wanted, she set her easel up and started sorting out the paints she needed. A glow of happiness spread through her as she picked up her brush and began the outline of the bluish-mauve hills she could see in the distance.

Knowing how quickly the light could change, she worked swiftly, trying to catch the delicate hues that were at the moment evading her.

Time passed, but it ceased to exist for Beth. She was in a world of her own. A hollow feeling in her stomach made her stop for a short while at lunch time, but her eyes scarcely left the picture or the view she was trying to capture. If she could just get that deeper green on that further tree ...

Mid-afternoon found her still working furiously

away at the canvas. The subtle changing light spur-
red her on, but she knew it was a race she couldn't
win, as dusk fell suddenly there, but at least she would
have more than an outline to work on when she got it
back home.

The sound of lapping water gradually seeped
through her consciousness and she glanced down at
the beach—or where the beach had been, for the
sea had completely invaded the area. She heard the
sound again, a soft sort of gurgling sound, that
sounded nearer than the bay below her. Puzzled,
she looked behind her and found to her consternation she was surrounded by water—on an island within an island!

Remembering where she had left the car, she
gulped, and scrambled over to the side she had left
it further down the hill. Her feet squelched as she
walked, reminding her of moor land, and indeed as
she peered closer at the ground, glints of water could
be seen among the tufted grass.

Almost frightened to look, she stared down at the
car, noting despondently that although it was still
there, its wheels were immersed in brown swirling
water, and was completely unusable.

In abject misery Beth stared around her. How
long, for goodness' sake, would she be stuck there?
She looked back at the car. Was there a chance she
could get it out before the water rose higher? Feeling
the damp rising through her thin sandals, she knew she
couldn't. Even if she managed to get to the car, she
doubted if she could move it free from the mud that
now encased it; and to be honest, she didn't fancy

making the effort. Marshland could be tricky; she was safer where she was.

Another thought struck her at this point that made her blink hastily—was it marshland or swamp? Oh, no! she hadn't parked the car on a swamp, had she? The thought made her go cold; how much, for heaven's sake, was a new car?

She glanced at her watch, and knew a spurt of surprise that it was close on six-thirty. That meant that it would soon be getting dark.

For the want of something to do, Beth got the coffee flask out, glad she had left some for later use, and her fingers curled round the mug, absorbing the heat it gave out, not realising until then that a thin cotton shirt and cotton jeans were no proof against a stiff sea breeze.

However much she tried to forget her position, the swamps were uppermost in her mind, and swamps, with Beth, were connected with crocodiles. As the light dimmed yet further, she told herself stoutly that there would be no such creatures on the island, although her feverish imagination whispered back, 'Why not?'

It was then that a voice floated up to her from the bay; it sounded resigned. 'So there you are!'

Beth had never been so glad to see anyone before in her whole life, even Gavin Patterson. She could not as yet see him, but he could evidently see her. She walked to the edge of the bluff and stared down at the bay. He was there sure enough, complete with boat —she wondered why she hadn't heard the boat's engine.

Looking up at her, he drawled sardonically, 'I hope the picture was worth it.'

Beth wasn't too sure about this. There was the car, for one thing, and she felt a guilty pang. He didn't know about that yet!

'I'm coming up,' he called. 'Here, catch this, there's nowhere to moor it down here.'

Catching the rope that he threw at her, Beth walked back to her easel. She ought to start packing up. When she told him about the car, he would be in no mood for pleasantries—not that he ever was, she thought miserably, at least not with her.

Her eyes alighted on her still wet canvas, and she sighed. She had been very pleased with the result, now she wasn't so sure. It was going to be a very expensive picture indeed! Her eyes blinked as she had a vision of him tucking the picture under his arm, not only getting spattered with paint but ruining the picture in the process. She had to act quickly, for he would be with her at any moment, she was sure.

As her anxious hands started to grasp the canvas, she found she was hampered by the rope she still held, and looked around for somewhere to moor it. Her eyes alighted on a short tree stump a little to her left, and she dashed over to it. Securing the rope to the stump with a knot she had learnt as a Girl Guide many years ago, never dreaming at that time when it would come in useful, she rushed back to her easel and removed the canvas. By the time Gavin had joined her she had it safely stowed away in a protective cover, and was now putting her paints away.

'I'll take the easel and the case,' he said curtly.

Beth noticed he said nothing about the car, but she had a nasty suspicion that he knew exactly what had happened.

'Where's the rope?' he asked, staring at her empty hands.

Beth walked to where she had left the rope, but there was no sign of it—or the tree stump. She frowned in bewilderment. 'It was right here,' she said. 'It couldn't have come undone. Even the stump's gone,' she added indignantly.

'Are you telling me you moored it in a mango swamp?' he said in a voice that held a certain amount of incredulity in it, then as if his patience were exhausted, he shouted, 'To a mango stump? I just don't believe it!'

Beth swallowed; how was she to know it was a mango swamp? She stole a look at him and was relieved to note that he appeared to be lost for words, for which she was exceedingly grateful. Of course she had to ruin everything by stupidly asking, 'What do we do now?'

The question so irritated him that he found his voice, and very vocal he was too. Fortunately for Beth, she didn't understand a word he was saying, but she was sure he was swearing in what was probably an old native dialect.

Wisely keeping her distance, she eyed him warily, noticing a little sadly that his outburst had not helped much, because he was still furious with her when he had finished.

Grabbing her easel and stool, he jerked his head in the direction of the bay. 'Come on,' he said tersely, 'and watch where you put your feet. Follow my steps exactly.' He gave her a glare. 'Do you think you can manage to do that?'

Considering the question not worth answering, Beth followed his tall back, as he slowly retraced his steps to the edge of the bluff, glancing round every now and again as if he couldn't trust her to carry out even this simple task.

It was very slow going, and Beth was glad she had only her box of paints to carry, Gavin having swept everything else up. Eventually they arrived at the edge of the bay, and it was a very thin edge, for there was only just about room to stand. The tide had evidently started receding, although it would be a slow process.

The boat, Beth saw, had not been carried out far, and her anxious eyes searched for traces of the rope that might have got caught up somewhere on the slight incline they had just descended, but there was no sign of it, and her gaze returned to the boat now bobbing up and down with the motion of the tide.

Beside her, Gavin unceremoniously dumped her gear down on the damp slip of land they stood on, and slipping off his sandals, then removing his heavy sweater, he waded into the water and was soon striking out with practised strokes towards the boat.

With a certain amount of relief, Beth watched as he reached it and climbed aboard, and soon the welcome sound of a motor springing into life was heard, and it was heading back towards her.

Bringing the boat in as near as he could, Gavin signalled her to wade out to him. He was taking no chances of leaving it again, she noticed, and knew she would have to make more than one trip out to the boat with the amount of stuff she had to convey to it.

As she had picked up his sweater and sandals the moment he had gone to rescue the boat, taking no chances of them getting wet, she felt that they were first priority, and grabbing her easel she made the first trip out with them. For a moment it looked as if he might insist that she got in the boat and left the rest of the stuff right where it was, but Beth had no intention of doing this. Her picture was getting more costly as time went on, and she felt she deserved some compensation, and was off to collect it before he could do anything about it.

At last they were off, and by now it was dark. Beth, sitting facing a grim Gavin, shivered as she felt the first force of the cold evening breeze, and began to worry about the silent man steering the boat wheel in front of her. His sweater still lay on the seat opposite her, and his brawny chest was bare; the thick hair still held water, from which small rivulets trickled. If she was cold, so must he be. She picked up the sweater and managing to catch his attention held it out to him. His curt, 'Not to bother,' made her feel terrible. He might just have said he had had enough of her help for one evening.

She hadn't even thanked him, she realised with a pang of remorse. 'I haven't thanked you,' she said quickly. 'I don't know what I would have done if you ...'

She was not allowed to finish, for he cut in with a

biting, 'It's Janice you should thank. Luckily for you, she had to go back to the cottage, and saw the map you'd been looking at.'

Beth bit her lip and gazed out to sea. Why had Janice asked for his help, of all people? Why hadn't she got Johnny to look for her? Because Johnny didn't own a power boat, that was why, she told herself bitterly.

'I must say,' he went on coldly, 'she seems to understand the workings of your mind remarkably well, and was convinced you wouldn't have had the sense to realise that such things as tides exist. She put it down to your artistic bent—said you'd still be painting away while the water was lapping around you. And she was right, wasn't she? Although I don't share her view on the subject of artistic talent—crass stupidity, I'd call it. The areas of swamp are clearly marked on that map, but you didn't take the trouble to note that, did you?' he flung at her.

Beth did not answer—there was no point. From his point of view it *was* crass stupidity, and there was no getting away from it. In a way, she deserved the lecture he was giving her. If it made him feel better, she didn't mind a bit.

The twinkling lights of the harbour now came into view, and Beth wanted to shout with relief that her ordeal was over, but soon found that she had been a little presumptuous.

'In future,' he said harshly, 'you will provide your sister with your exact movements each day. I do not intend to allow another incident of this nature to take place. I shall feel a great deal easier in my mind if I know your whereabouts each day. That way,' he added sarcastically, 'I can judge what services, land, sea, or air, might be deemed necessary to accommodate your next rash move.'

Still Beth remained silent. Land, sea, and air!—she had impressed him, hadn't she?

'This arrangement,' he went on, 'will be continued until Janice's wedding, after which, I presume, you will be leaving.' Beth, gazing out to sea, felt the hard stare he gave her as he added meaningly. 'Any other arrangement is quite out of the question. I trust you understand me?'

She understood only too well. So he did know of Janice's plans for her, and was telling her quite categorically that there wasn't a chance. Well, she knew that, didn't she? As if she wanted to work for him anyway! Managing to inject a note of acid sweetness into her voice, she murmured, 'Janice can be so simple at times.'

He nodded grimly. 'So I've noticed,' he replied cuttingly. 'She's certainly got a blind spot where you're concerned—seems to think you want looking after. In one sense I entirely agree with her, only I would say you need watching out for, rather than looking after!' He gave her another piercing look. 'Isn't it about time you grew up,' he asked harshly, 'and stopped leaning on your sister?'

Beth's sudden start did not go unnoticed by him and he looked gratified that he had got under her guard at last. 'Oh, I've heard about some of your escapades as a child, and how Janice had to smooth things over for you—not that I saw it that way at the time, but

having since become acquainted with you, I can see
how it must have been. I think Janice deserves some
peace now, don't you? I also intend to see that she
gets it,' he added ominously.

Beth sat very still; through her shocked senses came
the thought of Janice's reaction had she been privi-
ledged to hear her boss's summing up of their relationship. Of all the pompous, misguided, hateful men ... !
She bit hard on her lip to stem the words she wanted
to shout at him. But worse than this was the feeling
that she wanted to cry. She had never leant on anyone—least of all on Janice. It was the main reason
why she had left Nicholas. He had tried to turn her
into just such a creature, and here was this ghastly
man levelling this charge against her ... It was the
last straw!

When the boat came up against the harbour steps,
she leapt out, and still clutching her picture made her
way up the steps. The rest of the stuff could sink to
the bottom of the bay for all she cared! The man,
too!

She had almost reached the top of the steps when
he caught her up, and she gave no sign that she had
heard his authoritative, 'Wait here,' as he walked
over to one of the harbour offices and disappeared inside. But Beth kept on walking, keeping her lips
pressed together tightly to prevent them trembling,
hoping to hold the tears at bay. She walked out of
the harbour and into the town, having no clear idea
of where she was going but just wanting to put a
healthy distance between herself and that man.

A few seconds later she heard the sound of a car,

and it slowed down when it reached her. Opening the door, Gavin said curtly, 'Get in. I'm late enough now.'

'Then you'd better get a move on,' snapped Beth, done with politeness. 'I'm getting a taxi.'

She had only gone a few yards when she found herself picked up as if she were a rag doll and taken back to the car, and thrown into the back seat. Her dander was well and truly up by then, and she smartly started to get out again.

He stood surveying her, with hands on his hips. 'I shouldn't if I were you,' he threatened. 'If I have to collect you again, you'll get the good hiding I've been wanting to give you for some time.'

As much as Beth disliked Gavin Patterson, she respected the fact that he was a man of his word, and sank back slowly on to the car seat, contenting herself with a glare at him. On no account was she going to give him the satisfaction of carrying out his threat.

When he had settled himself back in the driving seat, he met her furious eyes in the driving mirror. 'I'll give you some good advice for what it's worth,' he ground out. 'Go back to the poor devil you jilted. You're not likely to find anyone else willing to put up with your tantrums.'

Again the urge to cry came over her, and again she smothered the feeling. He'd only put it down as a childish act to gain his sympathy.

The minute the car pulled up outside Chartways, Janice rushed out of the house. 'Did you find her?' she asked.

'All safe and sound,' Gavin replied harshly, as he

got out of the car. 'How much time have I got?' he asked, dismissing the subject of Beth as if of no consequence.

'Fifteen minutes,' answered Janice, now back to being the efficient secretary.

'I'll just make it, then,' he answered as he strode towards the house. Beth, watching his departing back, gave a sigh of relief, only to be gasping with indignation the next as, suddenly recalling her presence, he looked back towards the car. 'Find something for that sister of yours to do. It's time she made herself useful,' he said sharply.

Janice, about to accompany him back into the house, turned and walked back to the car, then bent and peered into the back seat. 'Beth?' she asked, in a surprised sort of way. 'I thought Gavin might have dropped you off at the cottage.'

'No such luck,' answered Beth feelingly as she got out of the car.

Catching the misery in her voice, Janice placed a comforting arm round her shoulders. 'I do wish you'd told me where you were going, pet,' she said. 'I could have told you about the swamps, and how you'd have to watch the tide. Was it very bad?' she asked.

Not half as bad as the time she had had to spend with her maddening boss, Beth thought, but she answered truthfully enough. 'I kept thinking of crocodiles,' she told Janice, 'and tried to convince myself there weren't any.'

Janice's eyes opened wide. 'I never thought of that,' she said slowly. 'I must ask Gavin about that.'

The girls walked towards the house, and Janice

gave Beth's arm a squeeze. 'Thank goodness you're safe,' she murmured in a heartfelt voice, and gave a slight shudder. Beth knew she was considering the possibility of the reptiles actually being there. Her concern was touching; it was nice to know that someone loved her, she thought peevishly.

Another thought struck Janice as they entered the house, and she clutched at Beth's arm in excitement. 'Do you think Gavin's considering the possibility of you taking over from me?' she asked. 'He did say I was to find you something to do, didn't he?' she added hopefully.

Beth gave her a pitying look. Talk about incurable optimists! 'No dear,' she answered positively. 'We don't get on—or haven't you noticed?'

Janice sighed. 'Oh, well, you never know. Come on, I'll see if I can find something for you to do.'

However, after they had moved into the well-lit part of the house, Janice stared in dismay at Beth's muddied jeans and even more muddied sandals. 'You can't possibly stand around in those!' she wailed.

A light appeared in Beth's eyes. 'I'll go back to the cottage and change, shall I?' she asked innocently, with no intention of coming back.

Seeing the light, Janice shook her head. 'Oh, no, you don't,' she said firmly. 'If Gavin thinks you can help—then you'll help!'

'He's your boss, not mine,' retaliated a disappointed Beth.

'You did,' reminded Janice, a little unfairly to Beth's way of thinking, 'wreck his car. And he's John's boss as well, remember.'

Beth stared at her. 'Is that the way he thinks?' she demanded. 'Your boss, I mean? That I owe him something? I did offer to pay for the wretched thing, but he ignored the offer,' she added bitterly.

Janice grinned at her. 'Of course not, silly. He's not petty-minded. No, it was just that I thought it would be a good opportunity of showing him you can be useful. I also think it's time you two buried the hatchet,' she said confidently.

'In whose head?' queried the sceptical Beth.

Janice giggled. 'Well, you know what I mean. You could at least try,' she argued soberly. 'To please me?' she pleaded coaxingly.

Beth shrugged noncommittally, then sighed. For Janice's sake only, she might just do that, the only thing she could be sure of was that it wouldn't make a bit of difference as far as her boss was concerned. If he went down on his knees, she still wouldn't take the job as his secretary! A little voice inside whispered, 'Chance would be a fine thing' and she smiled at her thoughts, then looked back at Janice still anxiously watching her. 'Very well,' she said, adding warningly, 'And don't say it's my fault if things don't work out.' She looked down at her jeans and sandals, and sighed again. 'I'll have to change, you know. I'll be as quick as I can,' she promised the now happy Janice.

After a shower, Beth changed into a dress. She saw no reason to wear evening dress—she was going to work, wasn't she? As she left the cottage, she looked longingly towards the studio door, and wished she hadn't made such a rash promise to Janice. She simply couldn't think what she could do when she got back there—or just what Gavin Patterson had in mind for what he'd consider suitable labour for her kind of talents—washing-up, probably, she thought miserably. Not that she minded that, it would keep her out of his eagle eye. Her thoughts drifted on as she walked back to Chartways. Janice had denied that he was of the opinion that she owed him something, but Beth was sure that those were his exact thoughts on the matter. It was for this reason really that Beth had agreed to fall in with Janice's suggestion—apart, that was, from pleasing her, for she hadn't been able to get the uncomfortable thought out of her mind that she did owe him quite a lot, and as he wouldn't send her a bill for repairs, some other way had to be found for repayment.

When Beth arrived, Janice looked a little askance at the dress, as if to suggest that Beth should have worn evening wear. However, she said nothing, but took her through to the vast kitchen area and introduced her to the cook. Beth, thinking Gavin Patterson really had found a job for her, prepared herself for the washing-up duty, enquiring where the aprons were kept.

Janice chuckled. 'Stupid!' she scolded mildly. 'I've a more entertaining job for you than that. You're going to help me serve the drinks in the drawing room after dinner. Mrs Jackson will find you some food, so that you can have your meal in here while we're at dinner.'

Beth would have preferred the washing-up! She didn't fancy trailing about with a tray of drinks under

the no doubt watchful eye of Gavin Patterson. Something was bound to go wrong—it had on every other
occasion—so it would on this. 'Must I?' she pleaded.
'Honestly, I'd rather stay out here.'

Janice gave her her schoolmarmish look. 'Beth!'
she exclaimed exasperatedly. 'You promised!'

A miserable Beth nodded her head at her. 'I'll help
in the drawing room,' she agreed wearily.

The summons, and that was just how Beth looked
on it, came in no time at all to quash the hopeful expectation that Janice had let her off the hook, and she
joined her in a small ante-room off the drawing room,
where Johnny was busy dispensing drinks to be cir-
culated among the guests.

With hands that slightly trembled, making the
sherry in the fine cut glasses slop over on to the tray,
Beth made her debut. As soon as she entered the well
appointed room she knew without looking on which
side of the room her arch-enemy stood, and stayed
well out of reach by serving the groups of people
nearest the ante-room, noting with a sigh of relief that
Janice had taken on the other side of the room.

No matter what, Beth was not serving Gavin Patterson or any of the small knot of friends gathered
around him. When her tray was empty, she returned
to the side room to replenish it again. There seemed
to be a lot of people there; Janice had said it was a
business dinner, some sort of a trade conference, but
even so, thought Beth, it hadn't taken Gavin Patterson's mind off her, for he watched her constantly—
waiting, she presumed, for her to trip up and spill
sherry over some dowager's expensive gown.

Her chin tilted a little at this thought. Well, he was going to be disappointed. Just for once, she was going to make things go right. After all, there wasn't much that could go wrong, as long as she was careful not to tilt the tray. Nearly everyone was standing up, except the old gentleman who had sat himself in a club chair near the side room, in a position, Beth suspected, to be first in the drinks queue.

It was on her return after her third trip out to collect more drinks that Beth's certainty that nothing could go wrong received a rude awakening. A man stood by the drawing room door, hesitating a little as he looked round to find his host, and Beth very nearly dropped her tray. Nicholas! Her frantic eyes searched for Janice, who at that particular moment was having a cosy chat with an elderly woman. Janice, then, had not yet seen him.

When Nicholas moved further into the room, heading in Gavin Patterson's direction, Beth did the only thing she could think of at the time, and ducked down behind the club chair, the occupant of which she had just provided with another sherry.

Now she was safely out of sight, it only remained for her to get out of the room. The tray of drinks she left on the floor, and crawled on all fours towards the side of the room. The chair provided an excellent screen for her from the rest of the room, and having safely negotiated the distance without mishap, she crawled through the swing door, thanking providence for her quick-witted action.

Had Johnny not chosen that particular moment to bring in the canapés, Beth's escape would have been

successful. As it was, having no reason to suspect that
he would meet someone on their hands and knees, he
cannoned into her, propelling his tray through the
swing doors in an action not dissimilar to that accredi-
ted to flying saucers.

Beth's amazed eyes watched Johnny's exit, and she
hoped he had a soft landing, although judging by
the resulting crash she rather doubted it. She sat back
on the floor, and seeing that she had collected a few
delicacies from the tray Johnny was carrying, carefully removed a sardine and a few radishes from her
lap. There was a suspiciously damp feeling on her
forehead, which she suspected was another sardine,
and she was just about to investigate when her eyes
alighted on an immaculate pair of size nine shoes
standing right in front of her.

'I might have known it was too good to last. Have
you anything else up your sleeve to ensure that my
evening's ruined?' demanded a furious Gavin. 'Because if so, forget it. The first act was a roaring success!'

Beth couldn't think of anything to say except to
ask if Johnny was all right.

'Oh, you do think about other people, then. Well,
that's something. He's fine—due, only I might say, to
his acrobatic training.'

Beth had now lost interest in the conversation and
continued brushing her dress down. 'You might at
least apologise!' he ground out.

Her attention focussed on a dish of some grey-
looking mixture, probably horseradish, within tempting distance of her hand. 'I'm sorry,' she said, hoping

that would be that, and he would leave her in peace, but he wasn't through yet.

'I've a good mind to make you go out there and apologise to my guests, but you'd probably make a hash of that, too. I can't think, Miss Knight, what we did for excitement before you came to this island. I only know that if I had my way, your sister's wedding would take place tomorrow.'

Beth's fingers curled round the dish in front of her, and she hurled it at him. Seeing it coming, he ducked, and the man who had just appeared on the scene caught the full blast of the sticky pottage on the front of his evening jacket.

'Beth!' exclaimed Nicholas.

Gavin Patterson was clearly confused, and Beth noted the fact with pleasure as she watched him help Nicholas to clean his jacket, profusely apologising all the time.

When that was done they turned their attention to Beth, who still sat there, under the vague impression that if she kept quiet they would both go away. Feeling their eyes on her, she sighed, and looking at Nicholas, said, 'Sorry, Nicholas.'

'I should think so! What a greeting!' he replied rapidly.

Beth got up slowly, and Nicholas, taking another white handkerchief out of his pocket, began to wipe whatever it was off her forehead, just as if she had been a child.

'I gather you know Miss Knight,' Gavin commented dryly, watching Nicholas's tender administration with some amusement.

'He's what you might call my keeper,' said Beth bitterly.

Nicholas gave a smug smile. 'She means fiancé, of course.'

'Ex-fiancé,' Beth returned firmly.

Ignoring this, Nicholas, now satisfied he had removed all trace of food from Beth's forehead, pulled her to him and gave her a hard swift kiss, completely taking her by surprise, to her fury.

The fact that Gavin Patterson stood by watching made it worse for her. She wrenched herself free, and to take that sardonic look from Gavin's face announced that it was time she went, as she had to wash the dishes.

Nicholas stared at her. 'You've to what?' he demanded.

'Wash the dishes,' Beth repeated sweetly. 'It's the least I can do. I'm up to my neck in trouble as it is. And if you knew my boss . . .' She ran for it.

When she got to the kitchen, that was exactly what she did do, only she hadn't washed many plates when Gavin caught up with her.

'Put that damned dishcloth down,' he shouted. 'You know damn well we employ staff for that job!'

'Temper, temper!' admonished Beth, determined not to put up with any more browbeating from this man.

'As I've just spent the last five minutes explaining to Harbin that I do not employ you as a kitchenmaid, perhaps you'd be good enough to explain your extraordinary behaviour. I may be a little slow on the uptake, but I did gather that his appearance might have had something to do with what happened earlier. Am I right?' he demanded.

Beth dried her hands slowly. She didn't want to explain why she had acted as she had, or the blind panic she had felt at the sight of Nicholas. He wouldn't understand anyway.

'Put that cloth down,' he ordered, 'and sit right there. I'm going to get to the bottom of this.' He pointed to a kitchen chair and perched himself on the table, one leg swinging, showing his impatience for Beth to get on with it.

Beth's lips set mutinously. She had no intention of enlightening him.

She was saved by the sudden appearance of Janice, who rushed into the room, and catching sight of Beth announced dramatically, 'He's here! Nicholas is here, Beth!' She glanced wildly round the room as if seeking somewhere to hide her sister. 'What are we going to do?' she wailed.

Beth sighed. 'You don't have to do anything,' she told the frantically worried Janice. 'I shall have to do the disappearing act again, that's all.'

Gavin stared from Janice's white face to Beth's set one, and a grin of unholy amusement appeared on his. 'This Harbin must be quite a character,' he drawled. 'I must cultivate his acquaintance.'

Janice frowned at his levity. 'It's no laughing matter, Gavin,' she said sternly. 'I see he's got his name down for the trade conference.' She looked at her sister. 'Isn't that just like him?' she asked the thoughtful Beth who was busy making plans for her early departure. 'To kill two birds with one stone, I mean,

fix up a deal for his business, and collect you on the
way back!' Her hands clenched into fists. 'Only he's
not going to take you back with him. You're here,
and you're staying!'

Gavin's brows raised at this vehement statement.
Beth could imagine his thoughts. Janice was doing
the mother hen act again. She felt him look at her, as
if to provoke her into action. He was also reminding
her of his advice given earlier that evening, to go
back to Nicholas. It was also obvious that Janice
meant to keep her in her sights. Her previous idea of
making herself scarce wasn't going to work either.
Nicholas would just hang around. He'd know Beth
would keep in contact with Janice, and it wasn't fair
to leave Janice to cope with him. If she hadn't been
so spineless before, she wouldn't now be in this mess.

She took a deep breath. 'I'll just have to talk to
him, won't I? I couldn't have made it plain enough
before.' She sighed. 'I suppose he's still in the drawing room?' she asked the stunned Janice.

The question brought an immediate response from
Janice. 'Talk to him?' she echoed indignantly.
'You've already talked to him—and left a letter, con-
firming your decision. What more can you do? I
don't trust him,' she muttered. 'I've seen what happened before. No, Beth, you're not seeing him alone.
I'm coming with you.'

Before Beth could persuade her otherwise, Gavin
Patterson intervened with a smooth, 'Come now; it
seems a little common sense is needed here.' He gave
Beth a cold look. 'I'm sure your sister can manage
her own affairs, if given the opportunity, that is. She

may very well find that she's had a change of heart and decide to marry him after all.'

The mother hen became a vixen defending her young from a predatory attack, as Janice whirled on him. 'You know nothing about it!' she cried, and to Beth's consternation her large brown eyes showed signs of tears.

By this time Beth had had more than enough. She was even willing to marry Nicholas if she could bring a little peace into her life again. Her escape hadn't been very successful, had it? Nothing had gone right since she had left England. Her eyes fixed on the man now looking with some concern at Janice. None of this would have happened if he had had some sensibility, or shown some sign of that sense of humour Janice declared he possessed. He wanted her off his island, and he wasn't going to be too fussy as to how he achieved his aim. Nicholas's arrival would be seen as a heaven-sent opportunity to remove the thorn from his side. She, being the thorn. Beth knew that whatever she said to Nicholas would be undermined by the no less determined Gavin, who would do a little batting practice in his own part of the field. To give him some credit, he was looking out for Janice, and would very probably convince her later that his course of action was the right one.

It was this thought that made Beth stick to her guns. She wasn't being married off to accommodate Gavin Patterson! It wouldn't, she mused, be good policy, however, to say so at that particular time. If he thought his problem was solved, then he would let well alone, and Beth would be free to do a little manoeuvring of her own. She looked up to find his eyes on her, his expression plainly showing that he thought it was her fault that Janice was upset. Her eyes blazed back into his. How she hated him! 'I might very well do that,' she ground out.

'Beth?' there was a note of pleading in Janice's voice, 'You don't mean that, do you?' She turned to Gavin. 'Now see what you've done?' she cried, and rushed out of the kitchen.

Beth's look at Gavin as she went after Janice, echoed the same sentiments! It was harder for Janice, of course, for she had just realised that one of her champions had joined the opposition.

Beth was close enough to Janice to follow her into her office, and went up to the still figure that stood facing the window, although Beth knew she wasn't seeing the view, for her head was bent in silent misery.

She touched her arm gently. 'It's all right, love. I'm not marrying him,' she said softly.

'But you said you might,' gulped Janice. 'And that will be enough for Nicholas.' She swallowed. 'He'll probably make it a double wedding. He won't leave you here. I shall never see you again, I know I won't!'

Beth squeezed her arm. 'Now you know that's not true,' she scolded her mildly. 'Nothing's changed. I've had a taste of freedom, remember, I'm not likely to trade that in again.'

Neither of the girls saw the tall figure of Gavin by the open door, having followed Beth when she rushed after Janice.

'But why did you say you might?' demanded Janice, giving a loud sniff.

Beth sighed. 'Well, as you've just found out, your boss regards me as a disaster zone to be avoided at all costs. I said it for his benefit alone. I'm afraid, pet, I shall have to make other arrangements for my stay in this part of the world, find some place where I can get employment—there're scores of islands to choose from. Not too far, though,' she added, hoping to mollify the still miserable Janice. 'So that I can dodge over to see you every now and again, and vice versa. Just as long as I can keep out of you-know-who's way.'

Janice straightened her back. 'I'll talk to Gavin,' she said firmly. 'Once he knows about Nicholas, he'll understand.'

Beth gave a loud sigh. 'Janice! You've just not been listening to me, have you? There is no way—repeat, no way, that that man and I will ever see eye to eye. As for your crackbrained scheme of me becoming his secretary—I tell you, if it came to a choice of either marrying Nicholas or working for him, then I'd choose Nicholas—better the devil you know!'

'Beth!' exclaimed the scandalised Janice.

'I mean it!' said Beth. 'So don't you dare say a word to him. I want your promise on that, here and now!'

The figure by the door left as unobtrusively as it had come.

CHAPTER NINE

On the girl's return to the drawing room, Nicholas, who had been talking to Gavin, abruptly concluded the conversation and strode over to Beth.

Placing a proprietorial arm around her waist, he complained, 'Where have you been?'

Beth was saved the necessity of answering by Gavin, who had decided to join them, asking, 'How long are you staying, Harbin?'

Janice, torn between staying put by Beth's side and carrying on her duties as hostess by seeing off a few guests on the point of leaving, was left no option in the matter by Gavin's drawled, 'Janice?' and she shot Beth a look of, 'Don't give in, will you?' before she drifted away in the wake of the departing guests.

Nicholas took his time in answering Gavin's question, then looked at Beth. 'It depends,' he murmured.

On how long it took to bring her back to her senses, Beth thought, but having only just regained them, she wasn't likely to lose them again.

Gavin looked thoughtfully from Nicholas to Beth. 'I don't know your line of sport, but the island offers some good yachting facilities. We've a regatta to-morrow if you're interested, and I'd be only too happy to take you out, if you wish to take part in it.'

For once Beth applauded an action of Gavin Patterson's—even if he had an altruistic motive for gaining Nicholas's friendship. Under the circumstances he might even grant him the freedom of the island, if his mission was successful. As she could see Nicholas was wavering, for he was tempted to accept, she added her persuasion. 'You would enjoy that, Nicholas,' she urged, thinking of a whole day of freedom for herself.

'What will you be doing?' he asked, and Beth sighed inwardly. She was back to square one with him monitoring her every movement.

'Oh, I shall do some sketching,' and catching Gavin's eye, she added for his benefit, 'At the cottage. I promise to give the harbour a wide berth.' She thought she saw his mouth twitch, but couldn't be sure. Nicholas just looked bewildered.

'Why can't you come with us?' Nicholas demanded, and turning to Gavin, 'I presume there's a yacht club Beth can watch us from?'

Beth held her breath; he wouldn't like that at all, she thought. Why, she might even get near the starter guns! She was confident he would think up something though, but to her astonishment she heard him answer smoothly, 'Of course, why not?'

Why not indeed? Beth's eyes spoke her thoughts as they met Gavin's bland ones, and she felt like screaming. It was plain he was going to allow nothing to stand in the way of her reconciliation with Nicholas, and even the thought of a ruined regatta would not swerve him from that course. A tiny prick of panic went through her as she acknowledged that she had not one but two adversaries to conquer. Nicholas was formidable enough on his own—linked with Gavin Patterson, he was invincible. She felt like waving a white flag!

The fact that Gavin was to accompany them the next day allayed Janice's fears on Beth's behalf. It was as if his being there would give her protection, and although Beth knew otherwise, it would be a waste of time saying so.

Wearing a tan silk two-piece, which suited her Nordic colouring and gave Janice fresh qualms about her safety with Nicholas, because she looked adorable, Beth waited for Gavin to pick her up as had been arranged the previous evening, after first collecting Nicholas from his hotel.

Her hopes that it would pour, or that a thunderstorm would descend, ending all hopes of the regatta, were thwarted by a brilliant blue sky, and a reluctant Beth was forced to wish both men a 'Good morning' as she got into the car.

Her feelings were further outraged by a protective Nicholas who helped her into the back seat, after giving her another of those hard kisses that sealed his ownership of her, although Beth did her best to avoid the action by turning her head away, but Nicholas wasn't so easily deterred, and rather than put up an undignified struggle in front of Gavin she had to accept the kiss.

The yacht club was decked out with flags, and was a hive of activity when they arrived. Gavin, hailed on all sides, ushered his guests into the club, and seeing Beth installed on the verandah, in a position that gave her a commanding view of all proceedings, took Nicholas off to the quay section, where boats of all sizes and shapes were being lovingly prepared for the day's racing by their enthusiastic owners.

The air of happy anticipation affected everyone but Beth, who sat bemoaning the work she could have been doing. As yet she was the only observer, although there were plenty of women there, but they were, it seemed, all taking part in the proceedings, and dressed for the part, making Beth feel over-dressed in her suit. She could of course have worn her jeans and cotton top, but Nicholas would not have approved. She sighed; already he had got through to her, and she was automatically carrying out his wishes. She frowned. It wasn't that she was weak—well, she didn't think so; it was just that Nicholas had that effect on her.

In an effort to turn her thoughts elsewhere, she watched the last-minute preparations for the first race, and her eyes alighted on Gavin and Nicholas. Nicholas, as Beth had presumed, was crewing for Gavin, and wore a white silk short-sleeved shirt, while Gavin favoured navy blue; both wore navy slacks.

Beth's gaze lingered on them, noting that they were much of a height, but that was where the resemblance ended. Nicholas's dark good looks and lean wiry figure, as against Gavin's blond, muscle-bound frame, brought them in sharp contrast. They had a lot in common, Beth thought bitterly, for they were both of the same disposition, and each used to getting their own way!

Had Beth been in a happier situation, she would have acceded that they were quite the best-looking men in the vicinity, and this was borne out by the fact that several girls, either crewing for other boats or sailing themselves, found various excuses to carry out their preparations in close proximity to the two men.

The first race was won by Gavin and Nicholas sailing past the finishing line a few yards in front of their nearest rival, and Beth dutifully waved in acknowledgement of this as Nicholas caught her eye as they swept past on their victory run.

There was one more race before lunch, and Beth wished she had the courage to take a stroll along the quay and on to the beach, but daren't. Things were apt to happen when she least expected it, and she could no longer trust to luck, not with Gavin Patterson in the vicinity!

It was as well Beth had stayed put, as the next race was on a shortened course, and the men returned shortly, well pleased with themselves. 'What about that, Beth?' exclaimed Nicholas. 'Patterson handled her beautifully.'

'You didn't do so bad yourself,' grinned Gavin, as they settled down beside her.

Soon they were immersed in a discussion on the style and performance of the various boats that had taken part in the race, and Beth felt she might not have been there for all the notice they took of her. Not that she could join in the conversation. You could put all that Beth knew about boats on a postcard, and still leave room for a message!

For her, it was back to old times with a vengeance, for Nicholas never expected her to take part in any conversation, although he would allow her to con firm a point here and there depending on the subject raised.

Assuming the silent Beth was on her own, a young yachtsman attempted to engage her in conversation by asking her why he hadn't seen her there before. Grateful for the opportunity to while the time away until Nicholas or Gavin deigned to notice her presence, Beth was about to reply when Nicholas cut in with, 'Darling, this must be an awful bore for you. I'm afraid we've got two more races this afternoon, I daresay I could bow out.' He looked at Gavin. 'You could replace me, no doubt?' he asked.

Fuming inwardly at the cold way he had handed out a snub to the young yachtsman, who had got the message and walked away, Beth found herself now faced with the prospect of spending the afternoon with him, let alone the evening. 'It's all right, Nicholas,' she said swiftly. 'You carry on, I'm perfectly happy,' answering before Gavin could reply.

'There's a fair wind blowing up,' observed Gavin. 'Should make a good afternoon's sailing.'

If this remark was calculated to catch Nicholas's enthusiasm, it was perfectly timed, Beth thought, for there was no more talk of him pulling out, and they were soon discussing tactics for the next race.

A muted gong then sounded, and Gavin looked up. 'Lunch,' he commented brightly. 'Come on, we're in the first sitting.'

The small dining room was almost full when they walked in, but Gavin led them to a window seat set in an alcove, which Beth suspected was his personal table, for several people were looking for tables, and

they had arrived ahead of them, but they had by-
passed this one.

When Gavin stood aside to allow Beth to take her
seat, she almost did a double-take. It was the first
time he had shown her any deference, and when he
handed the menu to her with a 'Beth?' she was almost
overcome with confusion. It had always been 'Miss
Knight' or just plain 'You'.

Beth knew she had Nicholas to thank for her up-
graded status, but nevertheless she felt extremely uncomfortable, and preferred things as they were. She
was allowed no more than a perfunctory glance at
the menu before Nicholas commanded it, as usual
ordering for both of them.

'The steaks are good. I can recommend them,' suggested Gavin, who had observed Nicholas's action
and looked vaguely amused.

Still studying the menu, Nicholas shook his head.
'Er—no, I don't think so. Beth and I prefer a salad.
I'm a vegetarian myself, and Beth's gradually coming
round to my way of thinking, aren't you, darling?'

'Yes, Nicholas,' Beth replied, noticing the way
Gavin's eyebrows rose at the docile reply.

The same thing happened when liquid refreshment
was mentioned. 'We do not take wine with our meals,
except occasionally at dinner, do we, darling?'

Beth spoke her party piece again with a, 'No,
Nicholas.'

For this she received a hard look from Gavin, obviously wondering if Beth was taking the rise out of
the pair of them. But Beth had been well trained,
and was keeping out of trouble. She knew how to
handle Nicholas.

Gavin had been right about the wind. It was quite strong by the time the next race was due, and Nicholas fussed over her like an anxious mother. Was she quite comfortable? The wind was sharpish, hadn't he better leave his sweater with her?

Beth answered either yes or no, whichever was applicable, she did not feel it was cold enough for her to wear his sweater, but apparently he had decided it was, and handed it to her. Her firm, 'No, thank you, Nicholas,' was a mistake, for he just said: 'Put it on.'

She did not argue, but accepted it with a low, 'Very well,' and if she hadn't felt so miserable would have chuckled at the look on Gavin's face. He was obviously having trouble working out what had come over her.

By the time they had finished the afternoon's racing, Beth's thoughts turned to the cottage, and blessed peace. Janice would probably be there, and John too, for she would have brought him in for reinforcements should Nicholas take her home. The fact that he hadn't got his own transport would easily be overcome by his new ally, Gavin, who would probably offer him one of his own cars, just to help the course of true love to run smoothly!

But first there was tea to get through, and seated back at the same table, Beth found she was quite hungry. The tiny sandwiches were appetisingly laid out, and there were several plates of delicious-looking pastries, some with cream oozing out, and others covered with jam. Beth had never seen anything like them before, and wondered if they were a speciality of the island, and commented on them before she realised her mistake.

'Too rich, darling, try one of those almond-looking cakes,' ordered Nicholas, then seeing someone he knew across the room, he exclaimed: 'Why, there's Jimmy Darwell! He came over with me and promised to let me have an address—we're both in the same line. Will you excuse me, darling? Patterson?'

Beth could feel Gavin's eyes on her as she watched Nicholas go over to his friend's table, and when she turned back to him, she saw that he had picked up a plate of pastries and was holding it towards her. With a wicked twinkle in his eye, he said, 'I dare you!'

Beth looked back at him coolly; he was enjoying himself immensly. 'No, thank you,' she replied adding for good measure, 'Nicholas doesn't think they're good for me.'

Seeing the glint in his eye this answer produced, she knew they were back on the old footing, and he was about to make a reply when Nicholas returned, so he turned his attention on him. 'I presume you'll stay on for the prizegiving tonight? We've several cups to collect,' he reminded him before he had a chance to refuse.

'Well—er—yes, thank you. What do we do about dress, though?'

'It's informal,' replied Gavin. 'It has to be—there's no time for anyone to take off and come back again. We just see it through.'

See it through was right, thought a miserable Beth. There was no chance now of an evening at the cottage. At least she wouldn't be spending the whole evening with Nicholas, and she had to be grateful for that.

The dining room was cleared after tea, and one table was left in the centre of the room to accommodate the gleaming cups. Speeches were then made, and the proud winners stepped forward to collect their cups. Gavin and Nicholas took the lion's share, and judging by the ovation received on each occasion, they were popular wins, but Beth couldn't share the enthusiasm shown for either man!

To her dismay, the presenting of the cups was not the finale of the evening, for as soon as the presentations were over, a band appeared from a side door and settled down to entertain the members with some dance music.

Making certain no one else got a look in, Nicholas claimed the first three dances and would have taken the fourth, had not the young man who had approached Beth earlier that day made a valiant effort, and withstanding a caustic look from Nicholas swept her off for a foxtrot.

It was the only dance that Beth really enjoyed, for there were no clinging holds of the type that Nicholas was subjecting her to, and she had time to gaze around as she danced. She saw Gavin standing talking to Nicholas, and realised with a start that he had not taken the floor all evening, in spite of the hopeful glances several women were sending his way.

When Gavin asked her for the next dance, Beth could only assume he was being awkward. He must have thought she was enjoying herself and decided to put a spoke in the wheel!

The dance was a waltz, and suited her, for she knew she would not be able to concentrate on any

tricky steps—not with Gavin Patterson! A feeling
of embarrassment made things worse for her, and
she was stiff when he took her in his arms. He held
her correctly and seemed a little stiff himself, not due
to embarrassment, Beth thought, but distaste for
having to make a duty dance.

'How long have you known Harbin?' Gavin asked
her suddenly, taking Beth by surprise.

'Two years,' she replied, having a shrewd idea of
what was coming.

'Two years!' he exclaimed. 'And acting like that
all the time! Has he got a surprise coming!'

She couldn't pretend she did not know what he
meant. She stared up at him. 'You wouldn't understand,' she said coldly.

'Well, for once you're right,' Gavin remarked
dryly, adding conversationally, 'He looks sane,
doesn't he?'

Beth gasped; if he was trying to rile her, he had
succeeded! She judged it beautifully and her heel
came down on his foot with as much force as she
could produce in the given time. She was rewarded by
his quick gasp and a missed step. 'Sorry,' she said,
giving him a sweet smile.

'I think it's about time the scores were evened,
don't you?' he drawled, as he jerked her close to him
to prevent the likelihood of another retaliation. 'It's
also time someone took you in hand, and I'm not sure
Harbin's the man to do it.'

If Beth was uncomfortable before, she was doubly
so now. His nearness was beginning to affect her in
an odd way, for her knees felt like rubber, and her

pulse rate soared. It wasn't embarrassment and it wasn't fear, and she was completely bewildered by her feelings.

The rest of the evening passed reasonably well. Gavin did not ask for a second dance—his foot was probably sore, Beth hoped. However, there was a certain look in his eye whenever he looked her way, that gave her a few qualms. To all outward appearances he behaved as normal, but Beth had a nasty feeling that this time she had pushed him too far.

When it was time to leave the club she felt as if she were between the devil and the deep blue sea. On the one hand she did not fancy finding herself alone with Gavin—not in that mood!—and on the other, Nicholas's possessive arm round her waist gave her a foretaste of what was coming later, once they were alone. It was either clinches or a shaking, and she couldn't make up her mind which she preferred!

She soon found she had no choice in the matter, as Gavin dropped Nicholas off at his hotel, giving him no chance of a quiet session with Beth, and this did not please Nicholas at all, which was a pity, for when Gavin offered to take him on a tour of the island the next day, he was barely civil when he replied, 'Thank you, but I've arranged to take Beth on a tour of the islands.'

Whether he had actually done this or not, Beth couldn't be sure. It seemed quick work for someone who had barely arrived, but she could hardly say so. If he had accepted Gavin's offer she would have had a free day, knowing she wouldn't be expected to trail around after them, having seen most of the island.

The rest of the journey passed in an oppressive silence. Beth's thoughts were on the proposed trip with Nicholas, and that meant the whole day in his presence. Knowing him, she knew he would not be likely to forgive Gavin for the way he had dismissed him that evening, and would be all the more determined to remove her from the island. From now on, he would look upon Gavin as a rival, for he was intensely jealous. She sighed. At least it had quashed any alliance that they might have made; then she glanced surreptitiously at the grim-faced man beside her and swallowed. It didn't make any difference to her, she still had two opponents, even if they were on opposite sides of the fence!

When they had reached the grounds of Chartways, Beth wondered if he would drop her off at the house, and after delivering a lecture—at least she hoped that was the form the punishment would take—leave her to walk through to the cottage.

She ought to have known better. The car swept past the entrance to the house and continued towards the cottage. By this time Beth's imagination had passed the lecture stage, and she told herself stoutly that she wouldn't mind a shaking, but there was every possibility of being put over his knee and receiving the walloping he had threatened her with on other occasions. She gulped. She wasn't going to allow him to do that, no matter what!

In the end she decided discretion was better than valour, and the minute the car drew up in front of the cottage she had the car door open and sprinted for dear life towards the cottage.

If Beth hoped her earlier affront on Gavin's foot had impaired his speed, she was in for a disappointment, for he had covered the distance with an agility she wouldn't have believed possible for a man of his size, and now stood towering between her and the haven the cottage offered.

'Coward!' he said silkily.

Beth found herself marvelling over the fact that he wasn't even out of breath. She didn't know why she should think of such an irrelevant fact at that particular time—perhaps to take her mind off other pressing matters? She stared up at him, and knew she was beaten. 'All right,' she said wearily, 'you win. Do I bend over, or take it standing up?'

With a soft chuckle he propelled her forward, and Beth prepared herself for the worst. The speed she was pulled into his arms knocked the breath out of her, and she was never to know what had been his original intention, for as soon as she came into contact against his hard body, his arms folded around her, practically squeezing the life out of her.

'You're hurting me!' she managed to get out, staring up at him in some amazement. The next moment he was kissing her with a ferocity that frightened her. Beth had experienced hard kisses before, but nothing like this. Her soft lips were pounded under his ruthless ones. Vaguely she felt he was working something out of his system, but she wished he had chosen another way to do it.

Suddenly he released her, and she was forced to take a step back in order to regain her balance. She was too stunned to be indignant, but just stood there trying to get her breath back, absolutely lost for words.

Gavin was breathing rather hard himself, as he stood taking in her reaction. 'So that's what it takes to make you behave, does it? I rather suspected as much.'

Beth had no idea what he meant, she only knew that her lips hurt and her body felt as if it had been held in a vice. 'You needn't have been so brutal,' she said bitterly.

His voice was harsh when he answered, 'You asked for it. If you did but know it, you've been asking for precisely that from the day we met.'

Beth's surprised gasp and her indignant expression were duly noted by him and appeared to be expected, because he nodded. 'As I said once before, you've not grown up yet. Little girls play those sort of games on boys they've a hankering for. I guess you missed out on that phase—too busy getting into scrapes. But you're a big girl now, and it can get you into a lot of trouble.' He gave another nod at Beth's wide open eyes, as if unable to believe her ears. 'Think about it,' he advised her grimly. 'Someone had to tell you. It ought to be Harbin, but he prefers the answering machine he's made you into. I suppose you found that little act impressed him, so you carried on with it. Why don't you give him a break and show him what he's getting into?'

Her stunned brain had no answer to this taunt; she could only stand there blinking as the shock waves passed over her. As she did not answer, he gave a sigh and turned back to his car. As he got in and started up, he had one last stab at her, 'As I said, think about it.' The next minute the car swept past her.

For a long while Beth stood where she was, then as she felt the tears welling up in her eyes, she turned towards the door. Janice must not see her crying—she would put it all down to Nicholas, and for once it had nothing to do with Nicholas. It was only when the door refused to budge that she realised it was locked, and that meant Janice was still out. In her confusion Beth had failed to note that there was no light on inside the cottage, as the porch light was always left on, and it enabled Beth to find her key in her bag, although her vision was hampered by the blur of tears.

She had expected to find Janice anxiously awaiting the outcome of her day out with Nicholas, but she was grateful she had decided not to wait in. John, no doubt, had taken her out somewhere, and it did occur to Beth that maybe Gavin Patterson had had a quiet word with him on that score. It wouldn't surprise her—in fact after tonight nothing would surprise her again.

By the time Janice returned Beth had been through several stages of thought and now, in bed, was slightly calmer, and able to answer Janice's questions about how things had gone, with some equanimity. As Janice was still labouring under the impression that with Gavin in attendance Beth was safe, it was not hard to convince her that all was well. When she told her about Nicholas's plans for the next day, Janice gave an exasperated snort.

'Isn't that like him?' she demanded, 'I suppose he didn't give a thought to the fact that you might have your own plans.' She gave Beth a hard look, noting the shadows under her eyes even though the light was a muted one that came from a side lamp. 'He's not given up, has he?' she said. 'John can't understand what's wrong with him. I mean, you've made it quite clear how you feel, haven't you, and yet he still persists.' She sighed. 'Well, you'll just have to go on saying no until it gets through to him, won't you?'

After she had gone, it occurred to Beth that Nicholas wasn't the only one who wouldn't listen to what she told them. Janice was the same where Gavin Patterson was concerned. With both, it was a case of hearing only what they wanted to hear. This thought led her back once more to the subject she had tussled with, ever since Gavin had given her a piece of his mind.

No longer indignant or furious—she had been through that stage—she now had to face up to his diagnosis, because that was what it had been. Could he have been right? She only knew she had acted foolishly on each occasion they had met, that something about him had so riled her that she had wanted to hit out at him. At one time she had thought it was because of Nicholas, because he reminded her of him. Now she wasn't so sure, and was very much afraid that there was a grain of truth in what he had said. Was it some odd attraction that he held for her that had made her act as she had? Her lips twisted at this thought. Was it odd? He was an attractive man, and remembering the way she had felt in his arms she felt her cheeks grow hot, and her tongue gingerly felt her very sore lips. She couldn't—she wouldn't fall in love with such a man—and yet it was what he had hinted she had done. He had left her with no illusions on this score, for had she been aware of what she was doing she would have immediately recognised the 'keep off' warning he had taken such pains to give her. In any case, it seemed he was taking no chances. As he had wanted to bring Janice's wedding forward, so now did Beth. She never thought she would be grateful for Nicholas's presence, but she was, fervently so! In fact, if Nicholas decided to go back before the wedding, she was very tempted to go back with him— or at least part of the way. Just so that she could make her exit with flying colours, to prove that she wasn't 'hankering', as Gavin had put it, after him!

CHAPTER TEN

THE following week was taken up by pure sightseeing. Each day Nicholas would have a route mapped out— a visit to St John's, or St Croix, there were plenty of islands to choose from. The only place they did not explore was the island they were on. But Beth had suspected that this would have been Nicholas's reaction to Gavin's high-handed action the previous evening, and as it suited her purpose too, she did not demur.

Nicholas did not mention the engagement once. It was as if he were sure of his ground, and she noticed how a 'when we go home' would slip into the conversation, but before she could argue the point he would adroitly change the subject. Knowing it was his way of trying to make her accept his will, Beth said nothing, as she had no intention of going back.

On the last day of the week Nicholas made a mention of the work that was piling up at the other end, and how it was time to go home, and Beth, meeting his eyes resolutely, said casually, 'I shall miss you, Nicholas. I really have enjoyed this week.'

His lips thinned, and Beth knew they had got to the crunch. 'I want you to come with me,' he said crisply.

Beth shook her head firmly. 'No, Nicholas,' she said gently. 'I'm staying here.'

It took a minute or so for him to control his patience, but it was ebbing fast. 'It's Patterson's doing, isn't it?' he ground out. 'Oh, I've seen the way he looks at you, and I haven't forgotten the way he dropped me off so that he could see you home.'

Beth sighed. 'It's nothing to do with Gavin Patterson,' she explained patiently. 'If you want the truth, we don't get on,' and that was putting it mildly, she thought, and went on, 'When I said I was staying, I should have said in this part of the world—not on this island, but near enough to see Janice occasionally.'

'Where do you intend to live, then?' Nicholas asked abruptly. 'You can't live alone—no, I really can't allow it. Janice will be too busy looking after her husband to bother about you. Your place is with me. I'll look after you, as indeed I have done for the past two years,' he reminded her meaningly.

He was telling her that she owed him something, a subtle kind of blackmail, Beth thought, only it wasn't going to work. 'I'm very grateful, Nicholas, for everything,' she answered firmly. 'But I'm not going to marry you. It wouldn't work out. I'm very fond of you, but not enough for marriage.'

'I don't think you really know what you do want,' he replied irritably.

Beth did know what she wanted—her freedom— and she was about to tell him so when he abruptly changed the conversation. 'When's Janice getting married?' he asked.

Wondering why he had asked, she wasn't left long in ignorance after she had answered, 'In about a month's time,' and her heart sank when she saw him consult a diary, now realising what he had in mind.

'I think I can manage to take a few weeks off then,'

he said, and looked back at her. 'It will give you time
to think things over—and,' he added with a set jaw,
'I shall expect a definite answer by then.'

Beth wondered what he would accept as 'definite'.
and she had a vision of him haunting her existence
for years, until she came up with the right answer!

A day later he left the island, and Beth, waving him
off, felt a surge of relief pass over her as she watched
the plane getting smaller and smaller as it winged
into the distance. At best, she mused, she had been
given a month's reprieve, then it would start all over
again—in which case she had better enjoy what time
she had left. Nicholas had weighed things up pretty
shrewdly; with Janice on honeymoon, Beth was
bound to feel a little lost and lonely, and he meant to
be around to relieve that loneliness. Not only that,
she would have to find somewhere else to live, and
find a job of some kind, no easy task for someone who
had been as coddled as she had for the past two years.

Shaking these miserable thoughts away, she managed to secure a taxi and went back to the cottage,
walking in to find Janice in the lounge sitting with a
bandaged foot resting on a stool.

'What on earth,' queried Beth worriedly, 'have you
done?'

Over the top of the magazine she had been per-
using, Janice smiled at her. 'It's not as bad as it looks,'
she explained. 'I've only slightly sprained it. It means
I have to keep off it for a few days. I stupidly reached
for a book on a ladder, and it was higher than I
thought it was. The next minute I was on the floor.'

Beth gave a smile of relief. 'I'm glad I'm not the

only accident-prone member of the family,' she remarked airily.

The conversation then returned to Nicholas, and although Janice asked the question idly, it was plain to see she had been worrying about it. 'Has he really gone?' she asked in a hushed voice.

Beth nodded, and couldn't bring herself to tell her sister that he was coming back for her wedding. Time enough for that when it happened.

'Oh, thank goodness,' breathed Janice. 'My John couldn't understand him at all. I mean, you'd told him it was over, and left him a note, but he still persisted.' She smiled mistily at Beth. 'Well, it's all over now,' she said on a note of satisfaction. 'Now we can concentrate on the wedding. How do you fancy royal blue for the bridesmaid's dress?' she asked brightly.

Beth looked alarmed. 'Is it to be a very grand occasion?' she asked, then ran a hand through her hair. 'I know it's silly, but I'd never even thought of bridesmaid's and things.'

'You'd better start right now, then,' Janice scolded mildly. 'I'm only having one attendant, and you're it.' She laughed at Beth's dismayed look. 'And Gavin's the best man, of course,' she added mischievously, adding to Beth's misery.

Putting a brave face on it, Beth smiled back at her. Not for worlds would she spoil Janice's wonderful day. If she wanted her to be bridesmaid, then a bridesmaid she would be.

The telephone in the hall rang just then, and as Janice made a move to get up and take the call, murmuring that Mabel was shopping in town, Beth waved her back. 'You sit tight,' she ordered. 'I'll get it.'

'How's Janice?' queried the voice that had not plagued Beth for the last week.

Without realising it, she stiffened as she answered frigidly, 'Resting up,' giving no sign that she knew who was calling.

'Good,' replied Gavin. 'Er ... I presume he's gone back?' he asked conversationally.

Her fingers gripped the receiver. By 'he' he meant Nicholas, she supposed. Poor Nicholas, it appeared not only Janice was glad to see the back of him, though why Gavin Patterson should take that attitude was beyond her. 'Oh, you mean my fiancé?' she replied frostily. 'Yes, he went back this morning.'

'Your what?' he asked silkily.

Beth did not answer him; he knew very well what she had said.

'For a moment I thought you said "fiancé",' he went on smoothly. 'But of course, I must have misheard. He wasn't likely to have gone back without *his* fiancée, was he?' he asked, still in that smooth voice that made Beth's teeth grate.

To her credit she answered him politely, but it was no easy task. 'Why not?' she said casually. 'He'll be back for Janice's wedding, there was no point in both of us going back when I might spend a little more time with my sister.' Now chew on that, she thought viciously. 'Did you have a message for Janice?' she asked curtly, successfully giving the impression that he was wasting time.

His quick-drawn breath told her he hadn't liked

that one bit. 'No,' he said abruptly. 'It was you I wanted to talk to.'

Beth had been playing with the telephone cord, but now her hand stilled. He was going to ask her to let him know her whereabouts, and she was about to tell him in no uncertain terms that he would not be having any trouble in that direction, etc., when he took the wind out of her sails with a casual, 'I've missed you. It's been so peaceful.'

'And it's going to go on being peaceful,' Beth snapped back, wishing she could put the phone down on him. 'I've turned over a new leaf. From now on I stay put. Janice is laid up, so I couldn't do anything, anyway. So you can relax.'

He clucked admonishingly at her burst of temper. 'I was getting so well organised, too,' he said sadly. 'As for staying put, I don't think that will be necessary. Mabel's there, isn't she?' and he carried on before Beth could get a word in, 'I rather thought it might be a good idea if you got some training in while Janice is laid up. It's not so long now to the wedding; that way it will be a smooth takeover.'

Beth stared at the receiver in her hand. She couldn't have heard aright, surely?

He coughed, and Beth suspected he was laughing. 'Are you all right?' he asked solicitously. 'You haven't fainted or anything?'

'I think you've got the wrong number,' Beth grated out. 'The secretarial agency is your best bet.'

'Not from where I'm sitting,' he replied in a smug voice, adding in a 'by the way' tone, 'We eventually got the car back.'

Beth took a quick breath—it was blackmail!
Nicholas wasn't the only one capable of using it. She
swallowed. 'When do you want me to start?' she
asked bitterly.

'What's wrong with this afternoon?' he suggested
happily.

Beth took it out on the cushion she was supposed
to be plumping up before she sat down, and Janice
stared at her in some amazement. 'What's up?' she
queried. 'Who was that on the phone?'

'Your esteemed boss,' Beth answered sourly.
'Seems to think it's a good idea if I filled in for you
while you're laid up—and,' she added darkly, 'he
hinted at the possibility of my taking over from you.'

Janice's eyes opened wide, and Beth was surprised
to see that she looked anything but happy over the
prospect. 'Oh, dear,' muttered Janice, 'I'm not too
sure that it is—at least, not right now.'

Beth's eyes were wary as she demanded, 'Why
not?'

'Well,' supplied Janice, frowning, 'he's not been
what you might call in a good mood lately—for the
past week, come to think of it. We've all been a bit
worried about him, actually, because he's usually so
good-tempered.'

Beth was beginning to see a tiny light. Gavin must
have been terribly disappointed that Nicholas hadn't
whisked her off the island. She remembered his satisfaction after she had told him he was coming back—
so in his opinion all was not yet lost. But for goodness' sake, why had he wanted her up at Chartways?
Another stab of light pierced the darkness. He wanted

a whipping boy—and who better than her? Oddly
enough, she felt a little better after she had worked
that out. Things were beginning to make sense at last.
'What salary are you getting?' she demanded of the
surprised Janice.

Mentioning a figure that seemed a vast amount
to Beth, Janice asked, 'Why?'

Beth frowned back at her. She was busy working
out how much she could earn in a month, and having
reached the answer, she smiled at Janice. 'Well, that
should take care of any repairs that had to be done,'
she said satisfactorily.

It was Janice's turn to frown. 'The car, you mean?'
she queried, then as if a thought struck her, she
laughed 'That's if you last that long,' she commented.

Beth drew herself up to her full five feet four. 'I
intend to,' she answered coolly. 'And you'd be surprised what I can do when I set my mind to it.'

Janice, however, was still doubtful, and sighed. 'I
wish you luck, pet, but don't say I didn't warn you.
Gavin's not the man he was.'

On this doleful pronouncement Beth was left to
cope as best she might, and her thoughts were not
exactly cheerful ones as she made her way to Chartways just before two o'clock. The worst Gavin could
do was to shout at her, she thought glumly, and
steeled herself to accept all jibes and oblique references with fortitude, not allowing him to rile her into
throwing everything up. It was the only chance she
had of getting out of his debt, and she had to take it,
no matter what.

Her thoughts roamed on as she strode up the drive

to the big house. This would be the first time she had
seen Gavin since that night. Feeling the colour rise in
her cheeks, she wished she hadn't thought of that, not
at this time. The week she had spent with Nicholas
had helped her push that particular memory out of
her mind. It hadn't meant anything to Gavin Patterson, only as a method he had used to pay her back for
what he thought was deliberate provocation on her
part to catch his attention. She drew a deep breath.
Well, she had exploded that myth by saying she was
engaged to Nicholas, hadn't she? She frowned. Why
had he expected her to take over from Janice, then?
Because he hadn't believed her, that was why! Her
lips straightened. So it was a lie; but he didn't know
that, did he? Had Janice broken her word and told
him how things were between her and Nicholas? It
rather looked as if she had, and if so, Beth would be
wasting her breath if she contradicted her sister's mis-
placed confidences to her boss. And where did that
leave her? She swallowed. She would rather not dwell
on that.

On reaching the house, she noted with some concern that Gavin must have been on the look-out for
her, as the door opened when she got to the porch.
'Very good of you,' commented Gavin jovially,
making her dart a suspicious look at him, which he
met blandly, and Beth felt like the sacrificial lamb led
to the slaughter, as he led the way to Janice's office.

Entering the office, Beth glanced round the room.
Like Janice, everything was neat and tidy, no evi-
dence of its occupant having to take off in a hurry.
She glanced back at Gavin standing by the door.

There was a look in his blue eyes she couldn't fathom, and it worried her. Was he sizing up his next frontal attack? she wondered, and was sure he had something like that on his mind when he said casually, 'Sit down, Beth. I want to talk to you.'

'What about?' she queried suspiciously, thinking Janice wouldn't be a bit surprised when she returned to the cottage barely half an hour after she had left.

Meeting his eyes, she detected a hint of mockery in them, and to her furious chagrin found herself flushing. 'Am I going to work for you or not?' she demanded furiously. 'Or am I up here for a lecture?'

His brows rose at this, but he refused to be riled. 'To the first question, I sincerely hope so,' he replied airily. 'However, there are a few things that must be settled first—er—if you've no objection, that is.'

Here it comes, thought Beth wearily. She would have to promise to act with a certain amount of decorum as befitted the secretary to the owner of the island.

Seeing that she did not contend this query, he indicated the chair behind Janice's desk, and when she was seated, sat down opposite her.

Taking a deep breath, Beth prepared herself for complete servitude, reminding herself frantically that she was in his debt.

The first question, when it came, was so unexpected that she just sat and stared at him. 'Just what is the position between you and Harbin?' was what he asked, and giving a wicked smile at her stunned reaction to the question, he carried on blithely, 'As a prospective employer, I need to know how long I can expect to retain your services,' adding smoothly, 'Nothing personal, you understand?' Beth particularly noted the look in his eyes as he said this, and it rather belied his words.

In other words, she thought furiously, he wanted to know when she was going. Why he had to do it in such a roundabout way was beyond her. 'You might be a prospective employer,' she answered acidly, 'but I'm not a prospective employee! I understood you just wanted me to fill in while Janice is incapacitated, and that's why I've come,' adding haughtily, 'I intend to leave the island after Janice's wedding. I'm sorry I can't oblige and leave earlier.' She would post him a cheque for the repairs, she told herself.

'With Harbin?' he persisted, utterly ignoring the rest of her speech.

Beth was in a cleft stick. Why the wretched man wouldn't let be, she couldn't understand. 'Did you hope he'd got away?' she asked sweetly, still refusing to give him a straight answer.

'Are you asking for a dose of the last treatment?' he asked softly, 'because if you're not, I'd advise you to change your attitude. Now answer the question, one way or the other.'

Two bright spots appeared on her cheeks, partly through temper and partly through embarrassment. Trust him to bring that up! Well, he'd know sooner or later, she thought miserably. 'No,' she answered in a low voice. 'Although I don't know why it should be of any interest to you,' she added spiritedly. 'It makes no difference whatsoever to what we're talking about. I still intend to leave, so there's no question of my taking over from Janice permanently.'

'That's where you and I must agree to differ,' he drawled maddeningly. 'I think you'll find it's going to make a vast difference. However,' he said brightly, 'I'm glad we've got that little issue sorted out. Now let's get down to work, shall we?'

To Beth's confusion, that was just what they did do. There were no more interrogating questions, it was plain work from then on, and she had no time to work out the extraordinary remarks he had made, although it did occur to her that Janice had been right when she had said he was behaving oddly.

'Well?' demanded Janice the minute she got back that evening. 'Are you working—or a paid-up member on the dole?'

Beth tried to assume an indignant expression. 'Of course I'm working! I told you how it would be, didn't I?' she gave Janice a mischievous look. 'He said he thought I'd be a model secretary. I didn't chatter as much as the last one!' She ducked hastily as her sister hurled a cushion at her.

'Honestly,' pleaded Janice, 'did you get on all right? Does he really want you to take over from me?'

'Presumably,' replied Beth darkly, sober now. 'But I refused.'

'Beth, you didn't!' cried a scandalised Janice. 'Oh, how could you!'

'Very easily, as a matter of fact,' Beth replied, not a bit moved by her sister's rebuke. 'I told him the same as I told you—that I was standing in for you, and was willing to work up until your marriage.'

Janice's fingers nervously played with the tongue of her leather belt. 'I can imagine how well that went down,' she said miserably. 'Especially as he'd made a concession in your case. I mean, you haven't exactly got on, have you?'

Beth gave a wry smile. 'Not exactly,' she affirmed. 'And to be honest, I would probably have accepted, if I hadn't known the reason behind this kind offer.' She gave her sister an accusing look. 'You broke your promise, didn't you?' she said, 'He knew all about Nicholas and me; I must admit I was nonplussed as to why he should suddenly offer me this job—and not only that, actually be nice to me!—but I worked it out on the way back. It's pretty obvious he's sorry for me, and it's put me in a terrible position. Before I know it, I shall be bulldozed into accepting the wretched job. I told you he was like Nicholas, didn't I? Nicholas decided I'd make a suitable wife, and Gavin Patterson's decided I'd make a good secretary —and neither listen to a word I say!'

At that particular moment Janice wasn't listening either, at least not to the latter part of the narration, her mind was still grappling with something Beth had said earlier. 'Did you say nice?' she asked incredulously. 'Gavin?'

Giving her an impatient look, Beth nodded abruptly. 'That's what I said—and it's all your fault! If you'd kept your promise I wouldn't be in this mess.'

Janice stared, and seemed to be having some trouble in concentrating on Beth's accusation, then she gave her an indignant look. 'I didn't break my promise. I didn't say a word to him, although good-

ness knows he was curious enough ...' She broke off
suddenly as if a thought had occurred to her, and
whatever it was, it caused her some amusement.
'Well, well,' she murmured, 'so that was why he was
so bad-tempered.'

Beth gave her a suspicious look. Now what had
got into her? She knew that look of old. 'Janice?'
she said in a hesitant voice, 'you mean you didn't
say anything?'

Janice's wide grin confirmed her worst suspicions.
'You can take that smile off your face,' squeaked
Beth. 'You've had some goofy ideas in your time, but
if this one is what I think it is, you've hit the jackpot!'
The mere thought was mind-boggling, and although
she knew she ought to lecture Janice on the way she
sprang to conclusions, Beth had a sudden vision of
Gavin on his knees proposing to her, and it proved too
much. She burst out laughing. 'Oh, Janice ...' she
managed to get out in between paroxysms of laughter.
'How c-could you!'

Apparently Janice could, and did. For no amount
of straight talking would change her opinion on the
subject, and Beth gave up. As long as Gavin didn't
know what Janice had in mind, no harm would be
done, although, mused Beth, he seemed to catch on
to her train of thinking with an astuteness that was
discomforting, and she thanked her lucky stars that
he had granted Janice an extra fortnight off, ostensibly to prepare for her wedding, which meant in fact
that she would not be going back to work full time,
but would pop in to clear up any queries for the new

secretary. At least, Beth presumed for the new secretary, for she was more than ever determined to finish after the wedding, in spite of Gavin's refusal to take her decision seriously.

In the meantime, Beth was enjoying the work, and there were times when she was tempted to fling caution to the winds and accept the work permanently, but she had a vague uncomfortable feeling that Gavin was biding his time—over what, she had no idea. It was just that she felt that things couldn't go on as they were. It was somehow unreal, and she actually caught herself looking for signs of Janice's prediction coming true. She had now seen the other side of Gavin, and was beginning to understand why Janice had become so fond of him.

He was never too busy to spare the time to listen to what sometimes appeared to Beth as petty complaints from some of the island traders, and would give his opinion gravely on each trifling argument, and whatever side he supported, the losing contender would accept his judgment with a docility that was somehow touching.

All these things Beth noted, and stored away in a secret place in her heart. As for any confirmation of Janice's hopes, for that really was all they were, she had to admit sadly to herself, there was no sign. It was true he no longer teased her, or treated her as an adolescent, and she felt this was sad, too. It was as if they had started again, and Beth wasn't too sure she liked the new image. Hers—or his!

Perhaps that was what she was waiting for? For

one of them to break the treaty, for that was what she felt it was, and she wondered which of the two of them it would be. She was not to know at that time that it would take a third person to bring things to a head.

CHAPTER ELEVEN

THERE was now only one week to go to Janice's wedding, and the atmosphere at the cottage was one of feverish activity. Beth was only too pleased to leave Janice and Mabel to it as she left each morning for Chartways.

As Gavin had not said anything about getting a permanent replacement for Janice, Beth had left well alone, suspecting that he was determined she would fill the position, and her suspicions were given a kind of confirmation when a call came through for Gavin from Amanda Winton, and as he was in the office at the time, Beth handed him the phone.

'Good morning Amanda,' he said breezily. 'What can I do for you?' and after a moment or so replied in the same airy manner, 'Oh, well, I'm afraid we're not up to the dinner party stage yet, are we, Beth?' he asked the startled Beth, who wondered what it had to do with her.

'It's not up to me,' she said hastily. 'You're the boss.'

This appeared to please him, and his eyes twinkled as he remarked, 'It's nice to be appreciated,' making Beth colour. 'As I've said,' he carried on to Amanda, 'not yet. Perhaps a garden party after Janice's wedding. We'll see.'

Putting the receiver down, he met Beth's accusing eyes. He did mean her to stay on, she thought. 'I think

Amanda's missing the high life,' he commented. 'Thinks it's about time we threw a dinner party.'

Taking significant note of the 'we', Beth had all the confirmation she needed, and thinking about it afterwards, she knew she ought to have been furious at the way he had manipulated events to suit his purpose, but somehow she couldn't work up any such feelings, for she felt a tiny spark of relief inside her that her future was being taken care of. All right, she told herself, so he was another Nicholas—but in this case she had no objection—and it was no use trying to kid herself that it was because she would be near Janice!

The following day Janice brought her a letter that had been delivered to the cottage after Beth had left for work. Glancing at the small neat writing, Beth knew it was Nicholas, and she was almost afraid to open it; it either meant that he was still coming to the wedding, or that he had thought things over and had gracefully bowed out of her life. She read the letter, and felt a wave of depression settle over her. There was no question of him accepting her decision, he made that quite clear by the way he phrased, 'Mother sends her love, and hopes it won't be too long before we're settled back at home'.

Janice, who had perched herself on her desk, watched her closely. 'It's from Nicholas, isn't it?' she demanded.

Beth nodded. 'He's coming to the wedding,' she said slowly, adding heavily. 'He said he would, but I hoped he'd change his mind.'

Janice took the letter from Beth's nerveless fingers and read it. 'Well, of all the pompous ...!' she exploded.

'Hullo, who's upset our Janice?' asked Gavin as he strode into the office.

Thrusting the letter towards him, Janice muttered through pursed lips, 'Read that!'

'Janice!' exclaimed Beth indignantly. 'Don't mind me!' but as usual no one took any notice of her.

Gavin's eyes met hers after he had perused the contents of the letter. 'You don't seem to have convinced him, do you?' he asked amiably.

Beth stared at him—of all the people to talk! 'It seems to be a weakness of mine,' she replied furiously, taking refuge in anger, for his calm way of accepting Nicholas's determination to marry her now more than she had thought possible. She didn't know quite how she had expected him to react, but it hadn't been with amusement, she thought miserably. It appeared she was still one big joke with him. All these weeks had counted for nothing, and she had really thought they had reached some sort of understanding—Oh, nothing romantic, such as Janice had hoped—or to be honest, as she had dared to dream, but it wasn't a bit like that. For all she knew, he had probably already got a secretary lined up ready to take over at a moment's notice. He was just amusing himself by keeping her on a string. It was simple really, she thought bitterly, that way he could monitor her movements!

Feeling very near to tears, she held her hand out. 'May I have the letter back?' she said quietly, and tucked it away in her bag.

'What shall we do?' Janice asked Gavin, further infuriating Beth. Here she was dragging him into it now!

'It's not a question of "we",' she said firmly to Janice. 'This is my business, and my business alone.' She looked from her sister to Gavin, who stood watching her with narrowed eyes. 'I think it's about time I was left to manage my own affairs. This is between Nicholas and me, and however well-meant your interference might be, I prefer to do it my way.'

Janice gave an indignant, 'Beth!' taking exception to the 'interference' bit.

Beth's lips straightened. 'I mean it, Janice. What no one seems to remember is that I owe Nicholas something.'

Janice snorted at this, and Beth gave her a straight look. 'You had John, and Gavin,' she reminded her ruthlessly. 'Nicholas was my rod during that nightmarish time, and I haven't forgotten it.'

'And he won't let you forget it!' wailed Janice. 'He plays on that, and you won't see it!'

Gavin opened the door, and looked at Janice. 'Leave it, Janice,' he ordered.

Janice looked a little bewildered at him and then at the open door. He was telling her to go, and she had no option, she knew Gavin by now. She sniffed, 'Very well,' and glanced back at her sister's set face. 'Perhaps Gavin can make you see sense,' she muttered, and left.

'She's right, you know,' said Gavin, when they were alone. 'Owing someone something doesn't mean you have to marry them.'

Beth sat down at her desk. 'I've no wish to discuss

it,' she said waspishly, getting out some paper and carbons, meaning to start work.

'Leave that!' he commanded harshly.

Her lips set mutinously; he was the boss. She left it, and sat with hands twisting together, willing him to leave and let her wallow in her misery.

He sighed elaborately. 'There appears to be a sad lack of communication between us,' he told her, 'not to mention distrust, and I had hoped that by this time ...'

He left the rest of the sentence in the air, and Beth, glancing up at him swiftly, was surprised by the intense look of purpose in those very blue eyes of his, and her knees felt weak. Take no notice, whispered the voice of caution in her heart; he's doing the same as Nicholas is doing, playing on your sensitivities.

Whatever Beth had prepared herself for, it was no proof against the shock of his next words. 'You'll have to get yourself married off, won't you?' he said conversationally, adding as an afterthought, 'Engaged first, of course.'

Inside her, she felt the bitterness rise up and threaten to choke her. Who would he suggest? she wondered. There weren't that many bachelors around! Of course there was Mr Fisher! 'Poor Mr Fisher,' she said scathingly, 'I really don't think it's fair to embarrass the poor man, do you?'

'Who said anything about Mr Fisher?' he demanded. 'You could try me.'

Beth's outraged feelings were further enraged by the laughter in his eyes. 'For a consideration, of course,' he went on smoothly. 'With you as my wife,

I wouldn't need a secretary, would I? Could be quite a saving, come to think of it,' he mused.

Her hands clenched. How could he make fun at a time like this? It just went to show his real feelings on the matter. 'Thanks for the offer,' she managed to answer casually, 'but I won't scare you to death by accepting. Mr Fisher's more in my line!' she added a little maliciously.

'You have got it in for poor Mr Fisher, haven't you?' he said smoothly, though Beth caught an underlying dangerous note in his voice. 'I think,' he said slowly and very deliberately. 'I'm going to lose my patience with you any minute now. However,' he added airily, 'I did rather spring it on you. Sleep on it—the offer still stands, in spite of your determination to look a gift horse in the mouth.'

Now what, Beth thought, did he mean by that? Gift horse, indeed! Was he making sure she didn't try to capitalise on it? 'I've no need to sleep on it,' she answered quickly, 'I meant what I said to Janice. This is my affair. I don't need anyone's help,' adding hastily as she saw the glints appear in his eyes, 'but thank you all the same.'

'You might well find that you get that help anyway,' he growled. 'So don't say I didn't warn you,' and with that he left the office, leaving Beth with the definite impression that he was an exceedingly angry man.

As Nicholas had not given the date of his arrival, and Beth had assumed it would be a day or so before the wedding, she was a little confounded when he walked

into the office the next day shortly before she was
due to finish for the day. Having been given, as a defending counsel might have put it, no time to prepare
her case, she looked up at him blinking a little, as if to
assure herself that he wasn't a mirage. 'Nicholas!'
she exclaimed, glad that there was the desk between
her and him, as he strode into the office intent on
giving her his usual welcome.

'I didn't expect you until Friday at least,' she murmured, refusing to budge from the shelter of the
desk.

He glared at the desk as if it had done him a personal injury, and stood waiting for Beth to greet him,
and when she didn't, gave her a hard look and commented, 'Janice said you'd taken over her job. I
can't think why; it's not as if you'll be staying here
permanently.' He interrupted her as she began to
answer by, 'And I want no more nonsense about
finding somewhere to live either. I ought to have put
my foot down much earlier—Mother was right about
that. She's extremely upset by the whole thing, seems
to think it's something to do with her, but I'm sure
it's not. You never said you didn't want her to live
with us, did you?'

And so it went on; and was much as Beth had
feared it would be. Was it too much for him to expect her to give him some consideration for his love
and loyalty when she had been completely alone in
the world? Did her sister mean more to her than he
did? Was she so devoid of sensibility that she could
do this to him?

To all his condemnations, Beth had to plead guilty,

for she was guilty. She had taken so much from him, and given so little, not even her heart, she was made to feel the lowest of the low, and indeed had to agree wholeheartedly with all he said.

Her heart went out to him as he stood there with bent head, giving the indication that he was a broken man, and Beth couldn't take any more. It wasn't what she wanted, but ... 'Nicholas ...' and there was something in her voice that made him look up eagerly.

'I'm all for the last farewell bit,' drawled Gavin as he strolled into the office, 'but as a newly engaged man, I do wish to protect my interests.' He looked from Nicholas's astounded face to Beth's paper white one, and saw with a flash of fury that she was trembling.

Going to her side, he put an arm round her shoulders and held her tight against him. The action said more than words, and Nicholas's amazement changed to fury. 'Just what the devil do you mean?' he demanded.

'I should think it was obvious,' answered Gavin softly, and there was just as much fury in his voice as there was on Nicholas's face. He looked down at the stunned Beth. 'Darling, Harbin's a man of the world. He understands that these things happen. Stop whipping yourself. If he's half the man I think he is, he'll take it on the chin—perhaps even attend our wedding.' He gave Nicholas a challenging look. 'We're making it a double wedding,' he said meaningly. 'You're very welcome to come.'

Beth closed her eyes, if any remark was calculated

to infuriate Nicholas, that was it! She waited with bated breath for his reprisal.

'I'd like to see Beth alone,' he said stiffly, and glared at Gavin. 'I think I can say with some authority that I know her a little better than you do. I also know that she can be talked into something without giving it a great deal of thought.'

'You mean the same way you talked her into your engagement?' murmured Gavin goadingly. 'Well, I'm sorry, it's not on. She stays right here by my side from now on.' He gave Nicholas a warning look. 'I would advise you to accept the situation,' he said quietly, adding as a rider. 'This island is my home, and you're perfectly welcome to stay as long as you wish, on the understanding that you stay away from my fiancée. Break this condition, and you'll find yourself escorted to the airport within minutes.'

Beth was a little surprised at the fury in his voice—as if he really meant it. Nicholas, however, was in no doubt of this, for he drew himself up and looked directly at Beth. 'Well, you heard that, didn't you? It seems I have no choice in the matter. It's up to you now, Beth. You know how I feel. I'm at the Royal,' he said haughtily, and looked at Gavin with undisguised hatred in his eyes. 'I trust you won't object if Beth wishes to give me a note to take to my mother?' he queried sarcastically.

'As long as she sends it,' growled Gavin. 'She certainly won't be delivering it to you personally, in case that was what was on your mind!'

As there was nothing left to be said, Gavin escorted Nicholas out of the house, leaving a still trembling Beth to marvel at the way he had pushed Nicholas out of her life. He had only just arrived in time too, for she had been about to commit herself irrevocably to marrying Nicholas.

She curled her small hands into fists in an effort to stop them trembling. Somehow she had to get a hold on herself before Gavin came back—it was going to be embarrassing enough without her shaking from head to foot! She recalled his strong arm round her shoulders and the sheer relief his strength had given her when she needed it so badly. The tears dimmed her eyes. If he still wanted her to work as his secretary, then she would, and she didn't know what she'd do if he found someone else—she blinked the tears away. The idea was unbearable. She'd just refuse to go!

Having steeled herself to behave normally when Gavin returned, she was a little nonplussed when he didn't return, and although she waited five minutes past the time she should have left, he still did not appear.

With a sense of anti-climax, she picked up her bag and let herself out of the house. Was he now flaying himself for getting involved? she wondered, and was terrified she would expect him to go on with the farce. She gulped. And there was she hoping to remain as his secretary! She must want her head looking into! How could she possibly stay now? And what, for goodness' sake, could she tell Janice? 'Look, dear, there's a possibility of us making it a double wedding!'

On this thought she gurgled—it was absolutely

ridiculous! The whole thing had got out of perspective, and it was all Gavin's fault. He needn't have gone that far—a thought then occurred to her that made her stop in her tracks. Suppose Nicholas stayed for the wedding? And it was more than possible that he would. If so, she would be back to square one with a vengeance! Not so clever, Mr Patterson, she murmured. In fact, definitely foolhardy! Nicholas was nobody's fool. It wouldn't take him long to sum up the situation once he had had time to think things over. Beth had a premonition that she had better start packing. She wasn't even sure she had time to attend Janice's wedding—which would jolly well serve her right, she told herself. It was her fault Gavin had intervened, leaving her in this mess!

To Beth's untold relief Janice was out when she got back, and Mabel told her John had picked her up a short while before Beth's arrival, which meant an evening of blessed peace for her, and how she needed it!

So far she had done nothing about finding herself another job, but stupidly allowed herself to be lulled into accepting a position that was entirely unsuitable. Not that she had had much choice, she reminded herself, and to cap it all, she had to go and fall in love with a man who regarded her as a stupid child who required a firm hand now and again. She gulped. And how she was going to turn up to work tomorrow as if nothing had happened was beyond her comprehension. She could, of course, adapt herself to his way of looking at it—as an amusing incident—only it wasn't so amusing from where she stood. Mabel then called to her that her meal was ready, and she thrust aside the temptation to tell her that she wasn't hungry; it wasn't Mabel's fault that things were in such a mess.

After a valiant attempt to do justice to Mabel's culinary efforts, Beth settled down in the lounge to look through some of Janice's magazines. In some of them were advertisements, and as she had not only to get a job but settle on somewhere to live, too, she vaguely hoped to be given a lead in this direction.

At seven the phone rang, and Beth had a nasty suspicion that it would be Gavin with another of his laconic quips, asking if she was bearing up, and she frantically sought for something to say that would give him no inclination of her true feelings.

Her hopes that it might perhaps be a personal call for Mabel diminished when Mabel called her to the phone, and she braced herself as she picked the receiver up. But it was not Gavin, but Nicholas.

'I want to see you,' he said harshly. 'And I'm not going back until I do.'

So he had done a little adding up, she thought, and come up with the right answer, but it wouldn't make any difference. 'It's no use, Nicholas. I hoped by now you would have understood that.'

'Are you saying that you're not even prepared to say goodbye to me?' he demanded.

'You heard what Gavin said,' she answered, hating herself for having to bring that up.

'I repeat, I'm not going until I see you,' he replied obstinately. 'You know where I am; and I'm not likely to go anywhere—Patterson's seen to that,' he told her with a note of bitterness in his voice.

Beth drew in her breath. So Gavin had had Nicholas placed on what was no less than house arrest! Her sense of justice made her reply weakly, 'We'll see.' Not actually promising, but intimating that she was willing to think about it.

'Thank you,' he said on a note of satisfaction that told Beth it was settled that she would go to him.

Slowly replacing the receiver, she gave a deep sigh. She just wasn't up to this kind of cat and mouse game—she being the mouse, of course.

'Who was that?' asked a voice behind her, making her jump, and she turned to face Gavin, who stood watching her with a look on his face that told her not to lie to him.

She swallowed. 'Nicholas,' she answered slowly, adding swiftly in his defence, 'He just wanted to say goodbye to me.'

'And reminding you which hotel he's staying at,' Gavin ground out furiously.

Beth stared at his set jaw and blazing eyes, and had a suspicion of what was going through his mind. It must be galling for a man such as he, whose word was law in his part of the world, to come up against someone who was not prepared to be intimidated by him. He must also have come to the conclusion that Nicholas had not believed in the engagement story —no, she thought, that wouldn't have gone down at all well.

She met his smouldering eyes. 'I don't see how you could expect anything else,' she said, speaking her thoughts aloud. 'I mean, it was a bit too sudden, wasn't it? Nicholas, in spite of a certain remark you made once about him,' she pointed out firmly, 'is not stupid. He was well aware of the fact that you and I didn't exactly see eye to eye, and he hasn't been away that long!' She hesitated when she caught the look of amusement appear in his eyes again. She wanted to hit him; it was all a game to him, she thought bitterly and wished with all her heart she did love Nicholas and could tell him so there and then. 'If you hadn't gone overboard with the "Lord of the Isles" act, and invited him to our wedding,' she got out scathingly, 'I wouldn't be in this mess. Did it ever occur to you that he might decide to accept the offer?' she demanded furiously, adding bitterly, 'Of course not! You were convinced he'd take off in a huff, weren't you? Well, he hasn't—and that means I must!'

And she would, she thought distractedly; she had had about enough. 'And,' she went on, now thoroughly worked up, 'you can tell Nicholas I had a touch of pre-wedding nerves and made a run for it— he'll understand. It's what he thought I'd done before. You can commiserate with each other!' She flung out as she began to sweep past him, only to find that he had blocked her way.

'Let's go into the lounge,' he remarked conversationally. 'It's more comfortable there.'

Beth's eyes opened wide, and a wave of frustration swept over her. As usual he just didn't listen to a word she said! 'Sorry,' she ground out, 'but I've some packing to do.'

'I shouldn't bother,' he drawled, and to her fury calmly swept her off her feet and carried her into the lounge, kicking the door shut behind them. Placing her on the settee, he sat down beside her, pushing her back firmly when she attempted to get to her feet.

'Now it's my turn,' he said, a little smugly to Beth's way of thinking. 'And you can do some listening. Pre-wedding nerves or not, you're not breaking this en-gagement, my girl. True, I didn't have the oppor-tunity of actually asking you to marry me, but you'll do so, all the same.' He gave her a look as if to dare her to contradict him, then carried on blithely. 'Now that that's settled,' he said grandly, 'I shall begin to put you into a better frame of mind,' and he grabbed for the still gasping Beth, giving her a kiss that left her in no doubt of his feelings for her.

She was still experiencing some difficulty in accept-ing the fact that he did indeed love her, and when he allowed her space to draw breath, she managed to get out, 'You mean you love me?' in an incredulous tone.

He gave an exasperated groan. 'What more can I do to convince the woman?' he appealed to the room at large, and gave her another heart-stopping kiss. 'Are you convinced?' he asked a little while later, in a slightly husky voice.

Thoroughly shaken, Beth moved a little further away from him and tidied her hair with trembling hands. Things were getting a little out of hand, and she could no longer trust herself, or him. 'I think we'd better talk, don't you?' Her eyes pleaded with him to keep his distance, as did her voice, that shook a little.

Gavin looked a little disappointed, but gave a wicked grin, 'It's safer, you mean?' he said softly, then sighed. 'I have to admit that on this occasion you're right.' His eyes met and held hers. 'Three days, my love, that's all you're getting, I'm afraid. I meant it when I spoke of a double wedding.'

Beth's brain whirled. It wasn't long, was it? She glanced back at Gavin watching her with that certain look in his eyes, and thought it might be a good idea if she made him a drink or something—anything to take her out of his immediate vicinity! Well, she had rather wanted a white wedding, it wouldn't be the same somehow. Besides, Janice would be in white.

As if reading her mind, Gavin drawled, 'It doesn't particularly matter what you wear, as long as you say "I will" in the appropriate place. However,' he added as if it had been an afterthought, 'I've made arrangements for you to be fitted out in your wedding gear at a salon my family's patronised for some years. It's in St John's, by the way. I'll run you over tomorrow.'

Beth gasped, and forgetting her resolve to keep her distance flung herself at him. 'Oh, I love you so much!' she exclaimed.

Above her head, and with his chin resting on her ash blond curls, Gavin muttered, 'And to think it took a dress to make her say it!'

In a voice that was slightly muffled because her head was buried in his shoulder, she said, 'You're a fine one to talk! You never gave me a hint that you loved me, and I was so unhappy.'

Gavin gathered her close. 'I didn't want to do another Nicholas on you,' he said lovingly. 'He taught me a valuable lesson in not rushing my fences. Sure, there were times when I wanted to kiss the living day-lights out of you—when I'd decided I didn't want to strangle you, that was,' he gave a low chuckle, 'but I'd have scared you to death, wouldn't I? I called myself all kinds of a fool for forcing things to a head the night of the regatta. I could have lost you.'

Beth raised her head and stared at him. 'Do you mean to tell me you knew then?' she asked indignantly.

Another deep chuckle greeted this question. 'Let's say I got confirmation of a hair-raising suspicion that I'd gone overboard for a maddening little minx who took a delight in disturbing my peace. Not to mention pushing me into the swimming pool—or wrecking my car!'

'I'm not claiming any salary,' Beth hastily pointed out.

'But I'm claiming compensation,' said Gavin, against her lips.

Have you missed any of these best-selling Harlequin Romances?

By popular demand... to help complete your collection of Harlequin Romances

48 titles listed on the following pages ...

Harlequin Reissues

Harlequin Reissues

Complete and mail this coupon today!